Fleur McDonald has lived and worked on farms for much of her life. After growing up in the small town of Orroroo in South Australia, she went jillarooing, eventually co-owning an 8000-acre property in regional Western Australia.

Fleur likes to write about strong women overcoming adversity, drawing inspiration from her own experiences in rural Australia. She is the best-selling author of *Red Dust, Blue Skies, Purple Roads, Silver Clouds* and *Crimson Dawn*. She has two children and a Jack Russell terrier.

www.fleurmcdonald.com

Also by Fleur McDonald
Red Dust
Blue Skies
Purple Roads
Silver Clouds
Crimson Dawn

FLEUR McDONALD

Emerald Springs

ARENA

ALLEN&UNWIN

For the people in my life who have always held me up.
I'm thankful your hands are so strong.

First published in 2015

Arena Books, an imprint of
Allen & Unwin
83 Alexander Street
Crows Nest NSW 2065
Australia
Phone: (61 2) 8425 0100
Email: info@allenandunwin.com
Web: www.allenandunwin.com

Cataloguing-in-Publication details are available
from the National Library of Australia
www.trove.nla.gov.au

ISBN 978 1 74331 532 3

Set in 13/17.5 pt Garamond by Post Pre-press Group, Australia
Printed and bound in Australia by Griffin Press

10 9 8 7 6 5 4 3 2 1

MIX
Paper from
responsible sources
FSC® C009448

The paper in this book is FSC® certified.
FSC® promotes environmentally responsible,
socially beneficial and economically viable
management of the world's forests.

Prologue

Amelia took a deep breath, squeezed the keys in her hand and scanned the rodeo grounds. The squares of light from the atco hut windows didn't stretch far, and she was very aware that the shadows could hide anything or anyone; her hands shook a little at the thought. A moment more to calm her nerves, then she slid a key into the lock and pulled open the door to the treasurer's office.

She stood on the threshold, listening intently, checking that no one had snuck inside. Pale yellow light flooded the simple room: a couple of desks and chairs, filing cabinets, the trestle table where she'd stacked left-over promotional flyers, and the rickety stand where the old electric kettle sat beside teabags, coffee sachets and a mismatched set of chipped cups. Around the walls were posters of Torrica rodeos past: some faded, some still vibrant. And there, on the floor beside her desk, sat the bags, plain sand-coloured calico, *Torrica Rodeo Committee* printed on them in blue.

A round of drunken shouts and laughter rang out, then died away. It sounded close, but the camping grounds were about a kilometre from the ring. Noise travelled a long way on still nights.

Amelia wished the powerful towered spotlights that had shone down an hour earlier hadn't been switched off. She hefted two of the bags, her breathing shallow, a tremor running through her. Was it fear, exhilaration or anxiety? Maybe all three.

Outside, she briefly put the sacks down to lock the door. Walking quickly, she crossed the gravel to where her ancient car was parked. Fond though she was of Pushme the Mazda hatchback, she was regretting not accepting Paul's offer of his ute for the weekend. Pushme was getting less able to meet the demands placed on her.

Pausing as another lot of raucous yelling reached her, Amelia glanced around once more, acutely conscious of the huge amount of money in the bags. 'Come on, Gus, where are you?' she muttered, unlocking the back passenger-side door, lowering the bags onto the floor, then relocking.

When she'd been given the job of treasurer, she'd never thought about having to transport the whole of the organisation's takings to the bank's night safe in town. In the middle of the night. With only one escort, who should have showed up by now.

Amelia collected two more bags from the office and dumped them in Pushme. As she headed back for more, she heard the shouts of men and clatter of hooves on steel as a truck was loaded up with cattle. It was a comforting sound.

Then the crunch of tyres on gravel made her jump a couple of feet. A brand-new ute pulled up beside Pushme. Amelia held her breath.

'How you going tonight, Milly?' the president of the rodeo committee called as he got out and walked towards her.

'Gus!' she said, with a mixture of relief and annoyance.

He was about the same age as her dad, in his mid-fifties, his face weathered by the sun and wind. Never seen without his tattered hat and large belt buckle, he radiated dependability—and he had been one of her biggest allies on the committee.

'Who else would it be?' he said. 'Sorry I was late—got held up at the last minute. Scare you, did I?'

'Let's just say it was almost a job for the brown trousers.' She grinned, relaxing. 'Sorry, just a bit nervous with all the loot. Can't say I've ever seen four hundred k in one place before, let alone in my own car.'

Gus whistled. 'Four hundred k? That's a record for this little rodeo.'

'Up thirty per cent on last year,' said Amelia proudly. That would show 'em, everyone who'd given her sly looks, waiting for her to stuff up. Jim Green and Kevin Hubble in particular.

'Committee should be happy with that.' He paused before adding, 'You've done a great job in such a short time.'

'I hope so,' she answered, unlocking and pulling open the office door. 'I certainly had something to prove, didn't I?'

Without waiting for a reply, she stepped inside. Gus came in behind her and they grabbed the last four bags. Amelia gave the room a once-over, then nodded with satisfaction before turning off the lights and locking the door.

While she was happy to see Gus, the weight of responsibility hadn't completely lifted. She wished she'd been able to organise one other escort—even just her bossy older brother, Graham—so that her car could be flanked by two other vehicles. *Too late now, Milly*, she thought, and squared her shoulders, picking up the heavy bags. She turned around to see Gus kicking at the dirt, clearly anxious to get going, and said, 'Sorry, am I holding you up?'

'I just don't want to be gone from the grounds for too long. If something goes wrong, it's on my shoulders.'

She nodded and strode towards the cars, calling, 'Right-o, let's go.' It wasn't that far into town. Nothing could go wrong. Well, unless Pushme broke down . . .

'Do you want me to drive in front or behind?' Gus asked.

'Um, oh, I'm not sure. What do you usually do?' Amelia glanced around again.

Gus must have picked up on her nervousness, because he gave her a reassuring smile. 'I've just had a thought,' he said. 'Why don't we stick the bags in my ute, and you drive that? Just in case. I'll follow in Pushme. If I break down, you can pick me up and we won't have to transfer the money by the side of the road.'

It was as though he'd read her mind. 'All right, that sounds like a bloody good idea.' Amelia smiled up at him, her heart-rate slowing.

They worked quickly, putting the four bags in his ute and swapping the others over. Then Amelia grabbed her jacket from Pushme's passenger seat while surreptitiously tucking something into its pocket: a can of Bundy and Cola, to be enjoyed back in town. It was completely innocent—her version of a bottle of champagne—but she still hoped Gus hadn't noticed it.

She waved and smiled at Gus, then slid into the driver's seat of his ute. Feeling silly, she glanced over her shoulder at the bags on the back passenger-side floor—as though they could have disappeared while her back was turned! She took a look around inside the ute. 'Wow, pretty flash,' she whispered, before carefully turning the key in the ignition.

Testing the clutch and accelerator, Amelia drove out of the showground gates and onto the dark road, trying to get a feel for the ute. Gus followed close behind. She gave a huge sigh. 'Let's go.' Her voice came out high-pitched and nervous as she pushed her foot down on the accelerator. The vehicle shot away and she let her foot up. Fortunately she could still see Pushme's headlights, and she waited until they brightened. Then she cursed herself: why hadn't she thought to hire two-way radios? They wouldn't have mobile phone reception going through the hills. One day she'd learn to think ahead. One day.

'Bloody hell, bloody hell.' She'd entered the winding range road and there was no moon to cast its eerie light across the landscape. It was just dark, dark and more darkness. She checked for headlights behind her. Still there.

She was bone-weary, and as she leaned forward, peering into the obscurity, the tension in her neck pulled tight. The headache that had been threatening for the last few hours rolled in full force. *All you've got to do*, she told herself, *is get this money safely to Torrica. Only a few more k's.*

Rounding a bend, she glanced in the rear-view mirror and couldn't see Gus's lights. Looking down at the dimly lit dashboard, she realised she was travelling way above the speed limit. 'Whoops!' Once again she lifted her foot from the accelerator. It took a couple of minutes before the lights reappeared.

'Oh thank God.' Amelia's breath whooshed out and she rolled her shoulders and neck, trying to ease the tightness. Her gaze strayed to the passenger's seat where the Bundy and Cola was nestled in her jacket pocket. 'I can't wait to crack you,' she told the can, then returned her attention to the road and gripped the steering wheel tightly. Her eyes swept back and forth, alert for kangaroos and any other wildlife.

Soon she began to relax. 'Ten more minutes and it will all be over,' she whispered. 'Over.' She sighed and flicked a glance back to the money bags. Then, making a swift decision, she reached over and tugged the condensation-damp can from her jacket. 'We're just about there, and you, my friend, are all mine.'

The snap of the ring-pull was loud in the ute, and the first sip went down smooth as silk. Amelia felt a warm buzz creep through her as she took a gulp. A beeping sounded and she froze, before looking down to check all the alerts on the dash. Holy cow, well and truly over the speed limit! There was no way Pushme could keep up with a hundred and thirty. *Better just chug along at eighty, until Gus catches up.* Amelia crept along, casting frequent glances in the rear-view, until she noticed pinpricks of light. 'Ah, there he is.' She kept her speed down.

The lights grew closer and closer. That was strange—she wasn't going *that* slowly. A shiver went down her spine. Then she realised it was probably one of the trucks loaded up with cattle from the rodeo. *Stop being silly.* She put the can in a drink holder, thinking how different it was to the one in her car that was cluttered with bunches of coins, loose rubber bands and scraps of paper. How much nicer.

Then her breath caught in her throat.

The vehicle behind her was moving so quickly, it seemed to eat the night. It certainly wasn't a truck.

'What the hell?'

It closed in until there were only metres between the vehicles, then the driver flipped its lights onto high beam. With shaking hands, Amelia tipped up her mirror to take the glare away. Her throat felt as if it was closing over. Every bit of foreboding she'd experienced earlier returned. What could she do? She gripped the wheel, her knuckles white and posture rigid, staring at the road ahead.

She hoped that the vehicle would pass her and race off into the darkness. Just some idiot anxious to get home. She saw a flash of orange and realised it was an indicator. The vehicle—it was a ute, she thought, a big one, highset, a dark colour, with tinted windows—was pulling out to overtake. She started to breathe a little easier, her shoulders relaxing . . .

. . . until the other ute veered straight in front of her, cutting her off and hitting the brakes.

Chapter 1

Two months earlier

Gus thumped the table with his fist, trying to get everyone's attention. The rodeo committee members were standing around having a chat, making cups of tea and coffee, and grabbing at the biscuits that his wife, Pip, had made.

It's like pulling teeth, he thought wearily, then yelled, 'Come on, you lot, let's get this meeting underway so we can all get home.'

The gathering that settled in front of him, with much rattling of cups and spoons, was a sea of greying hair, dirty hats, denim jeans and coloured shirts, calloused hands and sun-reddened, deeply lined faces. Amelia Bennett, in her mid-twenties, was the only committee member under forty, and she was the first in years.

Well, that wasn't surprising. Agricultural areas were dying out. There were easier lives to be had and many parents sent their kids away from home: apart from anything else, there were no secondary schools out Torrica way. Few of the kids returned, and most were more interested in attending the rodeo nights than in helping to organise them. That wasn't surprising either—the local show was just about non-existent because no one was prepared to take it on. And when a rare youngster did show up at the committee, they weren't given anything to do because they wouldn't do it the way the oldies wanted.

But, Gus thought with an inkling of pride, *this crew hadn't frightened Amelia away.* Then he looked for her wavy dark brown hair and frowned. Every head was sprouting strands of grey—Amelia wasn't there. He suppressed a sigh; she'd probably forgotten again. Hopefully she was just running late.

'Okay,' he said, 'I'm calling this meeting of the Torrica Rodeo Committee to order.' He shuffled the agenda papers and looked across at the secretary. 'Cappa, you want to read the minutes from the last meeting?'

Cappa, with his vein-webbed nose and bushy brows, cleared his throat and stood, pushing his hat back. In his methodical drawl, he went through the minutes, then asked for a seconder. Fiona, her silver hair tightly curled from the day's visit to the hairdresser, put up her hand. Gus hid a smirk. You could count on her to second everything. Pip reckoned Fiona just liked to see her name in print.

'Right, new business,' Gus said before there was another outbreak of voices. 'I guess you all know that Ruby has had to resign because of her cancer treatments?'

There were nods and murmurings. Pip moved to send Ruby a card and some flowers, and everyone agreed right away—even Jim Green, who wasn't always the easiest bloke to deal with. *Their sense of community and friendship was so strong*, Gus thought. *If only there were some younger people here, it would be perfect.*

'Right-o then,' he said, when the banter had settled down, 'we need a new treasurer. Anyone want the job?'

The room went silent. No one made eye contact.

'Come on, someone has to take it on.'

Everyone was staring at their hands or the floor.

All right, Gus thought, *it's now or never.* 'What about Amelia Bennett?'

'Good one!' said Jim Green with a smirk, then saw Gus's expression. 'Oh no, you can't be serious. She's much too flighty.' He reddened, head swivelling from side to side. He'd clearly just realised that Amelia might be in the room. 'Where is she? Not here? Well, *that's* a good reason to get her to do the job,' he finished sarcastically.

❧

Right from the moment Amelia walked into the farmhouse, she knew that Paul had something important to say. The kitchen table, usually bare, had an embroidered tablecloth thrown across it. Two places were set with pristine blue-and-white Willow pattern china and engraved cutlery she'd never seen before. Velvet red roses—just like the ones her grandma used to grow at her family's farm, Granite Ridge—were on the bench in a big old coffee jar from the seventies. There'd be an orange lid lying around somewhere.

'Hey,' Amelia said, smiling at Paul and leaning in for a kiss. His gorgeous eyes, blue flecked with gold, seemed darker than usual. 'This looks impressive!'

As his fingers rested on her cheek and he looked down at

her face, Paul didn't quite meet her gaze. She couldn't work out if the news was going to be good or bad, but he was clearly steeling himself.

'You want to eat or talk first?' he asked. 'I've got some steak to cook up on the barbie and a salad to toss. Won't take long—'

'Talk first.'

'All right.' He stepped away from her and took a breath. 'The trouble is—and I know this sounds corny—I can't get you out of my mind. I really can't.'

She gave a playful laugh and raised her eyebrows suggestively. 'That's not a bad thing.'

'Listen, I'm serious,' he pleaded. 'I don't want to let you get away.'

'Get away?' She eyed him severely. 'I'm not one of your dogs that you chain on the back of the ute.'

'Shit. I'm stuffing it up.' Red-faced, he looked at the floor. Then he raised his head and met her eyes with an intensity Amelia had never seen before. 'I want to ask you to marry me, Milly.'

Her heartbeat sped up, an involuntary smile spreading across her face. Though they'd been going out for a little over a year and things were going well, she hadn't seen this coming.

'But I don't have anything,' Paul continued. 'I can't afford a ring. This place isn't a house—it's a bloody shack.' He swept his arm around, gesturing to the kitchen cupboards without doors, the fridge with more rust stains than white enamel, the woodstove that needed a tonne of kero to get started, the peeling paint . . . all signs of his late father's neglect. 'I couldn't expect you to live here, share it with the mice and cockroaches. I'm up to my eyes in debt and I can't afford to fix anything.'

'Honey—'

11

'Let me finish now or I'll never be able to say this again.' Paul took her hands and pumped them up and down, as though trying to release his frustration. 'I've got nothing to offer. Dad left it all in such a mess it's going to take me years to get back on track. By then, you'll have had enough of waiting.'

Warmth rushed over Amelia as she looked at his deeply tanned face, the dark blue eyes. The anguish there was clear, but she didn't know how to make it go away.

'Oh,' was all she managed.

Paul let her go and walked to the kitchen door, open to let in a cool breeze. There was no flyscreen, another thing the place needed. Looking over his shoulder, Amelia could see the moon rising, its soft light touching the land. She tried to organise her thoughts while the silence stretched out around them and grew uncomfortable.

The house was crumbling, there were no two ways about that. Wind whistled through the gaps around the windows in winter. Paul had to boil hot water on the stove for the dishes and the toilet was outside. Amelia made a point of going to the loo before she arrived and straight after she left.

Paul's father, Old Brian Barnes, had certainly left him in an awkward situation when he'd died. It was a miracle Paul had been able to convince the bank not to hold a mortgagee sale. All the time Amelia had known him, he'd been working his backside off just to make ends meet.

She walked over to him and put her hand on his shoulder. When he turned around, she stared into his face. His eyes were filled with concern and his handsome features were strained.

'You're not going to lose me,' she said and smiled. 'Idiot.'

He went still as he looked at her.

'It doesn't matter,' she whispered. 'We'll make it work somehow. I don't need a ring or a flash house. You've got me wrong if you think I want all of that stuff. I just need you.'

He stared at her, disbelieving.

'True,' she affirmed. 'Of course, if you're going to be speechless every time something significant happens . . .'

He blushed and grinned, then pulled her to him. He didn't kiss her, just held her close. 'So, you'll marry me?'

She gave a muffled laugh against his shoulder. 'Well, we have to get an indoor toilet before I move in. I'll take that over an engagement ring any day!'

Paul chuckled. 'I think that's fair. But there'll be a ring, I promise. One day, there'll be a ring.'

'Hmm, never thought you were so romantic!' She let him go, laughing.

He pulled her back and kissed her. 'I didn't either,' he admitted. He smiled down at her, then said, 'So, you want to wait before we get officially engaged, or tell everyone now?'

'Let's keep it between us for the time being. Though I'm not into long engagements. And . . .' She twirled around. 'How about we make some plans? A lick of paint here, a bit of no-more-gaps there . . .' She was smiling, but then she stopped at the look on his face. 'What's wrong?'

'Milly, you don't get it. Hopefully in the next few months I'll be able to get that toilet in, but there's absolutely no money right now. Not even enough for a sack of cement.'

'Doesn't mean *I* can't pay for things.'

'No way, Amelia. No way.' Paul shook his head firmly. 'I'm the provider. I'll make a home for you. You're not going to spend your money on this joint.'

What? She frowned. 'Don't be ridiculous—we don't live in the Dark Ages. I've got money set aside and if I'm going to live here, then what does it matter if I put some of it into the house? After all, we'll get to be together quicker. And don't pull all that macho "I'm the bloke" bullshit with me! You know I'm not a little woman.'

He took a breath. 'Milly, I'm serious. It's not a matter of me being stubborn, it's . . . it's a matter of pride. Look, I had no say in how Dad ran this place into the ground. I had to stand by and watch what he did. I need to get this house right for you, for me, for *us*. I have to do it myself.' He looked at her, his eyes begging her to understand. 'Don't worry, though. I'll make it work.'

Amelia stared at him for a long moment. In some ways, he was right: he needed to fix up his childhood home for his own self-respect. She also knew that when he was like this, he couldn't be swayed overnight.

'Okay then,' she said lightly. She reckoned she'd be able to wear him down eventually, at least on a few things.

❧

Gus was trying hard not to lose his temper. Bloody hell, these old bludgers could be so stubborn! 'We need to face facts,' he said. 'No one here wants to take on the job and we need a treasurer. It's time we let a younger person have a go. We're not gonna be here forever, you know.' Gus sat back and crossed his arms.

The room erupted.

'I reckon that's a really bad idea!'

'She's a nice girl, but . . .'

'What about the time she lost little Henry Marshall?'

Suddenly people who couldn't remember where they were last week were able to recall Amelia's stuff-ups from years ago.

'Well, boys and girls, the simple fact is that no one else is puttin' their hand up.'

'I think she'd be good at it,' Pip said firmly. All heads turned to her. 'Sure, she can be a bit flighty, but she has a kind heart and a big one. You saw the sort of passion she brought to her first meeting, all her dreams and hopes to make this year's the biggest and best rodeo we've had for a long time. She started that Facepage, or whatever you call it, and—'

'Well, why isn't she here now?' Jim cut in. 'She send her apologies?'

A few people nodded their heads.

'No, she didn't, but we've all been guilty of that,' Gus said. 'Won't give her life because of it.'

'I think it's a good idea, too,' Fiona said quietly.

'Do you?' snapped Kev Hubble, Jim's best mate. 'Well, when the till won't balance you can put the money in to fix it.'

'Enough!' Gus banged his fist down on the table. 'Kev, that's a bit harsh, mate.'

Cappa stood up, cleared his throat and spoke in his usual ponderous way. 'Why give Amelia such a responsible position? It's nothing against her personally, but she should work her way up to something like that. You have to understand the job before you take it on.'

'That's right,' Jim thundered. 'You can't just roll in and be treasurer.'

'I don't see you volunteering,' Fiona said, a surprising amount of heat in her voice. 'You're the reason this rodeo is going to die. You're a stupid man, Jim Green.'

Uproar broke out and it took Gus a few minutes to settle everyone down.

A thin, wiry lady, with soft grey curls to her shoulders, got to her feet. Anne Andrews had been silent throughout the debate. Pushing her glasses back onto her nose, she opened her mouth. 'You lot should listen to yourselves. Do you really think Amelia would be in this position by herself? Of course not!' She shook her head. 'She'd be doing it with our help, our support, which we should be happy to give. We can train her. Get her doing things the way we like them done.'

'But—' started Jim, and found himself silenced by the finger Anne pointed at him. She didn't talk too often, but when she did people listened.

'And what if she says no?' Anne continued. 'Where's that going to leave us as a functioning rodeo committee? I tell you: up shit creek without a paddle. You all seem to be forgetting something. Amelia runs her own bookkeeping business. She does my farm books and a few others around the traps. She has a degree in commerce, for crying out loud.' Anne strode to the front of the room and faced them. 'A young, passionate person is just what this role needs. I say we give her a crack at it. Go on.' Through narrowed eyes, Anne peered at the stunned committee and said, 'I dare you,' then went back to her seat with purposeful steps.

Good job, thought Gus. 'Right,' he said, 'I move that we nominate Amelia Bennett as our committee treasurer.'

⁓

As she drove up through the hills, Amelia glanced over the countryside. The moon was nearly full and the white glow it cast gave her goosebumps. She pulled Pushme off the road, killed the engine and got out.

Sitting on the bonnet of the car, she let her eyes roam the shadowy, bluish landscape. It was a nice change from how brown everything was in the daylight. March had been unusually warm. The bush was parched and waiting for those opening rains to sweep up from the sea.

Amelia heard a sharp bark in the distance, then sheep murmuring and the thud of hoofs as they bolted. The fox must have been looking for something to eat.

Turning her thoughts back to Paul, she tried to understand his need to provide for her. She sort of could, but it was still frustrating as hell. She was independent. The office work she did for her parents and other farmers around the district gave her an income, and she'd be happy to put her small savings into something she knew would be hers forever. Hers and Paul's.

Smiling to herself, Amelia hugged her knees as she replayed the night in her mind. His words, his touch, his love. From their first date, she'd been so comfortable with him. He didn't label her: with him she wasn't John and Natalie's little girl, or Graham's scatty sister. Paul just loved her as Amelia Bennett. She knew they'd have a great life together—she just wanted it to start sooner rather than later.

Thinking about Paul made her warm all over. She remembered the night they'd met, thrown together on bar duty at the local agricultural show. Despite the continual orders for beers, they'd introduced themselves, chatted and laughed. At the end of the shift, Paul had asked if she wanted to watch the fireworks with him.

Of course she had. She loved fireworks, and she didn't mind spending more time with this handsome stranger. But Paul didn't take her to the edge of the oval where everyone always sat. Instead, he put his big, warm hand on her waist and guided her up into the tumbledown grandstand that no one was supposed to use.

She whispered, 'Are we allowed up here?'

Paul shook his head and grinned. 'Don't worry, I know where to put my feet. Just stay with me and we won't fall through.'

After some giggling and stumbling, they settled down with a perfect view. As Amelia watched the fireworks, she felt like she was at the back of a movie theatre. She snuck sideways glances at Paul while colourful sparks reflected over his face and shone in his eyes. A spiderweb had attached itself to his brown hair and she wanted to brush it away.

He caught her glancing at him and—he told her later—couldn't pull his eyes away from hers. He put his hand to her face, pushed her dark brown hair back and gathered it at the nape of her neck, the whole time drinking her in.

Then they kissed.

And they'd been together ever since, mostly spending time at his farm, Eastern Edge. They avoided Granite Ridge. Natalie had a set against Paul's family that came from Old Brian's drunken exploits and some inappropriate comments he'd made over the bar one night. She'd mentioned, more than once, that the Barnes family seemed 'exceptionally common'. But that didn't worry Amelia too much—she was used to her mother's disapproval.

At least there was one family member who accepted Paul. That was Amelia's Aunty Kim, her mum's sister and polar opposite in both appearance and personality. A curvaceous lady, with long, curly dark hair that fell down her back, a wide smile and a ready laugh, Kim was an unmarried business-woman who ran the most popular roadhouse in the district. She'd been looking out for Amelia all her life, so if anyone would be happy for her and Paul, it would be Kim.

Sighing happily, Amelia let the future tumble around in her thoughts. The gains they could make on the farm, working together. Kids!

Wait, *kids*? She shook her head. Maybe that was getting a bit too far ahead.

In the back of her mind, something niggled. It was going to take a long time to make Eastern Edge profitable. If Paul was really going to be as stubborn as he appeared, it would be years before they could achieve anything. She'd be getting fitted for a wedding dress and a coffin around the same time. Her brow wrinkled.

On the breeze she caught the smell of eucalyptus and her frown turned to a smile. These sorts of nights were her favourite: she felt like dreams and wishes could come true. Tossing her head back, she stared at the stars until they blurred.

Then she realised something else was bothering her, lurking in her memory.

'Oh damn!' She jumped off the car and yanked open the door, then grabbed her phone from the charger and opened the diary app.

Rodeo committee meeting 7pm was typed under the day's date, with lots of exclamation marks. She checked the time on her watch. Ten o'clock. Too late now. 'Bugger, bugger, bugger!' Even too late to ring and apologise.

'When will you ever learn?' she muttered, all her happiness gone. She'd been wanting to make a good impression ever since she'd returned to town, yet no matter how hard she tried, she seemed to stuff something up at least once a week.

Fancy forgetting the rodeo meeting of all things! It was an event that she'd worked tirelessly for.

But that's just me, isn't it? she thought bitterly.

'Ah, our Milly,' she could hear her mother fondly saying to other parents when she was in primary school. 'Heart as big as a road-train. Such a *kind* girl. Such *good* intentions.' The *but* was always there, though. 'But she'd forget her head if it wasn't screwed on.' Then Natalie would pat her daughter's hair and smile, and Amelia's embarrassment would swell. The worst thing was, her mother seemed to be right.

Even now, after getting her degree and starting her business, Amelia had Post-it notes all around her bedroom, reminders of things she had to do. In Pushme, there were notes in yellow, blue, green and purple stuck to the dash. Her brain was always rushing; it would tick over and she'd jot something else down as she drove. She wanted to improve everything she was involved with. The trouble was, she had so many whirring thoughts that she tended to forget some of them.

As if on cue, Amelia's phone rang. She stared at the screen for a long moment before answering. 'Hi, Gus, I'm so sorry . . .' she began.

'Forgot, didn't you, Amelia?' he asked kindly. She could hear the laughter in his voice.

'Yeah. Paul invited me out to the farm for tea, and I didn't check my diary.'

'Not to worry. We would have had to ask you to leave anyway.'

'What?' Butterflies shot through her stomach. 'Just because I missed one meeting?'

'Because you were the point of discussion.'

'Oh no! What did I do wrong?'

'Now why would you ask that? Would you like the job as treasurer?'

Stunned, Amelia said nothing, her mouth moving as if she was a fish on dry land.

'You there? Hello?' Gus shouted into the landline. 'Damn mobiles,' he muttered. '*Hello?*'

'I'm here,' Amelia finally answered. A smile had found its way back to her lips. 'I'm *here*! Are you sure?'

'Yep. What do you reckon?'

'If I didn't know you better, I'd think you were messing with me!'

'Can you do it?'

'Of course,' she answered indignantly.

'Well then, the job's yours. See you tomorrow morning,' Gus said, matter-of-factly. 'And, Amelia?'

'Yeah, Gus?'

'Try to remember where the office is.'

Amelia could hear him laughing as he hung up. She was so happy she didn't even care. She hit Paul's name in the contacts—she had to tell someone her news.

Chapter 2

Amelia rolled over and checked the bedside clock.

Five-thirty a.m. Friday. The rodeo was a week and one day away.

Through the wall she heard her father's muffled voice, a sure sign that the house was about to wake. That meant time for her run.

She rolled out of bed and slipped on the running clothes she'd left on the hook at the back of her door. She didn't put her sneakers on inside, but carried them along the hallway with her. The front door opened silently on oiled hinges and she stepped into the clear morning. With a few careful hamstring stretches and a kilometre walk to warm up, Amelia kicked into her five-k track. Music pumping through the ear buds, she ran without thinking, sometimes in time with the beat and sometimes not.

To her delight, her father, John, had agreed to feed up some steers for the rodeo. Kept close to the house, they'd grown used to Amelia and no longer ran away as she followed her trail around their paddock. Instead they raised their heads, kept chewing, and watched until she passed. Amelia loved that; it meant not only that she belonged, but also that she could look at them and imagine them in the rodeo ring, ducking and weaving as horse and rider mirrored their moves, easing them along.

She noticed all the little daily changes in the paddock. Even though she wasn't a farmer, she still loved the land and stock. Occasionally she helped out in the yards, but if her brother was around she preferred to be nowhere near.

Her breath hissed in and out as she rounded a bend, then the sharp noise of the galahs made her smile. No matter how often she did this course, they rose in a squawking flock as she passed. A few metres on, she threw a quick glance over her shoulder: they'd already settled back onto the ground and were pulling at the onion weed growing along the edge of the track.

Running gave Amelia quiet time and cleared her head for the day, before all the thoughts started to crowd in. It kept her trim and fit. It also meant she could see her favourite place on the whole of Granite Ridge.

Well, she could look at the entry to it. Floods in previous years had made what her family affectionately called 'Emerald Springs' almost impossible to reach. Deep crevices, carved out by heavy rain, meant a ute couldn't drive in, and what had once been the Bennett family's picnic area had become over-grown with thick bush. No one had set foot there in ages, even though Amelia thought the long hike over granite boulders was probably worth it.

She blew out her breath, wiped a trickle of sweat from her brow, and ran on without stopping. One day soon she'd go up there, she promised herself. Every morning she remembered what the spot looked like. Circled by moss-covered rocks, where lizards sun-baked, was the main pool of water, which never went dry. Bottlebrush trees grew through cracks in the stones, their branches hanging over the water's surface, and wattle birds flitted between the tall red flowers.

Along the track before the main pool, up higher in the rocks, were two smaller pools. These often went dry because their water trickled down through thin waterfalls into the main one.

John had told Amelia that the main pool would have been used as a natural spring by the Aboriginal people: a place they knew would always hold water. In fact, there were precious rock carvings of circles, indicating water, en route to the springs.

As a kid, she'd spent Sunday lunches there with her parents and Graham. They carted the barbecue over the boulders, and it didn't take long before the smell of sizzling chops was wafting through the air. Amelia would never admit it, but the thinly sliced potatoes and onions had been her favourite, not the chops. And the sponge cake for dessert had certainly come a close second.

Later, her teenage birthday parties had been held there, and she and her three closest friends—Chelle, who also just happened to be her cousin on her father's side, Chrissie and Sav—had spent nights around a campfire, playing truth or dare and talking about boys. Or they'd go up during the day to lie on the small sandy beach and sunbathe, then take a dip to cool down. Amelia had loved to pluck flowers from the trees and put them in her hair, pretending she was on an exotic island. At night, they would break off branches and use them to roast marshmallows in the orange flames.

Emerald Springs had also been her daydreaming spot, the place where she could feel sand between her toes, float in cool water and stare at the sky. During wildflower season she would scour the hills for orchids.

When Amelia looked back, she thought how idyllic the area had been. Almost too perfect. Wistfully she wondered what it looked like now—if it was as gorgeous and wild as she remembered. She really wanted to take Paul there and show him how beautiful it was. To share it with him. Maybe even make love there on the sand.

✣

Amelia ran on and on, ragged breaths escaping her, until her wristwatch beeped time and she turned back towards the house.

'Morning, Milly.' Natalie was hovering over the stove, tongs in hand. Deftly she served up a plate of bacon, eggs and tomatoes and placed it in front of John.

'Morning,' Amelia puffed and headed towards the bathroom.

'Good run?' her father asked.

'Uh-huh. Back in a sec. Nature calls. Morning, Graham.'

Her brother nodded as she walked past, his mouth stuffed with the cooked breakfast his mum had just given him.

Amelia shook her head. Sometimes living at Granite Ridge was how she imagined things were like in the 1950s. Her mother, dressed in an apron, made it her business to tend to the every need of her menfolk. It was what Natalie had been brought up to do; the way her mother before her had treated her husband and sons. Even though Amelia could see how exhausting it was, she also knew her mother wouldn't change.

At the end of the hall Amelia paused and looked over her shoulder towards the kitchen. The table was encased in early morning sunlight and her family was laughing at something. No matter what, she loved them. Although her brother could be a pampered pain in the arse, he was also charming and told the best jokes. And John was kind, loving and supportive—everything a daughter could hope from a dad—and he treated Natalie with respect and kindness.

❧

Ten minutes later, washed and dressed, Amelia was sitting in front of a bowl of cereal. She drank deeply from a glass of water, then smiled at her family, wishing she didn't feel she had to try so hard with them.

'So, what's everyone up to today?' she asked cheerily.

'Just the usual for me, washing and ironing,' Natalie answered as she scraped egg fragments into the chook bucket. 'What about you, love?'

Reaching for the honey, Amelia wrinkled her nose as she thought. 'I've got to be at Pip's to do her monthly accounts by nine, and then I thought I'd go see Paul. Unless you need any help here, Dad?'

John shook his head, mouth full.

'We're fine, Amelia,' Graham said before their father could swallow. 'You go off and see your boyfriend.' He leaned back in his chair. 'I'm going to start shearing my mob of ewes today.' Graham was allowed to run two hundred ewes that were solely his on Granite Ridge, to supplement the pittance his parents paid him.

Amelia shrugged. 'No worries, just thought I'd ask.' She bit her tongue. It wasn't only her mother who had the 1950s attitude towards women. There were times she just really wanted to snot Graham, especially when he spoke down to her.

She'd wondered more than once why Danielle put up with it. Love could be blind, she reasoned. Especially when it was new and exciting. And Dani, at twenty-three, six years younger than Graham, had visions of being the grand farmer's wife with all the trimmings. A big wedding to begin with and then a lovely homestead. She wouldn't have a clue what it was like to manage the farm finances the way that Amelia did. Didn't mean she couldn't, but Amelia knew that Dani had a lot of maturing to do, as well as learning what real life on a farm was like.

The talk turned to familiar business matters and, half-listening, Amelia thought about Graham and his attitude towards money. In spite of his meagre income, he loved spending and never seemed to save anything. He never considered the future. Whenever he saw money sitting in the farm account, he wanted to buy something new, generally to replace equipment that was still in working order. He couldn't understand that the extra money had already been earmarked for something else, like a tractor payment or remitting GST monies. Graham certainly hadn't got Amelia's head for and love of figures.

Lately she'd seen some improvement in him. He'd started hanging out with Anne Andrews' three sons, Will, Mike and Tony, when some of his less savoury high school friends had moved on from town. Anne had raised her boys right. If only Natalie could have taken a leaf from her book.

Amelia tuned back in to hear her dad say: 'Not a partner, no, but Milly understands how it works. She's more than qualified, too, which you seem to forget.'

Natalie took her hands out of the soapy washing-up water. 'We should make sure that Graham can do it though, John. We've talked about this before. How can he take over Granite Ridge unless he's fully informed? He's going to be a married man soon enough, and I can't imagine Danielle being too happy about Graham not having more of a say about what goes on around here.'

There it was, just like clockwork. Amelia put her head down and tried not to grit her teeth. Then she started gulping down her cereal, wanting to leave the table as soon as possible and avoid an old, tired argument.

'Hell's bells, Nat,' John said, 'our Milly's got a degree in commerce! Surely we should be entitled to use her talents to benefit the farm.' He wiped a piece of bread around his plate to pick up all the egg yolk.

'Mum's right though,' said Graham, scratching behind his ear, a sure sign that he was getting angry. 'Not many farmers employ a bookkeeper, and you all seem to forget I do my own books for my sheep and my loan.' He looked at them all. 'Anyway, it's usually the wives who do the books and I know Dani's perfectly capable.'

Amelia tried not to cough. Not yet, Dani wasn't. It would come with time and there was still proof needed that Graham had a handle on his own affairs.

'John, no one's saying Milly isn't good at what she does,' Natalie said, 'but you know she's a bit flighty, just like Kim. At some stage she'll be swept off her feet by a man and leave. Then where will you be?'

'Um, excuse me? I'm actually in the room.' A surge of anger forced Amelia to her feet. 'Could you please not discuss my faults like I'm not here? And have you forgotten about Paul?'

'No need to get so fired up, love.' Natalie reached over and patted Amelia's arm. 'No offence meant, but one day Graham will take over here and his wife will be the one he turns to. We love you just as you are, but sisters shouldn't stand in the way.' She raised her eyebrows and nodded towards John as if to say: *I told you.*

'Let's change the subject,' John said. 'Graham, I've organised for the agronomist to take soil samples from the same GPS coordinates as last year. He'll be here at one-thirty. Can you meet him at the sheds?'

Graham looked embarrassed. 'Ah, no, I can't, Dad. Don't you remember I asked to have this afternoon off so Dani and I can buy our engagement ring?'

Amelia watched the delight spread across Natalie's face. 'I must call her mother and see if I can help with organising the engagement party.' She put her hands on her hips and smiled, her eyes thoughtful. 'I'm sure I could help decorate the footy club rooms, or do some cooking.'

Good, Amelia thought crankily. *Might keep you off my case for a while.*

'What time will you be back?' John asked Graham.

'Not in time for work. We'll go straight from Barker to Torrica, and I'll stay on for footy training. I'm gonna grab a tankful of diesel too.'

'No worries, son. Actually, while we're on that subject, there's been a lot of reports of fuel being stolen from farms, some chemical and sheep—there have even been bales of wool taken—and also drive-offs from remote service stations.

Amelia bought a padlock last time she was in town and I've put it on the bowser. The key's on the wall just inside my office. Don't forget to lock up when you've finished.'

'A padlock won't make any difference,' Graham said scornfully. 'They'll use bolt cutters if they really want to get in.'

'I heard they're sending a detective up from Adelaide to do a community talk about how to cut down on rural crime,' Amelia put in.

'Really?' asked her mother, her tone high in surprise. 'Still, what a good idea. Need to deter the little blighters somehow.'

'Yeah, they were talking about it on the *Country Hour* a couple of days ago.'

'You listen to the *Country Hour*?' Graham gave her a wide-eyed look.

'You'd be surprised by what I do,' she answered with a sweet smile. There was no point in telling him that she was up with the current agribusiness news, the prices of sheep, cattle and crops, and what was new in research and development. She needed to be, otherwise she couldn't be good at her job. But even if Graham listened, he'd forget as soon as she told him.

'So what type of ring do you think you're going to buy?' Natalie turned the conversation back to something of interest to her.

'Dani was talking opals and gold, but I guess it'll depend on what we see.' Graham put his empty coffee cup on top of his breakfast plate and handed it over to his mum, who took it with a smile.

'Aren't opals pretty expensive?' Amelia said before she could stop herself.

30

'Money is no issue. I've been saving up.'

Ha, I'd like to believe that, Amelia thought before she pushed her chair away and picked up her bowl to take to the sink. 'Nice for some,' she said. 'I guess I'll see you all at tea. Can't wait to see the ring, Graham. Will you bring Dani back here after training?'

'No, she'll stay in town. You can all see the ring when she comes to dinner next week. It'll be the talk of the town! Nothing ordinary for my girl.'

Amelia wanted to roll her eyes. Instead, she tipped her head to the side and surveyed him. Where was he going to get the cash to buy something as expensive as an opal engagement ring? She knew Danielle: that girl wouldn't settle for anything that wasn't flashy and showy. *Looks like Graham is overspending again.*

Chapter 3

Detective Dave Burrows tapped the steering wheel as he drove north. It had been three years since he'd last driven this road and so much had changed. Not the landscape so much, but him. His life.

He was no longer living in Perth; Adelaide was his base. He wasn't married, but separated. His two daughters still spoke to him, but less often than before the split; he cherished those phone calls more than ever. He was still a detective, but with all the funding cuts and lack of manpower in country areas, he spent more time in his car and less at a desk. That was the one change he liked.

The music switched to Cold Chisel's 'Flame Trees' and he felt a rush of cold run through him. The song reminded him of Melinda, his soon-to-be-ex-wife. He didn't need to listen to that. He leaned forward and changed the station to the ABC.

That helped. He could direct his thoughts a bit better. As he drove towards Clare, he thought back over the crimes that were the reason for his visit. There'd certainly been an unusual number happening in this area of the state. Of course, the towns got rougher and more 'wild west' the further north you headed, especially up around Coober Pedy and Mintabie where the opals were. Men—and women—could just disappear without a trace up there. A bit lower down there'd been a spate of fuel robberies, service station drive-offs and opportunistic sheep thefts, but one tanker theft stood out in terms of sheer audacity and quantity.

'The first of three robberies,' he said aloud. Talking to himself was one of the ways he reviewed evidence, as links were often clearer this way. 'Five hundred kilometres north of Adelaide. Eighty k's from the nearest town, Torrica. The farmer had been at the bowser the night before, filling his ute before he headed to a meeting. The diesel tank, all ten thousand litres of it, had just been filled that day and was still full when he was refuelling. So it was drained sometime between when the farmer left for the meeting and the next morning. No tyre tracks, but there was a strong wind that night. The question is, how did the crims know the tanker had just been refilled and he was off to a meeting? Inside information? Does that mean it's a local?' Dave thought for a bit, then continued. 'Ten thousand litres is a lot of fuel. You can't just fill up empty drums on the back of your ute and drive away. You'd need a truck with a tanker on the back.'

He reached over to the passenger's seat and found his notebook. Glancing between the road and the pages, he scribbled: *truck type? regos?* before chucking it back on the seat.

Then there were the other two thefts—fuel hadn't been stolen in those cases, but they had a similar pattern. Sixty k's in the other direction from Torrica had seen thirteen shuttles of chemicals taken. Once again, no one had been home on the night. There'd been truck tracks beside the loading ramp of the shed. If only the local coppers had thought to take a cast of the tyre tracks, but of course it had seemed like a random, opportunistic theft. At least they'd done enough to enable the victim to claim the insurance.

Dave kept spinning these thoughts around as he drove, then focused on the third crime, which had happened a couple of weeks later. A GPS guidance system had been stolen out of a tractor. Once again there was no one around. There had been tracks and footprints, but by the time the locals got out to the farm, they'd been destroyed by the farmer walking back and forth over the top of them. It had been frustrating when the locals had told Dave what had happened. It had been even more annoying when they hadn't thought to run a fingerprint kit over the inside of the tractor, even over the door handles.

Dave would have loved to have bawled them out for their incompetence, but he knew they were young and still learning. He also knew there were better ways to explain things to people than yelling. He prided himself on his casual but professional approach to dealing with staff members and the public.

He reached for his notebook and, steering with his knees, wrote: *Interview GPS owner, noise, lights etc*, before throwing the book back on the passenger's seat.

His daughters would laugh at him. 'Dad! Use Siri, you can just talk to her.' It had taken Dave some time to work out who 'Siri' was. 'No good me trying any new technology,' he'd told the girls. 'I'm too old to change my habits. And half the places I end up in don't have mobile reception.' The girls had pooh-poohed him for a while, but eventually given up.

Glancing out the window, Dave took in the paddocks and the dry brown land that stretched to the base of the majestic gumtree-covered Clare Hills. He allowed himself a small smile. He was almost at Kate and Sam's, and it was such a long time since he'd seen them. Dave and Kate had been as close as cousins could be when they were kids. Three years ago, she'd unwittingly become mixed up with a drug-running ring. He'd been so worried about her and Sam—as well as their friends, Matt and Anna Butler—that he'd almost broken all the rules and flown to South Australia to help them out. Instead, all he'd been able to do was advise from afar, and it hadn't been enough to stop Matt from being seriously injured in an assault.

Lost in thought, Dave missed the driveway. He eased his foot onto the brake, rolled to a stop, then yanked the wheel around and turned in through the gate, past a sign declaring that this was the home of Sam and Kate.

Dave pulled the unmarked police car up under a large pepper tree and shut off the engine. He looked around for signs of his cousin, but couldn't see her. He did, however, notice a diesel tank near the shearing shed, and went over to take a look. It was just a normal tank with a tap attached and a pipe that would let the diesel siphon down. He looked over his shoulder: the road was just over the rise and the tip of the shearing shed would probably be visible. It might pique the interest of anyone planning on stealing from an isolated farm.

Dave glanced at the sheds. Two tractors and a ute were parked inside. He strode over, climbed up the steps and looked through the tractor's window. Keys were in the ignition and the doors weren't locked. He shook his head.

'Dave?' He turned and saw Kate running from the house, her little Jack Russell, Zoom, at her heels. 'Dave, you're here!'

He grinned and walked quickly towards her, his arms outstretched. 'Aren't you a sight for sore eyes?' He pulled her to him, while Zoom's paws were busy on his jeans. The dog was checking him out, remembering his smell.

'It's so good to see you,' Kate said, muffled against his chest. 'Oh, Dave, you've lost so much weight. There's nothing of you!' He felt her pull away and knew she'd be looking at him with concern. Kate had to look everyone over.

'Yeah, I have,' he agreed, 'but I feel great and it was needed. Sitting at a desk all the time, it got out of control. Too many iced coffees and hot chips.'

Kate linked her arm through his and squeezed. 'It's lovely to see you, even though you've waited five months to get here. I should be severe with you, but I think you've had enough of that.'

Zoom danced around their feet as they walked towards the house.

'That's an understatement,' Dave muttered.

'Come on, I'll make you a coffee. Sam is out feeding the sheep, but he'll be back for lunch. Now I need to hear all of your news. Talk to me! Tell me everything.'

Dave grinned. Kate never changed: talkative, bossy, caring and loving.

'You know most of it! It's not like we haven't talked on the phone.' But Kate tugged on his arm and he knew his throwaway answer wasn't going to work. She wanted more details, and she wouldn't be happy until she'd dragged them from him and examined the situation from every angle. He steeled himself for the interrogation.

They went up the stairs and into the decades-old house. Its thick walls kept the temperature low during the searing summer. Today was warm, and Kate had drawn the curtains at one end of the kitchen to block out the heat. Even though it was April, the sun still had a sting.

Dave watched as his cousin bustled around putting on the kettle and slicing freshly made chocolate cake. Zoom hung at her ankles, hoping for a crumb, but nothing came his way. Dave's gaze fell on the photos hanging on one wall. There were his daughters: Bec and Alice, arms around each other, laughing, at Bec's fifteenth birthday party. The girls were like Kate's own children—she couldn't have her own. She would have been a beautiful mum, and that just made it all the sadder.

There was also a black-and-white of Kate's parents, who were no longer with them. They stood in front of some newly erected sheep yards, looking proudly at their work. More images of family and friends crowded the space.

Dave stooped a little and looked closely at one: a man, woman and young girl. He was pretty sure it was Matt and Anna Butler and their daughter, Ella. He was about to ask Kate when, out of the corner of his eye, he spied a photo that almost stopped his breath. His wedding photo. He let his gaze linger on Melinda for only a moment before turning away. He tried to work out what he was feeling, but it was all too mixed up. Kate's voice distracted him.

'Still white with two?'

'Huh? Oh, yeah, thanks.'

His cousin glanced over to where he'd been standing, and her face coloured. Dave was pretty sure she would have taken the photo down if she'd thought of it.

'Sooo,' she drew the word out as she placed the mug in front of him. 'Talk to me.'

Dave hoisted himself up onto a bar stool and took a sip. 'What do you want to know?' he asked. 'You've heard most of it. The split was mutual. She wasn't happy, I wasn't happy. I think we'd forgotten who we were. The girls grew up, left home, and we suddenly didn't have anything to talk about. You know I don't like to discuss my work and Melinda never talked about nursing. I'm too busy for hobbies and we don't have a lot of friends in common anymore.' He shrugged, staring into the coffee mug.

'Have you talked to her recently?'

Dave shook his head and looked up, catching the sympathy in Kate's eyes. 'There's nothing to say,' he said sadly. 'She's got a new bloke. That's why I left. Perth's a bloody small town when you don't want to run into somebody.'

Kate leaned over and placed her hand on his shoulder, not saying anything for a moment. Then she asked, 'Do you miss her?'

Dave thought about it and found he really wasn't sure. He certainly didn't miss the coldness in the house, the lack of conversation, and the distance there had been between him and Mel. There was no doubt, though, that he was lonely.

'I miss the idea of her,' he said slowly, realising that was what it was. 'I don't think I miss Mel herself. Towards the end, the house was so uncomfortable. We didn't talk. We were polite, of course, but it was like we were total strangers. I miss what we had in the beginning—we always had something to say. We'd laugh and muck around with each other.' He looked up at Kate. 'You know, it's bloody cruel the way time takes good things away. We get so caught up in our own worlds, we end up taking people for granted. We forget to make magic and keep that magic alive. Forget the little things, like please and thanks for meals. You say "I love you" but you don't mean it, it's just habit. And then you grow apart.'

He fell silent. The sadness made him feel hollow.

Zoom, who'd been curled up in his basket, let out a growl and barked. Kate looked out the window, then up at the clock. She smiled. 'Here's Sam. Nearly lunchtime.'

༚

Sam leaned back in his chair, rubbing his stomach. 'Thanks, Katy,' he said, smiling at her. 'That was really good.'

Kate leaned over and took his plate. Dave noticed her hand brush her husband's, and felt pretty sure they wouldn't let their magic die.

'So, Dave, what brings you up this way?' Sam asked. 'You said you were investigating a few things.'

'Yeah. I'm also doing a community crime prevention lecture in Torrica. There's been quite a few serious thefts lately. I did an interview with a reporter from the *Country Hour* a few days ago, but we've asked media outlets not to report too many details, because I'm hell bent on tracking these bastards down.'

'Torrica,' Kate said thoughtfully. 'Haven't you got an old friend somewhere in that neck of the woods, Dave?'

He grinned. 'Subtle as ever, Kate. You know I do. Kim Jenkins. Last time I saw her was when I was investigating stock stealing and Gemma Sinclair, all the way up at Billbinya. It will be good to catch up with her again—she's a bit of a character.'

A knowing smile spread across Kate's face. 'Hmm, did the flame ever really die? How long ago was it?'

39

'Oh bugger off! We were kids. Summer holiday fling. There was never really anything in it.' Dave shifted uncomfortably, not wanting to think too much about Kim. Maybe Kate had a point. Maybe she didn't. 'As if I need any complications right now.'

Kate chuckled and walked over to the freezer. 'Ice-cream?' she asked, brandishing a tub and waggling her eyebrows.

'Do you need to ask, love?' Sam said with a grin.

'Not for me,' said Dave. 'Watching my weight, you know.' He gave a half-smile. 'And, Sam, I wanted to talk to you about something. You gotta take the keys out of your machinery. You're so close to the road that anyone could walk in and take off with anything that's not bolted down. Insurance won't cover you if your gear isn't locked up. Not to mention your fuel tanks. Turn the power off to any pumps you've set up. Even better, have them turned off in a locked room, and you should lock the fuel tank cut-off valve rather than just the nozzle and handle. If you've got mobile tankers, keep them in sheds where people can't see them. Sight breeds temptation. Keep records and dip your tanks regularly.'

Sam grinned at him. 'Mate, it's just Kate and me here. We don't need to keep as much of an eye on things as those big pastoral companies.' Dave opened his mouth, but Sam continued. 'Don't worry, we haven't forgotten what it's like to be ripped off. It's only three years since it happened to us. We're pretty careful.'

'Well, mate, you need to be, 'cause even though this is happening a lot further north, this type of criminal often moves into other areas so they don't get caught. And these blokes could be dangerous.'

Chapter 4

Amelia pushed open the door of the atco hut and stepped into her office. Everything was silent except for a lone fly that kept banging into the ceiling, looking for a way to freedom. She waved her armful of files towards it, trying to guide it out the open door. It kept avoiding her and she gave up, opting for the tin of fly spray.

She had fifteen minutes before the phone interview with the newspaper. Somehow she'd not only inherited the treasurer's position, but also managed to get the media job. For a bunch of people who'd been reluctant to give her a go, the committee had decided pretty quickly that they liked her young, pretty face as the 'front' of the rodeo.

'Okay,' Amelia muttered, turning on the computer, 'mail first.'

Cappa, as always, had thrown the stack of mail on her desk even when it was addressed to him personally. She opened the envelopes and sorted everything into piles: one for treasury, one to be dealt with at the next meeting, and one for follow-up business. The last two she put into Cappa's manila file for him to discuss with Gus.

Amelia scanned the bank statement, making sure that the last two cheques she'd written out had been cashed, and then looked over the bills. After scribbling herself a couple of notes, she pushed the small mountain of paper aside. She grabbed the mouse and gave it a wake-up wiggle, before going through all the emails and forwarding them on to the right people. Finally, she opened up the rodeo's Facebook page. Uploading two photos of last year's event, she wrote: *'The countdown is on for the Torrica Rodeo. Only ONE week to go! Have you booked your tickets? Your camping space? If not, do it now or miss out!'*

A clatter of boots on the wooden steps made her jump, and she swung around in her chair.

'G'day there, Milly,' Cappa said as he walked through the door.

'Morning. How're you going?'

'All good, mate, all good. What have you got up there?' he asked, looking at the computer screen.

Amelia turned back. 'Oh, this is just part of the social media campaign I've been running on Facebook.'

Cappa moved closer and pulled his glasses from his pocket. 'Never understood this stuff. My daughter's into it, tries to get me to Headtime—or something-or-other—with her. My old brain just doesn't get it.'

Amelia burst out laughing. 'I think you mean Facetime, Cappa! Now you *should* get involved in that. It's like a video in real time, so you could see your grandies when you chat

42

to them. But take a look at what I've been doing here.' She pointed to the screen and Cappa leaned down next to her. 'I started a fan page. The main aim is to get as many fans as we can, so we can reach as many people as possible. And with a bit of advertising for a small cost, and sharing other rodeos' posts, we've got nearly four thousand fans! That's nearly four thousand people I can reach at the push of the enter button.'

Cappa nodded, but he still looked wary. 'How much does all of this cost?'

'The only outlay has been fifty bucks' worth of advertising, which netted us forty per cent more fans, so it was really worthwhile. Facebook itself is free.'

'Uh-huh. Free, you say?' He seemed startled and pleased.

'Yes. And look here.' Amelia clicked on a link and was taken through to a photo of a rider and bull. 'We can upload photos, and photos are what get people's attention. They can see what's going on and what we do.' She clicked again. 'And here. This is the program for the whole night, so anyone who's a fan of the page—they could be in Queensland or Tassie or anywhere in the world—can work out if they want to come.' Amelia smiled happily.

'So you're tellin' me that *anyone* in the world can see what this little rodeo is all about?'

'Anyone who's on Facebook and a fan of our page. When I first started it up, we had about a hundred fans, all local. That's good—we want the locals to know what's going on. But now, all these other people who like our page, they're rodeo riders who'll drive hours to be here on the night. Other committees have shared and liked the page too, so we're all connected, like one great big rodeo spiderweb.'

'Well, missy, to me it looks like you're doing a mighty fine job. But I'm sure there are others on the committee who wouldn't see this as a big contribution, 'cause they just don't get it.'

Amelia gave a rueful smile. 'Like Jim Green,' she said. 'But thanks, Cappa. That means a lot to me.'

'Credit where credit's due,' he said gruffly. 'Especially if we get all those people here on the night.' He took off his glasses and pocketed them.

'We might not get them all,' Amelia acknowledged, 'but going on the event that I've created, there's about half coming.' She shut down the page and started to pull up the bank website. 'So, what are you up to today?'

'Just got the tractor out to start preparing the surface. Everything closes in pretty quick when you're this near.'

'I know. Got a print media interview in a couple of minutes. The mail you need to look at is in your file.'

'Cheers.' He reached out for it.

They were interrupted by the phone ringing. 'Torrica Rodeo Office, Amelia speaking.' It was the journalist. 'Yeah, thanks for your interest.' She mouthed 'thanks' to Cappa, who smiled and ducked out of the office, manila folder in hand. 'So, the big day is in a week, and we couldn't be more excited.'

Keeping her voice bright, Amelia provided all the information she could until the journalist's questions dried up. Then she wandered outside, listening to the hum of Cappa's tractor. It pulled an implement that looked like a large rotary hoe; the ground had to be worked over until it was safe for both animals and riders.

Amelia jogged up to the top stand and looked down on what they called the 'ring'. The arena wasn't actually ring-shaped: it was an oval surrounded by high fences. Tight cables were stretched across the railings, and standing tall along the edges were powerful spotlights and tiered seating stands. At one end of the arena were the chutes where the horses would wait for the gate to open. Above them sat the caller's box, which wasn't used anymore. These days the announcers liked to be in the arena so they could interview the riders as soon as the event finished, and it was easier to see what was going on that way, too.

Amelia imagined the big night. The noise of the gathered crowd, the atmosphere, the booming voice over the PA, and the grunts of the horses and cattle. The yelling from the clowns as they lured the bulls away from fallen riders. The country dress-code would mean a landscape of plaid shirts, denim jeans and large belt buckles. Akubra hats and high-heeled riding boots would top and tail it. There'd be the smell of hot chips, cattle, fresh hay bales and horse mingling together.

Amelia's musings were interrupted when she noticed Gus's ute pulling into the parking lot. She readied herself as she walked down from the stand. It was time for the hard work to begin. Behind the arena were the cattle yards where the bulls were housed while they waited to go into the ring. Each year, the committee was called in to make sure everything was in working order. The others would be arriving soon.

'Hi, Gus!' Amelia got over to the back of the yards just as the committee president and Jim Green appeared. *Great*, she thought, forcing a smile. 'Oh hi, Jim.'

Jim didn't bother to reply, but Gus gave her a grin and said, 'Milly, how goes it?' He was carrying a toolbox and a checklist.

'All good,' she replied. 'There's some mail for you in the office. And I had the interview with the paper—went well.'

'Good! Not that I expected any less of you. Ah, here're Kev and Heidi . . . and they've brought the grandkids.' He sighed, eyeing the three blond boys.

'Little ferals,' Amelia said with a smile.

'Without a doubt.' Gus waved them over and everyone said their hellos. 'Right, Milly, you can check the troughs. Make sure they're working, clean 'em out and let 'em refill. Jim, you're on gates. Check they're swinging properly and the chains and latches are functional.' Gus looked down at his list. 'I'm going to head over to the spotlights to give 'em a test run and see that they're pointing in the right direction. Kev, I'll get you to give me a hand. Two days before the rodeo we'll do the PA systems and all the power systems. I've ordered in five generators, so we should be fine, but best to put them under load and see if we have any issues. Want everything perfect on the night.'

Amelia grabbed a screwdriver from Gus's toolbox and the trough broom from the small shed in the corner of the yards. At the first trough she undid the plug, and a gush of black and algae-filled water emptied onto the ground. The stale smell rose to meet her, but she ignored it and leaned under the trough cover to hold up the float.

'Don't waste too much water, Amelia. Don't want the water bill through the roof now, do we?'

Amelia looked up and saw Jim leaning on the rails.

'I'll do my best not to,' she answered flatly.

When she glanced up again a few minutes later, he was still there watching her, his arms folded over his chest.

'What's up, Jim?' she asked, struggling to stay polite.

'You'd better not stuff it up, girl,' he answered, his eyes narrowed. 'I'm well aware of your history. You should know that I was against you getting this position.'

As if I didn't know already! she wanted to shout. Several committee members had whispered in her ear about how she'd been elected, all with varying degrees of glee. It had been so good to know she had Anne's and Pip's support, as well as Gus's. Not so good to know about Jim and all the others. At least she had Cappa onside now.

Jim leaned towards her and pointed a finger in her face. 'I'm putting you on notice. You stuff up, everyone will know about it.'

Amelia's stomach squirmed, but she couldn't let him see that. 'I'll do my very best not to, then.'

'You think you're clever with all this Face-whatsit and interview stuff, but we'll have to see an increase on the night to make any of it worthwhile. I hope you understand that.'

'Loud and clear.'

Jim moved off with one last sharp look.

Blowing out her breath, Amelia turned her attention back to the trough. While that gasbag had been talking, the water had drained out, and now she had to scrub the scum from the cement. She didn't want any of the hardened committee members thinking she would shirk a job. She'd known all along that Jim would be watching her like a hawk, happy to find an excuse to complain. And Kev, too, as he was Jim's best mate. In fact, she'd caught Kev looking through the bank statements recently, so she was sure he was checking up on her.

She was concentrating so intently on her task that she didn't hear Anne come up behind her. When she felt a hand in the middle of her back, she jumped a little, then relaxed when she turned to see Anne's kind smile.

'Hi, Milly. Looks like you're showing that trough who's boss.'

Amelia stretched her back. 'Hi, Anne. We both know I've still got something to prove. How goes it?'

'Fine, and you?'

'Everything's getting so close, but I'm pretty sure I've got it all in hand.'

Anne leaned up against the trough and assessed her. 'The media coverage has been great. Are the entry fees coming in?'

Amelia nodded. 'There're only two teams that haven't paid yet and I'm expecting their monies to come through any day. I only checked the bank statement today, not internet banking, so it might even be sitting there.'

'Great. And the cash float, all sorted?'

Amelia knew that Anne's intervention with the committee had been one of the deciding factors in her becoming treasurer, so she wasn't offended by the close questioning. Unlike Jim and Kev, Anne was helping. 'I've put in an order with the bank, but would you mind having a look at what I've asked for? I went off last year's float, but I've got a feeling this year is going to be bigger and I'd hate to run out of anything. We've certainly got more riders coming from interstate.'

'Sure. And the prize money?'

'I've signed the cheques already, and Gus just has to counter-sign on the night. They're in the safe.'

'Anything else you need a hand with?'

Amelia shook her head slowly as she ran over her mental list. 'No, I don't think so.' She paused, then said with a half-smile, 'I'm just really trying not to muck it up. You know, it was hard to come back here after being away for so long. And even after all this time, I still get the feeling that what I was like as a kid goes in front of me. So this is me trying to prove to everyone that I'm not as bad as I was back then.'

'None of us are,' said Anne, rubbing her hands on her jeans. 'You're just what we need at the moment and don't let anyone tell you otherwise. So where's the float list? In the safe?'

'Yep.' Amelia scuffed the broom against a couple of stubborn spots of algae.

'I'll get back to you soon if I think we need any changes. Good luck with everything! Catch you later.'

Amelia gave Anne a grateful smile before the older woman walked away. Then, as she moved on to the next trough, Amelia let her thoughts drift. She *was* different to the teenager she'd been, wasn't she? She'd accomplished so much since then. But after what Jim had said, it was hard to focus on what she'd achieved. Instead, her head was flooded with all of her mistakes. Thinking about the day she'd babysat little Henry Marshall, she shuddered.

Saving up to buy her dream dress for the Year Twelve formal, Amelia had become the queen of odd jobs around Torrica: car-washing, mowing lawns, babysitting, whatever people would trust her to do. Henry's mum had asked her to watch him for two hours while she slipped over to Barker and did a big shop. It shouldn't have been difficult: Henry was a sweet, happy three-year-old, quick to smile and laugh—but also quick on his feet, which Amelia didn't realise until it was too late. After spending the first half an hour feeding him bread and vegemite, cleaning his fingers and face, and playing in the sandpit, Amelia had put him in the lounge room to watch *Play School* while she studied for a maths test.

Lost in the formulas and figures, she hadn't heard Henry slip out the front door, and it took a while before she realised he'd gone. The fear that had shot through her was like nothing she'd ever felt. She'd run outside like a mad woman, screaming Henry's name as she bolted down the street. Thankfully, she'd found him in the playground around the corner. When Mary Marshall had come home, Amelia had tearfully confessed what had happened, and even though Henry was unhurt and as happy as ever, it didn't keep Mary from gossiping about the incident. It had added to everyone's thoughts that ditzy Milly Bennett was not at all responsible.

'I'm not like that now,' Amelia muttered, scrubbing away. 'I'm not.'

By the time she moved on to the last trough, she realised the grounds had grown quiet. The tractor was standing still in the middle of the arena, and Gus and Cappa were deep in conversation. There was a fire truck off to the side, which meant the ground was about to be watered again; in the two weeks leading up to the event, the ring was watered or 'scarified'. There was a real trick to getting the dirt just right, but Cappa seemed to have it down pat after all these years: soft and smooth, no pot-holes.

Then Amelia noticed Kev and Jim, standing near one of the spotlights. They were watching her. She straightened up and kept her eyes on them. If they were going to try and intimidate her, she wanted to give it right back to them. When they glanced away quickly, she smirked and got back to work. She screwed the bung in and let the float down so that the clean, fresh water could run back into the trough.

Finished! Casting her eyes over the troughs, Amelia smiled and knew she'd done a good job. That prompted a surge of pride in herself and everything she'd accomplished. She knew that people in Torrica had been surprised when she'd decided to study commerce at uni, even her parents' friends who thought they knew her well. Everyone—including her own mother—had been even more surprised when she'd passed with honours. Nobody seemed to understand that when she looked at figures, nothing else existed; every mistake she'd made didn't matter when she was working with them. They entranced her. They made sense.

If she was to succeed here, Amelia knew she couldn't let any little thing go wrong again. Straightening up, she put her shoulders back and rearranged her face into a look of determination. Nothing was going to stop her from proving to everyone in the Torrica/Barker region that she was a hard-working and responsible person.

Chapter 5

'Can you keep a secret?' Amelia grinned at her Aunty Kim, knowing it was a silly question. No matter what Natalie said about her sister, the truth was that Kim had always been a vault.

Kim threw a tea-towel over her shoulder and rolled her eyes, putting her hands on the generous curves of her hips. 'Exactly how many years have I been keeping your secrets?'

'Just the whole of my life.' Amelia put lettuce and tomato on the steak sandwich Kim was cooking for a customer, then reached for the barbecue sauce. 'Cheese and beetroot?'

'Beetroot, but no cheese.' Natalie would have chided Amelia for not looking at the order form, but Kim didn't fuss. 'Anyway, what's so confidential that nobody can know?' She flipped the thin piece of steak, piled bacon, egg and onions on top of it, and then transferred it to the piece of toasted bread waiting on the bench. She was grinning. 'Remember when you had your first kiss and I promised not to tell anyone? And when you wagged boarding school, took the tram down to the sea and hung out with that bloke who was far too old and scary for you?'

'Oh my God, yeah! You know, he ran one of the rides at the show.'

Kim winced and nodded. 'I was horrified, but pleased you'd told me.'

'Well, he was weird. Can't believe I did that. I remember he kept saying, "You're a nice girl. You shouldn't be here."'

'I do believe he was right!'

'While we're tripping down memory lane, what about when you came to Adelaide and stayed so I could go out for my formal?'

'Ah, yes. I remember the begging and pleading from you, and the distinct lack of enthusiasm from your mother.' Kim laughed. 'I don't think Nat trusted me not to let you go out afterwards and have a few drinks.'

'I was well behaved.' Amelia pouted.

'You needed to be, because like I said to you back then, if something had gone wrong it would have been me who wore it, not you.' Kim looked over at Amelia. 'I think you had a pretty good time anyway.' Her wry half-smile made Amelia giggle.

'So did you! I remember something about you clubbing just as hard as all of us Year Twelves . . .'

'Shh.' Kim held a finger to her lips. 'Don't tell anyone.'

'Man, that was a good night.' Amelia leaned forward and hugged her aunty. 'I'm so lucky to have you. Now let me tell you another secret for your safe.'

'You're running away with one of the rodeo committee members?'

'Don't think *that's* likely.' Amelia wrinkled her nose. 'You know that Jim Green almost threatened me when I was helping out on Saturday. Said that if I stuffed up, he'd make sure everyone knew about it.'

'He's a small-minded bastard,' said Kim. 'Wouldn't take any notice of him.'

The bell jingled on the roadhouse door, letting them know a customer had entered. Kim would need to pop out of the kitchen in a second, and Amelia felt a surge of impatience.

'Anyway, my news—'

Kim chuckled. 'Quick, tell me everything!'

'Paul asked me to marry him!' Amelia's smile was wide enough to make her face hurt. She'd been hanging on to the knowledge for so long that she thought she might burst.

Kim stared at her, an incredulous look on her face. Then she held up a finger and said, 'Hang on. I'd better take care of business.' She wrapped up the sandwich and took it out to the counter. Chewing her lip nervously, Amelia leaned back on the kitchen bench and kept her eyes on her aunt over the swinging doors. She'd been hoping for joyful support, not incredulity! 'Here you go, Haydo. One steak sandwich, no cheese.' Kim turned to the new customer, then froze. 'Dave?'

'How are you, Kim?'

'*Dave?*' The high pitch to her voice startled Amelia. Kim wasn't easily rattled.

A tall, well-built man stood there with a huge smile. Amelia didn't recognise him, and she couldn't remember hearing the name Dave. She watched as Kim ran around the counter and threw herself into the man's arms. 'What are you doing *here*? How are you? Are you here for long?'

54

Amelia laughed under her breath when Dave staggered, obviously unprepared for the full force of her aunt's welcome. Then he swung Kim around, chuckling, before carefully setting her back on her feet.

'Still the same old Kim,' he said, smiling down at her. Amelia raised her eyebrows as his expression grew more serious. *Interesting.* He took a step back. 'It's good to see you.'

'And you, but why . . . ?'

'Work. I'm here for work. Not sure how long for, but I've got a forum on rural crime scheduled for next Monday. And I'm fine, thanks. Is that the order you asked the questions?'

When Kim laughed, Amelia was struck by how pretty her aunty looked. In fact, she was sure she hadn't seen Kim look quite like that before. Her smile was even wider than usual, and with a sexy tilt. There was definitely a history there—one that Amelia intended to find out about!

'I want to stay and catch up,' Dave was saying regretfully, 'but I can't right now. Thought I'd call in, let you know I'm around. And um, I also need to ask how to get to the Guild family farm. When I'm back from there, I promise we'll have a chat.'

'That's all right, work is work. The Guilds are on the north side of Torrica. Take the main drag and hang a left at the post office. Reckon they're about eighty kilometres out that road.' Kim cocked her head to the side and looked at him. 'So why are you heading out there? The Guilds keep to themselves. They don't go to the pub or any community events.' She leaned her hips against the counter and crossed her arms, which pushed her boobs up and made them seem even bigger, and they were pretty big. *Surely a strategic move*, Amelia thought.

Dave grinned and he suddenly looked younger. 'I can't tell you that, but rest assured I come in peace.' He held up his hand, warding off any potential blows.

'I'm sure you do, sweetheart, I'm sure you do.' Kim paused. 'It *is* good to see you, Dave. Really it is.'

'I'm looking forward to catching up with you. Do you want to have dinner?'

'Can't, really.' Kim gestured around at the roadhouse. 'That's my busiest time. But if you're looking for a meal, I'm open from six till eight. Kitchen closes at 7.30 p.m. sharp. You can call in on the two-way, Channel 40, if you're not going to make it before I shut. And I can sit with you if I'm not busy. Where are you staying?'

Amelia realised she should probably do something useful—and give them some privacy—so she went into the fridge to get out some lettuce and refill the containers. By the time she came back, the serving area was empty. Kim and Dave were walking out to his car, and Amelia smiled at her aunty's flirtatious body language.

'You hussy!' Amelia said with a grin when Kim walked back into the kitchen.

Kim laughed. 'That was Dave,' she said, her eyes sparkling.

'So I gathered. Do I get to know who Dave is?' Amelia crossed her arms and tapped her fingers, mimicking what Kim would do if she was wanting information from her niece.

'Dave is an old summer romance. Back when we were teenagers. And, sweetie, that's all you're getting for now, because I think you've got more news for me than I have for you. We were talking about a marriage proposal, I believe.'

She grabbed a sponge and started to wipe down the bench, and Amelia knew there would be no more information forthcoming today.

'All right, Paul's proposal,' she said. 'It was *way* out of left field.'

Kim shrugged and started chopping the lettuce. 'I had no idea it was so serious, so yeah, left field it is! Old Brian had those boys so under the thumb, I thought they'd never even look at a girl, let alone want to marry one. Frightening man, he was.'

Amelia hoisted herself up onto the sink and crossed her legs. 'But he's dead. He doesn't have any hold on Paul now.'

'Don't believe that for a second,' Kim huffed. 'That man could rule from the grave.' The bell jingled, and Amelia and Kim looked over to the doors as Kev from the rodeo committee walked in. 'Can you get that one, sweetie? He'll only want something from the fridge. I need to put on another batch of chips.'

Reluctantly, Amelia jumped down and went out to the counter. 'Hi, Kev.' She rang up his iced coffee and tried to smile.

He raised his eyebrows. 'You working here now, Milly?'

'No.' Was he implying that her bookkeeping business had failed and she needed extra income? *Yes, of course he is, the bastard!* 'Just came to chat to Aunty Kim.'

'You know, this would be a great place to put up some of the flyers we've had printed for the rodeo.' Kev handed over his money.

'Already organised,' she said, her hands in the till. 'Take a look at the front window.' *And don't let the door hit you on the way out.*

Kev nodded. 'Catch you round.'

'Yeah, see you.'

She watched as he opened the door and paused to check for her flyer, giving it a long look. What was it with him and bloody Jim Green?

Amelia went back into the kitchen. She'd used to love the smell of chips cooking, but after a few shifts in the cafe it had worn off. She still liked to eat them, though. Leaning over her aunty's shoulder, she pinched one before Kim could bat her hand away, and blew on it so she wouldn't burn her tongue.

'More information, please,' Kim demanded as she upended the greasy basket and shook chicken salt over the chips.

'It was about six weeks ago . . .'

'*Six weeks?* And you're only telling me now?'

Amelia grinned happily, polishing off her chip. 'He's putting in a toilet so I can move out there, and the job's just about done. That's why I'm telling you.'

'A toilet? Oh my Lord, Milly. Start at the beginning, would you?'

❧

Twenty minutes and a couple of customers later, Amelia had finally finished her story. 'Don't reckon Mum is going to be all that thrilled,' she concluded.

'If you're happy, sweetie, then she should be too. That's how being a family works.' Kim shook her head. 'Well, most families. So, you're going to move out to Eastern Edge this week?'

'Not until after the rodeo. I'm so bloody busy! I can't wait, though. Really.'

'I'm sensing a *but* . . . ?'

Amelia sighed. 'Yep, a huge *but*. I want to put some of my savings into the house. It's such a tip. But Paul reckons it's his job to fix all of that.'

Kim started to unstack the dishwasher. 'Ooh, now *that* is going to be a tricky one. Men love being the provider, especially when they have a new bride. You'll need to be careful about how you manage it. Softly, softly, sweetie.'

Amelia sighed. 'I know, I know . . .'

'You catch more flies with honey than you do with vinegar.'

'Don't talk in idioms, Aunty Kim.'

'I'm just saying, don't try to change his mind by being forceful and pushy. A man's like a horse—you've got to direct him with your knees!'

'Is that what you did with Dave?' asked Amelia, before falling into fits of laughter. They were both laughing when the bell sounded again and Kim looked over the doors. 'Speaking of a man being directed,' she muttered, 'here's your brother and his fiancée.'

Amelia jumped down. 'They were picking up the engagement ring today,' she whispered, 'after thinking about it over the weekend. Nothing too expensive for his special girl!' She wiggled her eyebrows. 'Let's check it out.'

They walked out of the kitchen to see Graham with his arm around Danielle, looking as proud as punch. Kim rushed up to the counter, pulling Amelia with her.

'Well, come on then, show us!'

Danielle held out her hand and they all gazed at the bright, beautiful thing on her finger. 'It's so lovely,' Kim breathed, and Amelia nodded. The ring wasn't as flashy as she'd expected:

a solitaire white opal set in an engraved white-gold band and surrounded by tiny pink gems.

'Pink diamonds,' Graham boasted, but his eyes were soft. 'You're worth every penny.' He dropped a kiss on Danielle's head, and she smiled up at him, moony-eyed.

'It certainly is amazing,' Kim said.

'Incredible,' Amelia echoed, her mind racing with dollar signs. 'So have you set a date?'

Danielle shook her head. 'Not yet, but the engagement party will be in two weeks. On the anniversary of the day we first had coffee—two whole years ago, if you can believe it! The workers' house on Granite Ridge will be renovated in the next few months, and then we'll be fine to move in. We'll have the wedding after that.'

Amelia opened her mouth but shut it again. Who was paying for all of this? Could it be their parents, or Danielle's? Had Natalie pressured John to contribute? The small amount Graham had made from selling his wool might have made the final payment on that ring. He'd said he'd been saving. Could that actually be true?

'That all sounds just perfect,' Kim gushed. 'Will you have many people at the engagement party?'

'It will be the biggest do around here in years!' Danielle said, beaming. 'It's going to be the party to be seen at.'

Kim squeezed her hand. 'Looking forward to it. Well, it's been lovely to see you both, but I really must get back to my chips. Can I take an order for you?'

'No, no, we just thought we'd call in and show you. It was a bonus that Milly was here.' Danielle gave Amelia a smile and then twirled to face the door. 'Come on, Graham, we'd better get on and show some of my friends now! See you tonight, Milly—I'll be over for dinner.'

Obediently, Graham followed. As they left, Amelia let her breath out.

'Aren't those two suited to each other?' Kim said, stalking back into the kitchen. 'That boy has got more of my sister in him than his father, that's for sure.'

'How much would that ring have cost, do you reckon?'

'Couple of grand, at least. Bloody hell!'

Amelia shook her head ruefully. 'Crazy. Imagine what else they could have bought with half of that—what it could have paid for on their house reno alone.' She sighed, thinking of all the renovations that Paul's place needed, with no money to spare. 'Anyway, I'll hear enough about them when I get home.'

'Tell me more about the rodeo.'

Amelia brightened. 'Not much to tell—everything is in place, I think.'

Kim put her hand on Amelia's shoulder. 'I know,' she said quietly. 'And I'm so proud of what you've achieved. Anne's been in here singing your praises, so from all accounts you've done a brilliant job.'

'I've really enjoyed it, especially the media and treasury side of things.' Amelia paused. 'I'm still so frightened I'll forget something, though.'

'If you've got Anne watching over you, it should be fine. You know she was the treasurer a few years back. She won't let you fall, of that I'm sure.'

'I hope not. All I want to do is prove to everyone that I'm a good person, not Muddle-Headed Milly. That I'm a grown-up.'

'I understand, sweetie, but the sooner you realise that it doesn't matter what anyone else thinks about you, the better off you'll be. You know in your heart you've done your best, and that's all that matters.' She gently pushed Amelia's dark brown hair back over her ears. 'Trust your Aunty Kim on that account, okay?'

Chapter 6

Dave shut his car door, locked it and looked around at the near-empty streets. There were a few cars parked across the road in front of the post office, and off in the distance he could see a young boy on a skateboard. Other than that, the town of Barker seemed to be asleep.

He'd quizzed Kim about the district the evening before, when he'd dropped by her roadhouse and tried a slice of her delicious cherry pie. Torrica, he'd discovered, had only a thousand people within its limits, but that swelled to over five thousand when the rodeo was on. There was Kim's Roadhouse, Torrica Farm and General, a pub, a bakery, the motel where Dave was staying, a bank, a small supermarket, a community centre and a footy oval with club rooms. There were a few shops, but from what Dave had observed on his way through the main street, a number of them were empty with boarded-up windows. The majestic town hall still stood tall and proud, a remnant of more prosperous times, beside a marble war memorial.

Barker, on the other hand, had over six thousand people in town, so there were cafes, a couple of clothing shops and many other stores, including a shopping centre—*maybe that was where everyone had congregated today*, Dave thought. And Barker had a police station. That was where he was heading now.

He was aware it was only a small operation, with two coppers and a lady who manned the phone and front desk. Taking care of a small town, the most these blokes usually had to deal with were pub brawls, the occasional theft, pulling people over for speeding, and randomly breath-testing drivers on weekends and public holidays. Unlike the poor coppers further south in infamous Snowtown, the worst thing the Barker police had dealt with was a little girl wandering away from a farmhouse and eventually being found dead in a dam—a tragedy but not a crime.

As he entered the cement-brick station, Dave smiled at the grey-haired lady sitting behind the high Formica counter. Peering over her glasses, she said, 'Yes?'

'Detective Dave Burrows.' He held out his ID.

'What can I do for you?' she asked, with a distinct lack of interest.

'I'm here to meet the local blokes,' he answered, puzzled. 'I've exchanged emails with them both.'

'Jack's out and Andy is off duty.' She pushed her glasses back up her nose. 'I can call Jack on the radio and get him to come back if you want? I think he's checking speeds in the eighty-kilometre zone.' She stood and moved towards the radio that hung on the wall at the back of the room.

'Thanks, I'd appreciate it. You weren't expecting me?'

The lady shrugged. 'I'm sure they are, but I'm not. I get told nothing and just do my job.' She picked up the receiver, made the call and, after they both listened to Jack's terse reply, hung it up. 'Guess he'll be back shortly,' she said.

'Guess so.' Dave wondered how much more laid back this office could be. 'Tell me . . . uh, what did you say your name was?'

She eyed him carefully. 'I don't believe I did. But it's Joan.'

'Pleased to meet you, Joan,' Dave held his hand out over the counter. She shook it with a firm, wiry grip. 'I'm Dave,' he reiterated. 'So, tell me about your job here.'

She sat back down. 'I man the station and help the boys with all the paperwork. Type up their reports and send 'em off, answer the phone, do the filing and basically be the dog's body.' She shuffled some papers on her desk, then looked up at him. 'Why are you here?' The first sign of curiosity.

'To investigate three crimes that seem to be linked. And give a talk on rural crime.' He leaned on the desk. 'Look, I don't suppose I could come around and sit down? And I'd love a coffee or a cup of tea if possible. I can make it, if you point me in the right direction.'

Joan waved him around, and he walked behind the counter. This station was so very different to what he was used to—and the lack of security was what interested him the most. He'd been in plenty of outback police stations, and certainly they were casual, but this one didn't even have a deadbolt on the door between the front foyer and reception! Obviously there was a lot less violence out here.

'Tea room's through there—' Joan pointed to an open door near the back of the room '—and toilets and offices are back there too. Oh, and the holding cell. In case you need it.'

'Thanks.' Dave found his way to the tea room, switched on the kettle and spooned some instant coffee into a mug. Leaning against the bench, he thought about the three crimes again. Yesterday he'd followed Kim's instructions and visited the Guilds—the family who'd lost their chemical, far off on the other side of Torrica from Barker—and now he was hoping Jack might be able to take him out to the two other farms that had been hit. He knew it would take most of the day, but he felt it was imperative he spoke to the farmers and saw where the crimes had taken place.

Out at reception, the phone rang and Joan answered it in a bored tone. 'Barker police department. How may I help you?'

Dave was looking around for a map, thinking there might be one on the wall, but there were only a few flyers pinned to a board. Disappointed, he made his way back out to the front once he'd filled his mug with boiling water.

'Excuse me, Detective?' Joan appeared before he got there.

'Hmm?' he said around the edge of the mug. Without thinking, he screwed his nose up at the instant-coffee taste as he gulped it down, and felt a twinge of embarrassment. *Adelaide's softened you up, mate.* Then, as he glanced up at Joan, he realised she was looking a lot more animated—and not in a good way.

'Linda . . .' Joan began, and swallowed. 'Linda Collins, a farmer's wife, she's on the phone sounding quite distressed. She says her husband, Ray . . . She says he's been attacked. Jack isn't answering the radio. It's out on a farm, a fair way from town.'

Dave stood still for a second, stunned. 'Was anything taken?' he asked as he moved towards the phone and set his mug down.

'She didn't say. Line two.'

Dave pressed the flashing button. 'Detective Burrows, how can I help?' He listened, asked some questions, and assured the woman he would be there as soon as possible. Then he hung up and turned to Joan. 'Can you call an ambulance to their farm? And does Jack have a mobile?' She nodded, and he punched the number into the phone as she recited it. 'Damn, message bank. Where the hell is he?'

'Who you looking for?' a male voice boomed as the door slammed.

Dave glanced up and saw a blond man in a police uniform, who looked like he'd just graduated from high school and was heading to a costume party. Dave had to stop himself from shaking his head. These kids in uniform were getting younger and younger. Sometimes he felt like a bloody dinosaur.

'Jack?' he asked, and the young bloke nodded. They shook hands. 'Good to meet you. Just had a phone call from—' He looked to Joan as he hadn't written the name down.

'Linda Collins,' she supplied.

'Her husband's been attacked out on their farm. She's not sure what happened but it seems the culprit took his ute with a load of chemical in the back.'

'Yeah?' Jack's pale eyebrows lifted so high they almost came off his face.

'So let's get going,' Dave said impatiently.

'Oh. Right. Sure.' He sounded just like Dave's daughters when they wouldn't get off their phones.

એ

On the way to the farm, Jack filled Dave in on recent developments. There were none.

'Not really sure why Adelaide seems to think we need you,' he added. 'All the burglaries around here this year have been different—well, maybe there've been a few more fuel thefts than usual, but prices are up. Isn't most rural crime just opportunistic?' He swung the car into a driveway lined with pine trees. There was a sign at the front gate declaring it to be the home of Collins and Son Grazing.

Dave checked his temper. 'As I said in my emails, I can see some similarities in the three most serious thefts over the past six months, so I believe they've been committed by the same person or persons. And yes, certainly, rural crime is eighty-five per cent opportunistic. However, I think these three were planned beforehand—planned well, too.'

It was inbuilt in Dave to observe everything, even when he was talking, so his eyes were roving over the landscape, seeing how close the sheds were to the house, where the tractors were and what cover, such as trees and bushes, was around. The ambulance was parked near the sheds. Jack drove over and leapt out of the car, and Dave followed. A man in his seventies was seated in the back of the ambulance, a blanket around his shoulders, while a paramedic examined his hip.

Dave introduced himself and Jack to the other ambo and got a quick update.

'He'll be okay,' the ambo said quietly, 'but this was an aggressive attack.'

Staring at the victim, Dave was unable to see any physical injuries. 'Why do you say that?' he asked, pulling his notebook from his top pocket.

The ambo gazed at him for a while before answering. 'He's been tasered.'

Bloody hell, Dave thought, and it must have shown on his face, because the ambo nodded grimly. Jack just gaped at them both.

Dave went over to the victim. 'Are you up to answering a few questions, Mr Collins?' he asked. 'I'm Detective Dave Burrows, Adelaide Metro Police.'

'Don't really know what happened, lad,' the elderly man answered with a wince. 'I had pulled up in the shed and was going to unload the chemical I'd bought in town. I'm getting ready for the opening break, you see. There was a movement behind me and then all I know is there was an electric shock and I couldn't move. Now I've got a damned thing in my hip.' He leaned forward so Dave could see the two little dart-like electrodes underneath the wrinkled skin.

Knowing they would probably have to be surgically removed, Dave felt a flash of anger on behalf of the old man, who seemed so small and defenceless. Whoever had done this was the worst type of coward.

'Can you tell me what was taken?' Dave asked, keeping his voice gentle.

'Me ute!' Mr Collins answered indignantly. 'And all the chemical on it. I didn't see anyone because when I went down I was facing the wall of the shed. All I could hear was shuffling, slamming of the car door, and then it driving off.' He paused, looking shaken. 'I'm pleased me dog wasn't tied on the back,' he finished in a small voice.

Dave jotted down a couple of things and glanced around. Jack was at his shoulder, listening intently. *Good. He might learn something.*

'Can you tell me how many car doors slammed shut?' Dave probed.

Mr Collins took a moment before answering, slow and thoughtful, 'You know, young man, I think I heard two.' He fell silent again, and Dave didn't interrupt. 'Yes, yes, I think there were two slams.' He nodded to confirm what he'd just said.

'Please think back to the movements you saw behind you.' Dave paused to give Mr Collins time to digest his words. 'What did you actually see?'

'I was undoing the side of the tray. Guess I didn't actually see anything, just sensed movement. Then there was a sound and I started to turn, but felt an electric shock—sort of like what you get when you hit yourself with a cattle prodder, y'know?' He pulled the rug tighter around his shoulders. 'Then me legs wouldn't work and I hit the ground, right flat on me face. Not sure how long I was down, then Linda found me and called you. Bit hard on her heart, the poor old girl. She's having a lie down.'

'Reckon you might have a bruise on your cheek, Mr Collins,' the ambo who'd been examining him said. 'Now, how about we get you to a doctor and checked out, and the detective can take a look around and talk to your wife when she's ready?'

Dave stepped back and gave a reassuring smile, and was pleased to observe Jack following suit. 'No worries. If you could just point us in the direction of the shed, Mr Collins, we'll do our jobs here.'

Chapter 7

'So who's going to christen the throne?' As they walked from Pushme, Paul put his arm around Amelia and she grabbed his hand.

'That'll be you,' she answered, grinning up at him.

'Me, huh? Why me?'

'No reason.' Amelia giggled. 'Whoever thought I'd be so excited about a loo? Funny the things people take for granted.'

Hand in hand, they walked up the steps of the Eastern Edge house and Paul held the door open for her. Amelia glanced around and saw the dirty footprints from the tradesmen—Paul obviously hadn't thought to clean up after them. *Oh well, can't have everything.* She walked down the hallway and peered into the bathroom. The place would still need repainting and she was determined there'd be a new vanity one day, but for the moment she was ecstatic. There, shiny white and brand spanking, stood a toilet where the bath had been. And perched delicately on the seat, with his head in the bowl, was Paul's fat ginger cat, Peanut.

'Yuck! Get out, Peanut!' Amelia clapped her hands and the animal streaked past her. 'Toilet's already been christened,' she called. 'Peanut thinks it's his local!'

Paul appeared behind her. 'Can't train a cat.'

'Thank you.'

'You're welcome.' He grinned. 'So you're still planning to shift in right after the rodeo? That's coming up soon.' He sounded a little nervous.

'Yep. Guess we'd better tell Mum and Dad.'

They were both quiet for a moment, staring at the toilet. Amelia pondered how such a simple thing had the ability to change her whole world. The thought of moving in with Paul filled her with equal parts happiness and apprehension. Without a doubt, he was her future, just as she knew Torrica was the right spot for her. She just had to prove that to everyone else. *Or do I?* she wondered, remembering Aunty Kim's advice. She knew Kim was probably right, but didn't know how to stop caring what others thought—especially the other committee members.

For the moment, she told herself, she needed to focus on Paul. 'This is so exciting,' she said, leaning up to give him a kiss on the cheek. 'I think I'm the luckiest woman in the world.'

'I'll remind you of that whenever you complain about having to cart hot water for the dishes.' He grinned and pressed his lips to hers. 'The feeling's mutual,' he said against her mouth. 'In fact, I really think you're far too good for me.' He manoeuvred her into the bathroom, laughing. Amelia gave a squeal, then laughed too as she heard the toilet lid flip shut.

Paul lowered her onto the loo, struggling to look solemn. 'You're my queen!'

She held his face in her hands. 'Does that make you my subject or my king?'

'Both.' He kissed her again and straightened up. 'Now, about the rodeo . . . You're going to be pissed with me, I know, but I can't help it. I'm not going to be here. I have to go to Adelaide for a couple of days, from Saturday morning. Stuff to sort out with Dad's will. I'm really sorry—I tried to change the dates.'

Amelia eyed him with dismay. 'Can't change it at all?'

'It's got to do with lawyers and courts, so no. Sorry.'

'But Paul, I wanted you to be one of the escorts for all the money.'

'Aw, c'mon, Milly, you'll find someone else. There's heaps of people on that committee.' He smoothed her frown with his thumb. 'Hey, are you free to come for a drive with me now? The stock agent is making a call and I've got to get the ewes in I want to sell.'

She glanced at her watch, then groaned. 'Nah, I can't. Meeting the girls for a coffee, and we need to make the most of the time Chelle is off-duty from the hospital. I haven't seen them in ages. Sorry, sweetheart. Besides, I'll be living here soon and you won't be able to get rid of me!' She got up and kissed him. 'Although even if you *have* annoyed me, I could still stay here all afternoon and kiss you.'

His arms tightened around her waist. 'Me too, baby, me too. But I guess that isn't going to sell the sheep or get this house sorted for you, is it?'

Amelia decided to ignore the way he said 'you' rather than 'us'. After one last, lingering kiss, they went out front and she jumped into Pushme.

'Have fun with the girls.' Paul tapped the roof as she started to drive off.

She put her foot on the brake. 'Oh hey, do you want to come over to dinner on Friday? We can tell Mum and Dad that I'm moving in.'

'If that's what you want.'

'It's not about what I want, but if I'm going to move in with my fiancé, we should tell them!'

Paul rubbed his hands through his hair, looking uncomfortable. 'It's just, the way your mum looks at me . . .'

Amelia tapped her fingers on the steering wheel. 'Paul, we've talked about this. I don't care what Mum thinks.' She eyed him. 'Are you trying to back out?'

'God no!' he almost shouted. 'But Natalie does make me nervous, all right?'

'Bloody hell, she makes everyone nervous.' Amelia touched his hand. 'Look, family's the baggage everyone brings with them. Including you.'

He nodded. 'You're right, babe. Friday night, then? And I'm sorry about the rodeo, I really am.'

'I'll let Mum and Dad know. And look, it's fine, I understand about getting the estate sorted. I've just got to remember to get another escort.'

'Look at you!' Dr Michelle Jenkins—Chelle to family and friends—hugged Amelia tightly. 'You look incredible. Country life must suit you.' She paused and searched her cousin's face, before adding, 'Unless it's something else?'

Amelia laughed and returned the hug. 'It's not been that long since you've seen me, cuz.'

'Hmm, so you're not madly in love? I've heard rumours about you and Paul Barnes . . .' She raised her eyebrows as if they were pulled up by twine.

'Well, duh! You know we've been together for more than a year now. Aunty Kim, can we please have two white coffees?' Amelia called through to the kitchen before they headed into the dining area. 'Wait, what rumours?'

'Oh, I hear you're shifting in with him. Anything to say on that?' Chelle tucked her long brown hair behind her ear and gave a wicked smile. 'Cat got your tongue?'

Amelia let the shock subside. 'How on earth did you find that out? I haven't even told Mum and Dad yet.'

'I've got my sources,' Chelle said mysteriously, grey eyes twinkling, 'and I can't tell you how I know this, patient confidentiality and all that, but I hear there's a new loo out at Eastern Edge. Anyway, you'd better let your parents know before someone else does! You know how people love to gossip.'

Amelia's reply was lost in the noise created when Chrissie and Savannah walked in.

'You've got a head start on us,' Sav said, flopping into the chair next to Amelia.

'You're actually late,' Chelle said, looking at her watch.

'And *you're* a doctor, so I can't believe you're early,' Chrissie quipped.

They all laughed. Amelia looked around at her friends,

who were all such different women, but had somehow clicked from an early age. Chelle was tall and lanky, always interested in science and sport. Chrissie, with her short, curly red hair, was small, round, feisty and book-obsessed. And Sav, blonde and seemingly prim, but with a wicked sense of humour, had always been planning her white wedding and longing to have her own kids.

Kim appeared with the two coffees and took orders from the others.

'So how are all the rug rats?' Chelle asked Sav, whose tales of her primary school students always seemed to get more outrageous as the year wore on.

'Feral, but gorgeous. And the store?' Sav directed the question to Chrissie, who worked for Torrica Farm and General.

'It's very quiet. Everyone's waiting on the opening break. That's why I could skip out a little early today.'

'I was out at Eastern Edge before I came here,' said Amelia, 'and it is really dry. Paul's hand-feeding all the sheep. Reckon everyone would like to see a break in the weather before the rodeo so it's not too late.'

'Nothing about rain on the seven-day forecast, but we all know that the Met office is always wrong,' Chelle put in. They fell silent. Three of them were farmer's daughters, and Sav a farmer's wife. They all understood the vagaries of life on the land.

'So tell us, Milly, how's the rodeo going?' Chrissie asked, leaning forward. 'I bet you're doing the best job. I heard you on the radio the other day and you came across so well. Anyone would think you've been doing interviews for years!'

'Really? I'm glad I didn't hear it! I hate the sound of my own voice.'

'No, it was fantastic. So professional. If I wasn't going already, I'd be coming now. Did you girls hear it?'

The others shook their heads.

Amelia laughed and her face grew hot. Chrissie had a way of making her feel so good about herself, but she didn't know what to say. She sipped her coffee and hoped for a change in subject. Then Kim arrived with the extra coffees and they all leaned back.

'So what else is happening down at the grounds?' Sav asked, stirring sugar into her cup. 'You've got a much more exciting job than any of us, so make us jealous!'

'Not much, but *everything*, if that makes sense.' Amelia paused and thought about the past week. 'It's a jumble of activity. People are rushing here and there, making sure that all the facilities work, we've got everything we need, et cetera. Then we all head off, and the grounds go back to being silent and still. It's beautiful when they're like that.' She fiddled with her spoon, clacking it against the table. 'But you know, I wish Jim and Kev would get over themselves. They won't leave me alone.'

'Probably want to get you into bed,' Chelle said blandly.

'*What?*' Amelia flinched away from the mental images. 'I don't reckon. They think I'm hopeless. They're waiting for me to trip up and prove them right.'

'As if that's going to happen,' Chrissie said indignantly.

'I hope not.'

Chelle shot her a concerned look, and she shrugged.

'Men!' Sav said, rolling her eyes. 'Wouldn't know a good thing if it whacked them in the face.'

They all laughed.

'Still, they're the only blemish in the whole show,' Amelia said with a smile, 'so I can put up with them.'

'Of course you can. You're strong, woman!' Chelle stuck her arm up with a clenched fist and grinned.

'Yeah!' Amelia said, nodding. 'I am, aren't I?'

'*Anyway*,' Chrissie drew out the word, 'I need some help. Once we've finished the coffee, have any of you got time to come to my place and help me put up some wall stickers?' She smiled wickedly. 'The important thing is that I have wine . . .'

ↄ

'Oh my God,' Chelle giggled, the curvy bits of the stickers' cursive writing stuck to each of her fingers. 'This is *crazy*!'

Amelia, her nose close to the wall, was trying to make sure the stickers were going on straight. She snorted. 'This is ridiculous!'

Chrissie stood back and admired their handiwork, while Sav poured more wine.

'This one's my favourite, from Christine Mason Miller,' Chrissie said, looking at the words that were stuck on her wall: *At any given moment . . .*

The rest of the quote—*you have the power to say: this is not how the story is going to end*—was still to go up. It had taken the four of them more than an hour to get the first four words up, so it looked as though the whole thing was going to take more than one sitting.

'Here, do it like this,' Sav said, putting down her wineglass. 'Smooth them on so they don't bubble. You just need to trace the letter with your finger.'

'That's all well and good for you,' said Chelle, 'but try keeping the bloody thing straight and not getting all the sticky bits stuck together. It's worse than bloody cling wrap, this stuff!'

'It'll be worth it.' Amelia drew another line in lead pencil, as a guide for the letters. 'I love this quote.'

'Me too,' Sav agreed, then glanced at her phone. 'Oh shit, is that really the time? I have to head home. Dean will be waiting. Date night.'

The girls oohed and aahed together.

'Young love,' cooed Chrissie.

After quick goodbyes, Chelle stuck a last letter onto the wall and stood back. 'We'll have another go next week. What do you think, Chrissie?'

'Yep, it's looking fantastic. Love all this positive affirmation stuff. Makes me feel so good when I get up in the morning.'

'You *are* a bit of a hippy,' Amelia observed with a smile. 'Now, who wants to head to the pub for tea? I'm not really ready to go home. Actually . . .' She half-grinned at the other two. 'I'm ready for a party.'

Chapter 8

The pub was cool after the warmth of the afternoon, and the three girls sat happily at the front bar, sipping their wine. It was too early for all the farmers to be appearing, but the old stalwarts Hughie, Terry and Marcus sat in a row with their beers half-drunk, staring at the horse races on the TV.

'So, I'm moving in with Paul,' Amelia said, dropping the bombshell on Chrissie, who almost spat her drink out. Chelle grinned and looked superior.

'Serious?' Chrissie said.

A small smile played around Amelia's lips. 'And I have even bigger news. We got engaged!' She paused and looked at her friends. Both their mouths hung open. 'Aren't you going to congratulate me?'

Both girls gave a little squeal and launched themselves at Amelia. 'That's such good news!'

'Congratulations, cuz!'

Amelia laughed happily. 'Yeah. But don't mention it to anyone yet. Haven't told the folks.'

'Can't imagine your mum's going to be too happy with that.'

'I don't care what she thinks. It doesn't matter what I do—it's never good enough. Dad will be fine, though.' Amelia took another sip of her wine. 'Mum just tends to ignore the fact we've been seeing each other.'

Raising her eyebrows, Chrissie said, 'Paul has an interesting family history.'

Amelia shrugged. 'Who cares?'

'Yeah, but you carry your family with you, no matter what,' said Chrissie, and Amelia frowned, realising that this echoed what she'd told Paul earlier.

Chelle nudged her shoulder and gave her a reassuring smile. 'My parents always say how lovely Mrs Barnes was, and I remember the other kids. They were all nice. Not Old Brian, of course, but he was an alcoholic.'

'Well, Paul is gorgeous and loving and special,' Amelia said.

Her friends nodded, and Chrissie waved to the bartender, Belinda, for another round of wine. Then she crossed her arms and gave Amelia an assessing look.

'The problem is, we've only ever seen you together once—that time you came to Sav's place for dinner. How do we know he's good for you, huh?'

Amelia smiled at her friend's protectiveness. 'It's been a bit of a challenge, 'cause we don't get much time together and we've never eaten out in town. You know he doesn't have much money, and he doesn't want me to pay for him.' She took a sip of her wine. 'It's just the way it's been. But don't worry, that'll change soon.'

'Oh man, we've got a wedding to plan!' Chrissie said excitedly.

'Forget the bloody wedding,' Chelle answered, a sly grin on her face. 'What about the hen's night? We'll have strippers! What do you like? Firemen, policemen? Oh, Milly, tell me you like a man in uniform,' Chelle gushed.

They all giggled and turned at the sound of the door opening. Four blokes in dirty jeans, checked shirts and filthy hats tumbled in. 'Give us a jug of beer, love,' the tallest one called loudly to Belinda, who frowned and cocked an eyebrow as they approached the bar.

'G'day there, girls.' One of the boys stopped to give them the once-over, but when his gaze got to Chelle, his eyes widened and he quickly followed his mates to the other end of the bar.

Chelle sighed and put her head in her hands. 'And there you have it, ladies, the reason I'm still single. No one wants to date the local doctor: she has seen and knows too much.'

Amelia laughed and patted her cousin on the back. 'You'll just have to find someone from out of the district. And unfortunately Paul doesn't have a single friend or a brother who would suit you!'

A few moments later, Anne Andrews' three sons came in, looking good as always. Much better than those other blokes, Amelia noted with approval. She waved at them but they didn't see her, heading straight for the bar. *Won't be long before they're snapped up*, she thought, then noticed Chrissie staring at them and smiled to herself. *Not long at all.*

'The Andrews boys, right?' asked Chrissie. 'They've come into the shop a couple of times, but usually it's just their mum. They seem to keep to themselves a bit.'

Amelia nodded. 'That's them. They're good mates with Graham, and I see them when I go out to help Anne with her books. The committee's hired two of them, the beefier ones, to do security for the rodeo.'

'Hmm, they're all pretty bloody cute.' Chrissie's eyes had a predatory gleam.

The door opened again, revealing another group—this time all girls, who made a beeline for the dining area.

'We should grab a table,' Amelia said, getting up, and the others followed.

Soon the bar was full and the patrons spilt over into the dining area. The noise of laughter and happy voices, and the smell of beer and pub food made Amelia feel at home. A few glasses of wine later, she was red-cheeked and laughing as loudly as some of the men in the front bar.

'That Andrews boy keeps looking over this way.' Chelle nodded towards one of Anne's sons. 'Reckon he's got his eye on you, Chrissie.'

Amelia and Chrissie turned at the same time, and were caught looking. He had a five o'clock shadow, dark eyes and hair, and a lazy smile. He nodded and tipped his glass to the girls. His brothers were deep in conversation and didn't notice.

'Oh, that one's Will. Nice bloke,' Amelia said. 'He's the middle son. The others are Mike and Tony—they're our security guards. Bit rough and ready, but all nice enough. I reckon Will is the pick of the bunch.'

'You know what? We all need more drinks,' Chrissie said slyly. She collected her purse and sashayed over to the bar.

'I'll have a softie, please,' Amelia called after her. 'Got to drive home.'

A path opened up for Chrissie, and Amelia could see Will watching. His eyes strayed to her friend's arse while she stood at the bar, then he went and waited in line alongside her.

'Ha, check them out.' Chelle nudged Amelia. Will was helping Chrissie with the glasses and coming towards their table. 'Fast worker!'

'Evening, ladies,' he said, setting two drinks in front of them and pulling up a seat. Chrissie slipped into her chair and took a sip of her wine, looking like the cat that got the cream.

'Will,' Amelia said with a smile, 'how's your day been?'

'Busy. Heaps of sheep work. We're preg-testing all the ewes so we can sell the dries.'

Chrissie leaned forward. 'The Jensons and Gotheries are doing that too. They were in the shop today and said they were about to start. You must have just got in before them.'

Amelia let the conversation flow around her and looked over the room. Her gaze came to rest on her brother and Danielle—she hadn't seen them come in. They were at the bar, chatting to Mike and Tony. She watched them for a moment: Dani tossing her hair and Graham, his head on an angle, smiling at her.

'Like two peas in a pod,' Chelle said in her ear. 'Both out to get what they can from that arrangement.'

'I think Graham loves her in his own way,' Amelia answered, glancing back over at the happy couple. Danielle caught her eye, but quickly looked away.

'Graham doesn't know how to love anyone but himself,' Chelle said.

'That's a bit harsh, Chelle.' Amelia turned to her, surprised.

'He's my cousin, I can say what I like about him. There's no doctor/patient confidentiality there!'

'Good point.' Amelia paused before going on thoughtfully. 'You know, Dani is still so young. I don't think she realises what's going to hit her. And that's mostly Mum's fault, you know. All the things Graham expects will be pretty hard on Dani.'

'Too true.'

They turned their attention to Will and Chrissie, who were getting on like a house on fire, and shared a smile. How nice it would be if Chrissie could connect with someone; she'd just been through a terrible break-up with her long-term partner.

Amelia was about to get up to go to the loo when someone walked past and bumped the back of her chair. Her lemonade spilt into her lap. 'Oh, bloody hell!'

'Sorry. Oh bugger, sorry.'

Amelia looked up to see Dave carrying a plate of salad and a beer.

'No worries,' she said, and grabbed a handful of serviettes to wipe her jeans. 'Hey, did you find the Guild place?'

He looked sharply at her, seeming a bit uncomfortable. She could tell he was trying to work out how he knew her—then she remembered that they'd never actually met! 'Sorry,' she said, blushing, 'I was at the roadhouse yesterday, working in the kitchen. You were chatting to my Aunty Kim.'

'Oh, right.' Dave coloured a little. 'I didn't know anyone was there.'

'I told Kim she was rude not to introduce me!' Amelia said, grinning. Then she noticed her friends were looking curiously at her and Dave. 'I'm Amelia Bennett, by the way.' She offered her hand. 'This is Chelle, Chrissie and Will.'

Kim's old flame nodded. 'I'd shake your hand, but I'm sort of full,' he said, raising his beer and plate. 'I'm Dave Burrows, Adelaide Metro Police.'

'Really?' Will's eyebrows went up. 'What's happening in our area?' He leaned back in his chair, staring at Dave with interest. 'Haven't heard of anything.'

'Oh, I heard something on the *Country Hour*, back a bit,' Amelia said. 'About fuel going . . .' She stopped mid-sentence. 'Is *that* why you wanted to know where the Guilds lived? Have they been done over?'

Dave smiled blandly, not giving anything away. She could tell he was good at his job. 'I'm here to run a community forum on rural theft and its prevention.'

'Sounds interesting,' Chelle said, reaching for her glass. 'Is there much rural theft going on?'

'You're welcome to join us,' said Amelia, smiling. 'Pull up a chair!'

Dave shook his head. 'Thanks for the offer, but I've got to get an early night. You'll have to come to the forum to find out all about it. Maybe you could help spread the word?'

'Happy to,' Will piped up. 'What are the details?'

'I can do you one better,' Amelia said. 'I'm in charge of all the media for the upcoming rodeo. Send me the info and I'll do up some flyers, and you can stick them around town. Happy to help a friend of Aunty Kim's.'

Dave glanced at her with a bemused expression. 'Would you really? That would be brilliant.' He put her number and email address into his phone.

'Leave it with me,' she said. 'I'll drop them off with Kim to give to you.'

'Right. Thanks very much. Well, nice meeting you.'

She nodded and grinned, and he headed off to eat.

Chrissie smacked Amelia's arm. 'As if you haven't got enough to do!'

Amelia smiled self-consciously and hoisted one of her shoulders. She wanted to send Dave in Kim's direction, but didn't want to gossip to her friends about it—the vault went both ways. 'I like helping, you guys know that.' She looked at her watch and yawned. 'I've got to eat. Ready to order?'

'I sure am,' Chrissie answered. 'You going to eat with us, Will?'

He gave her a slow grin. 'That'd be great.'

Chelle raised a knowing eyebrow at Amelia and she had to stifle a laugh.

When their meals came and Amelia dug into her big chicken parma, talk turned to the rodeo.

'Do you need a hand with anything, Amelia?' Will asked. 'I said to Mum I'd help out on the night if there was anything needing to be done.'

'Um, not that I can think of at the moment. I'll let you know if I . . . Oh, yeah! I *do* have a job for you.' Amelia slapped her forehead. 'Could you act as my second escort when I drive the takings to Torrica? It'll be just after midnight. Gus will be with me, and Paul was going to help, but he's got to be in Adelaide. It would put my mind at rest to have two blokes. I wish I could ask your brothers or the other security bloke, but their company doesn't allow them any responsibility for money, unfortunately.'

'Yeah, guess they've got to cover their arses. And of course I'll help out! Shouldn't be a problem, and I'll be around all night.'

'Thanks, that'll be a huge help. I'd really hate for something to go wrong.'

Will laughed and shook his head at her. 'What could go wrong?'

'I just don't want anything to happen on my watch.'

☙

'After saying I wanted to party, I reckon I've blown out,' Amelia confessed, when she'd polished off her parma and chips. She always got so sleepy after a big meal—and she was wishing her jeans weren't so tight! Grabbing her jacket from the back of her chair, she smiled at her friends and said, 'I'm heading home.'

'I'd better too,' said Chelle with a sigh. 'I'm on call tomorrow afternoon.'

Chrissie looked at Will out of the corner of her eye. 'I think I might stay for a bit,' she said, and smiled.

They all said their goodbyes, then Chelle and Amelia linked arms and walked into the cool night air. Amelia shielded her eyes from the bright lights of the car park and pulled her keys from her jacket pocket. 'Want me to drop you home?' she asked.

'Nah, I'll walk. Clear my head. Pubs always get so hot and stuffy.'

'Well, guess I'll see you when I'm looking at you then. Thanks for tonight.'

Amelia hugged Chelle and headed to her car. Instead of getting straight in, she leaned against it and threw her head back, trying to catch sight of the stars. They weren't as bright here because of the streetlights, but she could still make out the Southern Cross and Saucepan. She took a deep breath, closed her eyes, and let her body relax. She wanted to be calm before she headed home.

A man's voice filtered through the night. 'We do what we want to do and nothing you say will change it. *Nothing*.' There was menace in his tone and Amelia froze, holding her breath.

Silence. Was he gone? She didn't want to hang around and find out. Sliding down behind Pushme, she fumbled as she tried to get her keys into the lock.

'You reckon we're going to cave in?' the voice came again and Amelia realised he was probably on the phone. Or talking to himself. 'No show. None whatsoever. Listen to me again. Fuck off. *We* are the ones in charge, not you.'

She heard footsteps, leather soles clicking on the bitumen. They came towards her then changed direction. At last they faded steadily into the darkness.

Without looking around, she finally managed to jam the key into the lock. She jerked open the door, slid into the car and then locked herself in. Pushme smelt comfortingly familiar and she closed her eyes, taking deep breaths. Her heart was pounding, although she didn't really know why. *Just some bloke with a bee in his bonnet*, she told herself. With Pushme in gear, she drove out of the car park, keeping her eyes peeled. But she didn't see anyone.

Chapter 9

Amelia slipped out of the house an hour earlier than usual and threw on her running shoes. It was Friday morning—Paul would be coming to dinner, and she wanted some extra running and thinking time to clear her head before the inevitable awkwardness.

Each morning was a little crisper than the last and she could see her breath as she puffed outwards. The flock of galahs, the ones she always startled, flew up in the distance; she watched them swoop and glide until they settled in a large gumtree and started to decimate its leaves. They were so destructive, but she did love them. Every time they screamed it reminded her she was home. It was a much better noise than the hum of traffic from her tiny flat in Adelaide.

Her mind turned to the upcoming meal, checking off all the ingredients she'd bought the day before. She was pretty sure she'd got everything after dropping Dave's community forum flyers at Kim's. She was determined to do the cooking so she didn't have to listen to Natalie's complaints about all the trouble she was being put to.

Then there was the rodeo. Only one more sleep. She'd spend today in the camping grounds, making absolutely sure she hadn't missed anything. The committee didn't want to be having to unblock septics when they needed to be at the event.

Amelia was halfway around her track when she slowed to a walk. The gates to Emerald Springs were in front of her. Struck by an irresistible urge, and reminding herself that she had a bit more time, she climbed over and headed into the bush, looking for the path. The track was so overgrown that there was nothing to see, but she knew it by heart and pushed her way through the bush towards the first pool, leaving a trail of broken branches and crushed shrubs behind her.

It was a solid half an hour's walk. When she felt the first piece of granite beneath her foot, she closed her eyes and breathed deeply. The bottlebrushes weren't flowering, but they still had their own special scent that permeated the bush. Wattle birds and silvereyes flicked from tree to tree, and the Mickey minors put up a huge warning call as she passed their perch in the branches.

As she approached the first pool, she could see that it was almost empty. The puddle was covered in green algae and looked very unappealing, but a rain would fix that in no time. She followed the overflow until she came to the second, slightly deeper pool. After looking at it for a while, she picked up a pebble and threw it into the middle, trying to gauge the depth. It had to be around her knees, because she could see the slimy patch of stone where it still trickled, flowing into the main pool.

Holding her breath in anticipation, Amelia turned and kept going. Ducking under some straggly trees and climbing down into the crevice, she could hear water dripping. Then she saw the main pool. It was just how she remembered it— shaded in parts, sunny in others, edged with granite except for one tiny area, which almost looked like a beach. Grainy black sand framed the section that had been used to walk out into the water. Unlike in the smaller pools, the liquid here was crystal clear, reflecting the trees and hills. About six metres wide and a couple of metres across, it was a natural swimming hole.

Amelia slipped off her shoes and socks and dipped her toes. *Brr.* Then, without stopping to think, she stripped naked and slipped into the cold water. She was covered in goosebumps, but that didn't stop her diving under.

'Far out!' She broke the surface and took jagged breaths, doing a couple of strokes before flipping onto her back to stare at the sky. Drifting gently, she let her mind go blank for a few minutes. No dinner, no rodeo, just peace and contentment.

A few minutes later, she waded back to the edge. Shivering, she used her shirt to dry off before getting dressed. Then she glanced at her watch; it was definitely time to start back, and she'd have to hoof it. But her plan had worked a treat: the anxiety had gone. Her head was clear as the water, and her heart lighter.

∽

Knives and forks clinked against the plates as everyone ate in silence. Amelia glanced at Paul, who seemed to be concentrating hard on his roast lamb. Out of the corner of her eye, she could see her mother's mouth pursed in disapproval. Graham wasn't looking anywhere except his plate.

John cleared his throat. 'So, Paul, I guess you're hoping for an opening rain pretty soon?'

Paul swallowed, nodding. 'If it doesn't happen in the next couple of weeks, I'm going to have to look at buying in more lupins. The sheep are holding their condition pretty well, though.'

'Understand what you're saying. Our haystack is going down at a rapid rate of knots.' He put his fork down and leaned back in his chair, casting his eyes between Paul and Amelia. 'So, tell us more about your plans to move in together.'

Amelia looked up and smiled. Trust her dad to just go ahead and bring it up again. The stilted conversation over drinks on the lawn before they'd sat down to dinner had led to her breaking the news in a not-so-gentle manner, and she hadn't been sure if they'd discuss it any more that evening.

Her mother looked up. 'I am *loath* to try and change your mind, Amelia. I know how headstrong and stubborn you can be, but . . .'

Amelia felt Paul's eyes on her and looked at him. His expression of horror made her smile inside. She gave a slight shake of her head in a 'don't worry about it' signal, then turned her full attention to her mother.

'. . . surely you're not serious? This all seems rather sudden.' Natalie took a gulp of her wine as if it was the only way she could go on. 'Unless of course there *is* a reason behind it?' She looked steadily at Amelia.

Graham coughed and grabbed his beer to try and cover it.

'Now, Natalie—' John began, a look of thunder crossing his face.

'*Excuse me?*' Paul spoke at the same time as John and half-rose from the table.

'No, Dad, please, it's fine!' Amelia held up her hand, then reached across the table to grasp Paul's arm. 'Sit down, babe,' she said quietly. He frowned, but did as she asked. Then, keeping her voice even, she said, 'That was pretty uncalled for, Mum. There isn't a reason other than we love each other and want to be together. It's not just about moving in, it's about forever. We're getting engaged too.' There were congratulatory murmurs from her father and Graham. John reached over to shake Paul's hand.

'Well, it just seems so very quick to me,' Natalie blustered, raising her chin defiantly and twirling her wineglass between long, manicured fingers. 'I didn't realise it had gotten so serious. Why didn't you say something before now?'

'We wanted to keep it to ourselves until we were ready,' said Paul, reaching over to squeeze Amelia's hand. 'And we needed an indoor loo!'

Amelia grinned at him and squeezed back. She wished her mother had taken a bit more interest in her life, and not just in Graham and Dani's looming engagement party. She hadn't expected congratulations from her mother so she wasn't surprised by her reaction. But she also knew that Natalie's reaction to the news probably had more to do with her own problems than anything else. Amelia was sure her mother had things that she'd wanted but hadn't managed to do—dreams she'd never followed.

'When do you think you might move?' Graham asked.

'Some time after the rodeo tomorrow,' said Amelia.

Paul spoke up. 'I have to go away tomorrow morning for a few days, down to Adelaide, but we'll work around that.'

94

Graham nodded and thought a moment. 'Well, I guess you won't have time to do the books once you go, Milly? Maybe you could start showing Dani the office.'

John leaned forward and eyed his son sternly. 'Graham, I won't tell you again: that job is Amelia's until she doesn't want it anymore.'

'Of course I understand that, Dad,' Graham began, 'but . . .'

'No buts. That's how it is.' Then John's face softened and he turned to Paul. 'Now we certainly seem to be showing you our dirty laundry! I apologise for that. Let's start off again.' He looked at everyone around the table, an eyebrow raised, and Amelia felt a rush of love for her dad, giving him a grateful smile. He was the one who stood up for her and loved her without question. She was sure she'd disappointed him at times—after all, no one was perfect, least of all her—but he'd always been there and he'd never put her down, even after the little Henry Marshall incident.

'So, Paul, tell me more about your farm.' John rested his elbows on the table and fixed Paul with a friendly gaze.

'Eastern Edge has been in my family for two generations. There's six thousand hectares and I run the same as everyone else in the district: sheep, crops and a few cattle. It's fairly run down, but I'm working on that.'

'I'm sure you are.' John nodded encouragingly. 'How many sheep?'

'About eight thousand.'

'Rams?'

'White Suffolks mainly, put them over merino ewes for crossbred lambs.'

'Gee, the lamb market is looking good for this year, isn't

it?' John grinned. 'Been a few years since the outlook has been so decent.'

'Yeah, I reckon,' Graham put in. 'Pity the wool market's just fallen through the floor. Really going to affect the price I get on my wool this year.'

'Swings and roundabouts, lad, swings and roundabouts. That's what farming is all about.'

Amelia let the blokes talk, glad Paul was getting on so well. She collected the plates and cutlery while Natalie picked up the glasses, and they walked to the kitchen together. Amelia realised too late that she'd backed herself into a corner. As she laid the plates by the sink, she wondered about possible escape routes— but there was no way out. She'd have to talk to her mother.

'I'm just concerned for you, darling,' Natalie said, shutting the door firmly behind her. 'I hear that house is *very* run down. I can't see how you would be happy out there. You weren't raised in a tip!'

'Money and possessions aren't everything, Mum. Paul and I are just happy in each other's company. We talk all the time—we don't shut up.' Amelia gave what she hoped was a reassuring smile. She was worried about living out there too, and about Paul's stubbornness, but there was no way she'd admit it. 'He makes me happy.'

Natalie sniffed as she pulled the ice-cream from the freezer. 'Well, don't say I didn't warn you. And trust me, Milly, I know. I've been married to your father for thirty-two years. Things that I want or need always get put to the back burner because the farm always, *always* needs something. Even when there's extra money around.'

Amelia looked on, surprised, as Natalie's eyes glistened

96

and she plonked the ice-cream on the kitchen bench. She kept talking, but she was looking out the window, not at Amelia. Almost as though she was talking to herself.

'Do you know how long I've wanted to add a patio on to the house? There's money to do it, as you well know. But it just doesn't happen. It isn't a necessity. Somewhere between now and when I mention it to your father again, he'll say we need a new tractor or wool press. The cattle yards might need doing up or a new bore will need to be sunk. It's just the way it is.'

Amelia nodded but didn't know what to say, while Natalie finally turned to meet her eyes and kept talking.

'When there are bad seasons and there's even less money than usual, when the rains don't come, or there's too much of it and the crops look like failing, or the bottom drops out of the market, you need more than love. Men change. They get moody and withdrawn, and if you're struggling to make ends meet anyway, then it will hit you quicker than the rest of us. You need strength of character, my girl, and I'm not sure you've got what it takes to be a farmer's wife.'

Amelia had listened with a newfound compassion for her mother, but that last statement was a hard one to swallow. She decided to ignore it for the moment, and take the opportunity to ask a question that had sprung to mind. 'Mum, if you want a patio and can't have one, but Graham is having the worker's cottage done up, where is the money—and fairness, as far as that goes—coming from?'

Natalie's face closed up. She pulled out some bowls and started dishing up the ice-cream. 'You'll have to ask your father or brother about that. It really doesn't have anything to do with you.'

Chapter 10

When the gates to the rodeo opened, Amelia's stomach dropped. She was so nervous. All she kept thinking was: *It's finally here!* Her hard work was about to be put to the test. *Please don't let me have forgotten anything.*

By the time the bull riding was underway, the compère was talking quickly into his microphone. Amelia, stuck in her little office, could imagine the men milling around the chutes. In her mind, a rider settled himself on the bull and waited breathlessly for the gate to open. There'd be a constantly shifting sea of large hats and high riding boots, a clown in loud coloured clothing, and bulls bucking in the ring.

'Okay, ladies and gents, with a score of fifty-two points, competitor number thirty-two is about to ride Scorpion, the beautiful black bull from the south. This cowboy has made his preparations and is set to come out from chute number two . . .' There was a pause while the boys opened the chute and the bull leapt into the ring.

'Go bull, go rider . . .' the compère's deep voice took on an edge of excitement and Amelia walked towards the window to look out. She could only see glimpses of the ring, hats and a blur of movement as the men ran to follow the animal. 'Oh, look out, he's in trouble!' shouted the announcer.

She knew from the roar of the crowd that the rider had fallen, and now the clowns would be racing around to distract the bull. The rider would be scrambling to his feet and running to clamber over the steel rails on the edge of the ring. There was a collective gasp. Amelia's heart sped up and she stood on tippy-toe, trying to see what was going on and groaning with frustration when she couldn't.

'Scorpion isn't frightened of anything,' the announcer's voice called. 'Run, you clowns!'

Bored with seeing next to nothing, Amelia went back to her desk and kept on working, the rise and fall of the crowd's noise as her soundtrack. Eventually there was a knock on the door, and she looked up to see Anne's warm smile. She smiled broadly in return and got up to let Anne in. 'Hi! Can you believe it's just about finished?'

'Lotta hard work and it's all over in the flash of an eye,' Anne agreed, walking into the room. Then she crossed her arms and looked annoyed.

Oh great, what have I done? Amelia wondered.

'Just dropped by to tell you that you won't be able to rely on Will tonight as the extra escort. He's been drinking.' Anne shook her head, a disgusted expression on her face. 'Sorry 'bout that, love. He's normally the best of the three.'

Amelia digested that and felt a thrill of anxiety run through her. 'That's okay, nothing wrong with having a drink or two at the rodeo,' she managed. 'I should've known Will wouldn't want to be a designated driver tonight. Gus and I'll be right.'

'Bloody young idiots,' Anne grumbled. 'Got numbers through the gate?'

Amelia brightened. 'Yeah! Six thousand, three hundred and twenty-nine.'

Anne let out a low whistle. 'Well then, Amelia, the naysayers on the committee can put that in their pipe and smoke it. Most of that is down to you. Jim Green can choke on it. Good job, girl.'

Not knowing what to say, Amelia flushed with pleasure— Anne wasn't one to give out praise lightly.

Then, glancing at her watch, Amelia saw it was almost midnight. 'Better start to count all of this. Pretty sure that no one's going to want any more change from me!'

'Good idea. I reckon you'll find the bar will start to bring their money over soon. Obviously you've got the gate takings?'

'Yep, Fiona brought that over a while ago.'

A cheer went up and both women turned to the window, craning their necks. The crunch of boots on the gravel outside drew their attention back to the office, and Cappa rapped at the door. 'Anne, got a minute? I need a hand.'

'Sure. Catch you later, Milly. You've done a bloody good job.'

After they were gone, Amelia made sure the door was shut and locked. She drew the curtains, then sat down to count the money. Gus would soon turn up and they'd head into Torrica. Everything was going to plan.

The rest of the night passed smoothly. She and Gus switched cars and loaded up the money bags. Then she drove off along the dark and winding road.

ɛ3

Amelia stared, terrified, at the ute that had just cut her off. She kicked at her own brakes and reefed the wheel to the left, feeling the tyres leave the road for a few heart-stopping seconds. Then they crunched back down, off the bitumen, onto the loose scree and dirt, Amelia fighting for control as she rushed towards the cutting in the side of the hill.

Luckily she'd managed to cut her speed so that the ute bumped rather than crashed, but it was enough for her to hit her head and bang her chest against the steering wheel. She thought she saw stars for a moment, then realised it was a torch at the passenger-side window. She tried to move, but her seatbelt kept her from getting far enough.

The passenger's door opened and the light was shone in her eyes. She threw up a hand to protect them and dropped the other to release the seatbelt. Her fighting instinct kicked in and she screamed in rage, swiping at the flashlight but hitting nothing but air. Then she turned to open her door and run away, but there was a torch shining there, too. No way out.

Amelia heard one of the back doors open and smelt aftershave. Someone—a man, by the impression she got of bulk—started hauling the bags of money out, coins clinking together as they were shifted.

'No, you bastards!' She twisted around in her seat only to have the back of her head slapped none-too-gently. 'Ugh.' She rolled down her window and started to yell at the top of her lungs, in the hope someone, anyone, would hear.

'Bitch.' The word was mumbled but she could tell the voice was male. He opened her door and hauled her out. There was another slap, this one across her face, before hands came out of nowhere and grabbed her. Why hadn't she seen them? The thieves were dressed in black, she realised, invisible against the night. How many were there? Four or five?

Her arms were roughly pulled behind her back and she was dragged towards the road. She took a great big lungful of air to yell again, but felt a hand against her mouth and hot breath on her ear as the man hissed for her to 'Shut the fuck up!'

She started to concentrate more on her surroundings. Her eyes still had the white burn of torches on them, but she could hear men at the ute, talking quietly as they worked. Whoever held her seemed like he would welcome the chance to hurt her; she could feel her lips grinding against her teeth, taste blood.

Her fears were confirmed when he said, 'One more peep, you stuck-up bitch, and I'll break your neck.'

He let her go, but only for a moment, then slipped a blindfold over her eyes and tied it too tight. He did the same with her hands, trussing them behind her back; her circulation slowed immediately.

A man called, 'Is that all?'

'How many bags, bitch?' the voice rumbled beside her ear.

Amelia remained silent.

He tugged on her bonds, hoisting her arms upwards. A moan of pain rose in her throat and was stifled. 'I said, how many bags, *bitch*?'

She could smell his sweat and his ragged breaths, but still said nothing.

'Tear the fucking ute to pieces!' her captor instructed the others.

Terrified though she was, Amelia sensed that the man wasn't concentrating fully on her. She lifted her right leg and brought the heel of her riding boot down hard. It connected with his foot and, despite her fear, she smiled as she heard the air leave his lungs. She twisted away and for a moment she was free. She tried to run, blindfolded, struggling to get loose from the bindings around her hands.

The rope held. All too quickly she was grabbed and flung to the ground. 'You stupid bitch!'

Amelia curled into a ball, tensing for a blow. When it came, the air was pushed out of her lungs and she screamed. But her voice was cut off quickly as someone landed on top of her and smothered the noise. Trying to gasp for breath, but with an excruciating pain in her chest and the pressure of the man's body on top of hers, she couldn't get any air into her lungs. Panic flared within her stomach and she struggled, but once again the pain made her stop.

Moments later, the body lifted off hers and she heard an engine start. *Just leave*, she pleaded in the quietness of her mind. They had what they wanted, surely. *Gus, where are you?* she thought, but she knew Pushme was probably still a long way behind, around a few bends. Or had they run him off the road too?

Amelia tried to sit upright but was pushed over again. Obviously the man was standing near her—she just couldn't see him. Hot tears stung her eyes, and that, plus the pain, just made her angry. 'You won't get away with this!' she said breathlessly, hoping she sounded braver than she felt.

He ignored her. 'Where's the rest of it? We know you've got more than that! You won't like what happens if you don't spill. Keeping some on the side, eh?'

She recoiled as rough fingers grabbed the front of her shirt and pulled so hard the top buttons popped off. She bit her tongue, trying to take away the pain.

'Where's the rest of it?' he asked again, low and menacing. Silence.

'Where the *fuck* is the rest of it?' he shouted.

Her shirt received another tug and more buttons flew away. She pressed her lips into a cold, hard line to stop them quivering.

'Don't do that,' another man said. She thought she recognised his voice and her mind went into overdrive, but she just couldn't place it.

Something pressed into her back, two sharp prongs, and she stiffened. There was an unfamiliar noise before she registered more pain. Her body convulsed. It felt as though a thousand volts were coursing through her. She couldn't stop shaking, and it seemed forever before the pressure against her skin was removed.

'What the fuck did you do that for? A bag slipped under the seat, that's all.'

Through the fug in her brain she thought she could hear them panicking.

'You weren't supposed to hurt her! She's not going to like this.'

'Have you got everything? Let's get the fuck outta here.'

Amelia lay on the ground, unable to make her muscles move. Her whole body was hurting, her head pounding, and her chest felt like it was going to burst. Glass smashed around her and car doors slammed. The gears crunched and tyres squealed when they shot back onto the bitumen, leaving her alone in the darkness.

Chapter 11

Dave sipped his coffee and smiled at Kim over the rim. It certainly wasn't the uncomfortable morning-after that he'd worried it could be. He guessed that came from them being long-time friends—and former lovers. But even though he'd sort of hoped, he couldn't have foreseen last night's events. It must have been the country air and the smell of cattle and dust that had made him reckless.

Kim shifted and her toes slid up his leg. He closed his eyes, remembering the sensations he'd thought were long dead. It appeared they were anything but.

'More coffee?'

The waitress hovered next to their table and Kim turned away, rolling her eyes.

'Jackie, honey, you've asked that three times in as many minutes. Why not have some guts and ask the questions you really want to, or mind your own business?' Kim smiled sweetly as Jackie's face reddened and she hurried away.

Dave's grin widened. Kim was something else. In every way.

'Gossips?' he asked.

'The very best,' she confirmed. 'And don't you worry—' she leaned over and rubbed his arm '—what she doesn't know, she'll make up, and it'll be all over town before we walk out of here.' She stopped and cast a furtive glance to the side. 'In fact, if you look over at the door to the kitchen, the curtain will be parted ever-so-slightly and she'll be looking through it.'

Dave cut another piece of bacon, pushed it onto his fork with some egg and toast, and pulled his best policeman surveillance face. Casually he swung his eyes towards the kitchen—Kim was right. He wanted to laugh, but instead his mouthful of food caught in his throat and he coughed until he felt his face flush. Kim pushed back her chair and ran behind him, thumping him powerfully on the back.

Jackie hurtled through the door. 'Are you all right? Can I help?'

Dave shook his head and tried to wave her away, while Kim continued to whack him. 'Do you need mouth-to-mouth, sweetie?' she asked loudly and cackled as Jackie's eyes widened.

He'd just about caught his breath as she said that, and it sent him off on another coughing fit—this time with a smile on his face. Then, recklessly, he reached up, grabbed Kim around the waist and pulled her to him, planting his lips on hers.

A few moments later, he let her go. 'That should give 'em something to talk about,' he said, a cheeky grin playing around his lips.

Kim put her shaky fingers to her mouth and blushed bright red. 'I reckon it will.' There was a pause. 'More coffee?' They both burst out laughing.

Dave leaned back in his chair and looked at this wonderful woman, trying to work out his feelings. It wasn't like him to jump into bed with someone—he'd have bedded a few women since his marriage breakdown if that was the case. And he'd been faithful to his wife for their twenty-odd years together. It hadn't always been easy. While working for the stock squad in Western Australia, he'd spent many solitary nights away from home; it'd been lonely, no question. He'd missed Mel, and although he'd been in plenty of remote places where there weren't many women, several had shown an interest. He'd always found the willpower to reject them.

But the few weeks of romance he and Kim had shared about thirty-five years ago had never left his memory. He'd wondered many times over the years, especially in hard times with Mel, if it would have worked; if he, at seventeen, hadn't broken it off when he'd headed back to Western Australia. And through all this time, they'd stayed friends. He'd never understood why she hadn't married, but from what she'd said to him last night, it seemed she'd just never found anyone she thought she could spend forever with.

When Kim had organised to meet him at the rodeo, he'd been pleased. Pleased for the company and friendship, he'd told himself. Anything to stave off loneliness. She introduced him to people and he found himself holding court with four or five other blokes. It helped he hadn't mentioned he was a cop, but maybe there was more to it than that. His daughters had told him he gave off an authoritarian air, and he'd been trying to shake that off. It seemed he was succeeding.

Kim made him laugh with her down-to-earth observations and witty comments. It had been a long time since he'd done that without forcing it. Her face was animated and friendly, her eyes bright, and the curves she'd gained just added to the sexiness that radiated from her. Dave thought she was beautiful.

When one of the riders fell underneath the hooves of a black bull and the rodeo clowns weren't able to shift the animal's attention for a few minutes, Kim gasped and turned her face into his chest. Dave's arms automatically went around her in comfort or protection: he wasn't sure which—maybe both. Much to his astonishment, that was where they stayed for the rest of the night. A few hurried kisses, followed by a few slow ones as they walked to the car park and lingered under the stars, had seen him invite her inside his motel room when they arrived back.

Now here they were, having breakfast at the motel's restaurant.

Kim picked up a piece of toast and took a bite, just as a young woman came racing into the room, calling out, 'Kim! Are you there, Kim?'

'I'm here, Dani. Enjoying breakfast with this very sexy man.'

'It's Amelia,' Dani puffed, her face contorted in exertion. 'She's been . . . she's hurt. She's in hospital.'

Dave watched as Kim's face drained of colour and she shot out of her chair. Frantically she grabbed her handbag from the table and rummaged in it, pulling out her mobile phone. 'What happened?' she snapped, as she turned on the device and stared down at it, her hands shaking.

Dave stood and placed his hand on Dani's shoulder. 'Slow down,' he said gently, but with authority. 'Start at the beginning.'

Dani ignored him and continued to talk in a high-pitched, panicked tone. 'Natalie and John have been trying to reach you. She was attacked last night. Driving the rodeo takings into Torrica. All the money is *gone*!'

'Fuck the money,' Kim said as her phone buzzed with messages. 'Is Milly okay? Which hospital?' She half-ran towards the door, with the phone at her ear.

'Barker!' Dani called after her.

'Charge this to my account,' Dave said to Jackie, who'd come out of the kitchen after hearing the commotion. Then he caught up with Kim. 'In my car,' he told her and steered her towards the motel car park.

She went with him, her phone to her ear. 'Natalie?' she barked. 'What's going on?' Dave unlocked the door and held it open for her, while Kim clambered in, still speaking. '*What? Are you serious?*' There was a pause. 'I'm on my way.'

Dave concentrated on the road to Barker, while Kim tossed the phone into her bag and stared moodily out of the window. Dave knew better than to ask anything. His mind was whirling. Rodeo, attack, money stolen. Definitely a matter for the police, and he hoped the locals had done a decent job this time.

Kim was silent until they hit the outskirts of Barker. 'Take the first left here,' she said. 'The hospital is down the end of this street.' She sighed and rubbed her eyes. 'Thanks for bringing me over.'

'You're welcome.'

As soon as Dave pulled into a parking bay and turned off the engine, Kim got out and started striding towards the entrance. Not sure what to do, Dave followed, but at a distance. It was inbuilt in him to help wherever he was needed, but he was wary of walking into an explosive family situation.

Kim stopped and turned. 'Are you coming?' she called out.

'Sure.' He jogged a little to catch up with her. 'Want to tell me what's going on before we get inside?'

Pulling up to a sharp halt, Kim gave him a watery smile. She reached out and put her hand on his shoulder. 'It sounds like Milly was run off the road and forced out of the car. She was tied up and beaten. The rodeo takings were stolen. But that's not all.' Kim took a shaky breath. 'The ambos are sure she was tasered.'

Dave's insides froze but he kept his face impassive, professional. 'Tasered?'

'She's got burns. It must be the same bastards who attacked that old bloke last week, out at his farm.' Kim's voice broke.

'How did you hear about that?'

'Oh, it was in the *Barker News*, of course, and all my customers have been talking about it.' She walked into the hospital, Dave staying by her side this time as they approached the reception desk. 'Amelia Bennett, please?' she asked.

The ward clerk told them where to go and Kim hurried towards the end of the corridor, checking room numbers as she went. When she stopped, Dave watched her take a deep breath, pull her shoulders back and push open the door. He walked slowly down the corridor and leaned up against the wall. Pulling out his phone, he tried to ring Jack's mobile. He still hadn't met the other local cop, Andy.

Unsurprisingly, Jack didn't answer his phone. *So casual,* Dave thought with an inward groan. He considered calling Joan at the station, then shook his head and punched in the number for his supervisor in Adelaide. It rang once and then he listened to dead air. Looking at the screen, he realised the battery was flat.

'Shit.' And his charger was back in the motel room in Torrica. 'Damn it!'

He leaned up against the wall, looking at the ceiling and cursing himself. What a hypocrite he'd been about Jack—here he was, getting it on in his motel room and neglecting his duties! The pot calling the kettle black.

Before long he heard weeping from the hospital room, which immediately sobered him. 'Who would do this, Kim?' a female voice said, distraught and bewildered. 'And why?'

Chapter 12

Amelia couldn't remember why her head hurt so much. She wanted to open her eyes, but her lids were so heavy. Maybe she could reach up and peel them open. She tried to move her arm, but that wouldn't work either.

Fear shot through her. Flashes. Yelling, glass breaking.

The money!

'The money,' she managed to say out loud.

A warm, soft hand gently stroked her arm and moved down to squeeze her fingers. 'S'okay love, try not to talk. You've had a bit of a nasty accident.' Her dad's voice filtered through the fuzz.

'Accident! It wasn't an accident.' Amelia recognised her mother's voice.

Then a softer one. 'Sweetie, it's Aunty Kim. Can you open your eyes?'

She felt a hand on her forehead and smelt Kim's moisturiser. When she tried again to open her eyes, she was rewarded with a murky image of her aunty. There was a shadow on the other side, another person, and she turned her head to look. Shooting pain ricocheted up her neck and into her skull, and she gasped.

'Don't move, Milly. You're hurt. Just lie there and we'll look after you.' Natalie's voice was softer than normal. Gentle, even. 'The police are coming to interview you in a few hours. You need to be strong for them, so just rest, darling.'

'I'm okay,' Amelia managed. 'Water?'

There was blurry movement before a straw tickled her mouth. She put her lips around it. 'Can you suck?' her mother asked.

Even though her tongue felt dry and woolly, she managed to get a few gulps down, but the effort exhausted her and she shut her eyes again.

෪

Amelia wasn't sure how long she'd been asleep. Everything ached or hurt, but her head was clearer this time. Looking around the room, she saw her father sitting near the window, his face relaxed in sleep. At the end of her bed sat Aunty Kim, a magazine open on her lap. 'Ah, hello,' she whispered with a warm smile, 'you're back with us.'

'What time is it?' Amelia asked.

'Three o'clock.'

Her brow wrinkling, Amelia tried to understand.

'It's Sunday afternoon,' Kim explained. 'The rodeo was last night.'

Amelia's heartbeat sped up, her addled brain struggling to take everything in. Finally she gave up. 'Dad?'

Her father stirred in his chair and opened his eyes. Seeing Amelia awake, he came and sat on the bed, gently taking her hand. 'You're a bit banged up, love.'

'Feel like I've been run over by a truck.'

'We're all here, so if you want to go back to sleep, do that.'

'Where's Mum?' She tried to shift her body to a more comfortable position, but winced as more pain ran through her legs.

'She's gone to help Graham at home. She'll be back tomorrow morning.'

'Paul?'

John and Kim looked at each other with horror. 'Oh, sweetheart, we didn't think to call him. We're so sorry.' Kim's face crumpled and she pulled out her phone, dialling Paul's number, but he didn't pick up. 'I'll try him again soon.'

'I'd like him here.' Amelia craned her neck a little and looked down at her body, trying to work out why it hurt so much. Why was her arm in a bandage? 'What's wrong with me?'

'Nothing that's going to stay with you forever,' said her dad. 'Gravel rash.'

'And some burns.' Kim's face was set.

Memories filtered back. An electric shock. Gravel from the side of the road, pushing into her cheek as her body convulsed. Muscles not doing what she wanted them to. Feeling like she had fire burning through her.

'What happened?' she whispered.

'They used a taser gun on you,' her father answered, his voice low and distressed.

Amelia closed her eyes again and tried to remember. She'd put the money bags in Pushme, then Gus had turned up and

115

they'd moved everything to his ute. She'd driven off along the dark, winding road. There wasn't much after that, just snippets. She knew, though, that the money was gone, and that somehow it was her fault.

'I mucked up,' she said, as tears started to slip down her cheeks. 'What will everyone be saying?'

'Don't worry, love,' John said intently. 'It doesn't matter. Everyone is only worried about you—not the money, not anything else. Don't think about it, just concentrate on getting better.'

She couldn't help it. Tears kept trickling down her cheeks. Once again, she'd let everyone down.

Kim reached across the bed for the tissues and wiped Amelia's face. 'Listen to your father,' she said. 'He's right and he's wise. Everyone's only worried about *you*.'

The door swung silently open and a shaft of light from the passageway streamed in. 'Just come to take Milly's obs,' the nurse said, with a slightly too-bright smile. John and Kim got off the bed and retreated to the wall at the far end of the room, while the nurse wheeled in a machine to read Amelia's pulse, blood pressure and temperature. 'The doctor's doing her rounds—I'm sure she'll be popping in here soon. It's been such a busy day.'

As if on cue, Chelle entered the room and made a beeline for Amelia's bed.

'How you going?' she asked softly, holding her hand out for the chart.

'Okay. Bit sore.'

'Yeah, of course you are. Poor thing.' Chelle flicked through the information and gave it back to the nurse, before looking into Amelia's eyes and touching her arm. 'So,' she said, sinking onto the bed, 'it's mostly superficial. You've got a rather impressive black eye. There's rope burn, pretty deep around your wrists, and grazing on your arms and legs. We got quite a few stones out of your upper arms. Your legs aren't so bad because you were wearing jeans.' She gave Amelia a cheeky grin. 'I know those jeans were your old faithfuls, but we had to cut them off you, sorry!'

Amelia managed a small smile, but her heart was pounding. Those blokes had meant business and they had fairly banged her up. Something shifted in her mind. A man's voice. She tried to reach out and grab the memory, but couldn't quite catch it. Then she noticed Chelle watching her. 'What?' she asked.

'I'm just wondering what you're thinking.'

'Nothing really. I can sort of remember things, but . . . not much.'

'That's perfectly normal—you've had a trauma and a whack on the head. It's your body's reaction to protect you, and my guess is you'll remember in time.' Chelle paused. 'You're probably feeling a bit anxious.'

'Mostly I just feel really tired.' It was the truth—all she wanted to do was go back to sleep.

Chelle kept talking, her face sombre. 'Look, you do have a few bruised ribs and two cracked, which will hurt like hell when you laugh, breathe too deeply or cough. Don't get a cold if you can avoid it. And don't let anyone tell you jokes.'

Amelia half-smiled. 'I'll try not to.'

'All right, one last injury to discuss and then I'll let you rest. Two lots of taser burns. They aren't really concerning unless they get infected, because they're so small, like cigarette burns. They're on your left shoulder and just below your left shoulder blade. But look, these stun guns can cause heart attacks if you have an underlying problem, so I ran a few checks on your heart while you were sedated. No issues there—not that I expected one, but better to be safe than sorry. Especially with my cousin. And my best friend.' She squeezed Amelia's hand. 'The good news is that if you feel up to it, you should be able to go home tomorrow or the next day.'

'Thanks, Chelle.' Amelia tried to smile but her eyes kept drooping.

'Here, before you go to sleep again,' the nurse interrupted, holding out some tablets and a cup of water, 'take these painkillers.'

Amelia managed to swallow them before dropping into another deep sleep.

❧

A couple of hours later the two coppers from Barker, Jack Higgins and Andy Denning, appeared at the nurses' station asking to see Amelia. Chelle, who was filling in forms at the desk, took them down to her room but stopped in front of the door.

'Now you listen to me,' she said, pointing a stern finger at them. 'This woman is very dear to my heart, and she's badly beaten and fragile. Be gentle. If you're not, I'll report you to the highest authority I can.' She fixed them with a death stare, then pushed open the door. 'Milly?' she asked quietly. 'The Barker police are here—you know Jack and Andy. They need to ask you some questions.'

Amelia cracked open her eyes and looked at them all, and Chelle felt her heart constrict. 'I'll try.'

'How much money were you carrying?' Andy asked.

'Um, I can't remember exactly. Around four hundred grand. There'll be a copy of the deposit slip I filled out. At the rodeo office.' She was taking sharp, shallow breaths between every few words.

Andy made a note. 'And what can you tell us about the incident?'

Amelia opened her mouth and shut it again. Chelle could see the pain on her face, but knew how important it was that her cousin answer these questions. Even though Chelle hated it, she had to let the police do their job.

Finally, Amelia tried to answer. 'We left the rodeo grounds around one-thirty, I think. I remember that because I looked at the clock on the dash and that's when I realised the ute was going too fast. We . . . Gus and I, we transferred the money from my old car into his ute, and then I drove his ute, with him behind me. Um, I can't remember how I was stopped, or what happened after that.'

Andy looked at Jack, who shrugged.

Poor bastards are incompetent, Chelle thought as she watched the show play out. Well, maybe not incompetent, but so young and inexperienced. How the hell were they to know what questions to ask? Where was the hotshot Adelaide detective?

'Anything unusual happen at the rodeo that you can think of?' Jack asked.

'No. But I mean, not that I remember. There were a lot of people through the gate. I had the feeling it was going to be a really successful night. Of course, I spent most of it in the office, tallying up money and handing out change.'

Andy seemed to pounce on that idea. 'So your job is . . .' He left the question open-ended, a tactic Chelle had seen before.

'Treasurer. I collect the money for the entries, campsites and so on. I have change in the safe for whichever stall-owners need it, and then at the end of the night, I count it, put it in bags and take it to the bank in town. Or that was what was meant to happen. I was trying to do that.'

Chelle knew from the slurring of Amelia's words that she was too exhausted and it was time to intervene. 'Right-o, fellas, that's enough for the moment.' She smiled at Amelia's grateful glance.

'We need a bit more info than what we've got,' Andy protested.

'I'm sure you do, but not at the detriment of my patient. Enough is enough for today.' Chelle fixed them with another one of her stares and the policemen backed down. Following them out the door, she said, 'Maybe get your questions organised, then come back, huh?' And she shut the door with a firm *click*.

∽

Needing to go to the toilet, Amelia struggled to flick the sheets back. Her arms felt like they were being pulled tight and the burning pain took her breath away.

'What are you doing, young lady?' Kim appeared next to her, hands on hips.

'Need to go to the loo.'

'I'll get a nurse. Can you hold on?'

'Uh-huh.'

Within moments Kim was back with a nurse. 'You'll have to tell us if we hurt you.' Together they eased their hands under Amelia's armpits and slowly helped her off the bed, then over to the bathroom.

Sitting there in solitary, Amelia closed her eyes. She knew the police needed more than what she had told them. If only she could remember and wasn't so tired! The dreams she'd had the night before were rushing back. She was curled up on the ground. Even though the air felt warm, her body was freezing. She was shaking. There was a roar of an engine in the distance and then silence. She couldn't work out why her legs wouldn't work, and she couldn't free her hands from behind her back. Everything throbbed. There were pounding foot-steps coming towards her and a man's alarmed voice—Gus? Sirens and flashing lights; kind, calm voices and gentle hands. Then nothing, until the hospital.

She would have to think harder to remember the attack itself, but something was muddling her brain. She wasn't sure if it was the bashing or the drugs Chelle had her on. Managing to get herself off the loo, she shuffled over to the basin to wash her hands. As she looked in the mirror, her breath caught in her throat. That bruise was almost the size of a bloody dinner plate, extending from her eye down to her chin. Gently she ran her fingers over her face and tears sprang to her eyes. *Bastards.*

Then there was the missing money—and Gus's new ute! She remembered the sound of smashing glass. But what about Pushme? Why had Gus been so far behind? Then she remembered. She'd been driving too fast. She'd left him behind.

Unable to bear it, she leaned over the basin and let her tears fall, her sobs becoming louder until Aunty Kim opened the bathroom door, gathered her in her arms and held her, whispering that everything would be okay.

But how could it? Amelia wanted to wail. *How could it?*

Chapter 13

On Sunday afternoon, Dave pulled over about twenty metres from where Gus had found Amelia Bennett lying in the dirt. The local police had been over the area and sealed it off, and he'd met with them and examined their findings once his phone was charged, but he had to see it with his own eyes. He needed to try and understand how the theft had gone down.

The fact that Amelia was driving in front and Gus was so far behind had him puzzled. And how the thieves had got her to stop was also intriguing. Cutting her off was not only dangerous for everyone, but downright foolish. How could they be certain she'd be able to brake in time? Or *maybe* it hadn't been like that at all.

Dave leaned up against the car and slowly scanned the whole area. Here, almost at the bottom of the hill, how could they be sure that no one was going to come over the top? Did they have a decoy on the other side? If so, how would they have stopped another vehicle? Who do you stop for at night on a lonely country road?

Then there were the broken bushes and branches on the side of the road. The deep drag marks in the gravel, the width of a human body, were still visible. Dave ambled over to examine them, his hands behind his back. He followed the impressions until they stopped at the edge of the scrub. 'Right,' he said aloud, 'so that's where Amelia must have been left, until Gus arrived.'

Despite the fact that the furrows were obviously from someone being dragged along, they'd been interfered with by Gus and the ambos. This meant a lot of the footprints were hard to distinguish, too. Nothing was pristine; Dave could hardly regard any of the markings as nice, clean evidence.

He broke off a long stick and poked around in the thick bush. His search turned up a faded Coke can, an empty beer bottle, a battered sneaker and a whole lot of chip packets. Just the normal litter you'd find beside roadways anywhere. Then Dave paced across the bitumen, finding the black tyre marks and following them. They only lasted a few metres, so the brakes must have been applied quickly and heavily, but not for very long. He assumed—hoped—that Jack and Andy had photographed all of this and collected evidence to be sent off to forensics. They'd at least towed Amelia's car to a lot behind the police station in Barker, where Dave was headed next.

In the car he checked his mobile again, even though he knew what he would see—not a single bar of reception. When his battery was dead he'd missed three calls from his supervisor, Steve. The last message had been a very terse command to call back as soon as Dave saw fit. Dave had tried twice now, but the calls had gone through to message bank, and now he was out of range and might continue to be for most of the drive to Barker. He had a strong feeling he would soon be read the riot act.

ↄ

Dave headed to the hospital first thing Monday morning. Before he went in, he sat beneath a tree on a bench outside, looking at the phone in his hand. Five missed calls from Steve the day before, and then two more from him to Steve—well, it wasn't surprising on a Sunday night. The man had a family. Dave sighed, not really wanting to try again. *So much for technology.*

'Why so glum, chum?'

Dave looked up, knowing who it was but wanting to see her face. He indicated the phone. 'Haven't been able to get on to my supervisor and reckon I'll get a bollocking for letting my battery die.'

'Oh, you'll be right! He's not likely to replace you with another detective all the way out here.' Kim sat down on the bench beside him. 'So you'll be involved in the investigation, I take it?'

He nodded and brushed away a fly. 'How's Amelia now?'

Kim smiled. 'She's so much better. Such a strong girl.'

'I'm very glad to hear that.'

They were interrupted by the shrill tone of Dave's phone. He looked at the screen. 'Better take it.' He got up and answered the call, then walked a few metres away. There was no way Kim should hear this conversation. 'Burrows,' he said.

'Where the hell have you been?'

Dave apologised and explained.

125

'Damned inconvenient,' Steve grumbled. 'A full day's passed since this robbery was reported. I wanted you there with the locals when they interviewed her.'

'Well, I've been to the crime scene, I've looked at the ute the girl was driving, and I'm at the hospital now. I've also been told all about her injuries—'

'Yes, I know she was tasered like that man last week,' Steve interrupted impatiently. 'The crimes are obviously linked.'

'She was, but did the locals tell you that the violence has escalated? Amelia has got bruised and cracked ribs, her face looks like a bloody eggplant, and she's been bound, hands behind her back, and dragged through the dirt. She wasn't just tasered either. She was drive-stunned.'

Steve was silent for a moment. Drive-stunned meant that someone had put the gun on her skin and pulled the trigger, sending shock waves through her body—it was much more painful than being tasered from a distance. 'No,' Steve said, his voice low and gruff, 'the locals didn't tell me anything about that.'

'Those blokes are good kids, Steve, but that's all they are. Kids. You can't expect them to be able to manage this themselves. It's beyond their experience.' He paused. 'Look, my take is that Amelia was pulled from the car, bound and dragged to the edge of the road. Then she struggled a bit, gave him, her, whoever, a bit of lip or tried to escape, and was kicked. Pretty sure that's how her ribs got injured.' Dave kept walking, looking around him all the time. 'It happened halfway up a hill, so it seems pretty brazen. Desperate even. If someone had come over the top, they would have been seen straight away.'

126

As he spoke, he watched a florist's van pull into the hospital car park. A plump lady, carrying a large box of flowers, hurried up the steps and inside.

'I tend to agree. On all accounts. And we have this problem of a taser gun—where the hell did it come from? You don't just pull one out of your arse.'

'Exactly. My money's still on the black market.' Dave glanced behind to see where Kim was. She was still sitting on the bench under the tree, watching him intently. 'Could be organised crime. Bikie gangs.'

'Let's hope not. Good God, out in that neck of the woods? Still, as you and I know, anything is possible when it comes to organised crime. Well, you'd better get in there and ask the girl some questions. That's what you're bloody there for.'

Dave clenched his fist and drew in an angry breath through his nose. He *knew* that, for fuck's sake. He *knew* he'd fucked up. Did Steve really have to go on about it? Quietly he banged his fist on the fence between the lawn and parking area.

'Point taken,' he said through gritted teeth.

'Right, I'll be waiting to hear from you then. Good luck.' The phone went dead.

Dave stood at the fence a little while longer, his eyes narrowed and his mind spinning in different directions. Then, with purpose, he strode towards Kim. 'I'm heading inside to interview Amelia,' he told her. 'Do you want to be there while I do it? Or her parents?'

'I'll come with you,' Kim answered. 'Natalie and John are taking care of things at the farm. I said I'd stay until they both got back, but Milly was sleeping so I slipped out to grab a coffee.' Kim ran a hand through her hair and hoisted her large handbag up over her shoulder, and they walked together towards the hospital.

'You care for her a great deal,' Dave observed.

'Of course I do, she's like a daughter to me. I've loved her from the moment I first held her in my arms, and I can't bear to see her hurt.' Tears welled up in Kim's eyes. 'I've never been up close and personal to anything like this. How do you cope?'

'It isn't easy,' Dave answered quietly. 'I keep my mind on the job I have to do.' He didn't mention he couldn't let himself get emotionally involved. He'd seen that bring too many good detectives to their knees.

They continued towards the hospital in silence.

ᘓ

'So Amelia,' Dave began, once they'd exchanged pleasantries, 'can you tell me about the night of the rodeo?'

The young woman shifted uncomfortably. 'I spent most of the night in the office, so people knew where to find me—they had to drop off money for the safe and get change. I counted it as it came in, recorded it in all of the books and stored it. I wrote receipts for late entries and took the entrance fees. It was busy all night, so I didn't get out to see any of the events.'

'Was there anyone else in the office with you?' Dave had his pen and paper poised, but so far there hadn't been any information worth recording.

'No, just the committee members coming and going— Gus, Pip, Anne, even Cappa a couple of times.' She leaned forward to take a sip of water, but Kim beat her to it, grabbing the plastic cup, angling the straw towards her niece's mouth and holding it steady. Amelia wrapped her hands over Kim's and smiled at her before drinking. 'I could have done that myself, Aunty Kim.'

'I know, sweetie, but I was right here.'

Dave cleared his throat. 'What about people you didn't know?'

Amelia nodded. 'Yep, there were a few—those late entrants.'

'So tell me how they pay. Did they have to come into the office? Could they have seen the money sitting anywhere?'

'No and no. There's a window that acts as a counter. Like the ones in a movie theatre in the city, I guess. I sat behind it, taking their money and giving them change. You can't see very far in and I didn't leave any money lying around, if that's what you mean.' She sounded defensive and this intrigued Dave.

Kim leaned forward. 'No one is accusing you of anything, are they, Dave?'

'Not at all.'

Amelia just stared at him, distress in her face.

'You probably need to understand,' said Kim, 'that Milly seems to think people are going to blame her for this—'

'Aunty Kim!' Amelia cut in, a blush rising over her cheeks.

'Well, it was quite a thing for the committee to let a much younger person take on such an important role.'

Dave sensed there was more to the story but let it go for the time being, making a note on his pad to ask Kim about it later. He looked up at Amelia. 'Who else, other than you, has the key for the safe?'

'Gus and Anne. We needed a couple of backups in case they couldn't find one of us.'

Dave checked his notes again and decided to change tack. 'Judging from what Gus has told me, you were in his ute, in front, and he was in your car.'

'Yeah, that's right. I was going to go in my old car, but we swapped at the last moment. Gus thought it would be better if I went in his, in case mine broke down.'

'So you put all the money into Gus's ute?'

'Yeah, I already had a lot of bags in my car and we switched them over.'

'Right.' Dave looked at her intently. 'I'm assuming you hired some security guards for the rodeo?'

'Of course, it's a legal requirement. There's four guards, and they work in shifts.'

'Why didn't you have them around while you handled the money? And why didn't they escort you to the bank?'

'Oh, they're not proper security guards. More like crowd control. They're only there to break up fights or move people along when they're a little too drunk.'

Dave made another note on his pad. 'Where do you hire them from?'

'Two of them are locals—Anne Andrews' sons, Mike and Tony, and the other two came across from Barker. Harry King and Ian Pincott.'

After adding the names to his notes and making a note to contact them, Dave glanced up at Amelia again. 'Just so I'm clear, do you know why Gus wasn't right behind you on the road?'

Amelia looked miserable. 'I was driving too fast. I can remember looking down and seeing that I was above the speed limit, so I slowed down. Guess it was too late.' Tears formed again and she turned to Kim. 'Told you I stuffed up.'

Kim leaned forward and clasped her niece's hands. 'Whoever did this to you, that's whose fault it is. You, darling girl—' she put her hands on either side of Amelia's face and looked her in the eye '—*cannot* blame yourself for any of this.'

Dave studied Amelia's crumpled face, and was inclined to agree with Kim. He had to stay professional, though, and get through the rest of his questions.

Chapter 14

A quiet tapping woke Amelia. When she rolled over, her hospital bed creaking and complaining, she saw Pip and Gus standing in the doorway. Pip carried a blue plastic vase filled with brightly coloured blossoms: gerberas, chrysanthemums, a couple of deep red roses, all set in a forest of Australian native greenery. 'Hi there, you!' she said quietly, putting the flowers onto the side table.

'Hi.' Amelia tried to sit up without hurting her ribs, but failed. She gasped and clutched her side.

'Oh, Milly, let me—' Pip rushed over and helped her into a sitting position.

'Thanks,' Amelia breathed. 'Just got to learn to take my time.'

Gus stood at the foot of the bed, hat in hand, looking uncomfortable. 'Sorry this happened, Milly,' he said gruffly. 'Bit of a bugger really, considering how successful the rodeo was.'

'A *bit*?' Pip glared at him and shook her head. 'Men!' She turned her attention back to Amelia and raised her eyebrows. 'So how are you, love?'

'Pretty sore and tender, but other than that, not too bad.' Amelia felt as uncomfortable as Gus looked: all she really wanted to ask was if they blamed her at all. Or if there was any news about the money or the thieves. Everyone seemed on tenterhooks around her. She told herself that was just because they were worried, but she couldn't quite believe it. 'I just feel really bad about—'

Pip cut in. 'Everyone's saying what a wonderful job you did, all the media attention and so on. You really boosted the profile of our little rodeo. Everyone is so proud of you!'

'What, even with this classic Milly Bennett stuff-up?' Amelia couldn't help herself.

'It was *not* a stuff-up,' Pip assured her. 'It's something no one could have foreseen. Unfortunate, sure, and we're all so sorry you got hurt, but none of this is your fault.' She perched on the edge of the bed and smoothed Amelia's messy hair away from her face. Her voice was gentle when she spoke again. 'I think you're being too hard on yourself. I don't see anyone else sitting here in hospital with bruised and cracked ribs. You took the full brunt of the attack for the rodeo committee. We—'

Gus interrupted, putting his hand on his wife's shoulder and clearing his throat. 'Look, I've got an apology to make. I got a little, um, too relaxed, I suppose. I need to accept some of the responsibility. When you couldn't get a second escort, I should have found one and followed up on two-ways and everything else. I'm the president, the buck stops with me.' He scratched his head. 'I still can't believe this actually happened.

133

It shouldn't have. It used to be safe out here, but this sort of crap makes it seem there isn't much difference between us and the city.'

Though his expression was terribly sad, as if he'd lost something deeply personal, Amelia felt a great wash of relief. She didn't know about the rest of the committee, but these two didn't blame her, and their good opinion mattered the most.

'What about the money?' Amelia asked. 'Will insurance cover it?'

'Don't you worry,' Gus said. 'It's only the cash that's gone, not all the transfers that were already made into the bank. And yeah, the insurance'll cover about eighty per cent of what we lost. Not bad at all.'

Squeezing Amelia's hand, Pip said, 'Please say you'll come back, Milly, and be our treasurer again. You really did such a wonderful job. And we're going to give you another title.'

'What's that?'

'Media officer.' Pip grinned cheekily. 'You deserve it after all the extra things you did on the worldwide web.'

Amelia looked from one to the other, a wide smile forming. How could she say no? 'I'd love that. Thanks.'

The door opened and Amelia's mother came in, carrying a foil container with steam rising out of it. Greetings were made, then Natalie placed the meal on the wheeled table in front of Amelia. 'It's your favourite,' she said. 'Apricot chicken and rice. Thought it might be a nice break from the hospital food.'

'Oh, thanks, Mum,' Amelia said, grateful, then looked at Natalie properly: she was exhausted. There were shadows under her eyes, the lines around her mouth seemed deeper, and her face was drawn and pale. 'That's really kind of you.'

Unusually kind to me, she thought, pleased that her mother could still throw surprises her way.

'I guess you're busy out at Granite Ridge?' Gus asked Natalie.

'Yes, of course. The men are always busy, aren't they? That's the way of farming—Things don't stop just because . . .' Natalie flashed a smile instead of finishing her sentence. She started to tidy up around the room, gathering get well cards and newspapers and stuffed toys, rearranging the flowers in vases, pinching the heads off blooms that were wilting in their wet-foam boxes.

'And you've still got all the arrangements to make for Danielle and Graham's engagement party on Saturday?' Pip offered.

'Hmm, yes I do.'

Amelia tuned out the conversation and watched Natalie. She was clearly tired, stressed and agitated. *Seems like she's really taking this hard*. Whatever their differences, and despite all the discouraging things that Natalie had said over the years, her mum really did love her and want her to be safe.

The door was pushed open again and Anne, wearing dusty jeans and a checked shirt, strode in. She was carrying a large box of white daisies. Amelia realised her room was starting to feel like a crowded phone booth.

'I am so sorry, Milly,' Anne boomed without saying hello, walking straight to Amelia's bedside. 'I swear that boy of mine needs his head read. So unreliable. Don't know what got into him that night, I really don't.' She set the daisies down and put a hand on Amelia's shoulder, peering at her bruised face. 'Will has a lot to answer for.'

Tears welled in Amelia's eyes. 'Thank you,' she said. 'I've got to confess, I thought you'd all be so cross with me. Didn't think you'd want me back on board or to have anything to do with me. But you're all being so kind . . .'

'Why would you have thought that?' Natalie demanded, glaring around at the three committee members. 'It's quite clear that the blame lies elsewhere.'

Amelia gasped. 'Mum!'

'It's true. You're a first-timer. Everyone else on that committee has been through more than one rodeo and they should have known better. Been more prepared, more aware of the potential danger. The whole district's been talking about that old man who was tasered out at his farm last week.' She kept glaring at Gus, Pip and Anne. 'My daughter could have been killed because of your carelessness.'

Amelia watched, amazed, as tears welled in Natalie's eyes. 'Mum, it's okay. I'm okay—and that's not really right, or fair, what you're saying.'

Anne put her arm around Natalie's shoulders, and held tight for a moment before she was shaken off. 'You're right, of course,' Anne said softly. 'As a committee we *are* responsible for all of our members.' She paused and looked into Natalie's eyes. 'We're so sorry your precious daughter has been hurt. We'll do everything in our power to make sure nothing like this ever happens again.'

Natalie rubbed her hands over her face and tried to smile. 'Thank you,' she said with as much dignity as she could muster.

There was a heavy silence until Gus said, 'Have you heard anything, Milly, about the investigation?'

'Dave Burrows, that copper from Adelaide, has been here asking questions about all sorts of things—like whether or not anyone got into the office on the night, or who knew of our travel plans, and so on.'

'I've been wracking my brains trying to remember if there was anything untoward that night, but I just can't think of anything,' Pip said, frowning.

'No one's likely to recall anything,' Anne said, patting her on the arm. 'It was chaotic. We were all so busy trying to make sure everything went off smoothly. I wish there was something I could remember! Wouldn't that make a difference?'

'My oath!' said Gus. 'I've talked to everyone on the committee and a lot of the local attendees, and so has Detective Burrows. He got a big zilch, as did I.' He shook his head. 'You know, he's not a bad fella, that detective. He's pretty thorough. He checked on where we all were on the night and at what times we all left. Who had what jobs, et cetera.'

'When he was talking to me, he didn't rush. Got through what he needed to know,' Anne said. 'Same when he talked to Mike and Tony. They were really impressed. But how many people can he interview? I mean, there's only one of him, and those two boys from Barker. There's quite a few of us.'

Amelia sighed and nodded. 'And there was such a huge influx of people into Torrica over the weekend. It would be impossible to question everyone that was here, to track them down. We don't know most of the visitors' names!'

'I'm sure it was some blow-in,' Natalie said sharply. 'A local wouldn't do this.'

'I hope you're right,' said Pip. Amelia had never seen her look so worried and uncertain. 'Because if one resident could do this to another, to someone they know, live with, work with—well, our community is well and truly stuffed.'

Everyone nodded.

'Dave asked me about my financial situation,' Amelia said in a small voice. It had been bothering her, niggling at the back of her mind, since the detective had left. 'I guess he has to do that, to get to know and understand me better. Understand the situation. Doesn't he?'

Natalie stiffened. 'I'm not sure. Why would he need to know about that?'

'Guess he's just got to get a feel for the big picture,' Anne said. 'Did he ask you, Gus?'

Gus nodded. 'Yeah, he did. Just one of those questions he has to ask, I reckon. He also asked about the financial situation of the rodeo, and who else had access to the money. Suppose he's gotta discount what needs discounting and then, as he's weeding his way through all the information, he might find an important clue.' Gus shrugged and grinned. 'But what would I know about investigating a crime?'

Chapter 15

Dave tapped at the microphone and the feedback squeal made him put his hands over his ears. It was worse than fingernails sliding down a blackboard.

'Sorry, mate!' Kane, the boy in charge of the audio—who didn't look older than fourteen—adjusted a few levels and suggested he try again.

'Testing, testing . . .' This time it sounded right.

'There we go,' said Kane, pleased with himself. 'All good. Just don't touch anything and nothing should go wrong.' He took off the headphones and put them on the control board, then stood and stretched.

'Are you going to stick around for the event?' Dave asked. 'Or do you have a curfew?'

Kane laughed. 'A curfew? I don't reckon, mate. But I won't be here—got to head off now.'

'Is there someone else who knows how to work this thing if there's a problem?' Dave looked at the equipment;

he didn't have a snowflake's chance in hell of operating the set-up.

'Oh yeah, someone'll be around,' Kane said casually, throwing his rucksack over his shoulder. 'Everyone's had a bit of a go at using it, so you'll be right.' His boots clumped over the wooden floorboards towards the exit. 'Good luck tonight,' he called back with a flick of his hand.

Dave surveyed the sparsely furnished hall and sighed. He wished he could have brought a partner: there was safety in numbers. If something went wrong, there were two of them to fix it—or one to keep talking while the other pretended he knew what he was doing. But departmental budgets didn't stretch that far and, not for the first time, Dave felt the weight of responsibility on his shoulders. Plus, he was buggered after his full day of interviews and he'd had to skip lunch. The forum was meant to start in—he checked his watch—less than two hours. *Bloody hell.*

Dave straightened and told himself to get over it. He had to get across to the local farmers how important it was that they lock everything up. Times were changing and crime crossed all parts of society now. The country was clearly no longer immune.

In the corner of the big space were piles of chairs stacked up against the wall. His R.M. Williams boots clicked on the floor as he walked over to lay them out. Placing them in rows of six, he worked until the hall was filled with chairs.

Methodically, he took out the leaflets and pens he wanted to distribute, and slid them into brown paper bags with string handles. There were information sheets about what he'd cover tonight, but experience had shown these types of forums always worked better if there was a take-home package. Along with the sheets, each bag held a magnet emblazoned with the Crime Stoppers phone number, an SA Police pen and a notebook. Dave was hoping for at least a hundred attendees. He stacked the bags in lots of ten, so he'd know how many he'd processed.

'Helloooo?'

Dave turned as high heels clipped up the steps and into the dim room.

'Oh,' said Kim, stopping for a minute and peering around, 'Dave, you in here?'

With a smile, Dave went over to her. 'What are you doing here? Not that it's not a nice surprise.'

Kim smiled back at him and held up a plastic bag. 'Dinner. I skipped out early. Jackie from the motel's in charge.'

'I'm very spoilt!'

'Nothing less than you deserve.' Her smile widened. 'Do you want to go sit in the park or eat here?'

'I reckon some fresh air and wide open spaces would suit me down to the ground right now.'

He held out his hand, Kim took it, and together they headed outside. Even though the days were still warm, the evenings held the promise of winter. The clear blue sky and the sun dropping to the horizon didn't do anything to ward off the chill.

'How did you know I was here?' he asked as they crossed the road, making a beeline for the Lions Club park.

'And you're supposed to be a detective.' Shaking her head, Kim poked him in the side. 'Your car's parked out front!'

Dave gave a short chuckle. 'Yeah, I guess that's a bit of a giveaway.'

In the park they sat down on a bench and Kim handed him a steak sandwich, a Coke and a straw. Before he'd even started to unwrap it, ducks appeared at their feet, silent and brooding, watching for dropped crumbs. Dave threw a crust towards the pond and the ducks stampeded in a quacking, excited mass. The strongest one got there first and pecked the food up, preparing to swallow, but was thwarted by one of the smaller birds, who cheekily plucked the hunk of bread straight out of the other's beak. Dave smiled and took a big bite of his sandwich.

'It's beautiful here, isn't it?' Kim asked, looking around. The body of water was surrounded by tall gumtrees, all hand-planted forty or so years ago, and a small bridge ran from one side to the other. A grassy area off to one side was equipped with wood-fire barbecues, next to a brightly coloured plastic playground on tanbark.

There was no one else around but Dave could hear the passage of cars behind them every so often. He slipped his arm around Kim's shoulders and looked down at her. 'So how's your day been?'

'Busy! Had to dash back to work from the hospital in the morning. I've served dozens of buckets of chips, burgers, steak sandwiches. Thank goodness I've got Jackie to give me a hand in the kitchen. There were a couple of shearers' buses come through and put in big orders. But that makes me happy.' Kim smiled and flicked back her long curly hair, and Dave eyed it appreciatively. 'And there was a busload of oldies on a trip to the Flinders Ranges. They just wanted coffees and cake, so that was easy enough.'

'You love that roadhouse, don't you?'

He screwed up the wrapping and tossed it back in the bag. Opening the Coke, he took a sip and looked over at her. He was still getting used to having a woman back in his life, and the fact that it was Kim startled him every time he thought about her.

A woman back in his life . . . Was that really what Kim was? After all, it had only been a few days, and how could it work once he'd headed back to Adelaide? Dave decided not to think about that yet.

She reached out and took his hand, giving it a squeeze. 'I love being the boss of my own business—and I love talking to people, seeing them smile, hearing their stories. Makes me happy. When the coaches come in, a lot of the oldies like to chat about themselves and where they're from, what they've done with their lives and where they're heading to. I know it isn't a fancy career, but it works for me.'

She was so open about her life, so honest. Dave couldn't help himself. Her lips were full and just demanded to be kissed.

'Mmm.' Kim's mouth moved against his. '*You* make me happy too.'

'That's lucky, because the feeling's mutual.'

ᴄᴐ

Dave watched Kim serving cups of tea from the small kitchen at the back of the hall. He was so pleased she'd offered to help—it freed him up to walk around the hall and talk to the people gathered there. He caught her eye and grinned. She winked, then turned back to the next man in the queue.

It was a good turn-out. As Dave worked the room, he listened to snatches of conversation. Farmers were lamenting the need for opening rains and how it was unseasonably warm. Pretty standard stuff when a bunch of farmers got together. But then his ears picked up something a little more intriguing—it sounded like the local vet was laying into a group of blokes about paying their bills.

Just as he was edging closer to eavesdrop properly, someone tapped him on the shoulder. 'G'day, you must be the copper everyone's talking about.'

A man who was seventy if he was a day appeared at Dave's shoulder. He pushed back his terry-towelling hat to reveal a deeply lined face, but eyes that were clear and alert.

'Dave Burrows.' He held out his hand and the man shook it with a firm grip.

'Clive Frank. I just wanted to let you know there've been a few strange happenings around my place recently.'

'Have there now? Would you mind writing them down for me? In the bag there's a pen and paper—'

'Can't write,' Clive said. 'It won't take long. Me dogs have been barking at two in the morning for the last couple o'days.'

'Right,' said Dave, pulling out his own notebook and scribbling. 'Did you have a look outside?'

'Yep, couldn't see nothin', but it's odd, you know?'

'I'm sure. Where's your farm?'

'T'other side of Torrica.'

'Do your dogs ever bark when there's a full moon, Clive?' Dave asked, knowing full well there was a super moon due that night.

Clive scratched his head. 'Now that you mention it, they can have a bit of a howl when the lady is out.'

'When they do it next, maybe you should check if there's a full moon? If there's not, certainly get back in contact with me.' Dave handed over his card.

'Cheers, Detective. Me missus said you'd have a good laugh at me expense, but I thought I should say something. You never know.'

'Dead right, Clive, I'm pleased you did. Catch you a bit later on.'

Dave moved off into the crowd before Clive could say anything more. A spite-filled voice caught his attention, and he shifted over to the wall where he could stand without drawing attention.

'Of course she had something to do with it,' a man was saying. 'I've worked on the committee with her and there was *no way* she should have been allowed to have that job. Like I've said before, you work up to a position of responsibility—you don't just get it handed to you. Thought you agreed with me on that.'

'Jim, you're blowing hot air out of your arse. Milly and her family are respectable people. Why do you reckon she's involved?'

'Well, she's hooked up with that Paul Barnes for a start, isn't she? He hasn't got a pot to piss in. My theory is that she's helped herself to our takings to make their life a little easier. Don't know why you find it so hard to understand, Cappa.'

'Mate, you're making life hard for that girl, with no reason. And I wouldn't let Kim hear you saying any of that. You'll end up with egg on your face quick smart.'

It was Jim and Cappa from the committee: Dave had interviewed them, and he'd found out from various committee

145

members that Jim hadn't been keen on Amelia being treasurer. He listened for a bit longer before he looked up and realised Kim was trying to attract his attention. She pointed at her watch: it was time. He swallowed, then made his way to the front of the hall and tapped at the microphone. Happily there wasn't any feedback. When he scanned the sea of faces, all the people taking their seats, he was pleased to see the space was nearly full. Glancing over at the sideboard, he realised all the bags he'd made up were gone.

'Good evening, everyone, and thanks for coming along. I'm Dave Burrows from the South Australian Police. Until a few years ago, I headed up the stock squad over in WA, so I'm no stranger to rural crime or country life.' He paused as he collected his thoughts. 'Now, there were info packs over there, but it appears they've all gone. If you've missed out you can see me afterwards and I'll get one to you. It's important that everyone has one, because inside is a Farm Security Assessment form.

'One of the things the SA Police want to do is work with you to prevent all types of rural crime. Can be anything from domestic violence to pubs getting ripped off, to stolen property from farms or depots. I'll be at your disposal for the next few weeks, so if you'd like me to come to your property and do a security assessment, I'm more than willing to do that.'

There was a general shuffling of papers and people putting on reading glasses to look at the contents of the bags. For the next half an hour Dave addressed issues of safety for persons and property, as well as covering the best means of crime prevention, before turning his attention to the rodeo theft.

'Now, I'm sure you've all heard that a young woman was badly hurt in a robbery this week, and you might have heard

146

about other thefts committed in this area over the past few months, within about a hundred-k radius of Torrica. These crims aren't scared of hurting people. An elderly farmer was tasered during a theft last week—it seems they didn't expect him to be around. The woman who was attacked has injured ribs and was tasered. All I can do is encourage you to keep your eyes open and be careful. If you see anything odd or suspicious, please get in contact with me. Thanks for your time this evening.' Stepping down from the platform, Dave waited for people to come up and talk to him.

ᏚᏃ

'That went really well,' Kim said as she washed up the last of the cups. Dave was drying and putting away. She bumped her hip against his. 'We make a good team.'

'It did, and yes, we do,' Dave answered with a smile, but he was thinking hard about a conversation he'd found very interesting. He said casually, 'What can you tell me about the local vet? And what's his name?'

'Grant Hink. Oh, he's a nice enough bloke, I reckon. I don't have much to do with him, since I don't have any animals.' She looked at Dave. 'I don't suppose you're going to tell me why you're asking?'

'Strictly confidential, but I heard him and a few other blokes talking. Sounds like he's having trouble getting them to pay their bills, and he's struggling.'

'Nothing new about that.' Kim snorted. 'There're always people not paying their accounts. They don't realise how important it is for businesses to have a good cash flow. We have bills too.'

'Would there be many people in town with that problem at the moment?'

'I wouldn't know without looking at their bank accounts, Dave,' Kim said with a grin, but her eyes were thoughtful. 'I'd find it hard to pin it on a local . . . however, if you're looking for reasons for a robbery, I can probably name three businesses in the main street which are just about to go under.'

Chapter 16

On Monday evening Amelia was enjoying a brief moment of quiet. She was tired and, though her visitors' hearts were in the right place, she wasn't sure she could stand to answer 'How are you?' one more time; she was glad the room's other bed had stayed vacant.

She wanted to see Paul, of course, but no one could get on to him. Trying not to think about it, she opened up a gossip mag. 'How She Drove Her Man Away' screamed the headline above a photo of a scowling actress. *Perfect*, Amelia thought, snapping it shut and gingerly leaning her head back against the starched pillow.

Natalie had tidied the flowers and gifts into orderly groups, making the stark hospital room look like a cross between a toy store and a florist. A thin stream of late-afternoon sunlight cut across the floor and, as the door opened, caught on *Get Well* printed in silver and gold over a great bundle of balloons that seemed to push their way into the room.

Sav, Chrissie and Chelle appeared behind the mardi gras of colour. Their arms were full of boxes of chocolates, flowers and other goodies—Chrissie held up a bag of green grapes. Then Sav let go of the balloon strings and they floated to the ceiling like reverse confetti, bobbing up and down. Their brilliant impact matched Amelia's smile as she realised that these were the visitors she needed.

'Helium-filled happiness, Milly!' squealed Sav while she sashayed past the end of the bed, reaching up to tickle the bottom of the balloons.

'Ready, aim, fire!' said Chelle. She pulled a bottle of champagne from under her arm, tore away the foil and aimed it at the ceiling. The cork popped, loud as a shot, and they all laughed.

'Really, Doctor? Booze?' said Amelia with a grin, a little shocked.

Chelle held the bottle up for Amelia's inspection. 'Non-alcoholic, my friend. A good physician is always prepared.' She cleared a space on the bedside table and produced four plastic cups from her lab coat pocket.

Chrissie placed a card next to the cups after she'd removed the cheesy badge from its front—it read *No. 1 Patient* in big cartoon letters. She tried to hand it to Amelia, but Chelle grabbed it, opened out the pin and began poking at the silver balloon above her head. 'I told you not to buy silver.'

'You're a lunatic!' Sav laughed when the silver ball popped. 'Don't you know how to behave in a hospital? I could have you deported, or defrocked or whatever they do to badly behaved young doctors!'

Amelia snorted. 'Isn't defrocking what they do to clergy?' She giggled then gasped, holding her ribs. 'You've got to stop this. Chelle, you said no jokes!'

'Never fear,' commanded Chelle, passing Amelia a cup, 'the doctor is on duty.' She stopped and grinned. 'I'm also off duty!' Then she turned to Chrissie, who had seized the badge and started popping balloons. 'If you don't quit doing that, I'll use you for needle jab practice!' She took a pillow from the spare bed, giving it to Amelia. 'Here, hug this. It'll help.'

Chelle turned back to Chrissie, who scrambled to get away and dropped the badge. Sav snapped it up with a shout of triumph.

The multi-hued orbs bounced in the draft from the air-conditioning, creating a kaleidoscope across the ceiling. Amelia gazed up at them. 'The balloons are beautiful,' she said, as her friends collapsed in a giggling heap. 'Thank you!' She stopped and put on a sick patient's voice. 'But Doctor Chelle, are you sure this is allowed?'

'Certainly. In fact, it's compulsory!' replied Chelle, coming over to sit on the edge of Amelia's bed. Then she whooped and jumped up as Chrissie released the brakes from the bed and pushed it away.

'Oh sorry, Doctor,' said Chrissie, with a complete lack of remorse.

Amelia leaned back and straightened. 'Oh, stop! I knew you lot couldn't be trusted. Nurse! Help! You're killing me. Don't you know I've got cracked ribs?'

Chelle pulled out another pillow from behind Sav, who'd made herself comfortable on the empty bed. 'Here you go, hold both pillows like you'd hold Paul. They'll give you support when the pain starts . . . unlike a bloody man!'

Amelia hugged the two pillows close.

'I don't think that's going to be much comfort to her,' Chrissie interjected.

Chelle laughed again. 'Hey, Sav, where's that pin? Chrissie here needs a lesson in discomfort. Don't make Milly laugh too much. Each time you crack a joke, I'm going to jab you. Milly's in a lot of pain and I'd hate to let her suffer alone.'

'You're a bloody sadist!' Sav squeaked. She walked over to Amelia, reached down and pinned the badge to her pyjamas. 'Right, now I think we're all safe from the maniac medic in our midst.'

'Did you buy out the entire florist?' asked Amelia, hugging the pillow tighter.

'Every last blossom,' confirmed Chrissie, grinning wickedly. 'Except a few wilting chrysanthemums in a jam jar.' She leaned forward. 'Your future sister-in-law arrived to order for the engagement party.'

'Why would you order flowers for an engagement party?' Sav asked scornfully. 'You'd have to sell the top paddock to pay for enough to fill the footy club.'

'I wouldn't want flash flowers,' said Chelle, dreamily. 'Gum leaves and native bushes would be enough for me.'

'Dani doesn't do things by halves,' Amelia said, drawing a slow, steady breath.

'Ooh, yeah, we know. And if we didn't, one look at her left hand would set us straight quick smart.' Chelle surveyed the three boxes of chocolate, chose the Cadbury Roses and cracked the plastic seal. She took her sweet time selecting a

152

chocolate before she offered them around. 'Dani was carrying on about being on a wedding-dress diet. Maybe we could send her some chockies to help out.'

'You guys are really down on her! Has she done something I don't know about?' Amelia asked.

'Nah. Just being her usual endearing self,' Chrissie said.

Amelia shook her head, giving a wry smile.

There was a gentle knock on the door and a nurse pushed a trolley in. 'Oh, you've got visitors. How lovely. I just have to check everything, though—sorry to intrude.' She reached down and took the medical chart from the end of the bed, then realised Chelle was sitting in front of her. 'Oh, hello there, Doctor.'

'I'm not here,' Chelle answered in a sing-song voice. 'I'm off duty.' She turned her attention back to the chocolates.

The girls quietened, making their way through the Roses, while Amelia's vitals were recorded and her medication swallowed down.

'And what have you had to drink today?' asked the nurse.

'Lots of water,' Amelia answered, 'and a little bit of this fizzy grape juice.'

The nurse's face stiffened until she saw *Non-Alcoholic* emblazoned on the bottle. 'And your bowels? Have they opened?' She smiled apologetically.

Amelia glowed a bright red and nodded, before asking, 'Would you like a chocolate?'

'Oh, thank you so much! A nurse's main food groups are cold coffee and stolen chocolates. Sugar and caffeine see us through.' She grabbed a fistful from the box and stuffed them into the pocket of her uniform. 'Let me know if you need anything,' she said while backing her trolley out of the room.

Amelia noticed Chelle scanning her medical chart. 'Am I gonna make it, Doc?'

'Certainly. Don't even know why you're still in bed—malingerer!' Chelle hooked the chart back onto the foot of the bed. 'I reckon you can get out of here tomorrow morning, first thing.'

'Thank God!' said Amelia, relief swelling in her chest until she realised she sounded ungrateful. 'Not that it's been too bad in here. Mum brought me apricot chicken at lunch and you guys have completely outdone yourselves.'

'Best of all, we brought some fruit to make sure your bowels keep opening,' said Chelle with a grin, waving the bag of grapes.

'How's Paul going?' Sav asked, looking a bit more serious.

'How would I know?' Amelia muttered into her glass. She wished the wine was the real stuff, so it would warm her all the way to her stomach and chase out the cold feeling that settled there when she thought about Paul. 'The thing is, I haven't clapped eyes on the bugger since he left for Adelaide first thing on Saturday. He was meant to be back in town this morning. And he isn't answering his phone.' Amelia gripped her cup so tightly, she felt the plastic crunch a little.

'Loosen your grasp there, honey,' said Chrissie.

'How weird,' Chelle put in. 'Doesn't seem like Paul.'

'Who knows . . . maybe he's been held up. Maybe he forgot to take his phone off silent.' Amelia knew she looked as miserable as she felt, but at least it was a bit of a relief to have got the news off her chest.

Chelle squeezed her arm and they all gave her sympathetic looks.

'Let's not dwell on the mysteries of men,' Sav said brightly. 'Tell me some gossip! What about you, Chrissie? How's Will?'

Chrissie folded her arms. 'Well now, *that* would have to be the shortest relationship in the history of dating. Now-you-see-me, now-you-don't.'

'What? You guys looked good together,' Amelia said. 'He seemed so into you!'

'Yeah,' chimed in Chelle, 'when I saw you two having dinner at the pub, it was like no one else existed!'

'I thought so too, but he stopped returning my calls just after the rodeo. No sorry, no sod off, just haven't heard from him. His mum does all their shopping, and I can't exactly ask her about it.' Chrissie sighed. 'It's so frustrating! Anyway—' she swirled the liquid around in her glass '—you win some, you lose some.'

'Good Lord, look at us!' Chelle giggled. 'Hopeless in love. Only one out of four can maintain a healthy relationship.'

Sav crossed her legs primly, as though teaching a pre-primary class, then said, 'I think I should buy us all vibrators.' The girls shrieked with laughter while Sav held up her hands in a *What?* gesture. 'It would save a lot of heartache, don't you think?'

'What do you mean, "us"?' Chrissie asked. 'Aren't you getting seen to?'

Sav blushed. 'Some nights Dean's too tired.'

That set off another round of giggles and innuendo-laden comments.

'So,' Amelia began tentatively, when they'd all calmed down, 'what's being said around town about the robbery?'

There was the briefest of pauses before the three started to talk at once:

'I've not heard anything.'

'Nada, as far as I know.'

'Nothing.'

They were so obviously lying that fear rose up inside Amelia. She wasn't angry with them, though—just touched that her friends wanted to protect her. 'I can tell you're hiding something,' she said. 'Whatever it is, I want to know.'

They exchanged glances, then Sav opened her mouth. 'Okay. Well, you know what Torrica can be like. Sally, that genius from the bakery, is *positive* you've taken the money and hidden it somewhere. Tasered yourself, no less, 'cause you had to make it realistic.'

Chrissie rolled her eyes. 'Yeah, and Deb at the bank is doing her usual "I-know-everything-but-I'm-sworn-to-secrecy" act, which is a sure sign she knows nothing.'

'Some idiots,' said Sav, 'say your family's going bankrupt and—'

'Of course, we put whoever we hear saying that sort of shit right in their place,' Chelle said, and the others nodded firmly. 'No one's really taking it seriously, Milly, so don't let it get you down.'

But the aftertaste of the chocolates and grape juice had turned to bitter acid at the back of Amelia's throat. She set her plastic cup down. 'I'm sorry, guys. I need a bit of time alone.'

Chapter 17

Amelia got out of the passenger's seat and breathed in the fresh, clean air. True to her word, Chelle had released her into this fine Tuesday morning, and Amelia was so grateful to no longer be smelling hospital-grade disinfectant. Her father at her elbow, she slowly walked down the garden path, up the stairs and into the kitchen. Natalie was cooking lunch, fussing over a salad.

'You right, love?' John asked as he hovered by Amelia's side.

'I'm fine, I think. It's just so good to be home.' She sank into the kitchen chair that Natalie pulled out for her.

'And it's good to have you home,' her dad said, his hand on her shoulder.

'Where's Graham?' she asked.

'You should be able to see out there.' John pointed at the window.

Over near the shed, Amelia's brother was attaching the sheep feeder to the ute. Once it was secure, he drove over to the auger and backed under it, before getting out to start the engine. She watched as the grain flowed into the feeder, filling it up until Graham shut off the engine and climbed back into the ute. Soon he'd be driving out into the paddock, with the sheep running behind and bleating madly, in search of the grain they knew would be coming.

'Pretty dry, Dad,' Amelia said when Graham took off, dust flicking up from his wheels.

'Yeah.' John sat down and accepted the food-laden plate Natalie handed him. Before he tucked in, he said, 'Can you put the radio on, Nat? Just want to hear the weather report on the *Country Hour*.'

Sitting in the sunshine that streamed through the window, Amelia closed her eyes and let the sounds of home wash over her: the click of her father's knife and fork against the plate; her mother doing the dishes; the radio announcer talking up a cold front due to hit sometime next week. They were all comforting noises, ones that Amelia needed around her right now. She needed to feel safe. More snippets of the attack had been coming back. Last night she'd dreamed of fingers running down her neck to tug her shirt collar, and a low male voice making threats. Before she woke up she'd felt her shirt pop open, her heart thumping.

Amelia shuddered and opened her eyes, looking outside again as the dogs barked. A cloud of dust was swirling up the driveway like a cyclone, and her heart skipped a beat as she recognised the vehicle that caused it.

'Paul,' she said softly.

The ute pulled up in a mixture of spitting gravel and skids, and her fiancé almost fell in his hurry to get out of the cab.

'*Milly!*' he yelled, covering the path in three steps.

John opened the door to let him in. 'It's all right, son, she's okay,' he said, but Amelia suspected that Paul didn't hear a word.

He made a beeline for her chair and grabbed her hand as he sank to his knees in front of her. 'Babe, are you okay? Bloody hell, look at you.'

'Where've you been?' she asked, pulling her hand away. 'We've been trying to contact you.'

'Held up in Adelaide, trying to sort all this stuff out with the lawyers. I'm sorry, I left the charger at home so my phone's been dead. Never even really thought to look at it—you know I don't use it too much.'

Amelia took a deep breath and slowly went over the details of her attack, with Natalie and John chiming in with their own commentary. Paul listened, his face tightening.

'Oh babe, I'm so sorry. If I'd known I would've been here.' He reached forward and took her hand again, gentler now. This time she let him hold on. Tentatively, he reached up to run his fingers down her cheek, which was turning from purple to a browny yellow. His blue eyes hardened and narrowed. 'Who did this to you?'

John shook his head and sighed. 'If we knew that, the bastards would be locked away by now.'

'Well, they'd better not come across me,' Paul swore. 'I'll kill 'em.'

That sent a thrill through Amelia. 'How did you hear?' she asked.

'Soon as I got into town this morning, I called in to the store to grab some dog food on the way home. Chrissie told me, then I came straight out here.'

Amelia smiled. 'Can't beat the grapevine.'

'Not in Torrica anyway. So what's the doctor saying? What about the cops?'

Amelia filled him in on what Chelle had said—that she was healing nicely and soon the bruises would be gone and her ribs wouldn't ache when she laughed. 'As for the cops, I haven't really heard anything. I spoke to the two local guys on Sunday when I was pretty out of it, and yesterday I was interviewed by the detective who's come in from Adelaide to do a rural crime talk, but that was it. I don't know if there's been any progress. I wasn't very helpful. Couldn't remember much.'

'Can you now?' Paul asked, stroking her arm.

'Bits and pieces. Last night I remembered that a man pulled my shirt open—'

'*What?*' Paul exploded, jumping to his feet.

'No, no!' Amelia shook her head and held up her hands. 'Just at the neck. Nothing happened, but I could just remember him doing it and—' she paused, trying to think '—I reckon he said something, but I can't remember what.'

Paul sat back on his heels and shook his head.

'Would you like a cup of tea, Paul?' Amelia's mum asked.

'Huh? Oh, no thanks.'

'Here comes Graham,' Amelia said as her brother's ute drove into sight, the sheep feeder bumping along behind.

Paul put his hands on her shoulders and looked into her eyes. 'I should be off, but I don't want to leave you.'

'I'll be fine. Now I know you're back. Just come and visit me soon.'

He bent down and kissed her softly.

જ્જ

Amelia looked at her brother as he came in from the paddock, and took a sharp breath. Graham was dishevelled and unshaven, and his eyes were bloodshot. She realised her mum was staring at him too, her hand hovering over the board where she'd been chopping carrots. What was going on?

'Get the sheep fed, son?' John looked over the edge of the *Stock Journal.*

'Yep, all done.' Although he gave Amelia a look of concern, Graham didn't say anything before he went off to the bathroom to wash his hands.

'Tea?' called Natalie, putting the kettle on for about the eleventh time.

Amelia smiled. 'A cup of tea will fix everything.'

'Yes thanks, Mum,' Graham called from the hallway. When he returned, he sat across from Amelia. 'So how are you?' he asked softly.

'Getting better. I can't wait to sleep in my own bed tonight, away from all those bloody beeping monitors!'

'Does it hurt?'

'My ribs still do, but everything else is settling down. The burns are a bit itchy, which means they're healing, according to Chelle. So I'm on the up and up.'

Graham stared at the marks on her face. Finally he said, 'Not pretty.'

With a shrug, Amelia said, 'Not as bad as it was.' She stared at her brother and wondered why he was looking so seedy. 'We could be twins with our eyes,' she joked. 'Yours are as bloodshot as mine.'

He grimaced. 'Yeah, rough night.'

'What happened?' Amelia asked, shifting in her chair to get comfortable.

Graham opened his mouth, but didn't say anything as Natalie put a cup and saucer down in front of him. 'Nothing. Suppose I was worried about you.' He took a sip. 'Look, about the engagement party this Saturday—I haven't spoken to Dani yet, and Mum, I know you've been putting in the hard yards, but I've been thinking maybe we should postpone it.'

Amelia smiled and reached over to squeeze his arm. Every so often he could really knock her sideways with his thoughtfulness. 'Thanks, that's lovely of you, but please don't do that. I'll be up for it and I reckon we can all use a party. And you've all put in so much time and effort!'

'Right then, thanks Milly,' Graham said, but his expression was still very solemn. 'It's just been a bloody awful week. And I went to the Rural Crime Forum last night. That was pretty interesting. Informative. Didn't put me in a good mood, though, I've got to say.'

John put his paper down. 'Tell us about it.'

Graham summed up Dave's speech, and added that there'd been a good turn-out, which Amelia was pleased to hear.

'Did he say anything about the robbery?' Natalie asked. 'Any leads?'

'Um . . .' Graham mulled it over. 'Yeah, he said there are criminals targeting our area and that they're dangerous. That was all. Didn't sound like the coppers are getting any closer to finding out who it is.'

'Yeah, well,' Amelia said wryly, 'I can vouch for the crims being dangerous.'

Chapter 18

Sitting on the edge of his motel bed, Dave stared at the note he'd found tucked under his windscreen wiper after the forum the night before. Four typed words: *Look at Amelia Bennett.* He'd stuck it in an evidence bag, and today he needed to send it off for forensic analysis—along with the folded piece of paper that had been wedged in beneath it. His mysterious informant had either managed to get a copy of Amelia's bank statement or forged it, a cause for concern on a couple of levels. To his expert eyes it seemed like the genuine article, though, and it made him think of the conversation he'd overheard between Jim and Cappa. The list of figures showed that the young woman had only fifty dollars sitting in the account two weeks ago.

Of course, Amelia might have a separate savings account. But Dave was going to have to ask her about that, alongside other questions about inconsistencies in her story that weren't the norm for an interview with the victim.

He picked up the phone and rang the Barker police station.

'Joan,' he said without preamble, 'I have some evidence I need to get to Adelaide. Anyone going down?'

'Not from here.'

'Can you get on to the next closest cop shop and find out? It's important.'

'Leave it with me,' she said before clunking the phone down.

Dave dialled another number. 'Coops, it's Burrows.'

There was silence on the end of the phone before the voice said, 'Don't tell me. You need a favour.'

'Something like that.'

'You and the rest of the fucking police department.' Coops sighed like an old man. 'Right-o, whatchya got?'

'A note and a bank statement that was left underneath my windscreen.'

'Fingerprinting?' Coops asked.

'Yup. How long?'

'If I don't do the favour, it'll be months.'

'And if you do?' Dave tapped his foot, looking at the evidence bag in his hand.

'A few days.'

'Coops, you're a bloody legend.'

'Yeah, yeah, you're not the only one who's told me that. When can you get it here?'

'Tomorrow at the latest.'

'Contact number?'

Dave recited it, a smile in his voice.

'You owe me,' Coops said.

'I reckon I still might from the last case I worked on,' Dave answered dryly.

'Well, I'd better catch up with you and get paid, then. Catch you later.'

'Yep. And Coops? Thanks, mate.'

Hanging up the phone, Dave tried to ignore the hollow feeling in the pit of his stomach. Kim would not be happy. And, honestly, he *didn't* want to investigate Amelia. The most likely explanation for the note was that someone was throwing suspicion on the young lady because they had it in for her, or because they were trying to deflect attention away from themselves or someone else. Jim was an obvious suspect, of course.

Setting down the evidence bag on the bed beside him, Dave put his face in his hands. Even if he found nothing dodgy about Amelia, it wouldn't matter to Kim. Acting as though there was the remotest chance Amelia was a criminal might change everything.

'That would be bloody right,' he muttered, shaking his head at himself. 'I reconnect with Kim and it all goes pear-shaped.'

But he had to get himself together and do his job. His notebook was chock-full of questions for Amelia, and the only way to get them answered was to go and ask her. He just hoped he could send off the evidence bag and then get in and out of Granite Ridge before Kim found out where he was and what he was doing. He'd been a copper for a long time, and there wasn't much he was genuinely afraid of, but he was man enough to admit that Kim's inquiring mind wasn't something he wanted to deal with when she found out he was questioning her beloved niece.

એ૩

'Amelia, I need to ask about the alcohol in Gus's ute. When I opened the door I could smell it very strongly, and forensics removed a can of Bundy and Cola. Had you been drinking while driving, or was the smell there when you got in?'

They sat outside in the homestead's garden, Dave on a stone bench and Amelia on a beautiful old swinging garden chair. The jasmine vine beside them was in full flower and the scent was heady. He watched her feet touch the ground as she pushed the seat back and forth. The bruise on her face was now mottled, a bit of yellow creeping into the purple.

'I had that can with me,' Amelia answered frankly. 'I planned on opening it when I'd delivered the money.' She shook her head, staring at the ground. 'But I ended up cracking it on the drive into town. I had a headache and was really tired, so I thought it might help me get through what I still had to do. I just had a few sips. Is that illegal?'

When she brushed her hair gingerly from her face and looked up at Dave, he was disconcerted by how like Kim's her eyes were.

He made a note on his pad. 'You're in luck—it's illegal everywhere except SA. Though I'd discourage it.' Amelia let out a long breath of relief and he was almost sure she was telling the truth. 'Look,' he said, 'I know you're probably sick of this question, but have you remembered anything else about that night?'

Those familiar eyes stared into the distance. 'There's still not much,' she said softly. 'I told you that I went over the speed limit, didn't I?' Dave nodded. 'I remember seeing headlights in my rear-view mirror. I thought it was Gus, thought he'd caught up. Then I realised they were on high-beam, and by then it was too late—they cut me off.' She stopped and took a couple of shaky breaths.

'Can you explain why you were driving so fast?' Dave looked at her intently.

'Oh, I wasn't meaning to.' Amelia licked her lips and ran her hands over her arms with a shiver, but it wasn't cold—the sun was beating down strongly and a dry northerly wind had begun to blow, rustling the leaves. Amelia shivered again.

Signs of guilt? Dave wondered, then checked himself. *More like trauma.*

'I hadn't driven Gus's ute before,' Amelia explained. 'It's brand new, one of those ones that do a hundred before you realise it. I'm not used to that much power, not in my old car. I call her "Pushme".' They both chuckled. 'Anyway, the ute didn't feel like it was going extra fast, it just did . . . And I hadn't been looking at the speedo. I was too busy looking at the road. Then I opened that can—took my eyes off things for only a second, I promise.' She blushed and swallowed.

'Then you saw the headlights?'

'Yeah, thought it was Pushme. Then . . . I don't remember so much about what they did to me—there are big blank patches in my head—but I heard voices and there was more than one. And I had a dream last night about a man popping buttons off my shirt, but I'm sure it didn't go further than that. Honestly, Dave, that's all I can recall. I'm sorry.'

He nodded and gave her a reassuring smile. 'Okay, let's move on. When I interviewed you first off, you said you'd spent most of the night in the office and there were lots of people dropping in. You named a few of them, but do you know if all the committee members turned up?'

167

'Everyone was there at the rodeo, but not all in the office. I mean, I didn't see everyone, but I would've heard if someone was a no-show.'

'And did the whole committee know how, when and where the money was going to be transported?'

Amelia paused, then slowly nodded. 'Probably. I don't think it was discussed at any of the meetings, but as far as I know, what we did wasn't any different to any other year, so there's a good chance everyone just knew. They're all old hands.'

'Tell me about your role as treasurer.'

Natalie popped her head out of the kitchen door, and Dave wondered if she'd been listening in. 'Does anyone want more tea?' she asked brightly.

'No thanks, Mum,' Amelia said with a smile, and Dave shook his head. Natalie ducked back inside, and Amelia turned to Dave. 'Gus asked me to do it—be treasurer, that is. There was a bit of opposition, but he got around that.'

'Why the opposition?'

'Even though I have a degree in commerce and I'm an experienced bookkeeper, so I'm capable, *some* people thought I might be a bit flighty and irresponsible.'

She sounded defensive, and Dave remembered this issue being mentioned at the hospital—he'd forgotten to follow up with Kim. He'd have to get her take on the situation later. If she was still talking to him.

'You seem pretty responsible to me,' Dave told Amelia. 'Well, if we forget about drinking while driving . . .'

She blushed again. 'Yes, exactly. And you didn't see me as a teenager. I had something to prove, you see, and being the treasurer was part of that.'

Dave nodded sympathetically. 'Sounds fair enough.'

'Of course,' Amelia muttered, bowing her head and rubbing her eyes, 'it didn't exactly work out the way I planned.'

To make her feel better and butter her up a little, Dave repeated some of the things Kim had said: that it wasn't her fault, that she couldn't have known, that she needed to focus on recovering. When she'd calmed down, he changed tack. 'What about your financial situation, Amelia? I know I've asked you before, but—'

'Yeah, I'm good. I have some savings.' Casting him a sharp glance, she crossed her arms and sat forward.

'In a separate bank account?'

She raised her eyebrows. 'Yes, better interest rates. Why?'

It was a struggle to keep the relief from his face. 'What about the other committee members? Do you know of any financial problems they might have?'

'Don't know about all of them, but I do the accounts for a couple of members and they seem to be fine. I don't think I can tell you who I work for, though. Isn't that like breaking confidentiality?'

'It's not as though you're a doctor,' he said and grinned. 'If it's going to clear their names, I don't think they'd be worried.'

Amelia smiled. 'All right—Gus and Pip, and Anne. Actually, I do the accounts for quite a few farmers around the district, as well as my family. I'm sort of like an office manager who goes to your farm.'

'You must get around a bit, doing that. Have you seen or heard anything untoward in the district?'

'You know, I've been wracking my brains ever since I heard you on the *Country Hour*. But no, I haven't noticed anything weird or different. I certainly didn't think something like this would happen to me.' She wrapped her arms tighter around herself and a tear slid down her cheek.

'I know this is hard and you're tired, Amelia. I'm sorry. This won't take much longer.' Dave looked down at his notebook to refresh his memory. 'Can you tell me about your relationship with Paul Barnes?'

She sat up straighter and wiped her eyes. 'What do you want to know? We've been together for just over a year, we're moving in together, and—' she lowered her voice '—we're going to get married. We're doing the house up first, but there isn't much money so it's slow-going. He's such a lovely bloke.'

'I'm sure he is.'

When she smiled it was the happiest Dave had seen her since that night at the pub. Unfortunately, what she'd just said about Paul raised a red flag. Dave remembered Jim Green's words from the forum, the ones that had prompted his question about Paul: *Well, she's hooked up with that Paul Barnes for a start, isn't she? He hasn't got a pot to piss in.* It seemed that Jim, whatever his faults or motives, had been telling the truth about this.

Dave made some more notes. 'So things are a bit tight?'

'That's what I just . . .' Amelia paused, realisation dawning in her eyes.

'Amelia?' he prompted.

'Um, oh, well, you know, farming can be pretty tough. You spend your cash on the stock and the machinery, and there's not much left for the house. You've seen a lot of the places around here: there's a hundred-and-sixty-thousand-dollar John Deere tractor out back, but no glass in the kitchen windows.'

She gave a shaky little laugh. 'Once the opening rains come, we'll have a bit more to spare.'

'What about your savings?'

Annoyance crossed her face, but was it directed at her fiancé or at Dave's questions? 'Paul's not keen on using them. He wants to "provide" for me. He's old-fashioned—one of the beautiful things about him.'

It all sounded plausible enough, but on the other hand . . . Dave wondered if he should ask to see evidence of her savings. Well, not today.

'Right-o,' he said, closing the notebook and slipping it into his pocket. 'Look, I don't have any more questions at the moment. Glad you're out of hospital and feeling a little better.'

Amelia nodded. 'Thank you.' Her eyes—*Kim's* eyes—were fixed on him, and he shifted uncomfortably. 'You know,' she said, 'my aunt's a good person. She deserves to be happy.'

Taken aback, Dave wasn't sure what to say. 'Yeah, she is,' he managed, getting to his feet, 'and yeah, she does.' *Not sure I'm the one to make her happy, though,* he thought. *Especially after this.*

Frowning, Amelia looked away. He wondered how much she'd guessed about his questions, and hoped she wasn't too upset. 'See you around, Detective.'

He got to his feet. 'Yep, I'll be in touch soon.'

જી

When Chrissie arrived for a lunchbreak visit, Amelia was perched on the stone bench where Dave had been sitting. In her hands were a pencil and a sheet of paper that she'd grabbed from the house right after he'd left. Hoping a different medium would help, she'd been determined to recover her memories and write down everything about the robbery—but all she'd managed were a few scribbled words.

She glanced up as Chrissie walked towards her, then flinched when she noticed her friend's concerned look.

'You all right?' Chrissie asked, just as Amelia felt wetness on her cheeks and reached up to touch them. She'd been concentrating so hard on remembering, she hadn't noticed she was crying. She wiped the tears away.

'I've just . . .' Amelia screwed up the paper and chucked it onto the ground, anger and fear suddenly swelling. 'I've *got* to remember what happened!' she wailed. 'Chelle said the memories might never come back, but that's just not on.'

Chrissie wrapped her arms about her friend's shoulders and hugged her tightly. 'Okay, okay, let's start at the beginning and see if we can jog things along.'

'I don't want to be some bloody weak little girl,' Amelia yelled, pulling away and getting up. 'I *want* to remember, I *want* to be able to tell Dave what happened—every bloody detail. If I can't remember, I can't defend myself.' She grabbed Chrissie's hand. 'I think he's investigating me. He's asking about my finances . . . and Paul's.' Her hands were shaking and her face felt hot.

She heard movement behind her and spun around—at the shouting Natalie had come out of the house, but Chrissie waved her away and shook her head. Natalie made a despairing gesture and retreated to the kitchen.

'Come on, let's go for a walk,' Chrissie said, squeezing Amelia's hand. 'Just a slow one up to the shearing shed and back again.' She gently took the pencil away and put it on a white-painted iron table, then linked her arm through Amelia's.

Breathing deeply as they walked, Amelia started to relax. Chrissie talked about her day at work so far and some of the gossip she'd heard, and then about how Paul had come in first thing that morning. 'I was so pleased to see him,' she said. 'Meant I could send him straight out to you. Honestly, I don't think I've seen a bloke more upset. He left a trail of red dust behind him, he bolted so fast.'

'It was really good to see him,' Amelia said, even as she felt her stomach constrict at the thought of what she'd revealed to Dave.

'How did he go in Adelaide?'

Her stomach tightened further. 'I'm a bad fiancée. Never even asked.'

'I think you'll get away with it. Got a bit on your mind.'

Amelia swallowed, nodding. She took more deep breaths of the eucalyptus-scented air. 'Do you ever think about the times we used to have at Emerald Springs?' she asked. 'I love that place.'

'Oh yeah! I loved swimming there, although—' Chrissie leaned closer '—I have to say, I was always scared something would grab my legs from really deep down. I'd swim around with my knees up around my chest, and that took some doing!'

Amelia laughed. She was surprised at how good it felt, the mirth bubbling up from inside, even though her ribs still gave her a spasm of pain. 'Look, Chrissie,' she said, 'I want to move on from what happened, and I reckon to me that means remembering. Not just so I can report back to Dave—I need to do it for myself.'

'So just keep walking and don't think,' prompted Chrissie. 'Say the first thing that comes into your mind. How did you get out of the ute?'

Amelia opened her mouth to say she didn't know, but a word came out: 'Dragged.'

Chrissie didn't change pace. She tugged a little on Amelia's arm to keep her walking. 'Dragged,' she repeated.

'Yes. I remember hands on me and . . .' Amelia stopped, struggling with what she had to say.

Chrissie stayed quiet, her gait steady, while Amelia looked around her home. Everything was just as it had been before the rodeo. It was peaceful and quiet. The shearing shed still had a piece of tin that banged every time the wind blew, and the chook-pen gate had flapped open as it always did when there was a northerly wind. She loved this place and knew it by heart. It hadn't changed in those few minutes of the robbery, but she had.

Instead of the contentment she usually experienced at Granite Ridge, she felt fear. Dark places—like the shadowed insides of the sheds—were making her anxious. She realised that in her head was the idea that someone was lurking there, watching her, waiting for the moment to strike. She wondered if she could ever make it stop.

Holding tight to Chrissie's arm, she raced through what she had to say, the images filling her mind. 'They dragged me out, hit me. There was a torch, or a spotlight—something shining in my eyes.' She paused and licked her lips. 'A man tied my hands. Felt like he'd set me on fire—must've been the taser. Then he kicked me.' Amelia stopped, looking into Chrissie's wide, worried eyes. 'I know there's more—I *know* I heard them talking—but I just can't remember what they said.'

Chapter 19

Dave grabbed hold of Kim's hand as she put his late lunch on the table in front of him and turned to go back into the kitchen. She hadn't smiled at him once today.

'Sit with me a little while,' he said. 'There's no one else but me here.'

Kim sank into the chair opposite. 'Fine.'

'Got a question for you,' Dave said, as he attacked his steak.

'I'll answer it, if it's not the line of questioning you took with Milly this morning.' She gave him a stare that left him in no doubt she knew what he'd been up to.

'I'm doing my job, Kim,' he said softly.

'I know.' There was a defiant tone to her voice. 'Which is why I didn't mention it. Doesn't mean I'm happy about it.' She crossed her arms.

The only sound now was the buzzing of the flycatcher. Dave put down his knife and fork, and gazed at Kim. 'I'm sorry,' he said.

'What for? Can't help having to do your job. I know you're barking up the wrong tree if you really think Milly had something to do with it, but I won't interfere until I need to. You'll find who really did this, Dave, because you're tenacious. You won't look at Milly for long.' Kim sounded so confident, and Dave hoped he never had to break her heart with any terrible news about her niece.

'Okay, look . . . what can you tell me about Paul?'

Kim leaned back and eyed him. 'Paul. What do you want to know?'

'Anything and everything. No matter how small.'

Kim started at the beginning. She told him how Old Brian Barnes had pissed all his money up against the wall. How he'd driven all his kids, except Paul, away—and how, when he'd died, the bank had wanted to hold a sale.

'But Paul did everything in his power to stop that. He sold stock to cover the interest payments that were behind, and he sold some machinery too. I think it was called a dispersal sale, not a clearing sale, because he didn't want to get rid of everything, you see? He got enough money together to put a crop in, and the first harvest was a good one. He's been clawing his way back since, but it's been hard yakka.' Kim frowned. 'So, you suspect him, don't you? It's him you're mainly interested in, not Milly.'

Dave gave a sad smile. 'I can't say anything officially, and you didn't hear anything from me. However, I can say—' he held up a finger '—if it *is* Paul, she may be the cause.'

Kim stared at him. 'Right. Yeah, okay, I can understand that, but . . . look, there's someone else you might want to think about. This idiot on the rodeo committee,

176

Jim Green. He's been giving Milly a hard time since day one.'

⁊

It resonated with Dave that Paul had held a dispersal sale and put a crop in, but he couldn't put his finger on why. After lunch, he went back to his motel room and wrote up two names on the whiteboard he'd set up: *Paul Barnes* and *Jim Green*. And just for good measure he wrote *Grant Hink*. There was a motive for that man, without a doubt: whether he was capable of assault and robbery was another question.

Standing back, he looked over all the information he'd written down. On the top left-hand side was what had been stolen. Below, every fact they had on the crimes. In the middle was a map of the area. He'd marked in black where the two towns were, while in red he'd marked where the crimes had taken place. Then he'd drawn a line linking all of them together. He stared at the radius.

'Okay, I need to find the link here,' he muttered. 'There's nothing I can see on the map that links everything together. Not yet, anyway.' He stuck the texta in his mouth and tapped it against his teeth as he thought.

His eyes were drawn to the items that had been taken: *Diesel, Chemical, GPS guidance system, Ute.*

'Bloody hell.' Slowly the hand holding the texta went down to his side. 'There it is. The link. What a bloody idiot I am.'

He ripped the lid off the texta and connected the four items with a line. Next to it he wrote: *Cropping.*

'That's what it is. All these things are related to cropping.' It hadn't occurred to him until now, but it was pretty difficult to crop these days without a GPS system. It cut down the waste on chemical and seed, making the task much more efficient. 'And I bet they took the ute mainly because the chemical was on the back and it was quicker and easier to drive off with it.' He spun around to the motel table, which was serving as his desk. Flicking through his notes, he found his interviews with Amelia and read back through them.

'So,' he said, 'we have a boyfriend who is skint. It's common knowledge he's sold things to get himself out of debt. Everything that's been stolen has to do with cropping. Is Paul planning to put in more crop?' He made a note on his pad to ask.

'We have a girlfriend who has access to the money from the rodeo and could pass on information about the transfer. But she got hurt.' He paced the room. 'Do I assume the boyfriend could be merciless and beat Amelia up? Maybe he even coerced her into helping him. Or could he have paid someone else to do it? Did it get out of hand somehow? Maybe whoever did it went too far and Amelia wasn't supposed to get hurt.' Dave stood still and thought a bit more.

Now he had more questions than answers, but that was okay. He'd get to the bottom of it. Today he'd talk to Jim and then have the long chat with Paul that he'd been planning.

He snatched up his car keys and his satchel before carefully making sure the curtains were drawn, so no one could see in. That had been the biggest issue he'd had with the girls who worked in the motel. They were all gossips and desperate to have some idea of what was going on. He watched them when they came in to make the bed, doing their best to peer at the whiteboard. He'd had to cover it up with a blanket and lay all his notes face down on the table.

As much as he loved small towns and communities that looked out for one another, sometimes it was hard to keep secrets.

಄

Dave pulled up at Barker freight depot and looked around. There were forklifts piling freight onto the back of three trucks. Through an office window he could see a man on the phone gesturing as if angry. Dave couldn't see Jim, but that didn't mean he wasn't there. Depots were like rabbit warrens, with sheds and trucks everywhere.

'G'day, can I help you?' called a voice to his left.

Dave turned and saw a tattooed truckie with a big moustache and a blue singlet stretched over his ample belly. 'Yeah, I'm looking for Jim Green?'

'He'll be over in the lunch room. It's his break. Him and Kev's.'

'Kev?' Dave asked.

'Yeah, Kev Hubble. Can you shift your car, mate? Over towards that way.' The man pointed to a car park that Dave hadn't seen.

'Yeah, mate, sure. Sorry.'

He'd briefly interviewed Kev and Jim on the day before, along with all the committee members, but hadn't realised they worked together. They were clearly thick as thieves socially, but employment hadn't come up. *Interesting fact*, he thought.

He shifted the car and went in search of Jim and Kev. At the door of the gloomy shed-cum-lunch-room that smelt stuffy and enclosed, he heard voices.

'Get out of the bloody way, ya stupid mongrel.'

179

Dave took a step into the shed in time to see Jim kick out at a skinny yellow dog, who was slinking away into the darkness of the closest corner. Jim's foot didn't connect but there was a high-pitched yelp that told Dave the action had happened more than once.

'Dunno why the boss lets that mutt stay here, sneakin' around, eating scraps, the way it does. Full of fleas and worms.'

'I dunno why you've such a bloody bee in yer bonnet about the poor thing,' Kev muttered. 'It's just looking for a home.'

Knowing he hadn't been noticed yet, Dave stopped to see what Jim would do next. He wondered if Jim had a tendency towards violence.

'Ha!' the man snorted. 'I'd kick the bugger again if I could reach it, but I'm knackered after me run yesterday, so I'm not getting off me fat arse.' He sat down at a rickety old laminated table and plonked his dusty boots up on it, then took a swig of coffee from a dirty white cup.

Dave cleared his throat and walked further into the light, nodding at the men. 'Jim, Kev.' He grabbed a chair, turned it around and sat down straddling it.

'G'day,' said Jim, looking at him warily.

'How you goin', Dave?' Kev asked, amiable enough.

'All fine in my neck of the woods. How about with you?'

'No use in complaining,' Kev quipped. 'No bastard listens anyhow.'

Reading body language was so important in Dave's line of work and he was getting the impression that Jim really wasn't that happy to see him. Kev, on the other hand, was relaxed and comfortable.

'Just needed to ask a few more questions about the night of the rodeo.'

'Fire away,' Jim said, putting his cup down and taking his feet off the table.

'Did you think Amelia was going to do a good job as treasurer?' Dave asked as he got out his notepad.

'You recording this?' Jim asked suddenly.

Dave looked up at him. 'Uh, no, but I need to take notes so I don't forget what you said. You got a problem with that?'

'Nah, nah.' He waved his hands about. 'So get on with 'em, then.'

Dave repeated his first question.

'I was opposed to her getting that job,' Jim said in a loud voice.

'I gotta admit I didn't like the idea much either,' Kev added.

'Why was that?' Dave raised his eyebrows and made his tone sound surprised. Of course, he already knew these details from the interviews he'd conducted on Monday, but he needed to make sure the stories matched up.

'I didn't think Milly had the capability. You gotta work up to these types of jobs.' Jim leaned forward as he spoke. 'You can't be involved with any type of group and not earn yer stripes. Start as a lackey and work up from there. Coupla years runnin' around, doin' everyone's bidding, then take on a job.'

'Her and that fancy degree she's got,' Kev said in a snide tone.

Dave's eyes slid across to him. He made a gesture so that Kev would continue talking, but the man just shrugged as Jim took up the commentary again.

'I didn't like the way she sidled in here, pretended her past didn't play a part in the way we all thought about her. She twisted Gus and the others around her little finger, pretending she was changed.' Jim screwed up his mouth and shook his head. 'Let me tell you, a leopard don't change its spots. She's a silly little woman, coming in wanting to upset the pecking order that all of us had already worked out.'

'You don't like her, then?'

'It's not that we don't like *her*,' Kev broke in. 'Just that we thought she'd cause trouble. Jim 'n' me didn't want that. We've worked hard on the rodeo. Didn't want to see it go down the gurgler 'cause of some inexperienced girl.'

'Couldn't put it better meself,' Jim said emphatically.

Dave nodded his understanding and jotted down a few notes. 'So did you make her life difficult at all?'

The two men stared at him, then their eyes shifted away to glance at each other.

'Well, I don't reckon . . .' Kev started to answer.

'Nah, we didn't,' Jim interrupted. 'We told her a few facts about what would happen if she stuffed things up. That wasn't making her life difficult. Just putting it out there plain and simple.'

Dave suppressed a sigh of irritation. 'Got it.'

He asked a few more questions, but nothing came out of it, other than their complete lack of respect for women. He was glad Kim was nowhere around—she'd have eaten these two for breakfast!

When Dave got back to his car, he sat for a moment and took a few deep breaths to calm his irritation, hoping the talk with Paul wouldn't be quite like that one.

Chapter 20

As Amelia drove across the ramp into Eastern Edge, she was smiling. After two days in the hospital and one and a half at home, this was the first time she'd been able to get out by herself since the robbery, and she was looking forward to having some alone time with Paul. She'd been worried that driving by herself might trigger memories of the attack, but as soon as she'd headed off into the bright sunshine, she'd known it would be okay.

Paul had visited Granite Ridge the evening before, and Amelia thought she saw a thawing in her mother's attitude towards him. Her father, meanwhile, had come in early for a beer on the verandah with Paul, genuinely pleased to see the young man and to discuss farming with him. While Amelia wouldn't wish her experience on anyone, she was glad something positive seemed to have come out of it: a relationship between her parents and the man she loved. Natalie had even lent her car to Amelia for this trip—Pushme was off getting a full service, as Amelia didn't feel safe getting in the unreliable old car.

The driveway was long and winding, so it wasn't until she rounded the last corner that she saw the three utes, one with a trailer, parked in front of the house. On two of them was emblazoned *Smithy's Building Company* in bold blue letters, while the third belonged to a local electrician. With a small gasp of surprise, Amelia pulled up and climbed out of the car. She stared at the house, her eyebrows raised, listening to the noise coming from inside—then jumped at the sound of smashing glass.

'Ah, fuck it!' yelled a male voice.

In spite of her confusion, Amelia giggled until her ribs ached, then headed towards the house. Peanut was in his usual position as overseer, high in the branches of the pepper tree, washing his paws but keeping an eye on his kingdom.

'What's going on here, Peanut?' Amelia asked, pausing at the bottom of the steps. She opened the front door and called, 'Hello?' Then she walked in.

She didn't get two paces before she froze: the best word to describe the scene was 'chaos'. The old scarred wooden kitchen benches were gone, replaced by modern, sleek-looking ones in creamy-stone laminate. A new stove was sitting on a pallet in the middle of the floor, and the window above the sink was now missing its glass. *That* appeared to be covering the floor.

'Oh,' said Amelia, picking her way through.

A tradesman looked up. 'G'day, love. Don't mind the mess.'

'What are you doing?' she asked, then realised it was a ridiculous question.

'Guess you're Amelia, then? Paul's getting everything organised so you can move in as soon as possible.'

'But there's no money!' Amelia blurted out.

'Nothing for you to worry about,' answered the tradie with a grin, as he swept up the glass. 'Your bloke's got it covered.'

'Uh-huh,' she said, fixing a polite smile in place.

She wandered through the rest of the house, taking in the progress. A wall in the kitchen had been pushed out so that it now opened into the lounge room. The latter had barely been touched, except for some filling around the windows and a lick of paint—and a new TV set still in its box beside two recliner chairs, waiting for their plastic wrapping to be removed.

The bedroom had also been painted. The fresh white ceiling was a massive change from the dark water stains that had covered it before. There was even art on the walls: a couple of simple, lovely landscapes instead of the sepia photos that Old Brian had hung, so faded you could barely make out what was in their frames.

Picking her way back down the passage, Amelia heard a bang from outside. Looking through the front window, she realised that the tin roof of the verandah was being taken off. Sheets of forest-green mini orb were stacked close by to replace it.

Amelia turned around slowly, and kept turning until she felt dizzy. What the hell was going on? She walked outside and stood beneath the pepper tree, shielding her eyes against the sun as she surveyed the house again. Peanut jumped down and rubbed against her legs. Bending, she scratched his ears, while a sense of foreboding built in her stomach. She knew she should be happy with what she was seeing—obviously Paul

185

had found money somewhere. But where? It wasn't that long ago he was telling her there wasn't enough cash for a bag of cement.

'Don't be silly,' she muttered, trying to pull herself together. But her mind went back to the night of the robbery. To the voices. Could one of them have been Paul? Could she have been completely wrong about him? She shook her head at herself.

'You're being crazy,' she said, picking up Peanut and holding him close for comfort. 'Really bloody stupid.' She took a deep breath and buried her face in the tawny coat of the cat—then jumped at another crash of glass. Peanut leapt out of her arms and disappeared up the tree again, before remembering to look regal and haughtily staring out over the house.

Another tradesman in standard uniform of steel-toed Mack boots, dusty navy shorts and a grey shirt walked outside, carrying one of the pantry doors over his shoulder. He threw it at the pile of debris that was building up, where it landed with a *crunch*. 'You wouldn't believe the number of rat nests we pulled out from in between the wall and cupboards,' he said, wiping sweat from his brow.

'*Rats?*' Amelia shuddered, thinking of all the nights she'd spent in the house—and all the times she'd gone downstairs barefoot in the middle of the night to get a glass of water. 'That's seriously gross. Mice I can deal with.'

'Yeah, a total infestation, complete with baby rats. Puss-cat got an early dinner. I've cleaned it all out now and plastered up where they were getting in. They were behind the oven as well. I tell you, these old farmhouses have got more holes and cavities in them than a piece of Swiss cheese.'

'Swiss cheese?' Amelia repeated faintly.

'Reckon you'll be real happy we're pulling all this apart for you. I'm trying to get Paul to put insulation into the roof. With the amount of rodent shit and dirt up there, it's a bloody wonder the ceiling hasn't fallen in. Anyway, better get back to it.' The tradie gave her a cheery grin and thumbs up before returning inside.

She followed him. 'Sorry, how much is this costing?' she asked.

He turned and tapped his nose. 'Can't tell you that, love, but won't take long. Will get a bill to Paul after that.'

'So you haven't quoted on the job?' Amelia couldn't keep the anxiety out of her voice. *Has Paul got no idea what it's going to cost?*

'I guess the boss quoted, but I'm not involved in any of that. Just the hard labour!' He pulled a hammer from his belt and began to tap at the other pantry door. It came off easily. 'Anyway, if you ask me, you shouldn't be worrying about this. Just enjoy it when it's finished.'

Amelia nodded and managed a smile. There was no reason to get on this man's back. 'Yeah, true enough. Good luck with it all! Thanks for the rat removal.'

She went to sit in the car and wait for Paul.

೫

'You're early!' Paul pulled up next to her car and spoke through the window. 'I wanted to see your face when you got a surprise. What do you think?'

An hour of sitting, waiting and watching men pull apart the house, and replace it bit by bit, while she tried to work out where the money was coming from hadn't improved her mood. These weren't just the few small renos they'd been talking about, the ones he wouldn't hear of her paying for. These were *huge*! The whole kitchen was being demolished and replaced.

'I'm not sure what to think,' she said stiffly. As she said it, she recognised her tone as the one Natalie used when picking a fight. *Shit!*

Paul got out and opened the car door for her. She stood slowly, recoiling a little from his hug. He gave her a funny half-smile, his blue eyes puzzled, then shrugged and led the way inside. 'So here're my plans,' he said, gesturing around. 'A new kitchen. They've gutted the whole—'

'Yeah, I can see that.' Amelia said, arms crossed over her chest.

He didn't slow down. 'And by making the lounge and kitchen open plan, you'll be able to watch the kids while you're cooking or whatever you're up to.'

Amelia listened as he talked excitedly and led her from room to room. A couple of times she couldn't help but smile and get caught up in his enthusiasm, but then her fears would come crashing in like an icy shower.

When Paul finally finished, he took her hand and led her back to the kitchen. At some point the tradies had called out good night and left. The room was covered in dust, and strangely silent. The dim glow from the bare light bulb left dark shadows in the corners that moved as the light fixture swung in the evening breeze.

'So what do you reckon?' Paul stood with his arms outstretched, looking proudly at Amelia.

'It's . . . very impressive.'

'Oh, I forgot! Come with me.' He took her hand and guided her outside, around to the back of the house. The lawn, which had been dead and brown most of the time she'd known him, was newly turfed, with a sprinkler set on it. 'I'm trying to get it established before you move out here,' he explained.

She eyed the lawn, then him. 'You're putting in a lot of work.'

'I want it to be as good as it can be. Here, sit down.' He patted the space next to him on the large, smooth log that fenced the lawn, then when she sat down he put his arm around her and kissed her cheek. Amelia did her best not to stiffen.

Her mind was whirling. Surely Brian's will hadn't held any extra money. Even if it had, there certainly wasn't enough to cover the costs of all these renovations. Her fear and anxiety were heightened by the ache in her ribs and the bruises on her face. No matter how many times she told herself that it didn't make any sense, that Paul wasn't that good an actor—and anyway, if he *was* a criminal he wouldn't be stupid enough to spend the money like this—her mind span back to the question of how the hell he'd got his hands on so much cash.

Just ask him, she told herself firmly. *You don't have to imply anything. There must be a reasonable explanation, and knowing Paul he'll tell you straight out.*

'Stay there,' Paul instructed, oblivious to her tangled thoughts. 'I've just got to get something from the ute.' He jumped up and ran into the dusk.

Amelia looked out over the brown paddocks, dotted with gumtrees and spiky bushes. This was her favourite view. It was where she'd put a patio, if she ever got that far. The land stretched off into the distance. Sheep grazed quietly. There was a chook pen in the house yard, along with a vegie patch—not that she particularly enjoyed gardening, but she liked the idea of growing fresh vegies and herbs to use in her cooking.

Paul returned with a picnic basket in hand. He settled beside her and drew out a bottle of white wine and two glasses. Amelia held them while he poured.

'So here's to us,' he said, raising his drink.

'To us,' Amelia repeated, and sipped the cool, crisp liquid.

'And I've got more news!'

Her eyes widened. 'I can't see how there could possibly be more!'

'I've bought thirty White Suffolk stud ewes.' The pleasure in his face was clear. 'They're in lamb to the ram that won at the Sydney Royal.' He turned to her. 'So I want to get a stud up and going. Sell the rams to the neighbours. Bit of extra pocket money. And it will be something we can do together.' He turned back and looked out over his land.

She watched as Paul surveyed his farm. She didn't think she'd ever seen him look so satisfied or proud. It wasn't, she thought, the face of a man who'd been involved with a robbery in which his fiancée got hurt. No, she'd been worrying over nothing. Her heartbeat started to calm and she took some slow breaths. She'd check with him to see where the money had come from, that was all.

Peanut appeared and jumped onto the log, curling up beside Paul. He scratched the cat under the chin, and Amelia listened as the power-motor purr kicked in, before returning her gaze to the pasture.

'Milly,' Paul said softly. 'I know I've asked you before, but will you marry me?'

When she turned to look at him, he was holding out a small maroon box, its lid popped open so she could see the solitaire diamond ring sitting on a plush bed of dark red velvet. The style was vintage, with a delicate engraving around the gold band, and four smaller diamonds elegantly setting off the main stone.

'Oh,' she said, her hand involuntarily pressed to her mouth. 'Wow.'

Paul gazed at her intently as he asked, 'So will you?'

'I want to,' Amelia breathed as she reached to touch the ring.

Paul leaned back. 'But?'

Pulling her hand back, Amelia stared at the ring for a moment longer, then at Paul. The words rushed out. 'But where did all this money come from? You didn't have anything and now suddenly you're getting the house almost rebuilt. And this ring! What's going on?'

When Paul turned red and looked very uncomfortable, alarm bells sounded in her mind. 'I don't really want to get into that now, all right?'

'Well, I do. Come on, Paul, you've got to tell me. Now.'

She watched his expression as her words sank in. He snapped the ring box closed and shot to his feet. Peanut also shot up, yowling and darting off into the night. 'What do you mean?'

She bit her tongue, not trusting herself to speak.

'You think *I* was involved in the robbery? What the fuck, Milly? It was bad enough that the bloody detective came out here yesterday to ask questions!' Paul stalked towards the house.

'No! No, I'm not saying that.' Amelia stood and tried to follow him as he backed away from her. Why hadn't she kept her bloody mouth shut? 'No, that's not what I mean . . .' Her voice trailed off.

'But it is, isn't it?' Paul shook his head. 'Everything I'm doing here is for you. How the hell could you even think that?'

He turned on his heel and stormed off. No matter how hard she tried to force herself, she couldn't follow. Within moments, the sound of his ute roared to life and she heard the spray of gravel as he span his wheels.

Chapter 21

'Savannah! Hey, Sav!' Amelia ran across the road to catch up with her friend, who was going for her early morning jog. Breathless by the time she grabbed Sav's arm, Amelia gasped, 'Didn't you hear me?'

'Oh hey, Milly. No, sorry. In my own little world. Got to keep moving. I'm late for school.'

'Oh right.' Amelia was crestfallen for a moment. She'd desperately wanted to have a coffee and talk about what had happened with Paul the night before. 'What about lunch, are you free?'

Sav narrowed her eyes and pulled back as if something had bitten her. 'No, sorry. I'm on lunch duty. But I'll give you a ring tomorrow when things are a bit calmer.' She checked her watch and jogged off towards the school. 'Are you feeling all right?' she called back over her shoulder.

'Yeah, fine. Thanks for asking.' Amelia stood on the footpath for a long time after Sav had disappeared, bewildered. *Maybe she's really just having a bad day.*

With a shrug, Amelia headed through the sunlit streets to Kim's roadhouse and went into the kitchen. 'Hey, Aunty Kim!'

'Oh hi, sweetie.' Kim's face was red and her dark hair limp with sweat as she put in another batch of chips. A great cloud of steam rose. 'Getting ready for the lunchtime rush,' she called over the noise, which put paid to conversation for a while.

Amelia nodded and began to arrange paper buckets on the bench so they'd be ready when Kim needed them. Soon they were all filled with golden fingers of potato.

'You okay?' Kim asked as she shook salt over the chips, then shook the containers so the grains trickled down.

Amelia shrugged. 'Not really.'

Setting a container down, Kim looked at her. 'Well, what's going on?'

'Oh.' Amelia waved her hands around, not sure where to start. 'Paul is renovating the house.'

Kim beamed. 'That's fabulous, sweetie! You must be so happy!' Then her smile fell. 'Aren't you?'

'Well, yeah, I would be . . . but how is he paying for all of this? He had to scrimp and save to put the new loo in, and now there's this huge reno happening! And it's not on the cheap, either: they've pulled the whole kitchen out and replaced it, as well as putting new tin on the roof.' She rubbed her hands across her face. 'He has a diamond engagement ring, too. Suddenly he's all cashed up. And when I asked him about it, he didn't want to explain.'

Kim crossed her arms. 'I think you'd better start at the beginning.'

Amelia took a deep breath and repeated everything that had happened out at Eastern Edge.

'So, do you really think he was involved?' Kim asked, a strange expression on her face. 'Because if you do, you should report it to Dave.'

Dob Paul in to the cops? Amelia's stomach twisted up in knots. 'No, the thing is, I don't. Not really. I mean, I trust Paul, but I just can't work out how he's funding everything.' She bit her bottom lip. 'Paul loves me. He wouldn't put me in a situation where I'd get hurt or have people thinking I'd done something wrong.' She slumped against a bench, feeling absolutely miserable. *Would he?*

'Sweetie, I hate to be the one who tells you, but you're not the first person to have thought of this. I've heard talk around town. Everyone knows that Paul's on the bones of his arse— you know he was really lucky not to have the farm sold out from under him when his father drank himself to death.' She stroked Amelia's hair.

'But Paul wouldn't hurt me.'

'I don't think he would either, but maybe he got involved with someone dangerous. Maybe he got in too deep, love.'

Amelia stared straight ahead, trying to make sense of what she was hearing. 'I've got to go,' she said and scrambled to her feet. She ran out the door before Kim could offer another word.

⁓

Amelia had to get to Emerald Springs. It was a long and hard walk from where she'd left the car, longer than she'd done since getting out of hospital, but it was the only place that would calm her down and give her some peace of mind. The

195

only place where she'd be able to think clearly. She moved gingerly, trying not to jar her ribs as she started on the uphill hike. As she walked, she found it hard to keep her anxious thoughts at bay—she just didn't have the energy. Fears and suspicions accosted her, but she forced herself to keep going.

Forty minutes later—a bit longer than it usually took her—she was pleased to kick her shoes off and sink her bare feet into the sand. Lying on her back on the little beach, she closed her eyes and listened to birds flitting from tree to tree, the sounds of their wings seeming so close to her ears. Her fingers ran through the sand as she moved her arms up and down in a soothing motion. Tears spilled out of her eyes and for a while she let them fall.

She kept thinking about the things her friends had told her at the hospital, about the gossip around town. Chelle had said no one was taking it seriously, and not to let it bring her down, but she'd had the most terrible thought. If Dave was harping on about her finances and asking her about Paul, where was he coming from? Maybe he'd heard the talk around town. The more she considered it, the more it made sense.

Everything Paul had set in motion would appear to have been made possible by ill-gotten gains—if the thought had occurred to Amelia, it would definitely have occurred to others! And if people in Torrica believed that Paul had something to do with the robbery, then it would stand to reason they'd assume Amelia was involved, too. As far as they were concerned, she would benefit from the theft.

So did *Sav* think that? Was that why she'd been so strange and distant? Amelia pushed the idea away.

What could she possibly do to clear their names? She sighed, rolled onto her stomach and propped her chin on her fists. She gazed at the deep water while a willy wagtail jumped around the edge of the pool, chattering and preening.

'Am I interrupting your swim?' Amelia asked quietly.

Chat, chat, chat, the wagtail answered, his backside wagging from side to side as he eyed her still form.

Feeling a bit more serene, Amelia sat up and looked around, then closed her eyes and let her head drop to her knees. But she still wasn't completely comfortable, not like she usually was here. Her eyes snapped open. Something wasn't right.

She peered around again, her gaze roaming over the bush near the wagtail. The branches were broken, as if something or someone had crashed through. Getting to her feet, she went across to the other side of the pool—the wagtail hopping away from her—and looked closely at the disturbed foliage. She examined the ground for kangaroo or emu tracks, but there was nothing obvious in the churned dirt.

A shiver ran down her spine, cold radiating out and covering her body in spite of the heat. For a moment she couldn't put her finger on what it was, but then she realised: it felt as though she was being watched. She swallowed hard, trying to push her fear down, and scanned from side to side, slowly.

The birds kept singing and a gentle breeze blew, making the water ripple and shimmer. There was nothing else. Nothing that she could pick up on, anyway.

You're losing it. No one else was here; she was the only one who made the trek anymore. She hated that these irrational fears were haunting her here, in her safe, special place. Shaking her head and shoving all her thoughts aside, Amelia sat on the edge of the pool and dangled her feet in the water.

Once again she thought about the night of the rodeo, trying to relax her mind and hoping that, this time, something jumped out at her. She took deep breaths, remembering Chrissie's calm voice as she'd talked her through the process, not trying to grab at anything. There was something—something in the depths of her memories that she still hadn't quite caught. Something important. Unbidden, recollections of the man's hands hard and insistent against her shirt engulfed her.

'No,' she muttered. 'No. Just *go away*. I want to remember everything but that.'

She found she needed to move, so she rose and walked around the pool. Then, as panic crept up and almost overtook her, she went faster. Keeping her gaze on the uneven ground to make sure she didn't trip, she suddenly stopped. Bending, she peered closer at the marks.

There were boot tracks in the sand leading *into* the pools. She knew instantly they weren't hers—she was barefoot, and anyway, they were much bigger and she didn't own boots like that. Who'd been here? It was such a difficult spot to get to, and really the only people who knew it well were her family and the few friends from town that they'd brought in. Why would there be someone hanging around?

It's probably just Graham, she told herself. *It looks like a Blundstone boot mark.* He'd probably been up here getting cold feet about the engagement party on Saturday. *Honestly, Milly, you'll give yourself a heart attack.* But she was still unnerved as she retrieved her sneakers and headed away from the springs, back towards the homestead. She was going to have a lie down and then head back to Kim's to apologise and have a slice of cake.

Chapter 22

'So Sav blanked you this morning?' Chelle asked as she poured a cup of coffee, then sat next to Amelia at the roadhouse table. It was the quiet time of a mid-Thursday afternoon and they were the only ones in the room, so they could talk freely. 'Are you sure she wasn't just rushed off her feet?'

'I'd like to think that,' Amelia muttered, 'but she hasn't replied to the text I sent, and you know how often she checks her phone. Anyway, if she does have a problem with me, serves me right. Look how I just treated Paul. I think that bang on the head scrambled my brains.'

'Don't be ridiculous.' Chelle took a sip. 'Oh man, that's good. I'm exhausted. I think I had about two hours' sleep.'

'Busy night then?'

'Babies choose the most inconvenient times to arrive,' Chelle said with a sigh.

Amelia thought it would be amazing to watch a new human life come into the world—she'd seen many animals born, and it never got old!—but she knew better than to say that to Chelle in this mood. And the thought of babies made Amelia think of Paul and some of the ideas about the future she'd been having before their fight. She took a few deep breaths, inhaling the delicious smells of the roadhouse. Kim was sizzling up some steaks for a late lunch order she'd walk over to the garage.

Chelle sighed again. 'So, what are we doing here? With my lack of brain power today, I don't think I'm going to be much use to you.'

'Dave's investigating me,' Amelia began. 'I'm sure of it.'

Leaning her chin on her hand, Chelle looked at Amelia with tired eyes. 'You know, I hope you don't mind, but Chrissie mentioned that to me. She's worried about you. We both are. She said it was really important to you to remember what happened that night. Are you sure you're not overreacting and pushing yourself too hard?'

'No, I don't think so. Dave's interviewed me twice and both times he's asked about my finances.' She held up a hand. 'Yeah, I know, I know, he's asked everyone, but from talking to Gus and Pip and Anne, he hasn't gone back to them for seconds. Look, Dave's an outsider—he doesn't know me, or Paul. So how could he not suspect us when we've got such a good motive? I mean, even I'm not sure about Paul.'

Chelle drank more coffee. 'Okay, so say you're right and Dave is looking at you. Why would you get yourself tasered *and* have your ribs cracked?'

'To make it seem realistic.'

'Too many TV shows for you, my friend.'

'Yeah, think what you want, but I know I'm right.' Amelia's voice rose in frustration. Why couldn't her friend see how serious this was? They weren't just talking about one robbery—there was the other crime, too. Maybe more.

'Come on, get to the crux of all this before I fall asleep.'

'Well, let's look at the facts.' Amelia held up her hand and flicked each finger as she spoke. 'One: Dave asked me about my financial situation and Paul's. Two: He's been told by me and everyone that Paul is broke, and now it turns out Paul's got oodles of cash and we don't know where it's come from. Three: Dave also asked why I was driving so fast. Maybe it looks like I was actually trying to get away from Gus.'

Chelle waved her hand in a give-me-more gesture. 'All circumstantial and can be explained.'

'Yeah, but enough to get Dave to look elsewhere? That's what I'm going to have to do, Chelle. I'm going to have to give him other people to investigate so he doesn't keep coming after me. But I can't just randomly throw people under the bus—I actually have to believe they could be responsible.'

'So what are you wanting to do?'

'I want to do some investigating. I want to find plausible suspects.'

Chelle shook her head. 'You're forgetting a couple of things. One, you're not a detective, you're just obsessed with *Bones*. Two, it's probably not anyone local.'

'I think it has to be,' Amelia said stubbornly. 'Who else could have known we were shifting the money that night, at that time?'

'Anybody with half a brain! No one would leave that amount of money on site overnight.' Then Chelle's eyes narrowed and she asked, 'So you're saying it's someone on the committee?'

'Or someone with access to them.'

'Babe, you're the one with access to half the town's bank accounts. You'd know if there was something funny going on there.'

Amelia rubbed the back of her aching neck. 'I know, and that's the trouble—believe me when I say that I've thought about all those accounts, but there's nothing funny in *any* of them.' She slumped, despondent.

'Bloody hell, of all the days to be feeling like death warmed up.' Chelle paused. 'Okay, so I guess we have to work out who else in Torrica would have been desperate enough to get the money. So, precise bank details aside, who has money woes? And here's another question. Has anyone bought anything really big and expensive since it happened? A new header, ski boat, any so-called toy that would have been classed as a luxury unless they came into excess money?'

'I guess . . . I guess we should start with Paul. I want to be absolutely sure.'

'Hell, Milly, if you really need to look into him about this, how on earth can you think about marrying him?' Chelle crossed her arms in disgust.

'I know!' Amelia's eyes stung with tears. 'But I just . . . I just need to know. I don't understand why he couldn't tell me where he got the money. And he certainly fits the bill.'

'Ugh. What a bloody mess. I think I need another coffee.' Chelle got up and helped herself. 'Okay, here's a couple of options. I know from Chrissie that Grant Hink, the vet, is having trouble.'

'You know, that's the second time I've heard that, but I find it really hard to believe when you see the flash surgery and new ute and so on. People don't think clearly when it comes to treating their pets and throw money hand over fist at the guy who looks after them.'

'Yep, totally right, but it's not the way you're thinking. Clients haven't been paying their bills, so he's having trouble meeting his. His bill at Torrica farm merch store is over ninety days.'

'How did you get talking to Chrissie about this?' Amelia asked.

'The invoices were printed on different-coloured paper and I asked why.' Chelle shrugged. 'I just thought it was a way of coding customers. I guess it is, in a way. The ones who are in big trouble get bright red, the ones in a smaller amount of trouble get green ones, and if you pay on time, you're lucky. You get the plain, basic white.'

'Right,' Amelia said. She thought for a moment. 'Were any others getting the red treatment?'

'No, Grant was the only one, but there were a few greens.'

'Many? Anyone we know?'

'I only saw three and the name on the top envelope. It was Jim Green. Green for Green. It's kind of funny.'

There was a pause. 'Jim? From the committee?'

'Your favourite person.'

Amelia closed her eyes as she processed that. 'But it only means he hasn't paid last month's accounts?'

'I think so, but you should ask Chrissie. I was only in there to kill a bit of time, while I was waiting for my afternoon surgery to start. We walked to the post office together.' The bell on the roadhouse door tinkled and Chelle's eyes widened. 'Ah, I think I'll head off, Milly. Looks like someone's looking for you.'

Amelia turned around and saw Paul making a beeline for them. She found she couldn't talk, so she waved to Chelle, who said hello to Paul on her way out.

'Well, I have to say, you really shocked me last night,' Paul said as he sat down. 'Not quite the reaction I was after.'

'I don't suppose I expected to see so much work going on either,' Amelia countered.

'No, I guess not.' Paul was silent as he picked at his nails before looking back at her. 'That really hurt, Milly. I don't understand how you could think that of me.'

Amelia leaned across the table and grabbed his hands. 'I don't really think that of you, but I couldn't work out how you could afford all that! There's never been any extra cash and then suddenly all these renos were happening—and there was a ring! I wasn't expecting one of them for months yet, maybe years.' She squeezed his fingers, but he pulled his hands away. 'I just . . . I've been so scared of everything since that last night of the rodeo. My head filled up with all these horrible thoughts, and—'

'That doesn't show a lot of trust in me.' Paul smiled sadly. 'I'm sorry. I'm not sure what to say.'

'Can you just think about it from my point of view for a moment?'

'No, I reckon you should think about it from mine,' he retorted. 'The person who's supposed to stand beside me, no matter what, asked me where the money came from when I gave her an engagement ring.'

'That was all I did, Paul. Just asked. I didn't actually accuse you of anything. You assumed I did.' She tried to put it as gently as she could, but even to her own ears it sounded horrible and harsh, like something her mum would say.

Paul leaned back in his chair. 'The reason I went to Adelaide wasn't to do the probate on Dad's will,' he said. 'I've already done that. I'd finally had an idea to make some money. For ages I'd been wracking my brains, trying to work out how I could get some cash to fix the house, make it a home so you could move in quicker.' His voice broke and he ran his hands over his face. 'So I came up with this idea. It took a while to organise and for it all to go through, but I finally got it done.'

Amelia couldn't help herself. 'What did you do?'

'I subdivided off forty hectares.' Paul looked into her eyes, unflinching. 'I was reluctant to do it—it's some of my best land, and it might come back to bite me—but I did it for you. For us. Felt I had to.'

'Um.' Amelia's stomach sank to her feet. 'I . . . um . . .'

Paul continued. 'So when I knew the subdivision had been accepted, I had it listed with a real estate agent. And it sold. I had to go and sign things on the Saturday, then there was more stuff to finalise with the bank on the Monday, and then I bought the ring. I'd had plans drawn up for the house months ago—I'd always wanted to fix it up, but more so knowing I wanted you there with me. The builder was organised last week. I could do that knowing there was money coming.'

Amelia's face was burning. She closed her eyes to hide her acute embarrassment. And not just embarrassment: shame.

'I'm sorry,' she managed. 'I'm really sorry.'

Paul was silent, looking down at his hands on the tabletop.

'What else do you want me to say?' she pleaded.

'Well, Amelia, I wanted you to know how I came by the money and now I've told you.' Paul stood up. 'As I told Dave Burrows when he came to see me.'

Amelia tried to catch Paul's eyes. 'He's been to see me too. I reckon he's investigating me. Or at least us. But if you've told him how you subdivided the land, that should clear your name, shouldn't it?'

'I wouldn't reckon,' Paul answered, his face grim. 'The simple fact is that I'm still short on cash flow for the farm operating expenses.' He shrugged and stared down at Amelia, a sad expression on his face. 'But whatever happens now, I wish you'd reacted differently last night.'

'I do too.' Amelia rose and reached for him. 'How can I make it up to you?'

He gave a short, sharp laugh. 'I'm not sure. I'll have to think about it.' And with that he turned and walked out, slamming the door, leaving her alone with the terrible fear that she'd completely ruined something precious.

Chapter 23

Amelia drove home, took a long hot shower and cried. Then she got dressed and stared at herself in the mirror, suddenly knowing what she had to do.

It was five o'clock, and the dirty grey clouds that had begun to roll in during the early afternoon had set fast. 'Opening rains,' Graham said to Amelia, his fingers crossed, as she headed out the front door.

'Be great, wouldn't it?' she called over her shoulder with a smile, knowing how important this rain would be to all the farmers in the area.

As she got into her mum's car, the drizzle had just started. Taking a deep breath, she drove out the driveway. To stop her thinking about what she was about to do, she turned up the radio and sang along to the McClymonts' 'Going Under'. Then she felt a stab of pain as the lyrics brought Paul to the forefront of her mind. Somehow, *somehow*, she had to fix things with him. She'd been in the wrong, so it needed to be her who made the first move. But how?

She flicked on the windscreen wipers to clear the small droplets that had blocked her view, then turned them off again. The drizzle seemed to be just that: nothing more than a sprinkle. Glancing at the still-cloudy sky, she swore under her breath and hoped the rain would get a move on.

As Amelia drove on, her stomach constricted with fear. She'd told no one of her intentions; she'd decided this was something she needed to do by herself, hoping it might jog her memories and help her heal. No more nightmares would be a good start.

Squeezing her eyes shut for just a second, Amelia inhaled deeply through her nose, then released the breath and turned her full attention to the road. The spot where she'd been cut off was getting closer. Goosebumps rippled over her skin and whispers began in the back of her mind. The sound of tyres on gravel. The smell of sweat mingled with men's deodorant. A rush of fiery pain through her body.

Amelia took her left hand off the wheel and shakily ran it over her hair, which was tied back in a ponytail. 'Come on, you can do this,' she muttered. When she glanced in the rear-view mirror, her heart quickened. The road was empty, just a long stretch of bitumen with white lines. But still the thumping wouldn't subside.

Pulling off at the place where she'd been attacked, Amelia sat in the car for a long time, listening to the rain patter against the roof, a little heavier now. Finally she cracked open the door and got out. She hadn't brought her Driza-Bone, she realised. It was quiet save for the raindrops hitting the leaves of the bushes alongside the road. The leaden clouds made the late afternoon dark, and Amelia shivered even though it wasn't cold.

She walked off the road to the place on the gravel where she'd been dragged. Bending down, she let her fingers trace the ground, her eyes shut. She could almost feel the burn of the torch they'd shone in her eyes, her hand rising to her face to block it out. Of course, it wasn't there now.

Sighing, Amelia sank to her knees, the rain falling on her as though washing her clean. She thought back to the moment when she'd slid into Gus's ute and started the engine, then remembered everything that had happened while she was driving—the speed of the car, the clink of the coins in the money bags, the taste of Bundy and Coke. She rested her elbows on her knees, her head drooping into her hands, and decided not to think at all. The rhythmic sound of the rain settled her nerves.

After a while she curled up on the ground. The rain was running under her collar and her jeans were soaked, but it didn't bother her. She tried to put herself in the position that she'd been found in, but placing her hands behind her back pulled at her ribs, so she brought them to the front and let them flop on the gravel.

She shut her eyes. The drumming of rain. The wetness drenching her body. She didn't do anything but lie there and immerse herself in the environment.

Soon she could feel the fingers hard against her neck and hear the popping of the buttons on her shirt. An unfamiliar voice yelled in her face: *Where the fuck is the rest of it?* She realised she hadn't felt any skin against hers. The man must have been wearing gloves.

Don't do that. The steadiness of another male voice filtered through her mind, but Amelia didn't move. *Don't do that,* she heard again, and with a sharp intake of breath she sat up, clutching at her chest. Paul? That sounded like Paul.

'No,' her mouth formed the word just as the guilt kicked in. It wasn't him. It couldn't be. She already knew that. But she was convinced she knew that voice! How? She struggled to put a name to it. *What the fuck did you do that for?* Panicked voices as a car engine started and doors slammed. *You weren't supposed to hurt her! She's not going to like this.*

Amelia sat there, still and shaking. What had the man meant by that? It didn't make sense—of course she hadn't liked being kicked and tasered.

Unless they were referring to another 'she'. Another woman. Someone who was working with them.

Amelia got up and paced the ground, wiping away the water that trickled down her face. Then she hurried to the car, jumped in and gunned the engine, the wheels splashing through puddles as she sped towards Torrica. She had to find Dave, and she knew exactly where to start looking.

ço

Dave was pleased to be sitting in the roadhouse talking to Kim, instead of staring at his whiteboard or his mountains of paperwork. All the words had seemed as if they were blurring together, and he'd needed some air and company.

One of the best things about Kim was that ever since she'd scolded him for questioning Amelia, she hadn't asked him about the case. She would talk about everything else unless he asked her about something in particular.

On Monday, when Dave had requested the bank records for the Torrica rodeo committee, he hadn't yet been thinking about anyone else's. Now he was putting a report together to look at Paul's, Amelia's and Jim Green's.

He'd questioned Amelia's brother, Graham Bennett, but other than the fact he owned his own mob of sheep, there didn't seem to be anything odd about him. And Graham had a seemingly airtight alibi: at the time of the robbery, he'd been helping his dad load up cattle from the rodeo and take them home.

Then there was Grant Hink. Dave had spoken to him the day before, but had come up with nothing. The man had made no attempt to hide his financial circumstances and also had a bloody good alibi.

The door swung open and a blast of cool air entered when Amelia rushed in from the rain, looking soaked to the skin.

Kim leapt up and ran towards her bedraggled niece. 'Milly, you all right?'

Pushing back his bowl of chocolate pudding, Dave followed her.

'Yeah, fine,' Amelia puffed, giving her aunty a quick hug before turning to Dave. 'I need to talk to you. I've remembered.' She bent over, clutching at her chest.

'Milly!' Kim grabbed hold of her, panic in her voice. 'Are you okay, sweetie?'

Amelia caught her breath, then slowly started to stand upright.

'Let's sit her down,' Dave said. He put his arm around the young woman and helped her over to the table, while Kim rushed into the kitchen to get a glass of water.

Dave sat opposite Amelia and gazed at her as she squeezed water out of her sodden ponytail, wondering what had put her in such a state. 'What happened today?' he asked in his gentlest professional voice.

'I went out . . . I went to where the attack happened,' Amelia said slowly.

'You did what? By yourself?' Kim put down the glass, then handed Amelia a clean tea-towel to dry her face and hair.

'I've been trying to remember. I thought it might help.'

'Oh, Milly, why didn't you ask me? I would have gone with you. You didn't have to do that by yourself.'

Dave noticed Kim glance out the window and was pretty sure she was thinking about the darkness and rain, and how frightened her niece must have been out there. He had to admit, it took guts to go back to where you'd been badly injured.

Or did it? That voice of suspicion was still niggling.

'Did it help, Amelia?' Dave asked, in that gentle voice, feeling in his top pocket for his ever-present notebook.

'I hope it will,' she answered, and took a breath. 'First, a tiny thing. I'm pretty sure that whoever ripped my shirt was wearing gloves. Not rubbery like you'd get in a kitchen, or rough like woollen or synthetic gloves can be. They were soft and smooth, so I wondered if they might be leather.'

Nodding, Dave jotted down *leather*. That certainly made sense from what he knew about the crime scene. 'What else?' he asked.

'Voices, I've mentioned voices before, but now I know what they said. And I'm sure I recognised one of them, but I have no idea how. He said, "Don't do that. What the fuck did you do that for?"'

Dave was feeling a bit sceptical, but he kept his face blank. 'How do you know you're not imagining this, Amelia?' he asked softly.

She faltered. 'Well . . . I . . .' She looked down at the table and Dave ignored the filthy look Kim threw his way. 'I guess I can't be completely sure, but I think I'm right, Dave.' She looked up and Dave was impressed with the conviction in her eyes.

'You said one of them. How many were there?'

'I don't know,' Amelia said immediately. 'I know the man who hurt me shouted at me, really loudly, in my ear: "Where the fuck is the rest of it?" And I reckon he asked me that a few times, or something like it.'

'Was the voice definitely male?'

'Yes, all the voices were. But the big thing I remembered, the thing I needed to tell you, is that one of them said, "You weren't supposed to hurt her! *She's* not going to like this." My first thought was that of course I didn't like being beaten and so on. But then I got to wondering if they meant someone else. Like there's a woman involved, working with them.'

Dave glanced at Kim out of the corner of his eye. She was sitting upright and listening intently, a set look on her face.

'She's not going to like this,' Dave repeated as he wrote it down, underlining it with bold, black lines. 'Interesting.' It did open up the possibility of a mystery woman being involved, although he had to take everything Amelia said with a grain of salt. He gave her an encouraging look, but no more information was forthcoming.

'That's all I can tell you about that,' she said with a shrug.

Dave thought for a moment, then changed tack. 'So, Amelia—' he leaned back in his chair and pushed his notebook

213

to one side '—tell me, what do you think they meant by "Where's the rest of it?"'

Amelia frowned, staring into the distance. 'They must have been talking about the money. I think they couldn't find all of it.'

'And was it anywhere else other than Gus's ute?'

She shook her head. 'No. We'd transferred it all across before I left. So . . .' Her eyes narrowed in concentration. 'You know, I think a bag slipped under the seat, but then they found it.'

Was she just making that up on the spot? Dave studied her for a moment before asking, 'That was what you heard?'

'I think so. I mean, maybe I heard more.' She took a shuddering breath. 'I don't think they were supposed to hurt me, but somehow everything got out of hand and that's what happened. And they were worried that this woman wouldn't like it, so that would put her in charge of them, wouldn't it?'

That sounded like a bit too much of a leap at this stage, but Dave just gave a reassuring nod and said, 'Don't worry, leave it with me.'

Chapter 24

'Right, Graham?' John called from the cab of the front-end loader. He wiped his hands on his dusty jeans and waited for the thumbs-up sign from his son. Over the rumble of the tractor engine, he heard the clanking as Graham pulled and tightened the chain through the underbelly of the sheep feeder and hooked it up.

'You're right!' Graham yelled from below.

John pushed the lever forward to lift it off the ground. He knew the chain would slip until the slack was taken up, so he was being extra slow and patient. It was always dangerous shifting big pieces of equipment; after having a hay bale nearly fall on top of him when he was younger, John was as careful as he could be.

'Gently does it,' he muttered to himself, all the while watching Graham for any hand signals.

The loader shuddered as the chain tightened and John breathed a little easier. He backed out and slowly drove towards the truck, in position for the feeder to be loaded, all the while keeping his hand on the lever, slowly raising it so he could slide it straight onto the trailer. Graham had jumped up on the truck now and was waiting to unhook it all.

'Excellent,' John said as the chain was unhooked and Graham waved his hand in a 'back out' motion. John swung the tractor around and drove towards the next feeder in line.

Selling the feeders had been Graham's idea. John still wasn't sure it was a good one, but he agreed with his son that there needed to be a little cash flow so the worker's cottage could be done up without putting any extra pressure on the bank account. They hadn't used the feeders for a few years, preferring to trail lupins along the ground. That was the opposite to what other farmers were doing—so many swore by the feeders—but John had seen too many sheep die around them when they clambered over one another to get at the grain. He was happy enough to trail feed still, even though it was old-fashioned.

Graham hooked up the second feeder, John put it in the trailer, and then they repeated the process another four times. 'Last one,' Graham called loudly.

John got out of the tractor. 'Need to take a leak. You jump in and I'll hook it up as soon as I'm finished,' he said, walking around behind the truck.

Within minutes he was back, his work-roughened hands deftly bringing the chain through the legs of the feeder and pulling it tight. He gave the thumbs up to Graham, who let out the clutch with a jerk. The feeder swayed precariously as it left the ground.

'Steady, mate!' John called, grabbing at the edge to stop the feeder from swinging wildly. 'Shit.' He gestured quickly for Graham to slow down, but his son wasn't looking, his eyes focused on the truck. John shook his head. *There's something seriously wrong with that boy today.* Actually, if John was being honest with himself, there'd been something different about Graham for a while.

John thought about this as he walked, both hands on the feeder; the swaying was getting more furious now and he had to hold on with all of his might. Maybe Graham had changed when he got engaged? That'd be enough to do it to anyone, John thought ruefully. Anyone who wasn't totally and utterly committed. He glanced up at Graham, trying to read his face. Blank.

'Up higher, son!' John yelled as they got closer to the tray. 'Higher!' He made frantic motions with his hands as it became clear the feeder was going to hit the side of the trailer. Then he let go of the feeder and jumped out into a space where he knew Graham could see him, gesturing upwards. 'Higher, higher, higher!'

Finally seeing the motions, his eyes widening, Graham reefed on the lever and the feeder started to move up. John breathed a sigh of relief. It made it over the side of the trailer and Graham lowered it down, with John jumping onto the truck and manoeuvring it into position, before the slack was taken off.

'Right-o, all good!' John called and started to take off the chains.

Graham backed the tractor out and turned off the engine after lowering the bucket to the ground. 'Sorry, Dad,' he said as he climbed out of the cab.

John jumped off the back of the truck and felt his knees jar as he landed. *Getting old had knobs on it*, he thought, not for the first time. He regarded his son and realised the dark rings under his bloodshot eyes had deepened.

'What's going on, Graham?' he asked in a gruff voice, looking out over the dry paddock towards the bush that held Emerald Springs. 'There's something not right with you.' He leaned against the truck and waited for an answer.

'Don't know what you're talking about.' Graham reached up to itch behind his ears—a sign of agitation since his boyhood, John recognised—then grabbed the chain and started to tie the feeders to the back of the trailer.

'I think you do. When was the last time you slept through the night? You're looking like you could fly to bloody America with the bags under your eyes. Noticed a few empty stubbies in the bin in the shearing shed. Drinking won't help, you know.'

'There's nothing wrong, all right?' Angrily, Graham yanked the chain hard and it made a clattering noise as it scraped across the steel.

John watched him for a bit longer. 'Mate, I don't believe you, but when you're ready, you come and talk, okay?'

Graham stilled. He didn't turn around but said, 'I think I'm in trouble with that loan.'

John closed his eyes. *Shit.*

The loan would be the one that Graham was using to pay off the house repairs, the ring and the engagement party. The one that, against his better judgement, John had agreed to go guarantor for.

'Do you?' John asked. 'What's happened?'

Graham turned around and raised his eyes to his father's. John read nothing but hopelessness and despair.

☙

Amelia sat at her home office desk, staring blankly at the computer screen. Her head was fuzzy and the accounting program she used, Agrimaster, blurred in front of her eyes. She'd gotten up bright and early on this sunny Friday, thinking she'd try to forget her troubles while getting stuck into the work that had piled up. But instead she'd found herself trying to work out how to talk to Paul. To apologise.

'Milly, do you want a cup of tea?' Natalie called. 'I've just put the kettle on.'

Hearing her mother's voice, Amelia pulled her thoughts away from Paul and back to the job at hand. 'No thanks, Mum, I'm fine.'

Between Paul and what was going on with the investigation, she felt as if her brain was fried. Amelia was desperate to give Dave as much information as she could, to help clear her and Paul's names. And the memories that had flooded back the day before were swirling through her head, the voices taunting her. Somehow it seemed even worse that a woman might have been involved in doing this to her. Maybe even a woman in town. Amelia would keep searching quietly in the background until she found out something—for her own peace of mind, if nothing else.

She thought about what Chelle had said to her. *Has anyone bought anything really big and expensive since it happened?* How the hell would Amelia know? And how could she find out?

A smile began to spread across her face. 'Of course!' Amelia grabbed the mouse and clicked on the internet icon, bringing up Facebook.

In the search area she typed in the first name she thought of: Pip Clinton. Because she was friends with Pip, the woman's page came up straight away and Amelia scrolled down through the timeline. There were photos of the rodeo events and ones with her daughter, but nothing unexpected or strange.

Then Amelia remembered the names of the people with overdue accounts at Chrissie's store and typed in *Grant Hink*. She was pleased to see that his security settings weren't high and that his personal page doubled as one for his vet clinic. She looked through it carefully, feeling like a stalker. There were lots of comments from people who were grateful for the care he'd given their pets; photos of Grant shoeing a horse and of his vet nurses holding a Jack Russell puppy, 'free to a good home'.

She came across a photo of Grant dressed in leathers and astride a motorbike. A silver badge on the side read Harley-Davidson—although with the settings on the handlebars, Amelia had known that the moment she saw it. Checking the date, she was disappointed to see the photo had been posted four weeks before the rodeo.

Well, she thought, *that doesn't mean it wasn't him, just that he hasn't advertised if he's bought some new toy. And maybe he was involved with the earlier robberies. Why would you buy a new Harley when you haven't paid your bills at the local shop?*

Clicking back into the search area, she typed *Jim Green* and wasn't surprised when there wasn't a hit. She tried the other committee members, just in case, but there weren't any hits. Well, most of them didn't have a clue what Facebook was. Frustrated, Amelia clicked back to her office work. She focused on the Agrimaster cashbook and looked at the statement in front of her. Ticking off each invoice against the statement, she entered the total due and clicked on the 'Save' icon. She opened the next envelope, from Barker's small engine shop.

'What's Graham buying now?' she muttered, staring at the invoice: a chainsaw, lawnmower and hedge trimmer. 'What the . . . ?' Pushing back her chair, she went into the kitchen. 'Mum,' she said, brandishing the paper, 'did Graham talk to you about this? Is the farm supposed to pay for him setting up his own gardening shed?'

Natalie held out her hand for the paper, took a look at it and shrugged. 'Of course it's fine. Who else is going to pay for it?'

'But it's not in the budget. There's nearly two grand worth of tools here. I can claim the chainsaw for tax, but not the other two.'

There were boots on the verandah outside and the door opened: John, mopping at his brow. Now the rain had been, the weather had turned humid.

'Dad—' Amelia began.

'I said it was all right, Milly.' Natalie glared at her.

'What's up?' John asked.

Glancing at her mother, Amelia tried to work out if it was worth bringing it up with her father. Probably not, she decided. 'Nothing.'

John looked from one woman to the other. 'What's that?' he asked.

'Oh, just an invoice Milly was asking about. But it's fine.'

It was John's turn to hold out his hand. Natalie passed the invoice over, her mouth forming a thin line. Amelia watched as her dad's brow wrinkled and an odd expression passed across his face.

'It's okay,' he said in a heavy voice. 'Just pay it.'

As Amelia went back to the office, she heard her mother offer John a cup of tea. 'Yep, please, love.' There was a pause as Amelia settled into the office chair, then leaned towards the door hoping to hear her parents' discussion—no luck, so she got up and silently moved to the door. That was better.

'You know it's not okay, don't you, Nat?' John asked quietly.

'He's got to get some perks, John. Lord knows we don't pay him much.'

'We pay him what we can and he gets cut in to the profits.'

'Of which there haven't been any for the last two years,' Natalie pointed out, her voice hard and cold.

'And what do you want me to do about that?' John answered in a tone that Amelia had never heard him use before. 'I can't make it rain and I can't make the prices go higher than they are. This is how it is. Graham needs to learn to be more responsible than this—he can't hide behind you forever. And he can't just go about booking things up willy-nilly. He'll have us in the mire before we can blink.' There were boots on the floorboards and then: 'Don't worry about the tea.' The screen door banged.

Amelia raised her eyebrows and backed away from the door to her chair. Clearly this was a well-worn argument. The cups and saucers started to rattle as Natalie banged them down on the kitchen counter.

An engine's roar sounded from outside and Amelia swung round to look out the window. She caught a flash of bright yellow—Chelle's car. She was about to rush out to greet her cousin when she realised she should give her mum a couple of minutes to get her public mask back on.

After listening to Chelle and Natalie say hello and exchange pleasantries, Amelia walked out into the kitchen. 'Hi!' She watched as Chelle held out her arms and her mother turned away.

'Hey there, you! How are you feeling?'

'Not bad. Bit tender, but not bad. What about you?'

'Fine.' Chelle half-smiled and Amelia realised she'd picked up on the tension in the house. That was the problem with having a doctor for a friend and cousin: Chelle was trained to watch for this sort of thing. 'Check out this cake your mum's made! Isn't she clever?'

Good old Chelle, Amelia thought. She was incredible at putting people at ease.

'Yeah, it's amazing.' The two love heart-shaped cakes were slotted together like ying and yang symbols and coated with white fondant. Little chocolate love hearts were scattered over the top like confetti.

'What type is it, Aunty Nat?' Chelle asked. 'Please tell me it's mud cake on the inside!'

Natalie smiled but shook her head. 'Sorry, it's actually an old-fashioned fruit cake.' She laughed as the girls' jaws dropped. 'That's Dani's favourite.'

'That's nothing short of disappointing,' muttered Chelle, looking crestfallen.

'Sorry about that!' Natalie turned back to the chicken satay skewers she was putting together.

'Come on down to my room,' Amelia said with a grin, gesturing for Chelle to follow her. 'We can chat there.'

'Ooh,' said Chelle as she started forward, 'just like we're teenagers again. See ya, Aunty Nat!' To Amelia she said, in a stage-whisper, 'Tell me you've got One Direction on your iPod.'

Amelia rolled her eyes. 'Not that teenager-ish,' she answered as they went down the stairs, before saying in a low voice,

'Sorry, Dad just had words with Mum when I questioned some of Graham's spending.'

'Oh, nothing new with your brother then?'

'Apparently not. So what's going on with you?' Amelia asked as she sat down on her bed and leaned against a pillow. She reached out, grabbed the other pillow and hugged it to her still-sore chest.

'Ha! You're organised,' Chelle said with a laugh. She plopped on the other end of the bed and put her feet up near Amelia.

'What?'

'Getting ready to laugh, aren't you? With the pillow?'

'Oh Chelle, I wish I was, but I really don't feel much like laughing. This whole thing is pissing me off. I've been hopeless with work today. Can't concentrate.'

'Well, no wonder,' Chelle said as she pulled off her shoes and massaged her feet. 'You've been through so much in such a short time . . .'

But Amelia suddenly couldn't focus on what her cousin was saying. 'Do you *have* to put your dead skin all over my bed?' she asked, her face screwed up as she eyed Chelle's cracked heels. 'That's just gross. And you being a doctor!'

'Oh shut up! I'm rubbing my feet. They're tired. It's been a busy day.' But Chelle swung her legs around and lay on her tummy, facing Amelia. 'So which bit is pissing you off the most?' she prompted.

'All of it. I can't decide what's upsetting me most today.' She took a breath. 'And what you told me about Jim Green and Grant Hink has really got me thinking.'

'Tell me about it, then,' Chelle said, dropping her head to the bed.

'Well, who has the ability to go on to farms all the time without causing suspicion?'

'A stock agent,' Chelle answered, her voice muffled.

'Yeah and a vet. And a truckie who carts wool.'

'True.'

'But look, I have to tell you something. I reckon there's a woman involved—and I have no bloody idea who it could be.'

Chelle looked up quickly, her eyes wide. 'A woman?'

Amelia nodded before telling her cousin exactly what she'd remembered when she was out at the crime scene.

Chelle listened in silence. 'Interesting,' was all she said with a frown, before adding: 'But, look, those other names and the fact they've got access to farms, that's worth mentioning to Dave, I reckon. If he doesn't already know.'

'I thought so.' Amelia wondered if her cousin didn't believe her about the mystery woman, but what was the point in arguing about it? She let it go.

'Okay . . . and to completely change the subject, because we don't actually work for the police force, what about Paul?' Chelle cocked an eyebrow. 'We need to organise a "make-up" scene.' She paused and put her finger up, like a teacher instructing a class. 'Involving make-up sex, of course, but first we need to set the scene because you made a little stuff-up.'

'Thanks, Chelle, like I needed reminding,' Amelia said with a groan.

'Look, you weren't yourself. You've had a belt on the head and understandably you've been pretty emotional. You were bound to overreact.' Chelle shrugged. 'I'm pretty sure Paul will come around.' Then she grinned and cocked an eyebrow. 'Especially if you get a Brazilian . . .'

'What?' screeched Amelia, starting to giggle. 'Oh God, don't make me laugh!'

'. . . and lie on the bed in sexy black or leopard-print lingerie.'

'I don't think so!'

'Maybe you should even have a note stuck to you. In a love heart, of course: *Beautified just for you,* or *I am your sex slave for the evening.*'

Amelia snorted, then her eyes widened. 'How did you just think of that?' she gasped. 'Oh no!' She waved her hands in front of her. 'Don't tell me. You've already done it, haven't you? *Chelle!*'

Her cousin smiled a very wicked smile.

Chapter 25

'Here you are, Belinda,' Amelia said, dropping a couple of bags of frozen chips onto the bar. 'Aunty Kim says to give her a yell if your order doesn't turn up tomorrow and she can send some more over.'

'Cheers, Milly. Can't believe we've run out! A lot more meals on the weekend than we expected. Appreciate you running them over, especially with your ribs being so sore.' Belinda eyed her and Amelia wondered if she was looking for some gossip.

'Oh, it's fine. I can handle a couple of kilos. It's been a whole week and I'm nearly back to my old self.' That wasn't completely true, but now the whole town would think it was.

Belinda grabbed a wine glass and poured a healthy slug into it. 'Here, on the house. Thanks for your help.'

Amelia was about to thank her when a voice boomed out.

'Give us three beers, love.'

She took a sip of her wine and watched as Belinda poured the beers for Mike Andrews then picked at the coins on the bar to get the amount she was owed. Mike slid one down to his brother Tony, and the other to Jim Green who was further down the bar.

Geez, she thought as they downed them in a couple of gulps and ordered another round. Friday night was looking like a big one! She walked away from the bar and sat at a table, then picked a few peanuts out of the bowl in front of her and popped them into her mouth, just as Mike yelled, 'Get that into ya, Jimbo! It might shut you up for a bit. You and your bloody mouth.'

'You can talk, ya mug,' Jim called back. 'Always yappin', you are.'

Chrissie pulled out a chair opposite Amelia, sat down and met her eyes. 'Full of shit, that one,' she muttered, taking a slug of her wine.

'Hello to you too.' Amelia smiled. 'I didn't know you were coming in tonight.'

Chrissie put a finger to her lips. 'I'm not here,' she said with a grin, 'but I needed a wine before I went home. Anyway, I wouldn't have thought you should be here either, with your ribs. What if you get bumped?'

'The pub was out of chips, so Kim asked me to drop a couple of bags over when I called in to see her. Anyway, I need some Dutch courage. I'm heading out to try and fix everything up with Paul after I leave here tonight.' She'd told Chrissie all about the Paul situation in a long phone call.

'A pub without chips would have to be better than a pub with no beer,' quipped Chrissie, who'd always loved Slim Dusty, before taking another sip. 'So, fixing it all up with Paul, hey. How do you think it's going to go?'

'Buggered if I know.' Amelia sighed, twisting her glass around and mopping at the wet ring with the hem of her T-shirt. 'I don't want to think about it, so change the subject please! Why was your day so full on?'

'Just busy. That little bit of rain has got all the croppers excited. They're coming in to pick up their chemical orders so they can start spraying. Spent most of the day on the fork-lift.' Chrissie glanced around, then leaned forward. 'People can't stop talking about all the thefts that have been going on around here, and the things Dave said at the crime forum. The whole town's spooked, waiting for the next—'

Above Chrissie's head there was a flash of movement and then a crash of glasses. Amelia stood up so quickly that her chair tipped over behind her. One man had another in a headlock, their backs to her. More glasses smashed. The men twisted for a second, not long enough for her to work out who they were.

Chrissie grabbed her arm, pulling her towards the wall. The movement caused a twinge of pain in her ribs and she caught her breath.

'Bloody idiots,' she said above the yelling and grunting.

There were shouts of 'Hey!' and 'Stop!' as others tried to pull the men apart. Or were they joining in the fight? Amelia stood frozen, her heart pounding—she hadn't seen a full-blown pub brawl before.

Belinda yelled out from behind the bar, 'I'm calling the cops!'

From the side, Danielle came running in. 'Leave him alone!' she screamed and jumped on the back of a man who had someone in a headlock.

'What . . . ?' With growing fear, Amelia realised it was Graham at the bottom of the pack, and Jim Green was the one who held him. The two hefty Andrews brothers had their hands on both men, their faces red with exertion. '*No*. Dani! Graham!'

Amelia tried to go to them, but Chrissie put a hand on her shoulder and slid an arm in front of her, holding her back as gently as possible. 'Don't be stupid, that's the last place you need to be. You'll get hurt again.'

'But Graham . . .'

'Is old enough to look after himself.'

'I just want to make sure he's all right. He's got his engagement party on tomorrow night. What the bloody hell is he doing?'

They watched as more people joined in. Amelia wasn't sure who was really helping. Jim's mate Kev was somewhere in the mix, and Grant Hink had managed to pull Danielle away and was holding her firmly around the shoulders so she couldn't go flying back in there.

Two tables were upturned, crockery smashing across the ground. A chair splintered. There were yells and the sound of fists thumping into flesh. Things seemed to be escalating. A man stumbled back from the scrum and crashed into the wall close to Amelia, making her jump.

'All right, time to get outta here,' Chrissie said.

Amelia nodded, her eyes wide. They walked gingerly towards the dining area.

A siren sounded and a few seconds later the two Barker policemen ran in through the front doors, yelling, 'Stop! Police!'

Amelia and Chrissie ducked into the dining area, then out the back way to the street. 'What the hell was that all about?' Amelia asked, her hands twisting nervously. 'And Graham and Dani? I have to see if they're all right.'

They walked to the front of the pub where the police car was parked. There they watched, Amelia's heart sinking, as the cops marched out Graham and Jim. Danielle ran after them, mascara dripping down her face.

Amelia followed her and put a hand on her arm. 'Dani!'

Rounding on her, Dani shook her off before narrowing her eyes and getting in Amelia's face. 'Leave me alone,' she said, her voice high and shaky. 'You're the reason this has happened. Just leave us alone!' Then she turned and strode away.

'What the hell was that all about?' Chrissie hissed to Amelia.

Stunned by the ferocity in Dani's tone, Amelia shrugged and stood back, even though her impulse was to run to her brother's side. 'I have no idea,' she muttered, trying to contain her shock. 'Maybe she reckons Graham was standing up for me.' Was Amelia really going to be at their engagement party tomorrow? It was hard to imagine. She watched as Andy asked Dani to move back and the young woman refused. He took hold of her arm, opened the police car door and ushered her in before shutting it. Amelia could see she was crying.

'Good move,' Chrissie said with a smirk. 'Those doors have got child locks on them. She won't be able to get out.' Then Chrissie seemed to spot something, and her voice changed. 'Hey! Look who's here.' She nudged Amelia, who turned and saw Dave hurrying towards the flashing lights.

231

'Right-o, you lot, show's over.' Dave's voice boomed out across the night, before he turned to the small gathering who'd come out of the pub to watch. 'Head back inside and have another drink—a softie.' He paused before adding: 'And don't any of you even *think* about getting in a car and driving home. Jack and Andy here are going to be busy with the breatho once we've dealt with these two.' He turned to Graham and Jim, who were standing sullen-faced, their arms crossed and with a policeman on either side of them. 'What's going on here, eh? Bit of a lover's tiff?'

'Nothin',' Jim said. 'It was nothing. Just got a bit hot under the collar after I'd had a coupla drinks.'

'Pretty hot for nothing,' Dave observed, taking out his notebook. He stepped closer to the men and lowered his voice as he continued to question them.

'That was the best "get out of here now" line I've ever heard!' Chrissie said with glee. 'Did you hear that?'

Amelia shook her head, her gaze still trained on the body language of her brother and Jim.

'Go home now,' Chrissie said, in a terrible but hilarious imitation of Dave's deep, commanding voice, 'otherwise you'll be breath-tested!'

That made Amelia glance at her friend and smile, despite the butterflies in her stomach. She moved closer to Chrissie, who looked at her strangely.

'What's up?' she asked.

Amelia screwed up her nose. 'This is just so weird. I've never known Graham to get in a fight. How much trouble is he going to get into? I really should help him somehow. No matter what Dani says.'

Chrissie nodded. 'It's strange for him to fight, yeah. Always thought he was a bit prissy.' She shot Amelia an apologetic look. 'Sorry, but you know what I mean.'

Amelia gave a half-smile, but fear was getting the better of her. 'What if . . . ?'

Chrissie held up her hand. 'This has *nothing* to do with you and the attack,' she said sternly. 'This is Jim and Graham we're talking about here. Two idiots in a bar. Nothing more. Graham's probably shitting himself over the engagement party and sealing the deal with Dani. Men always lose it at times like this.' She put her arm around Amelia's shoulders. 'Don't be paranoid.'

'You know, I look around here and see all these people, and I can't help but wonder if any of them were involved. Stupid, I know.' Amelia leaned into her friend and Chrissie stroked her hair.

'I wouldn't think that's silly. I'd say that was normal. Now, didn't you say you were going out to see Paul?'

Amelia nodded.

'Well, like Dave said, you'd better head off. Otherwise he'll get Andy and Jack onto you with the breatho.'

'I need to stay for Graham.'

Chrissie shook her head firmly. 'Actually, you don't. Dani's here, even if she's gone slightly mad.' When Amelia hesitated, Chrissie gave her a push. 'Go on, Milly, get going and fix your love life. Graham can look after himself.'

❧

Driving out to Eastern Edge, back in good old Pushme, Amelia's anxiety grew and grew. The knot in her stomach made its way up to her throat and she felt sick. If she'd been driving out here two hours ago, it would have been the fear of what lay ahead with Paul. Now she was also worried about Graham.

She tugged at her lacy black bra. It was the scratchiest thing she'd ever come across, compared to her well-worn, comfortable sports bras. And as for the French knickers . . . *Bloody hell!* Cursing Chelle for talking her into this plan, Amelia glanced down at the box beside her. It held rose petals, candles and another sexy outfit she could put on later in the night. She also had wine, beer and tinned oysters. Thinking about them, Amelia made a face. She couldn't stand them, but she knew Paul loved them. She'd brought brie and biscuits for herself.

But it was so late now that she figured Paul would probably be in bed. There might not even be a chance to seduce him and make things right. Still, maybe, if everything went according to plan, they could have a midnight feast.

Graham pushed back into her thoughts and she shoved him out again. Now was the time to concentrate on Paul.

Pulling up and parking under the pepper tree, Amelia saw that the house was bathed in darkness, so it looked like he was definitely in bed. Moonlight lit the path leading to the kitchen door. Clutching the box of goodies with a heavy heart, Amelia walked up the steps and knocked. Silence. She knocked again, then pushed open the door and called out, 'Paul? Are you here?'

There was a rustling and a *tap-tap-tap* on the floor—then something brushed past her legs and she gave an embarrassing squeal. She turned to see Peanut running into the bushes. *Bloody cat.*

Fumbling for the switch, she turned it on and light flooded the room. For a moment she stood, speechless. The changes inside were incredible—it looked like they were almost finished. The stove was now in place and the wood-stained cabinets shone brightly. The Pigeon Pair freezer and fridge were stainless steel, and the kitchen sink sparkled.

Amelia stood there, taking it all in, before tiptoeing over the newly polished wooden floorboards and pulling open the pantry door. It was huge! Looking up, she saw a fan in the ceiling, then realised the small shelf to her right had a power point just above it. She was sure that was where Paul's bread maker would go; he loved his homemade bread.

Shaking her head, Amelia felt a sense of shame. How could she have been so stupid? Chelle's voice echoed around her head: *You weren't yourself.*

'Totally,' she muttered, 'but is that a good enough excuse?'

She went down the hallway, calling softly as she went. 'Paul?' When no answer came, she stopped, confused. Then she went to the bedroom. It was empty. So where was he? Again, the butterflies started in her stomach. As she paced the kitchen, their fluttering grew stronger and stronger. She imagined him injured in a paddock somewhere, no one knowing where he was. Maybe he was unconscious.

Or maybe he's stealing something else, the devil's advocate in the back of her mind said loudly.

'Piss off,' she muttered, closing her eyes and trying to banish the wayward voice. 'You know that's not true.'

Finally she went outside and stared into the gloom, hoping to see a flash of light or hear a noise. Something to indicate that Paul was out with a lambing ewe or some other job that would need his attention at nine-thirty at night.

Then she saw it. A beam of light bouncing across the land as if a ute had hit a bump. Relief flooded through her and she raced back inside to set up her plan.

Ten minutes later, there were rose petals strewn across the bedroom floor and over the sheets. She'd placed candles in strategic positions leading down to the bedroom and set up a romantic picnic on the lounge-room floor.

Just as she'd finished, Paul opened the kitchen door and stared at her. He was holding his shotgun. 'What are you doing here?' he asked, his expression hard to read in the soft glow of the candles.

Amelia looked at him for a second before saying, 'Oh, you've been fox shooting. I was wondering where you were.'

Paul didn't say a word and Amelia, overcome by emotion, didn't know what to do or say, but finally acted on her heart. Walking over to him, she put her hands on his shoulders and looked straight into his eyes. 'I'm really sorry, baby. I don't know what I was thinking. I've been so emotional.' She took her hands away and stepped back, giving a tight-lipped smile of regret. 'Not an excuse, I know. I can't change it, but I can say I'm sorry.'

Paul nodded and moved around her. Pulling open the fridge door, he got out a beer and leaned against the new bench. 'I have no idea what you were thinking either,' he said quietly. 'I can't believe the woman I love so very much would even contemplate those thoughts about me. And only the day after some hotshot detective from the city comes and asks me the same questions. Makes it seem like he thinks I could hurt you. Got any idea how that makes a man feel?'

'Oh, no. No.' Amelia shook her head. 'Well, I didn't . . . not really.' She glanced down, her face hot.

'But you must have,' Paul said, with a thoughtful look. 'You accused me of—'

Suddenly Amelia saw red. 'Actually, I never said anything about the robbery. If you remember, I asked you where the money had come from, giving you a chance to explain, and you wouldn't tell me. *Then* you were the one who put two and two together.'

Paul gave a faint grin. 'Ah, there's the fighting spirit I know.' He breathed in deeply through his nose and gazed at her, his blue eyes brightening. 'I'm pleased to see that. You hadn't really shown it lately. Oh wait—' at her sharp look, he held up his hands as if to ward off a blow '—I didn't mean that the way it sounded. It's just . . . you've been kicked pretty hard and you were taking a little while to come back.'

'And how would you know?' she asked icily. 'Other than the conversation at Kim's, you haven't really been around.'

Paul seemed ashamed. 'I know. I need to apologise for that. I was still angry and I didn't even give you a chance to explain.' He paused and gave her a slight smile. 'What was really going on? Honestly, why did you suspect me?'

Amelia took a breath and let it out slowly. 'It was so weird. One moment there wasn't any money to buy a bag of cement, and the next there were all these renovations and an engagement ring. It made no sense. And it was only just after everything had happened.' She stopped, took another breath. 'The way I felt . . . I'd been having nightmares. Somehow you being involved with the robbery came into my head, even though I knew it didn't make sense. And when you wouldn't explain . . .' As she stared at him solemnly, her voice cracked. 'Paul, I'm terribly, terribly sorry.'

Paul moved over to her and took her hands. 'I'm sorry too. I know my pride gets in the way too often and look where we are. I should have told you why I went to Adelaide.' He made a face. 'I just *hate* having to pinch and scrimp and save, and watch the bank account all the time, when all I want to do is give you the best.'

'Why won't you let me put some of my savings in?'

He sighed. 'I'm sorry, Milly, I just can't. I was brought up to be independent, and I had to be that way when Dad turned out the way he did. I want to know I can look after you and whatever kids come along, without needing your money. Let's use that for fun things, like holidays and stuff.' He gave her a gentle smile. 'Listen, I know this is hard, but I'm still really hurt and it'll take me a bit of time to come back from that. See where we go from there.'

'That sounds fair.' Amelia vowed that she would put everything right, as of now. She pressed up against him and tried to put a sexy look on her face. 'These French knickers are driving me up the wall. How about we take them off?'

ॐ

The glow of the bedside table clock read 3.30 a.m. Amelia rolled out of bed and went to get a drink of water. The moonlight streamed in the window above the kitchen sink and seemed to pool over her feet. Staring out at the land as she drank, she let herself contemplate what had happened the previous evening.

She knew that Paul was still holding back from her, protecting himself. His caresses and kisses hadn't been given with the same openness as before. He was trying to hide it, but the slight detachment had chilled Amelia to the bone. Had she pushed him too far? What if she couldn't make it right? Guilt and shame flooded through her.

The shadows the moon cast across the kitchen floor made her think about her soul. There were patches of light that weren't hidden from anyone, but there were also dark places that she was trying to rid herself of: the self-doubt, the need to please others and the desire to be accepted. There was the fear and paranoia that still lingered from the attack—but also the strong wish to find out who had hurt her.

Quietly, Amelia padded back to the bedroom and hopped beneath the warm covers. Paul was breathing steadily next to her. She curled herself around him, putting her arm over his hip, and gently pulled him to her. The words *Please let this be all right* ran through her head like a mantra until she fell back to sleep.

Chapter 26

The man was dressed in a woollen beanie and face mask, his hands covered in soft leather gloves. He put the truck into gear and drove quietly down the hill. His companion sat silent in the passenger seat, staring as the truck seemed to eat the white lines that marked the middle of the road.

They drove about ten kilometres then gradually slowed down before coming to a complete stop. The driver didn't pull off the road, but sat and waited, the engine idling. Seconds later another man emerged from the bush, dressed the same way. He climbed into the sleeper cab that lined the back of the truck and they continued on their way.

'How did you know about the stud sheep?' the driver asked, breaking the silence.

'Town gossip at the farm merch store,' the woman in the passenger's seat answered. 'The ewes are Paul's engagement present to them both, and another way to make a bit of extra money. Got to give it to him, he's thinking outside the square by starting up his own stud. It's a good plan to add value to what he's already got. But I'm not having that.'

The bitter tone made the driver look over at her. She was staring straight ahead, hands folded in her lap, and holding her body in a rigid posture. He sighed and turned back to the road.

Half an hour later, she signalled with her hands and the truck started to slow down. 'In here. Get the gate, will you?'

The man they'd picked up climbed over the seat and jumped down to open the wire gate, dragging it to the side.

'Pull the truck up in a corner,' the woman said, 'so we can make a forcing yard to push the sheep up onto the truck.'

The country was swathed in gentle moonlight as they worked quickly to set up the panels they'd brought. In the crate of the truck were two black and tan kelpies, whining with anticipation. While the other man fastened the panels together with a roll of wire, the driver pushed open the crate and the dogs rushed out. They danced around his feet, standing on their back legs and jumping to reach his face. 'Sit!' he growled. Immediately they sat at his feet and looked up at him.

Together the men lifted up a loading race to the gaping hole in the crate, then made sure it was sitting in tight and couldn't fall under the weight of the ewes when they were being loaded onto the truck.

'There's a rope under the passenger's seat,' the driver said. 'Can you get it and we'll tie this to the crate?'

The woman opened the door and fossicked under the seat until she felt the rough rope. She pulled it out and turned back to give it to the driver, but thought she felt something else pull out too. She looked on the ground and felt around, but couldn't find anything. She decided that she must have imagined it.

'We right?'

'Reckon so.'

The woman glanced at the sky. The stars and moon were visible, and there were drifting cotton-bud clouds. Turning to the south, where their weather usually came from, she made sure there wasn't an approaching bank of cloud that hadn't been factored in. They couldn't afford not to have the moonlight. She'd watched the weather carefully over the past week with this plan in mind. Taking these sheep would leave a big hole in Paul's income.

They would win. After everything that had happened, they would win.

The woman nodded and turned back to the two men. 'Let's get on with it, then.'

The driver gave a low whistle and threw his arm out in the direction of the paddock. 'Way back,' he said to the dogs and they shot off without a backwards glance: one to the left, the other to the right.

The three stood and listened as the dogs' footfalls faded. A gentle breeze puffed at their faces and the rustle of the bushes made them all look around. Standing with their hands in their pockets gave them a relaxed look, but in reality they were tense, their eyes darting around, watching and listening for anything unusual. The bush on the road verge shielded them from view, but even so they didn't want anyone driving past on the road while they were in the middle of the operation. It was unlikely—the road was rarely used because it had only one farm entrance, to Eastern Edge.

The dogs' owner gave a loud, short, sharp whistle once every few minutes. Before long they heard the dogs puffing, hooves thundering across the paddock and the occasional bleat. In the pale light the ewes looked white, the same colour as the moon, as they were herded across the paddock by two dark shadows. The dogs crisscrossed back and forth, not letting any escape. The men walked either side of the sheep until the dogs herded them into the forcing yards and the gate clinked shut behind them.

'Right-o, on the truck with you all,' the driver said and pushed the sheep towards the narrow race. With as little noise as possible but much encouragement from the men, they made their way into the crate one by one.

The woman slid the door shut. 'Done.' She wanted to smile, pleased with their efforts so far, but there was still work ahead. 'Let's go,' she said briskly.

On the road back home, she listed everything that needed to be done with the ewes to make sure they couldn't be recognised. 'We need to take their tags out and replace them with our own. We're going to need to change the earmark. We can do that by using a pocket knife and making an extra slit in the ear, through the mark that's already there. That will make it unidentifiable.' She talked on and the men listened. 'They'll have to stay in the back paddock, up near the bush for a while—at least until the heat dies down.' She looked at her companions. 'And there's to be no more after this one. You hear me? No. More. They're investigating hard since you idiots hurt that girl. God knows why he made you lot so stupid.'

The driver looked across, his mouth open as if to say something, but the woman held up her finger and pointed it at him.

'Don't say a word,' she hissed. 'You're the worst of the lot.'

☙

243

Amelia woke to a thump on the bedside table. Reaching across the bed, she realised Paul wasn't there. Simultaneously she smelt coffee and opened her eyes. Paul was sitting beside her, a steaming mug in his hands. 'Morning, sleepyhead,' he said, pointing to her mug on the table, which was sitting in front of the clock.

'Have I slept in?' she asked.

'Not that much, but I'm ready to head out—just got to refuel the ute. Do you want to get dressed and come and see those stud ewes I bought for us?'

She'd forgotten all about them. 'Yes! Of course I do.'

'Right, see you down at the shed in fifteen minutes then.'

As soon as he was gone, Amelia gulped down her coffee, leapt out of bed and headed for the shower. While she was soaping her hair, she realised that Paul hadn't smiled at her once. That set warning bells ringing in her head. 'Argh!' she groaned, then quickly rinsed her hair and jumped out. Throwing on a clean set of clothes and dragging a brush through her hair, she grabbed her phone and ran to the shed, texting as she went.

Graham, just wanted to check in with you this morning and see if you were okay. What was last night all about?

After hitting send, she stuffed the phone in her pocket and kissed Paul good morning.

'Who were you texting?' he asked as he hung up the diesel hose and put the lid back on.

'Graham. He was in a fight last night at the pub.'

Paul turned and stared at her. '*Graham?* In a pub brawl?' He sounded even more surprised than Chrissie. 'Isn't the engagement party tonight?'

Amelia nodded and explained what had happened.

'That's strange,' Paul said, shaking his head. 'Maybe he's getting cold feet or something? Anyway, jump in and I'll show you these ewes. They're really impressive with their size and bone structure.'

As they drove off, Paul spoke with passion about the ewes and his plans for them, and Amelia let his voice wash over her. She enjoyed this so much: heading out in the ute with him, looking at the country and planning. It made her believe they still had a future together.

'So really,' Paul continued, as he slowed the ute and came to a stop in front of a gate, 'this is going to be a good money-making venture, but it'll also be fun. I love genetics and I think this would be a great thing for you to be involved in too, Milly. We've got to record all the birthdates and weights and so on in a special computer program. Then it gets sent off to New England Uni, and all the data is put in some great recording program that spits out EBVs we'll use to help sell the rams.'

EBVs? Amelia thought. *Oh, of course, estimated breeding values.*

She straightened up. 'I'd love to be involved.' Out of the corner of her eye, she saw Paul stiffen—maybe he was regretting his enthusiasm. He didn't say anything more, so she got out of the ute, opened the gate and let him drive through.

Paul circumnavigated the edge of the paddock, following the fence line. Amelia stared out the window, keen to catch a glimpse of the sheep before he did.

'Weird,' Paul muttered.

'What?'

'Can't see them anywhere.' He stopped and pulled out a set of binoculars from the centre console next to the handbrake. Slowly he canvassed the whole area. While he did that, Amelia got out and climbed onto the back of the ute, hoping the extra height would help.

'Are they over there underneath that cluster of trees?' she asked, leaning down to Paul's window.

She watched as he refocused the glasses. 'Don't reckon,' he answered. 'Hang on, we'll go over there.'

From her vantage point on the back of the ute, Amelia looked every which way as they drove. The wind whipped her hair over her face, making it hard to see, so she took off a hair lacky from her wrist and tied it back.

'I can't find them,' Paul said after another ten minutes of driving. 'Jump in here and we'll check the next paddock.'

Two hours later and they'd found nothing. The panic was plain on Paul's face.

'We've got to ring Dave,' Amelia said, taking charge of the situation. She'd never seen him look so lost before. 'With everything else that's going on, it would be silly to think it couldn't happen to you, babe. Come on, let's go back to the house.'

☙

'Burrows,' Dave barked into his mobile phone. He'd just spoken to Coops, who'd given him bad news about the note and bank statement—clean as a whistle.

'Dave, it's Amelia.'

'Yes?' He pulled his pen out of his pocket and picked up his notebook from the table, then glanced at his whiteboard, seeking the place where Amelia's name was written in red.

'I'm at Paul's,' she said breathlessly. 'His stud ewes are gone.'

Dave put the pen down and pressed the phone closer to his ear. 'Stud ewes?'

'Yeah, we're out in the paddock they were in, but they're not here.'

'Are you sure they haven't escaped? What sort of ewes?'

'White Suffolks. We've checked the road verge and other paddocks—'

'Crossbred-type sheep like to crawl. Could they have crawled out?'

'We know that! We're not idiots,' Amelia said in a stronger voice. 'Dave, we've looked. They're not here. And just to be slightly pedantic, they're not crossbred, they're purebred White Suffolk. And we think we've found truck tracks.'

That made Dave sit up and pay attention. He looked at the whiteboard and his eyes slid to Paul's name. 'Okay, I'll be there as soon as I can. Give me the directions to the paddock.'

Amelia told him and he hung up. Hoping to get one of the locals, he dialled the Barker police station. Jack answered and Dave gave quick and precise instructions about meeting him at Eastern Edge. Then he gathered up his evidence kit, phone, notebook and camera, and hurried out the door.

On the drive over, Dave talked himself through everything he knew. 'Five crimes, four on farms. Chemical, GPS equipment, diesel, ute. All to do with cropping. But it's sheep this time—doesn't fit. So have they changed or is it someone else acting under the cover of the previous crimes? Do we have two different lots of people doing it now?'

He turned onto the road that bordered Eastern Edge and drove slowly, looking for the cocky gate on the left-hand side that Amelia had told him about. He rounded a corner and saw her standing in the middle of the road like she'd promised. She waved to him and he pulled up. 'In here,' she called, gesturing him towards her.

Dave ignored her, parking on the opposite side of the road and getting out. 'Have you walked or driven through the gate?' he asked as he grabbed his trusty rucksack—packed with everything he'd need—from the back seat and walked over.

'Yeah, we drove through.'

Dave said nothing, but surveyed the ground. Truck tracks, with ute tracks over the top, he was sure. He took the camera out of his bag. Clicking quickly, he zoomed in on the clear part of the truck tracks, thicker and wider than those of the ute. And there was something about them . . . He leant even closer. It looked like one of the tyres had a chip of rubber missing. That could be a crucial piece of evidence.

'Where's Paul?' Dave asked, still clicking.

'He's gone to check some of the other paddocks.'

Dave stopped and looked at her. 'I thought you said you'd already done that?'

'We have!' she protested, her lips turning down. 'You don't trust anyone, do you?' Then she gave a short laugh. 'Huh, why would you, you're a copper.' She shook her head before saying, quietly and clearly, 'We have. We both have. We've spent over two hours looking for them and they are certainly not here. Back at the house is the paperwork that came with them, if you want that.'

'I do.'

She looked taken aback, and he realised he'd gone a bit too far.

'I'm sorry if I sound brisk and abrupt,' he said. 'I get like that when I'm investigating.'

'It's okay,' she said, shrugging.

Dave cleared his throat. 'Right, can you just stay here for now? I'm waiting for Jack Higgins to arrive. If you can show him where to go, that would be great.'

'Sure.' Amelia folded her arms across her chest. 'No worries.'

Dave grabbed his rucksack and put it on his back. Picking his way through the gate, he made sure he didn't step on any of the tracks. He followed their progress into the paddock. Deep grooves in the sand showed that the truck had turned to the left, and he took more photos before following them along the fence line.

The roadside bush was high and thick—there was no way anyone could have seen what was going on from the road. He knew the moon had been almost full, because he and Kim had walked down to the Lions Club park and sat by the pond. The moon would have provided enough light to see the ewes and load them. He'd also been following the moon cycles on the weather site he used. Most rural crime happened leading up to or on a full moon—the crims needed to see what they were doing.

Whoever did this would have needed dogs, though. Unless . . .

He turned and yelled, 'Amelia?'

'Yeah?'

'You drove through this gate in a ute?'

'Yeah, we did.'

He didn't answer. Okay, well, that meant it wasn't the ute that had been stolen in a previous robbery. They had to have dogs, and some type of panels or gates. He kept following the tracks until he came to the corner of the paddock. He looked back to the gate and judged the distance to be about three hundred metres. Standing there, he examined all the marks in the ground before getting out the camera again and shooting several more photos. He could see where the truck had been parked, as well as a mixture of tracks leading into where he assumed the back of the vehicle had been.

This was clearly where the ewes had been loaded on. Without disturbing the scene, Dave walked to the fence and looked around some more, his eyes raking the ground for anything that had been left behind. Once again, to his frustration, it seemed the scene was clean, bar the tracks.

'Damn,' he whispered. But then his eyes caught on something.

There was a small pool of black liquid on the ground. Watching where he put his feet, Dave looked at it closely and realised it was oil. Raising his head, he checked out the scene again. 'Yeah, yeah, this is where the cab of the truck would most certainly have been,' he muttered. Dumping his rucksack on the ground, he grabbed an evidence bag and used his pocket knife to scoop up a bit of the oil to cross-match when they finally found the truck. Searching for the tape measure he knew was in there, he finally found it and looked up just as someone called his name.

'Dave!'

He saw the young cop walking towards him. 'G'day, Jack! Got another one.'

250

'This is tough, hey? Paul Barnes can't take a trick. Sells a bit of land to get a bit of cash. Buys a few special sheep to make a bit of extra money, and then they get stolen.' Jack shook his head. 'Poor bastard.'

Dave looked at him curiously. 'How do you know they've been stolen?' he asked.

'Well, of course they've been! Just like all the other robberies around here.' Jack seemed affronted.

'Right.' Dave shifted from foot to foot. 'I understand what you're saying, but how do you know, without looking at the scene, that Paul Barnes hasn't made it look like they've been stolen so he can get the insurance money?'

'I . . . uh . . .' Jack mumbled, looking stunned.

'Exactly, you don't. That sort of attitude affects cases,' Dave said severely. 'Now, grab hold of this so we can measure.' He held out the measuring tape.

Jack's brow furrowed. 'Measure what?'

'Look here.' Dave pointed to the oil. 'We've got an engine leak. If we measure from here to where the sheep were loaded on, we can work out the length of the truck and do a check on who owns trucks like this one.'

'Right.' Jack grabbed the end of the tape and together they walked around, taking measurements. Dave wrote everything in his notebook with an excited feeling beginning to bubble in his stomach. They were getting closer to solving this, he was sure. He'd arrange to have the diagram and measurements sent off to Adelaide as soon as he got back to Torrica. He was pretty sure that Coops and the crew would be able to give him an idea of what type of truck he was looking for. Then he'd pull all the rego records on the trucks in the district and be able to narrow down a list of suspects—hopefully a shorter list than he had right now.

Dave kept circling the scene. The sand was deep and it was likely that if something had been dropped, it had disappeared under the surface. He stooped over, peering at all the tracks again. Finally he was rewarded. There *was* something else!

Using a pen, he shifted the sand from around the object. 'Bloody hell,' he muttered. Reaching into his pocket, he pulled out a pair of gloves and put them on. 'Pass me the tweezers from my evidence kit, can you?' he called to Jack.

'Here!' Jack ran up to him with a pair.

'Got an evidence bag?'

'Ah . . .' Jack glanced around. 'No.'

'In my rucksack pocket. Back left,' Dave said. He bent down, shifted a little more dirt and latched on to the item, drawing it out and holding it up.

Jack was holding a plastic evidence bag open. 'What is it?' he asked.

'A used canister cartridge from a taser gun.'

Chapter 27

'The after-sport rush will be here shortly,' Kim said to Amelia as they sat together with iced coffees in front of them. 'All the junior netball and footy players and their parents will be wanting a coffee and piece of cake before they go home. Reckon we've got about two minutes.'

Amelia stood up and looked out the window. 'No, I think you've got about thirty seconds. And it looks like there are a few grandies in among this lot!'

'There goes the peace,' Kim said, sighing and getting to her feet. 'Can you take the orders? I'll get the coffee machine warmed up and do some prep in the kitchen.'

Amelia didn't shift from where she was perched on a stool, but watched as they all walked in. These were people she'd known forever and had trusted implicitly—until the attack. Now she wasn't sure who to trust. Especially after the memory of that voice saying, *She's not going to like this*. Who could that woman be?

Over the past few days Amelia had found herself watching people as she walked down the street or shopped in the supermarket. People she knew well and people she only knew by name. Assessing them, wondering if they had the ability to mastermind and carry out such a violent attack.

She'd even, just for a second, suspected Sav, after she'd blanked her the other day. But Amelia had got cross with herself over that—surely she'd learned her lesson after opening her mouth before engaging her brain with Paul. Now, however, she was even more determined to try and work out who had done this. Paul's sheep had been taken—what would they do next? It seemed personal.

'There's got to be a local involved,' Amelia heard Gus say, as he and Pip walked into the roadhouse.

'Surely not,' she retorted. 'We're such a close-knit community. I can't think of anyone bad enough to do these sorts of things. No, I'm sure you're wrong.'

'What about Justin Croaker? He was always hurting little kids when he was at school.' They stood at the counter, completely absorbed in their conversation. 'Maybe he's turned out even worse than he was when he was a kid.'

'Now, you can't be saying things like that out loud and in public, Gus.' Pip frowned at him, then noticed Amelia. 'Oh hi, Milly, how are you? Your face looks *much* better.' With a grin, Pip opened her arms for a hug.

Gus patted Amelia on the shoulder. 'Good to see you. You going all right?'

She smiled up at him. 'Fine, Gus, thanks.' Then she noticed Pip glancing behind the counter, looking for Kim. 'Did you want me to take your order?'

'Thanks, love,' Pip said, beaming. 'Two coffees to go and a bucket of chips.'

'No cake?' she asked, thinking of the huge chocolate mud cake and the banana bread that were sitting in the kitchen.

'Oh, no, I don't think so,' answered Pip, patting her stomach.

Gus rolled his eyes. 'And chips are much less fattening,' he said with a patient grin.

Amelia wrote it down and took it through to the kitchen, where Kim was grilling up a steak. 'First couple don't want cake! But you were right about the coffees.'

'Thanks, sweetie! Won't be long.'

'Sure.' Pushing back through the kitchen doors, Amelia saw Anne walking up the path to the roadhouse. The bell tinkled as she walked in, and Amelia returned her broad smile. 'Anne! How are you?'

Amelia hugged her, and Pip and Gus said their hellos.

'Terrible business this stealing, isn't it?' Pip started.

Amelia listened from behind the counter, hoping there was some new information she hadn't heard yet.

Anne shook her head. 'Just shocking. I can't believe this could happen in a town like Torrica.'

'Paul's just had thirty White Suffolk stud ewes stolen,' Amelia put in.

'Really?' Anne turned to look at her in astonishment. 'How dreadful. When?'

'Happened sometime last night. Got to be after nine-thirty because Paul was out fox shooting until then and he didn't see anything. We went looking for them, but we had to call Dave in. They've completely disappeared.'

Kim came out with Pip and Gus's order. 'Here you go, guys.'

Gus thanked her and went over to pay. 'Now there's another example of why someone local has to be involved. Obviously they knew there were prize sheep and what paddock they were in. It's like the diesel that was taken a while ago. The tank had just been filled.' He handed over the money and gave everyone a significant look.

Amelia took a sharp breath. That was exactly what she and Chelle had discussed yesterday. The crims had to know what was on the farms, therefore maybe it was someone who had access to people's properties without attracting suspicion. There were those two names that sprang to mind: Jim Green and Grant Hink.

Amelia had also considered the local stock agent in Barker, but she was sure he couldn't be involved. For one thing, he was almost seventy not out, and for another he was incredibly overweight. Last time he'd been at Granite Ridge to look at some mutton, he hadn't even got out of the car, just stared at the ewes and offered the price.

'Gus, how on earth can you say that?' Anne asked. 'Are you forgetting Mr Collins? Nobody in this area could possibly use a taser gun on an old man. We've all been brought up and raised our kids to have respect for people, possessions and animals. For everything in life. That's just ridiculous.'

Pip lifted her eyebrows at her husband in a told-you-so manner.

'But who says the local person isn't working with thugs from out of town?' Gus asked, raising his hands. 'Even if they're all locals, don't you see my point?'

'I do,' Amelia said softly.

'So do I,' Kim agreed. 'But as far as that goes, a "local" doesn't need to be someone that's been raised here. Maybe there's a new workman on someone's farm, or a person who's shifted into a caravan park. There are plenty of reasons why it could be someone in this district. Anyone with an ear to the ground could have heard these types of things. Especially if they hang out at the pub.' She shrugged her ample shoulders and flicked back her curly hair.

'But if they're hanging out at the pub, we would have seen them,' Anne argued.

Kim shrugged. 'Just throwing ideas out there.'

Interesting ideas, Amelia thought, although she wasn't sure about them.

The bell on the door jangled as Cappa walked in. 'Ah, we got a committee meeting I didn't know about?' he asked as he spotted everyone.

'We can't possibly start—Jim's not here,' Amelia said in a sarcastic tone, and everyone laughed.

'We're just discussing if the criminals are local or not,' Pip said, sipping her coffee. 'Got any thoughts?'

Cappa grimaced before shaking his head. 'Gotta say I haven't given it a lot of thought. To me it doesn't matter if they're locals. The fact is, they need to be caught and I don't want them on my place. I've beefed up security since going to that detective's crime forum. Bloody amazing, the things he came up with. Things I never would have considered. I've put security cameras at my front gate now, and I've got a couple around the sheds too.'

Anne looked shocked. 'Bloody hell. I remember Dave suggesting that, but I thought it was going a bit far.'

'Don't think we can be too careful,' Cappa said, pushing his hat back and scratching his forehead. 'We're in a situation where we have to change *our* way of thinking. Not be so trusting. It's a bugger, really.'

Amelia thought that was the whole point. *Not be so trusting.* She felt a shiver run down her spine. This wasn't about what people thought of her anymore, not even Dave: it was about wanting to know herself. She couldn't feel safe in Torrica. She didn't think she'd feel safe anywhere until these people were caught.

'Fancy having to lock our front doors at night,' Anne was saying. 'Never even considered doing that until now.' She sighed. 'Times are a-changing.'

'You got that right,' Pip said.

Kim picked up her pen and pad. 'Right, let's talk about something far more encouraging,' she said, putting a huge smile on her face. 'Who wants to order, and who's going to Graham and Dani's engagement party tonight? Should be a blast!'

'Oh yeah,' Pip said, with pleasure in her voice. 'We're going. Great to see something positive happening here.' She grabbed at a chip from the bucket Gus was holding. 'Goodness, they've spent some money though, haven't they?'

Gus closed his eyes. 'Come on, Pip, time to go. You ladies just love to gossip, don't you?' He started towards the door. 'Good to see you all! Catch you tonight.'

Pip rolled her eyes and followed him, before turning back. 'Gossip's what we're supposed to do, isn't it?' She gave a cheeky grin and winked at Amelia. 'See you!'

Kim, Anne and Amelia all chuckled, while Cappa stood there with a bemused look on his face. 'Never understood women,' he muttered. 'You're a funny breed of cattle.'

'*Cappa!*' Amelia squealed indignantly.

'All right, all right, break it up, you two,' Kim said with a grin. 'Now, orders?'

'Steak sandwich, please,' said Anne, 'and I'll grab a Coke from the fridge.'

'And you, Cappa?'

'Toasted ham, cheese and tomato sandwich, please. And I think I need a coffee too. And . . . I can't resist a slice of your scrumptious mud cake.'

'Milly, can you ring these up?' Kim went back into the kitchen.

Amelia told Anne and Cappa the amounts, took the cash and put it in the till. Cappa turned to the noticeboard and started to read all the 'for sale' and community notices. A big group of customers trickled in; Amelia took their orders and handed them over the swinging doors to Kim, while the group sat down by the front window.

Anne was still sitting at the counter, drinking her Coke. 'Are you looking forward to the party then, Milly?' she asked.

Amelia half-shrugged. 'Of course I am. After all, he's my brother.'

'You're sounding very enthused,' Anne said with a wry grin.

'We're a bit different,' Amelia hedged. 'And Dani is . . . different again. Still, I'm sure it will be a lovely night. It'll have to be, with all the money they've spent. Even if Graham has a black eye!'

Anne looked intrigued. 'I heard something about a brawl last night. Only heard Jim's name mentioned, though. Tell me more?'

'Just your regular punch-up at the pub. Not the usual for Graham, but he must be nervous about the party.' Amelia paused and glanced over at Cappa, who was wiping his glasses with his handkerchief, the paper spread out in front of him. 'You know, Anne, between you and me, I can't work out why they couldn't just have a barbecue and a few drinks at the Granite Ridge shearing shed, rather than having to go all out on a massive party with all the trimmings. I saw the cake yesterday morning. Bloody hell, it looks like a wedding cake! I think this party is almost like having two weddings.'

'Do I hear a bit of the green-eyed monster?' Anne said with a teasing smile.

'Milly!' Kim called. 'Anne's order is ready.'

Amelia turned and grabbed the order that Kim was holding out over the swinging doors, then handed it across the counter.

'Smells bloody beautiful,' Anne said as she took it. 'Right-o, best get on. The boys will be wondering where I am. Was supposed to be back out there about half an hour ago. See you tonight!'

'Yep, see you, Anne!' Amelia said. 'Oh, I reckon I'll come out to you and catch up on the office work sometime next week.'

'Sure. Whatever day suits you. Don't know where the time goes—only seems like yesterday you were over doing last month's. I'll bake some scones for you.'

Amelia watched as Anne drove out of the car park across the street in an old beat-up ute. You'd never know just by looking that she and her boys were so well off. The Andrews family had always been careful and prudent farmers—the best sort.

Kim came out with the sandwich, coffee and cake for Cappa, who thanked her and then regarded her carefully. 'What does your bloke really reckon about all these thefts?' he asked in a low voice, as he unwrapped his sandwich and took a bite.

Holding up her hand, Kim shook her head. 'Oh no, Cappa, you're not getting anything out of me. Anyway, Dave doesn't talk to me about it. It's all confidential, you know.'

'Mmm, thought it would be. But I've been thinking.' Cappa put down his coffee and took another bite. 'I understand everyone's discomfort in it being locals, but how can they be anything else?' He spoke around his sandwich and Amelia had to look down at the counter so she didn't see the food moving around in his mouth. *When people live by themselves*, she thought, *they forget about manners!*

'To be honest,' Kim said, 'I feel the same, and I've had a lot of customers telling me that. But going over this isn't bringing us any closer to knowing who the culprits are. My vote is that we all back off and leave Dave to do his job.'

'Fair enough,' said Cappa, polishing off the first half of his sandwich. 'Well, it's been a pleasure, as always.' He stood up, tipped an invisible hat and headed out.

Kim went to sort out the next batch of orders, while Amelia held her tongue about her plans to investigate. She'd always trusted Kim to put things in her vault, but this was about more than trust—she didn't want to worry her aunt. She just couldn't let this go. *I have to do my best to work out who's done this.*

Chapter 28

Even from out in the car park, the atmosphere inside the footy club rooms sounded buoyant. The rain that had pelted down in the afternoon had given everyone a much-needed boost; the chatter was noisy and the laughter loud above the pumping of party music. Amelia slipped her hand into Paul's as they walked towards the front door.

'Don't be nervous,' Paul said as he gently extracted his hand from hers and put it on her shoulder.

Between Paul's distance and her nervousness about facing Dani and the whole community tonight, Amelia was a walking mess. Even though she was trying her best not to be. 'I still don't get why Dani said that I caused the fight at the pub. I haven't been able to ask Graham, because he hasn't responded to any of my texts and he hasn't been home.' Her voice rose in agitation as she spoke.

With a sigh, Paul stopped walking and pulled Amelia around to face him. 'Stop panicking, Milly. Who cares what she thinks? I really don't think it's important. I think you're more worried about what everyone's going to say to you tonight—if they're going to want to get up close and personal with you, chat to you as if they're your friend, and then go and talk about you behind your back.'

Amelia looked down. She wanted to stop caring what other people thought about her—but it wasn't that easy.

'I'm right, aren't I?' Paul urged.

'Yeah, I'm worried about it all.' She wasn't going to mention that she kept looking at every woman as a suspect, which made her as jumpy as hell.

'I've told you how amazing you look. Don't let anyone spoil tonight for you.'

Amelia looked down at what she was wearing: a long black skirt, knee-high, heeled boots and a silver shirt. She'd covered her yellowed bruise with makeup. Paul had told her that she looked as beautiful as the night sky, and she'd chided him for being a silver-tongued charmer.

With a small smile and a gentle tug on her hand, Paul led her up the steps and into the clubhouse. Amelia caught her breath. 'Bloody hell!' She slowly turned around and took in the decorations.

A wall of hay bales was set up at the front of the room, with hundreds of photos of Graham and Dani pinned to them, following the couple's whole history together. To the left a banner was strung out, printed with *He Asked and She Said Yes* in a country-style font. The trestle tables were covered with white cloths, each portion of cutlery held in a small calico pouch with a purple bow around it. Everything else was decorated with purple. On the ceiling hung Chinese lanterns and fairy lights.

'Might as well be a wedding,' Paul commented.

'I said exactly the same thing this morning. Far out, did they invite the whole district?'

'Probably.'

Amelia looked around, wondering if there was someone in this room who had orchestrated the attack on her. She'd keep her eyes peeled for anyone acting even the slightest bit different. Yes, maybe she was being paranoid, but she had good reason.

'Hello, Milly.' Gus appeared from the throng. 'Paul, g'day. Good to see you.' The men shook hands, then they all chatted about the rain for a bit.

'Better go and say hello to the happy couple,' Amelia said as she caught sight of Graham and Dani greeting their guests closer to the front of the room. Paul groaned and she elbowed him gently in the ribs before propelling him towards them. They were intercepted by Kim, who had Dave following in her wake. He was wearing a slightly better tie than usual and looking a tad uncomfortable.

'There you are!' she said, throwing her arms around a startled Paul before focusing on Amelia. 'I've been keeping an eye out for you. Paul, I'm so sorry to hear about your sheep.'

'Thanks, Kim,' said Paul, his voice rough and his blue eyes earnest, before shaking hands with Dave. *He's been so brave today*, Amelia thought.

'So, what do you think of the decorations?' Kim spun around with her arms held out, gesturing at the extravagance.

Amelia grinned. 'The whole thing is even more than I imagined.' She turned her back slightly, as Paul and Dave started talking about the missing ewes. Then she whispered to Kim: 'I'm not enjoying this at all.'

Realisation dawned in her aunt's eyes. 'Don't you be worrying about what people think. Defiance, my sweet, defiance! Go to the toilets quickly and practise this look in the mirror.' Kim put her head on the side and lifted her chin, while her eyes widened in a manic glare.

Amelia snorted, then turned to Paul when she felt his hand on her arm.

'Come on,' he said, 'let's go have some fun!'

'Ha!' Kim said, her hands flying to her hips. 'Charming, that is!' She kissed Amelia on the cheek and winked. 'Defiance,' she reiterated, before putting her arm through Dave's and walking off.

They made their way to the front and waited until Dani and Graham were free. The couple were dressed up to the nines and couldn't have looked more different to the pretty disgraceful picture they'd presented the night before.

'Hello, you two.' Amelia gave them a polite smile, which they both returned. *So that's how it will be. All right, then.* She leaned forward and kissed Dani, then Graham. 'What a beautiful setting, Dani. It looks amazing.'

Paul shook Graham's hand before nodding at Dani.

'Thank you. We worked hard to get it just the way we wanted, didn't we?' She turned to Graham, who opened his mouth to say something, but she hurried on. 'Such a shame that Graham was hurt last night. I suggested he put makeup on his black eye, so he didn't ruin the photos . . .' She shot a glare at Amelia.

Amelia blinked before glancing at Graham, who was looking uncomfortable. 'Ruin the photos? Oh, but surely he wouldn't *ruin* them with just a black eye?' She wondered how shallow her soon-to-be sister-in-law actually was.

'Oh, not ruin them, of course . . . well, I'm sure you know what I mean.'

Amelia really wanted to say that she had no idea, but bit her tongue.

'It's always nice to have good photos,' Dani finished. 'Memories, as such.' She gave a tight-lipped smile and pulled on Graham's arm. 'Come on, we'd better be good hosts and talk to some other guests. Thanks for coming.'

'You're welcome,' Amelia said, falling back on politeness. Then she got hold of herself—she bloody well wanted to sort things out with her brother. 'Hang on, Graham? Got five seconds?' She ignored the look that Dani sent her and gave Paul a reassuring glance, pulling her brother to a quieter part of the room. 'Are you okay?'

'Fine,' he said shortly, not meeting her eyes.

'What's wrong?' Amelia's brow wrinkled. 'What's going on with you?'

'Nothing, Milly, honest.' A soft expression shifted across his face, but it was replaced quickly. 'I'm fine. Sore as hell, and I reckon my pride is a bit shot, but that's all. Man, you wouldn't believe the shit I got from Dani when she saw my face!' He shrugged. 'Can't be helped. I'm sure there have been worse things happen the night before a wedding, let alone a bloody engagement party. Still, wish it hadn't happened. This party has been such a big deal to Dani. And to Mum.'

'What was it all about? The fight, I mean.'

'Nothing. Just being stupid drunken idiots. We're both old enough to know better.' He glanced over his shoulder and Amelia could see Dani shooting daggers at them, so she gave Graham an awkward hug and told him to enjoy his night.

She watched him go, thinking that he wouldn't have been at the pub long enough to get really pissed. It was reasonably early in the night and she'd been there before him, hadn't she?

The 'happy' couple stopped to talk to Anne and Will, and Amelia saw Graham throw an apologetic look over his shoulder at her. She half-shrugged and gave him a sad smile. What was her brother getting himself into with Dani?

'Milly!' Chelle waved and jumped up and down to attract her attention.

'Ah,' said Paul, grabbing Amelia's hand and dragging her over, 'I owe this woman some thanks.'

Amelia blushed as Paul gave Chelle a kiss on the cheek. 'I hear I need to thank you, future cousin-in-law,' he said.

'Thank me? What for?' Chelle took a sip of her wine and smiled coyly.

'Let's just say the French knickers were much appreciated last night.'

Chelle burst out laughing. 'Pleased you put my advice to good use.' She nudged Amelia, who was staring at the floor in embarrassment. 'Lighten up, cuz, it's all for a good cause!'

They laughed and Amelia squeezed Paul's hand, happy that he'd said *future cousin-in-law*. He was being so good to her tonight. Maybe the cracks could heal after all, and sooner than she'd expected.

'So, what a bloody big spend-up,' Chelle said, her eyes on the ceiling.

'Well, we always knew it would be.'

'Have you seen Chrissie and Sav yet?'

'No. And I'm still not sure if Sav's talking to me. I haven't heard from her since she stonewalled me on Thursday morning.'

Paul put his arm around her shoulders; she smiled up into his blue eyes and leaned against him.

'Speak of the devil!' Chelle said, raising her eyebrows.

Chrissie and Sav were shouldering their way through the crowd. 'Hi, we're here!' sang Chrissie, her hips moving in time to the music. 'Can't wait to dance.'

'Hey.' Amelia smiled at them both, but watched Sav carefully. Her face seemed happy and open, just pleased to see everyone, and Amelia started to relax.

'Gotta looove dancin',' Chelle said, bumping hips with Chrissie.

'Where's Dean, Sav?' Amelia asked.

'Probably at the bar. That's where he always feels most comfortable.' Sav put her head on the side. 'Can I, um, talk to you for a moment?'

A pang of fear ran through Amelia, but she grinned and said, 'Sure.' She gave Paul a little smile and said she'd be back in a while.

Together they walked outside. The rain had started again and the drumming on the tin roof soothed Amelia's nerves. They moved down to the end of the verandah and Amelia tucked her hands under her armpits, shivering. 'Whoa, it's a bit chilly.'

'Yeah, a culture shock after the hot days we've been having. I've never worked out why Mother Nature can't gradually go from hot to cold so we don't really notice it. Not these extremes we always get.'

'I'm with you. Crazy weather. But it's climate change and all that, apparently.'

'Of course!' Sav smiled, then her face fell. 'Look, I owe you an apology.'

Amelia stood there watching her, waiting.

'I snubbed you last week and I'm sorry. I got so caught up with the kids coming to school and talking about you, blaming you. And listening to everything their parents were saying . . . I started to suspect you, too.' Sav looked down and hopped from one leg to the other. 'Great friend, I realise. Leaving you in your time of need and all that.'

'It's okay,' Amelia finally said. She was still struggling to put aside the indignity and mortification of knowing the community had been talking about her and Paul, but it was really difficult. Especially when it came from one of her best friends. 'Look, a couple of days ago I blamed someone inno-cent as well. It's a horrible feeling when you realise there was no way they could have been involved. I think everyone's looking for answers when there aren't any to have yet. It's a shit of a situation.'

Sav nodded, and they hugged. Amelia honestly wanted to forgive and forget. She kept reminding herself that what was happening was almost exactly the same as between her and Paul. But there was something holding her back—probably the same kind of distrust and disappointment that Paul was feeling towards her.

'Hey, Sav!' Dean stuck his head out the door. 'You coming or what?'

Sav turned back to Amelia. 'Sorry, better go. I'll catch up with you inside.' She ran off to her husband.

Amelia watched her go and sighed, leaning back against the wall of the club rooms. It still hurt her knowing that people had talked about her. But not as much as that taser and kick in the chest had hurt, she reminded herself. Not as much as the hurt of losing her trust in Torrica. The rain continued to fall and goosebumps broke out over her arms. *Time to go inside.*

A movement caught her eye, and she turned back and stared out into the dim light. Over at the barbecue shed, she saw someone pacing up and down. It was Graham, and he was talking intently on the phone. Who could he possibly be talking to on such an important night?

In her mind's eye Amelia saw Jim holding Graham in a headlock. No, it couldn't have just been a random dust-up, she decided. There'd been something more going on there than met the eye. And her gut told her that Jim was at the bottom of it.

Chapter 29

'Ladies and gentlemen, we are gathered here tonight to celebrate the love of two very important people.' There was a round of applause as Dani's father, Max, started his speech. Amelia wondered how much he'd had to drink: his cheeks were a bright rosy red and his glasses kept slipping down his nose.

John stood next to him, his hands held in front of him, looking very proud. Amelia saw him glance towards Natalie, who was standing to the side, next to the incredible cake she had created, and give her a nod. 'Now, you'll have to forgive me for making this sound like a wedding speech, but to be very honest, I really had no idea how to start and that was the best I could come up with . . .' He paused while a smattering of polite laughter rounded the room.

Amelia pressed closer to Paul and turned to smile at him. Her breath caught as she saw he was already watching her, desire in his eyes. Yes, maybe things between them could go back to normal quicker than she'd hoped. Her grin widened as his hand slid down to rest on her bum, and she gave him a small shake of her head and roll of her eyes when he pinched it lightly.

'Dani and Graham have been together two years to this day,' Max continued, 'and I think you'll agree with me, they are more than suited to each other.'

Chrissie caught Amelia's eye and gave a 'whatever' look, and Chelle nodded in complete agreement. Amelia had to look down to hide her expression.

'I'm pretty sure you don't want to hear too much from me, so I'll ask the happy couple to come up here and cut the cake,' Max said. 'And I think they're also going to announce the date of the wedding! But first I think John has a couple of words to say.'

John stepped forward and cleared his throat. 'On behalf of Natalie and I, we want to wish Graham and Dani the very best. We're pleased to be welcoming Dani into our family, and grateful that Graham has chosen so wisely!' Everybody laughed and John grinned. 'Can I also add what a fabulous job Natalie has done with the cake, and acknowledge everyone who has helped out for tonight. Now I won't keep you waiting anymore. I give you, Graham and Dani!'

A cheer went up around the room, while Max and John stood there waiting for Dani and Graham to appear. When neither of them emerged after a few seconds, both men began to look very uncomfortable. 'Dani, where have you got to, sweetheart?' Max called into the microphone.

Amelia looked around but couldn't see either of them.

'Goodness! I wonder where they are,' Anne said with a sly look on her face.

Amelia gave her friend a surprised glance. 'Anne! I never suspected you had such a dirty mind.'

'Not at all—you're the one who leapt to conclusions! Should have employed some security guards to keep them inside.'

'Yeah, where are your boys when you need them?' Amelia asked with a laugh.

'Will's the only one here. Other two got called in to be actual security guards over in Barker tonight. New little bar opening up that they're busy at.'

The crowd began to get a little restless before starting to clap and call out, '*Dani, Graham! Dani, Graham!*'

A little flustered, Max bent down to talk to his wife, and John gave Natalie a confused glance, but then another cheer went up when Dani and Graham came through the open door, looking sheepish.

'Gawd, can't keep your hands off each other, even out in public?' yelled a man's voice.

Amelia looked around and realised it was Kev Hubble, whose face was even redder than Max's. *Bloody typical*, she thought. *Uncouth bugger, just as bad as Jim*. She wasn't even sure why he'd been invited—then she remembered that he was Dani's great uncle. Well, that just went to prove you couldn't choose your family.

There were wolf whistles. Will Andrews and a few of Graham's mates started to stamp on the floor. 'Good job, Benno!' they yelled.

Benno? Amelia hadn't heard Graham called that in years!

Paul bent down to whisper in her ear. 'Surely they wouldn't have?'

273

She gave him a look. 'Of course not,' she whispered back. 'The opposite if you ask me—they've been arguing. Look, Graham's scratching the back of his ear. He always does that when he's pissed off.'

Paul stared at her. 'How do you know that?'

Amelia shrugged. 'He's my brother. I've lived with him for years!'

Paul was giving her another strange look just as Graham took the microphone and started to speak. 'Thanks for coming,' he said, still scratching behind his ear. 'Sorry to hold you up. We were just talking about some of the arrangements for the rest of the evening . . .'

The wolf whistles and stomping started up again.

'. . . contrary to common belief!' Graham held his hands up and smiled broadly until the noise died down. 'Seriously, thanks all for coming.' He reached over, took Dani's hand and held it up to his heart. 'My gorgeous fiancée and I are thrilled you could make it tonight. It's a big thing when you ask the love of your life to marry you and she actually says yes.' He paused and looked down at the woman beside him.

The chatter had become non-existent and Amelia noticed that even the clinks from glasses had stopped.

'To be really honest, I never knew if Dani would say yes. I hoped she would, but I couldn't be sure. After all, she's much prettier, funnier, kinder and gentler than what I ever thought I deserved.' He looked over at Dani as if trying to convey everything he felt for her through his eyes. Then his hand strayed back to scratch at the spot behind his ear, and he coughed. 'Anyway, without getting too emotional, thanks again to everyone who's come tonight—a few out-of-towners drove long distances to be here.'

He stopped and spoke with Dani briefly, and she took the microphone. 'Thanks to our parents for your love and support,' she said in a shaky voice. 'To all of our family and friends who helped set up here tonight, you've done a great job. Haven't they done a great job?'

The room erupted with clapping and calls of 'Yeah!'

'I really want to acknowledge Natalie and my mum for all the effort they've put in too. And finally, I want to say to Graham—thank you, honey, for asking me. There was no way in the world I wasn't going to say yes!' Dani leaned up and kissed him, and all the boys went wild again.

'That's almost sickening,' Chelle said in Amelia's ear.

'You're just jealous,' she answered.

'Maybe, but it's still revolting.'

'And—' Dani waved with her hands to get everyone to quieten down '—we'd like to announce that our wedding is on the twelfth of February next year, so . . .' She paused before shouting, 'Save the date!'

Max took the microphone from his daughter and asked everyone to raise their glasses to Graham and Dani.

'Where's your drink, Chelle?' Amelia wanted to know, as she raised her own glass with everyone else and repeated: 'Graham and Dani.'

'Got to drive home afterwards.'

They stood together, watching as the couple worked the room once again, shaking hands with some people and clapping others on the back. Graham took off his jacket and hung it over the back of a chair, before slipping his hand around Dani's waist and dragging her to the dance floor.

~

Later in the evening, Amelia wandered outside again to cool her cheeks. The room had become stuffy, and smelt of beer and the body odour of dancers. Glancing up at the sky, she realised the rain had stopped. Clouds chased one another across the inky expanse, leaving glimpses of stars behind them.

Amelia wondered how much rain had fallen and hoped it was widespread. She leaned back against the wall, her hands behind her back, and shut her eyes, before sliding down and sitting on her bum. She had to give Dani her due, but she couldn't have done it without help from loads of other people, her mum included. It had been a good night. The band was exceptional, the food lovely, and even though it seemed so over-the-top, the whole idea had worked really well. And she'd heard Dani's mother say that it had all run on time, down to the last minute, even with Dani and Graham being late for their own speech. 'I'm not asking why they were,' she'd added hastily.

As Amelia had said to Paul, she was sure they'd been arguing. Graham's tell-tale sign of anger had been a giveaway, and so had the tightness in Dani's face. It was likely anyone who knew the couple well would have noticed the same thing. And the argument probably had something to do with the brawl.

A voice filtered over to Amelia from the barbecue shed and she opened her eyes. She peered through the slatted verandah rails and once again saw Graham talking intently on the phone. She frowned—this was definitely weird. Graham was never on the phone much; in fact, he didn't like mobiles. Only carried one in case there was an emergency out on the farm and he couldn't get to the ute to call on a two-way.

She watched him pace back and forth, gesturing angrily. Before she knew it, he was scratching behind his ear again. She wished she could hear what he was saying.

'Milly?' Paul came out on the verandah. 'You okay?'

She held up her finger to silence him and scooted closer to the edge of the verandah. Still couldn't make out the words, just her brother's muffled voice.

'What's up?'

'Graham's out there on his phone for the second time. Just strange he isn't inside with everyone. Dani must be wondering where he is.' Amelia glanced around.

Paul looked down at her in exasperation. 'Does it really matter, babe? Come on, let's get another drink and have a dance.'

Amelia got up and, with one last look over her shoulder, followed him inside.

⁊

Around midnight everyone had left except for the closest friends and family, and only the young ones at that. There were serviettes and other bits of rubbish strewn around the room. Amelia and Paul went to say their goodbyes and found Graham patting down his coat and putting his hands in his pockets. 'Where's my phone?'

Amelia shrugged. 'Don't know.'

'Put it in my pocket after I was on it last. It's got to be here somewhere.' Frantically he searched again, but came up empty.

'Darling, it'll be here somewhere, dropped on the floor.' A rather tipsy Dani got down on her hands and knees to have a look. 'Nope, nothing here,' she sang.

Amelia watched, worry tingling at the back of her mind, as Graham's expression changed from frustration to fear. 'Shit,' he muttered. 'Someone's taken it.'

'Oh, don't be silly. No one would've done that. Not in our circle of friends!' Dani backed out from under the table. 'Come on, let's go home. We'll come back and look tomor—Whoops!' She pitched forward and fell heavily against Graham. They both staggered until he somehow got them upright again.

'You right?' Amelia asked. 'Want Paul and me to drive you home?'

'We're good,' Graham answered, his eyes still searching the room for the missing phone.

'We'll get you another one, baby.' Dani giggled. 'Don't sweat the small stuff. You tell me that all the time.' She put her face up to his. 'Kiss?'

'Bloody hell.' Amelia turned away and shook her head at Paul, thinking, *Dani is a pitiful drunk!*

She expected her brother to be amused, but Graham's face was set like stone. 'You're right, Dani, we can look for it tomorrow. It's fine.' He put his arm around his fiancée in what seemed like a vice-like grip. 'Right, well, I guess we'll see you later,' he said and started to half-carry, half-drag Dani towards the door.

'Thanks for a lovely evening!' Amelia called out after him.

'Yeah.' He didn't look back. 'No worries.'

Chapter 30

Amelia stumbled out into the kitchen and poured herself a glass of water. The heavy clouds made the morning darker than it should have been at this hour. She'd woken at 6 a.m. with the dry horrors.

'Ugh,' she mumbled, as she pushed her tangled hair back off her face. 'I swear I didn't have that much to drink, but I'm as dry as a . . .'

'Talking to yourself?'

Amelia jumped and let out a little squeak before she turned around to see Graham sitting at the kitchen table, sipping a cup of coffee. He looked like he hadn't slept at all, and his stubble made his chin black to match his eye.

'Shit, you scared me.' Amelia put her hand on her chest as her heart tried to punch its way out. 'And I thought you were at Dani's.'

'Oh,' Graham said, guilt flickering over his face. 'Sorry, I didn't think.'

'S'okay.' She poured herself another glass of water and sat down opposite him, putting her hands on the glass and twisting it around. Not saying anything, she gazed out the window at the looming clouds. She shot a quick glance at her brother and saw he was staring at the table. 'Did you find your phone?' she asked, finally, when it became clear he wasn't going to speak.

'Nah.' He shook his head to emphasise the word. 'Shits me. Lost all my contacts, everything.'

'That's a bugger.' She took another sip of water. Surely he'd want to talk about the engagement party more than his phone. *But you asked the question,* she reminded herself. *And he looks like he isn't thinking clearly.* 'It was a lovely night,' she ventured. 'And with the rain on top of it, you should be really happy.' She was prying now. The way he looked, there was no way he was happy.

Graham smiled briefly. 'It was a good night. Dani did a great job to put it all together.' He took another sip from his cup and the silence stretched out in front of them. 'Did Paul enjoy—'

'What are your—'

They both gestured for the other one to speak, and Amelia shook her head. 'It's okay. Mine wasn't important. What were you going to say?'

'I was just going to ask if Paul enjoyed himself. But tell me what your plans for the day are.'

'I think Paul had a great time,' Amelia answered before pressing the heel of her hand to her forehead.

'First, I think I might go back to bed. I can't believe the way I feel, considering I didn't drink very much at all. And then, well . . . maybe I'll go to Paul's, or just hang here and finally catch up on some work. Not sure yet. What about you?'

'I'm going to get the steers in and weigh them.'

'You really need to do that today? Why don't you go and open all of your presents with Dani?'

Shaking his head, Graham said, 'She can manage that without me. Anyway, we opened some last night.' He stood up and stretched, before putting his coffee cup in the sink.

'I wouldn't have thought she was in any fit state to open anything,' Amelia said without thinking, then clapped her hand over her mouth. 'Sorry, Graham. Shouldn't have said that. Foot in mouth disease!' She watched for any sign he was angry—he'd certainly never liked anyone casting aspersions on Dani's character.

Instead he shrugged. 'Yeah, she had a good time. That's allowed!'

'Totally. And I'm not one to talk today!' Amelia opened the fridge door and grabbed the orange juice, before pouring herself a glass. 'Well, I think I'm heading back to bed.' She turned to go, desperate to say something about how much he'd been on the phone the night before. 'Hey, Graham?'

'Hmm?'

She hesitated for a moment, not wanting to upset the fragile truce they seemed to have arrived at since she'd been hurt. Then she said, 'Don't you need Dad to help you get the steers in? They're in a pretty big mob.'

જી

Graham backed his ute out of the shed and automatically patted his shirt pocket to make sure he had his phone. Feeling nothing, he cursed again. It hadn't been lost, of that he was certain. It had been taken. Angrily he hit the steering wheel and took his foot off the clutch a little too quickly, causing the tyres to spin.

The ute splashed through a puddle and brought his thoughts back to the job at hand. Twenty-four millimetres overnight was a godsend. The feed would be a bit short for the first couple of weeks, until it grew long enough and had enough oomph in it to feed the stock, but if they had another rain in a week or two, they'd be able to stop hand-feeding. That would free up a lot of time and give him the opportunity to start thinking about spraying to put the crop in.

The chemicals were in the shed and now that he'd shorn his own ewes and sent his wool away to be sold, he was sure the cash he needed would be available. Sometimes he got so furious with Amelia and her high and mighty ways when it came to money. Didn't she see that so many of his mates didn't have to answer to their family—to their father or sister? And they didn't have their mother walling them in. They were free to farm their land as they pleased. That was one of the reasons he was so keen to have Dani involved. If she took over the books, he'd have a bit more of a free hand. But no, that wouldn't be happening, no matter how hard he or Natalie pushed. John was too set in his ways and too one-eyed when it came to Amelia.

Graham's eyes narrowed and he let out a growl. Then he took a few deep breaths to calm down before reminding himself that John didn't actually favour Amelia. Deep down

Graham knew that, but he had to blame *someone* for the fix he was in, and Amelia was an easy target.

Nothing was supposed to turn out the way that it had. Harmless fun and the chance to make some extra cash—pay off his loan—had turned into something far darker. The taser had changed everything, as had the violence. Graham had to make things right after what had happened to Amelia, but he still needed money. Blackmail had seemed the only way to handle things.

He drove past the gateway into Emerald Springs and startled a flock of galahs who'd been bathing in the puddles the rain had left behind. As he glanced in the mirror back at the entrance, a feeling of foreboding came over him. He slowed the ute, turned around and drove back. Standing in front of the gateway, he could tell that Amelia had been in here a few times, because the path was a little more obvious.

On foot now, Graham pushed his way up the path, ignoring the drips from the trees that seeped through his shirt and the mud that was building up on his boots. Within half an hour he was standing in front of Emerald Springs. Overtaken with childhood memories, he lingered there for a moment, allowing himself to recall the shouts of joy and sounds of splashing. The smell of the barbecue sizzling and the sun on his skin. In a time when things were a lot less complicated.

Emerald Springs had always been Amelia's special spot, but what no one knew was that it had also been his secret hiding spot. He'd used it in high school when he'd had to keep his stack of *Penthouse* magazines and the exam he'd stolen from his maths teacher's desk away from his mother. That was the trouble with having a parent who insisted on cleaning his room and making his bed every day. His own bedroom had never been a sanctuary, so he'd had to find his own.

Being a cool, cloudy Sunday, it was the perfect time for Graham to check that what he'd hidden was still in place. For his own peace of mind. Plus, he'd have a better idea of where to hide things in the future, just in case.

∾

The steers thundered across the paddock and Graham sped out to the wing to turn them towards the gate. With the ground wet, the sound of their hooves reminded him of *The Man from Snowy River* movie, his favourite, and the way the brumbies had thundered across the mountain country.

He wished he was on a horse or a motorbike. Even with four-wheel-drive engaged, the bloody wheels still couldn't find traction and kept spinning in some spots. And these steers were feral! Not having been handled very much and feeling energetic because of the cooler weather, they were giving him the run-around. Graham swore at himself for not thinking to bring one of the work dogs. But they were his father's and he rarely used them, unless he was working sheep—they didn't work so well on cattle.

After much to-ing and fro-ing, swearing and cursing, he managed to get the lead steers through the gate and the rest followed. The difficulty of the job did nothing to help his temper.

'Fucking cattle,' he swore, finally able to relax once they were trotting down the laneway, confined by a fence either side. 'Who wants the fucking things?'

With a rev of the engine and a beep of the horn, he had them confined in the holding yard. Latching the gate, he climbed back into the ute to go to the shed and grab the weighing platform and readout. He'd leave them there for a little while, give them a chance to catch their breath. He'd go have a bit of breakfast, then come back and weigh them. John and Natalie were at church, so there would be no one to help him. Or bother him.

⁓

A few hours later, Graham was back at the yards and starting to push the cattle inside. He heard a vehicle driving up and turned, expecting to see John. His eyes widened and his face paled when he realised it wasn't his father.

Graham walked carefully through the cattle, tapping one on the nose with the piece of poly pipe he was holding as it huffed and stamped its feet. 'Don't be like that,' he told the steer. 'I'm not going to hurt you.' Then he faced the approaching vehicle and muttered, 'Now what the bloody hell do you fuckwits want?'

He stood with his hands hanging over the rails, watching the ute pull up. Graham tried to show he was in control, that he wasn't frightened. But it was hard. 'G'day!' he called. 'Didn't expect to see you here.' He had to keep his anger in check. He knew these two were dangerous and he didn't want to give them any extra reasons to get nasty.

'We didn't expect to be here,' came the answer.

Graham watched as one of them walked down behind the cattle and the other approached him. The ominous feeling that had plagued him this morning was back, and he swallowed hard, all the while staring his visitor in the eye.

He had to stand up to them. Had to get as much extra money as he could. The bank was hassling him and he knew this was the only way he could pay the loan back. John had told him just before the engagement party that he wouldn't be making any payments—it was up to Graham and Graham only. He couldn't let his family down, and what would Dani say? *God, Dani.*

'You're a liability, Graham.'

'Not as much as the bloke down the back there,' he shot back, his voice sounding much tougher than he thought possible. 'He's a nasty bastard, him and his stun gun.' He glanced down at his watch. Damn, he knew there was no way his parents would be back yet, and he'd noticed that Pushme wasn't where Amelia usually parked it when he'd gone back for breakfast. She must have gone to Paul's.

So there was no one else on the farm. He was in trouble and he knew it. His heart was pounding and he was drenched with sweat.

Without warning, a gunshot sounded and the cattle jumped in panic. They moved together like the sea, swarming towards Graham, their eyes wide with fear. A few let out terrified bellows. To Graham it seemed to be happening in slow motion as they bore down on top of him.

'Fuck!' He scrambled to get over the fence, but the first steer was on him before he could manage it. He heard the clicking of their feet on the yards as the pressure of the bodies piling up on top of one another gave way and they spilled out into the openness of the paddock. The rest of them trampled on top of him and he was rolled over and over, beneath their bellies and through their legs.

His last conscious thought was that now maybe he could be free.

Chapter 31

Dave was sitting on his bed, looking at a photo he kept in his wallet, when there was a knock on the door. 'Coming,' he called, quickly stuffing the picture back inside.

He didn't know why he still carried this image of his ex-wife. It had been taken at a party three years before they'd split: when they'd still been happy, or at least thought they were. Mel's smile was wide and beautiful, and her eyes stared straight at him. But lately Dave had realised the ache he'd used to feel when he looked at it was fading. Did that mean he was finally moving on?

Did he want to? That was a whole different question.

His cousin Kate, in her wisdom, had asked if he actually wanted to get past what he was feeling. He'd looked at her, not fully comprehending. Since then he'd been thinking a lot about her question, when he was awake in the long hours of the early morning, while it was still dark.

Was he going to be the aloof, scared, lonely and remote

detective? Or could he find his way back to the man he'd been before? The one who laughed easily and told dirty jokes. The one who'd always been the first on the invites of his workmates, because he was fun to be around and good value. The one who held and loved his daughters and would move mountains for them.

And the big one: could he love again? That question kept going around in his head as he walked over and opened the door.

Kim rushed in, her mascara smudged with tears. 'Oh, Dave,' she sobbed.

'What's wrong?' He put his arms around her and held her close, wondering what on earth could have happened now.

'It's Graham.' She hiccupped as she pulled back and stared up at him. Instinctively he held her face in his hands, using his thumbs to wipe away the tears that were running down her cheeks. 'He's dead.'

Dave stilled. 'Dead?' he asked with trepidation in his voice. 'How?'

'He was working with some cattle in the yards and they were spooked.' Kim paused as a fresh round of tears stung her eyes. 'They ran over the top of him.'

'Faarrrk.' Dave let his breath out with a whoosh and tilted his head to look at the ceiling as it sunk in. Kim wrapped her arms around him tighter and buried her face in his chest. He dropped his arms around her waist, gave her a kiss on the head, and they stood there for some time.

In among the shock and horror, he realised that this woman, who felt so good pressed against him, might just have the power to make him love again. The detective in him wanted to rush to the scene and make sure there weren't any signs of criminal activity—and the truth was, that was where he needed to be. But in that moment he was a man, not a detective. He was holding Kim and that was where he wanted to stay.

∽

Before heading to Granite Ridge they stopped off at the road-house where Kim clunked around the kitchen, dishing up two casseroles and a chicken bake. She'd thrown in a whole mud cake that she'd made the day before and raided her freezer to see what other sweet treats might be hidden away.

Dave knew from experience that Kim's sister wouldn't feel like cooking for a long time, but the way Kim was throwing meals together, she wouldn't have to.

'Can you put this in the car?' she asked Dave.

He grasped the containers she held out to him, but she didn't let them go. He looked into her vivid blue eyes. Even reddened and puffy, they still reminded him of the sea on a clear, sunny day, as they always had.

'What?' he asked gently.

'Thank you,' she said, a catch in her voice.

He gave her a tender smile. 'It's all right. I'm just pleased I'm here.'

'Surely nothing else can go wrong now?' she asked.

'Things happen in threes,' Dave answered automatically, hoping he sounded reassuring. But then he realised that, of course, only two things had happened.

'That means there's one more thing.' Kim sounded miserable.

Dave backpedalled as quickly as he could. 'It's just a saying. Nothing in it.'

Kim shrugged and let go of the containers, and Dave took them out to the car, stacking them neatly in the boot. He was shutting it when his mobile rang.

'Got a death,' Andy Denning said as a way of greeting.

'So I heard.'

'When the ambulance got to him he was still alive, but he snuffed it before they could transfer him.'

'Bastard of a way to die,' Dave said, looking over his shoulder to make sure Kim wasn't anywhere nearby.

'Are you coming out?'

'Yeah, we'll have to send a report to the coroner's office.' He sighed. 'And considering everything that's been going on, we're going to need to go over the scene with a fine-tooth comb. Make sure there isn't any sign of criminal activity. Don't let them move the body until I get there. I'm heading out to Granite Ridge in about fifteen minutes. Where are you?'

'At the station, so I can be there in about half to three quarters of an hour.'

'So, Jack's at the scene?'

'Yeah, he went when the ambos called.'

'Get on the phone to him and make sure no one touches anything.' Dave was about to hang up when he thought of something else. 'Oh, Andy, where's the family? I'm just assuming they're still at the farm because that's where Kim is heading.'

'The father has identified the body already, so I've asked them to stay at the house.' Andy lowered his voice. 'I didn't really think Nat and Milly needed to see Graham in this state.'

'That's good. Really good thinking.' Dave kept the surprise out of his voice as he praised the young policeman. 'Right, I'll get there as soon as I can.' He punched the disconnect button and turned just as he heard Kim walking up behind him, her arms full of more food.

'Get where soon?' she asked quietly.

'Andy Denning. We need to have a look at where it happened,' he answered, his voice gentle, opening the boot again and taking the load from her arms.

'But it was an accident.'

Dave's heart ached as she gazed at him, her eyes wide.

'I have no reason to think it's anything else . . . but Kimmy—' he tucked a stray strand of dark hair behind her ear '—it's just standard procedure.' He placed the containers next to the others, slammed the boot shut and held the passenger's door open for Kim.

'I put a note on the roadhouse door saying I didn't know when I'd be back. I would have got Jackie to help but she was at the motel.' She sighed and leaned her head against the window. 'Still, knowing Nat, she won't want me around for too long. Always got her Great Wall of China up, she has.'

✧

Kim bustled straight into the kitchen at Granite Ridge and folded a sobbing Natalie into her arms. She didn't say anything, just let her sister cry and cry. Kim couldn't understand what it would feel like to lose a child, but the pain in Nat's face, no matter how distant they were, was confronting.

Although Kim had no clear idea how to handle this situation, she knew to make sure she loved everyone, whatever happened.

She was a firm believer that love could fix and heal everything. She didn't care if it was fairytale stuff: that was the way it worked in her world. She felt Dave's reassuring presence behind her.

Amelia sat slumped on the couch, her face white. Paul sat next to her, his arm around her shoulders. She stared at nothing but the floor, while John stood next to the window, his back very stiff and upright. He didn't respond when anyone spoke to him, just continued to stare unseeingly.

Finally Natalie started to hiccup and lifted her head from Kim's shoulder. Her face was covered in tears and snot, and Kim felt her heart melt a little when Dave handed over one of those big men's hankies, neatly folded.

'Does anyone want a cup of tea?' Nat asked after wiping her face, in a voice that was husky from crying.

Amelia gave a giggle that turned into hysterical laughter. 'Good old Mum,' she managed, the tears beginning to flow. 'That's your standard line in a crisis.'

Kim watched Paul pull her closer and thought how lucky Amelia was to have him—and reflected on how glad she was that he'd proved to be one of the good guys. She turned back to her sister, her hand still on her shoulder. 'I'll make a cuppa, if you'd like one, Nat.'

'No, no, I don't need one.' She looked at Dave as if seeing him for the first time, then gestured towards him. 'But your friend might.'

Dave shook his head. 'No thanks, Mrs Bennett, although it's very kind of you to offer under the circumstances.' He paused. 'I'm very sorry for your loss.'

Natalie sank down into a chair at the kitchen table, the hanky crumpled in her white-knuckled hand. 'He was such a good boy,' she muttered. 'Such a good boy. Even when he was a baby, he never cried.'

There were sounds of a vehicle pulling up outside and Kim watched out the window. Dani, sobbing hysterically, threw open the car door and tore down the path, her mother following behind her. A few seconds later, Dani burst into the room and stared around at everyone wildly.

'It's not true!' she screamed. 'It can't be!'

Kim moved towards her, since no one else seemed to be able to. 'Oh, sweetie.' She tried to guide Dani to a chair, but the young woman shook her off. The anger in her face took Kim aback and she let go without an argument.

Dani ran across to John, put her hands on his tense shoulders and made him turn around to look at her. 'It's not true. It can't be. We've got our whole lives in front of us. We have plans! Dreams!' She stopped, her chest heaving.

John reached out and touched her face, before a tear slipped down his grizzled cheek. 'It's true,' he managed to say. 'I'm sorry.'

Dani stared at him for a moment, still disbelieving, then let out a wail and crumpled to the floor. Kim and Dave were beside her in a second, helping her to the couch, while the three Bennetts looked on numbly, wrapped up in their own grief, and Paul stayed by Amelia's side.

'In the sitting room there's a bar, Dave,' Kim said. 'Can you get me the whisky from there, please?' She flicked the kettle on and started to get out mugs from under the cupboard. 'Paul, can you leave Milly for a second and go out to the car? There's food in the boot to bring in.' She started to put the tea bags into the cups. 'Milly, sweetie, sit next to Dani, there's a good girl.'

Kim had worked out that today everyone needed to be told what to do—gently, of course. They didn't know how to operate on their own, so she needed to put her own feelings aside and get on with helping her family. *That's what families do.*

An image of Graham standing on the stage the night before, smiling at Dani, came to her. Then another one of him as a little boy, with his brown hair flopping over his eyes, a chook tucked under one arm and his face covered with freckles. A smile that would have lit up any room. It was such a shame his mother had spoiled him the way she had, but he'd been able to turn on the charm.

Kim heard Dave come up behind her and reach around to put the bottle on the bench. 'Thanks,' she said in a shaky voice, trying to rid her mind of the memories. They needed to come later. When she was alone.

Dave whispered in her ear. 'I have to go out to the scene, but I don't want to leave you here by yourself.'

'I'll be fine.' Kim reached up and put her hand to his face. 'Honestly, I will. You go do what you gotta do, and I'll handle things here until you get back.' Kim managed a watery smile. 'I can do this,' she said, her eyes misting over. 'Because that's what families do.'

Dave kissed her cheek and, with a last lingering look, walked out the door.

Chapter 32

As he drove towards the cattle yards, Dave knew he should be thinking about what had happened, but he couldn't focus. He was overwhelmed with how kind and steady Kim was in a crisis. She just put her feelings aside and pitched in, helping anyone who needed it. She was the opposite to his ex-wife, Melinda, who'd spent her days giving to others as a nurse, coming home with nothing left for her family.

Kim's heart was as big as a lion's, Dave was sure. And that, he decided, was very attractive.

In the distance he saw the glint of the lights flashing from the police car. Someone had forgotten to turn them off. He made an exasperated sound—those boys would end up with a flat battery.

He started to cast his eyes around his surroundings and he put Kim out of his mind. It was time to concentrate on the job. The cattle had recovered from being spooked and made themselves at home, grazing around the sheds. Some had jumped a fence into a different paddock, but most were in the hay yard, scoffing as much as they could get into them. He suspected there might be a few with injuries—broken legs or the like—but at first glance he didn't see any.

The cattle lifted their heads and watched him curiously as he walked over to the ambulance. He could see a tarp stretched out over the body, not far away.

'Dave.' Jack nodded to him.

'How you going?' Dave asked as he studied the young policeman, who was rather pale and a bit green around the gills.

'Fine,' Jack answered shortly.

Dave didn't push the young man. Seeing your first dead body was always confronting and even worse when it was in a small, close-knit community. You didn't need to be close to the deceased to know how hard their death would hit everyone.

Turning to the ambos, Dave thanked them for coming. 'I seem to be seeing quite a bit of you blokes,' he said. 'Wish I wasn't.'

'Yeah, we wish you weren't too,' one of them replied. 'This is nasty.'

'I'm sure it is.' This would be the first time Dave had seen a cattle stampede death, but he knew what to expect. While the bruises and grazes looked terrible, it was the injuries you couldn't see that killed. The fractured skull. The broken chest. The ruptured liver or spleen.

Dave also knew that Graham's mother, sister and aunty should never see him the way he was now: lying in the muddy yards, covered in fresh blood, with unseeing eyes. It was bad enough that John's last image of his son would be of what was lying underneath the tarp. He would surely be haunted by what he'd seen for years to come.

'Right, let's have a look,' Dave said, snapping out of his thoughts.

All four of them went over to the body, and one of the ambos lifted the edge of the tarp and pulled it back. Graham's corpse lay just as Dave had expected him to: twisted and broken. At first glance, Dave was sure an arm and a leg had been snapped, considering the unnatural way they were angled. There was blood pooled around the body's mouth, nose and eyes. It was a mangled mess.

'Damn,' Dave muttered. 'Okay, Jack, let's shoot some photos for the coroner. I'll show you what angles I want.'

As Jack snapped and Dave directed, he also looked around. The forcing yard had been constructed with pine posts placed close together and ringlock wire leading up to the gates. No bloody wonder the steers had gone over the top of the yards—there was nothing holding them in! If they'd been yarded—contained by the sturdy steel panels—this wouldn't have happened. Well, Dave conceded, it may have, but not in the same way.

The wire had been torn from its nails on the posts and strewn across the paddock. Some posts had been snapped at ground level and were lying broken on the ground. The cattle had left the deep imprints of their hooves in the damp, muddy earth. In short, the scene was carnage.

'I can see why he's been so badly injured,' Dave said, as Andy, who'd just arrived, appeared at his shoulder. 'Because the fence snapped so easily under the weight of the animals, he was tumbled under their feet.' He made a rolling motion with his hands. 'Four hundred k-gees of beef running over the top of you isn't going to leave you looking pretty.'

'No,' Andy said, going pale.

Dave clapped him on the shoulder and turned to Jack. 'Okay, get some shots of this too. Once you've finished with the body, the ambos can take it away.'

While they'd been examining the scene, the clouds had rolled in and a light drizzle had started to fall. 'Let's work quickly, fellas,' Dave said. 'If this isn't an accident, we need to find the evidence of that before the rain spoils it.'

'Not an accident? You've got to be kidding,' Andy said. 'Look at it. The cattle have been spooked and they've crushed him. How can it be anything but?'

Dave turned around. 'Might be my suspicious nature, but how were they spooked? Why'd they go crazy when Graham was in that spot? Look around—there was nowhere for them to go. They ran, hit the fence and then the gates. Sure, Graham might have been on his way up there to open the gates and push them into the yards, but he was at the front when they were spooked. Why is that? If I didn't know better I would have said there was something down the back that set them off.'

Andy and Jack stared at Dave, their heads turning from the back of the yards to the crumpled fence. He could almost see the cogs turning in their minds.

'I'm not saying it wasn't an accident.' He softened his voice. 'It probably was. But we're doing a disservice to Graham if we don't look into it properly.' Dave checked the sky. 'We're going to need to get a hurry on. Have you noticed how the birds have stopped singing and the wind has dropped? It's going to pelt down in a minute. Let's get going.' He strode off towards the other end of the forcing yard.

෴

Dave ran his hands over his face before turning off the ignition. He'd found it a lot more draining to deal with a scene when he was in love with the aunty of the deceased, than he would have if it had just been a run-of-the-mill incident.

His hand stilled as he realised what he'd just thought. *Love?* And that morning he'd been wondering if he *could* love again.

'Hmm,' he muttered, then opened the door and went in search of Kim.

Having so much experience in this situation, Dave found the house as he expected it: teeming with emotions—shock, disbelief, fear and sadness. Some neighbours had arrived to help out, so Kim was sitting on the couch next to her sister.

When she saw him walk in, she smiled and came over to him.

'You're all muddy,' she said.

'Yeah, it's a bit of a mess down at the yards. Can I wash up somewhere?'

Kim led him to the laundry and stayed with him while he washed. 'I can't be here long, Kimmy,' he said. 'I'm going to have to write up my report and send it through. We need to get Graham's body on the way to Adelaide for an autopsy, and the quicker we do all that, the quicker you will all be able to make arrangements.' He dried his hands and looked down at her. 'How are you holding up?'

'I'm okay,' she said quietly. 'I wish I could take some of their pain away, though. John isn't good at all. I'm worried about him. He's so quiet and just staring all the time. He doesn't hear anything when we talk to him.'

'That's normal. It's only just happened. What about Natalie?'

'She's devastated, of course.' Kim sniffed. 'She and I have never been close, but I'll be there throughout this, holding her close. I can't imagine how things can ever be the same for any of them.'

'And Amelia?'

'Sad, at a loss, but she'll be okay. She's a fighter. Always has been.'

Dave closed his eyes and held Kim's hands as he said, 'I need to talk to them before I go. I'm sorry, but I do. I'll make it quick.'

Kim nodded. 'Come on, let's get it over and done with. Then we can both go. I'd like a bit of time to myself.'

ॐ

It was almost dark as they pulled up in front of Kim's house.

Dave switched off the car and looked over at her. She was rubbing her neck.

'Headache?' he asked.

'Yeah. A bad one.'

'Come on, I'll take you in and get you settled. Then I'll head back to the motel and write up my report. Got your key?'

Kim handed it over, and he unlocked the door and switched on the lights before Kim walked inside. He watched as she flopped on the couch and shut her eyes.

'Where do you keep the Panadol?' he asked, opening cupboards in the kitchen.

'In the bathroom above the sink.' Her voice was dull and flat.

Dave found the packet and punched two pills out of the foil packaging, then filled a glass with water and took it to her.

'Thanks,' she said, and swallowed the pills. 'You know, I think I'm going to miss you when you have to go back to the city.'

Dave gently took the glass from her and set it on the coffee table, before sitting next to her, putting his arm around her shoulders and leaning into her neck. He breathed in her scent and closed his eyes, trying to commit the sensations to memory. He *would* miss her. More than she would ever know.

Dave knew it was imperative that he solved these crimes so he could get back to Adelaide and sort out his life. He needed to move quickly. So he stayed silent.

Chapter 33

Amelia ran from her thoughts and feelings, as hard and as fast as she could. She pushed her way through the bushes and let the branches scratch her arms and face. The only thing she let herself think about was that she was going to Emerald Springs. She would be okay once she got there. Her safe place.

The oppressive atmosphere in the house was driving her mad. Amelia knew that parents should never have to bury their child: that wasn't the way of nature. She understood John and Natalie were grieving and would forever. But it was hard to face the sadness that threatened to engulf what was left of her family. Amelia needed space, air and freedom. The only spot to get that was Emerald Springs.

As she half-ran, half-stumbled through the bush, she brushed beads of sweat from her eyes. The air was heavy with humidity and little green shoots were pushing their way through the red soil. Now that the rain had washed away a layer of dust, everything had become more vivid. Even the sky looked bluer than before.

By the time she arrived at the springs, Amelia was breathing heavily. Her ribs had the dull ache of an injury that was nearly mended, but not quite. She doubled over, her hands on her knees, trying to catch her breath. Closing her eyes, she could smell eucalyptus oil permeating from the leaves of the gumtrees, made more pungent by the rains. Birds flitted from branch to branch, calling to one another, and there was the hum of bees in the distance.

After letting herself slowly fall to the ground, Amelia dug her hands into the sand and felt the grains slide between her fingers. Then she rolled over onto her back and stared straight up at the sky. It didn't take long for the fuzz in her brain to disappear, and she began to feel as normal as she could.

She missed Graham. It was hard to believe something like this could have happened to her family. To anyone. But it had. Amelia had read countless newspaper stories of people who'd been killed while mustering or working on farms. Stock work was always unpredictable.

A tear slid down her cheek. Angrily she sat up and brushed it away. She'd already cried so much and she wanted to be strong. She had survived being attacked and robbed, and she would survive this too.

Amelia stripped off her clothes and dived into the pool, staying underwater for as long as she could. Just before her lungs were about to burst, she opened her mouth and screamed hard. Bubbles rose around her and she kicked to the surface. Her lungs crying for air, she gulped deeply, all the while treading water. The freezing liquid against her hot skin sent goosebumps skittering across her body, but it felt good.

With her heart pounding in her ears, she flipped over and floated, using her hands to propel herself around the pool. She shut her eyes and focused on the silky feel of the water. After a while she paddled towards the waterfall that was flowing strongly because of the rain. She manoeuvred herself under the cascade, letting it fall over her head and trickle down her face.

Something brushed against her leg and Amelia's eyes flashed open. Instinctively she drew her legs up to her stomach, and Chrissie's comment about always being scared of what might lurk below flooded back to her. Her heart, which had settled, began to thud again.

'Don't be ridiculous,' she said out loud. 'There's never been anything in here.'

Even so, she scanned the pool for ripples. It had never bothered her before that the bottom couldn't be seen, but now the uneasy feeling wouldn't leave her. Moving as little as possible, she shifted further under the waterfall, closer to the bank. There was a ledge she could hoist herself up onto if it happened again.

Nothing.

Feeling a little braver, Amelia pushed her leg out into the depths of the water and felt around.

Still nothing.

She decided she'd imagined it and her heart started to slow.

Then she felt it again and let out an almighty scream. Panic made her splash towards the ledge and she grabbed at the rock, scrambling to get out of the water. With a heave she managed to push herself up onto the ledge. She sat there, her knees up to her throat, her chest heaving. 'What the hell is it?' she asked, her eyes raking the water, trying to catch a glimpse of whatever was down there.

Then her hand brushed something and she glanced down. Right next to her was a thick rope. As her eyes followed the length of it, she realised it entered the water.

Trepidation ran through her. She leaned over and pulled the rope. Her arms strained: it was attached to something heavy. Slowly at first, then faster and faster, she hauled the rope in, desperate to know what was on the end of it.

Finally Amelia saw a dark shape emerging from the inky blackness. Time stopped. She couldn't hear the gushing of the water or the birds singing. She didn't feel the sun on her skin. Her total focus was on the object as it came closer and closer, and finally broke the surface.

Amelia stared at the bag uncomprehendingly before yanking the rope up further and bringing it onto the ledge. It was small, black and waterproof. She looked it over carefully before taking a deep breath and unzipping it. The contents were shadowed, so she angled the bag towards the sun and saw the zippered top of a second bag. She reached in, grabbed it out and opened it, her hands shaking.

Her anxiety level raced up the scale when she saw what was inside. Not stopping to think, she took out a handful of small plastic bags filled with folded banknotes in every denomination. Her handwriting was on the outside of each bag.

It was the rodeo money.

ↄ

'You touched everything?' Dave asked, trying to keep the despair out of his voice. The most decent lead so far and it looked like the evidence had been compromised.

'Well, yeah,' Amelia answered. 'I wanted to know what was inside.'

'Right. I'll be there as soon as I can. Can you please not touch anything else and move away from the scene?' He rubbed his hand over his face.

'I'm not out there now.' Amelia was speaking quietly into the phone and Dave struggled to hear what she was saying. 'I'm back at the house.' Ah, now he understood. She didn't want her parents to hear. 'Graham was involved, wasn't he?' she asked in a small tone.

'I can't say, Amelia. Let me get all the facts first. I'll be there soon.' Dave hung up and grabbed his keys before heading out the door.

It only took him half an hour to get to Granite Ridge. As he pulled up, he saw Amelia was waiting outside. By the time he was opening his door, she was standing right beside it, bending down to talk in a low voice.

'I don't want Mum and Dad to know about this until you're sure of what Graham did.' She stared at him hard. 'They're dealing with enough at this point.'

'Totally agree with you,' he said as he got out of the car. 'Where are they now?'

'Mum's lying down and Dad's out in the paddock. He won't be doing anything, just driving around aimlessly.'

Dave nodded. 'The Barker cops are coming too. Will they be able to find their way or do we need to wait?' He didn't want to wait; he was impatient to see what she'd found, but he needed either Andy or Jack with him to help take photos and collect evidence. He turned as he heard a vehicle approaching behind him. 'Geez, they were quick,' he muttered.

The young cops pulled up and got out. They were grim-faced, their eyes compassionate, as they said their hellos.

'This way.' Amelia gestured and started to lead them towards Emerald Springs.

Dave grabbed his rucksack, which contained evidence bags, a finger-printing kit and a few other investigative tools, and his camera bag. They followed Amelia, who was setting a cracking pace down the road.

'Should we drive?' asked Andy.

'You can't get a car in there,' Amelia called over her shoulder. 'You can drive a few metres through the gate if you want, but it's only just over here.' She motioned with her arm and kept walking.

'Here, grab this.' Dave thrust the camera bag at Andy and hoisted the rucksack up over his shoulder, starting to follow Amelia.

Ten minutes in, Dave was wondering where on earth they were going. He thought he could make out a faint path, but Amelia was so sure-footed that finding the route didn't seem to bother her. She pulled back branches and held them as they passed, only speaking to indicate how far there was to go.

'How did you find this place, Amelia?' Dave asked, as he patted his brow with a handkerchief.

'Used to be our family's barbecue spot,' she said, and Dave noticed that she wasn't even puffing. It seemed she was in very good shape—just over a week ago she'd been lying in a hospital bed. Jack also seemed pretty fit. Andy, on the other hand, was red-faced and sweat-stained beneath his armpits and down his back.

'And who knows about this place, other than your family?' Dave asked.

Amelia stopped walking and thought. 'Graham and I used to bring friends out here, and so did Mum and Dad, although that didn't happen often. And everyone who came here could have told others about it. It's a rare and beautiful spot, so I wouldn't be surprised if heaps of people know about it.' She started to walk again. 'I hadn't been out here for ages though, until a couple of weeks ago, and I'm pretty sure I was the first one in years. The track was so overgrown. We stopped coming out here after we left school. Silly, really. It's such a special place.'

'And have you noticed anyone out here recently?'

Amelia nodded. 'Last time I was out here—last Thursday, I think it was—I got pretty spooked. At first I thought I was just nervy after the robbery, but then I saw there were some snapped branches, like someone had bashed through. Then I thought it was roo, but I noticed a boot print in the sand. It was just Graham, though.'

'How do you know that?' asked Dave, raising his eyebrows.

'The boot was a Blundstone. That's what he wore all the time.'

'How could you tell they were Blundstone boots?'

'The tread. It's the same as when he walks into the kitchen with mud on his boots.' There was a pause and Amelia's eyes closed briefly. 'Walked, I mean.'

'But how does that make it Graham? Lots of men wear those boots.'

'Um . . . well, I guess I don't know for sure. But why would it be anyone else? It'd be so hard for them to get out here without being noticed on our property. Risky, too.' She shrugged. 'Anyway, we're nearly there.'

When they entered the oasis, Dave drew a breath. It was as beautiful as Amelia had described. He looked around carefully, but nothing caught his eye. Jack and Andy were looking around too, wide-eyed.

'So explain where you were and what happened,' Dave said. He set his bag down and took out his notepad.

Amelia went through, methodically, why she had been out here, how she'd been swimming and where the rope had brushed her leg, before finishing with how she'd realised it was the rodeo money.

'So are you saying I have to swim over there to get to that ledge?' Dave asked, looking at the water with trepidation.

'No, I'll take you around this way.' She walked along the edge of the pool and climbed up a bushy outcrop, then fought her way along the top and pointed to where Dave could drop down to the ledge. He swung his legs over the side and, holding his breath, dropped the couple of metres before landing safely next to the black bag.

He pulled a pair of plastic gloves from his back pocket and put them on, before looking inside the bag. 'This thing should hold fingerprints.' He turned and called across the water to Andy and Jack: 'I need a big evidence bag and it'll have to go back to Adelaide—I can't pull prints off this one.'

Dave snapped a few photos, handed the camera up to Amelia, then turned his attention to the plastic money bags.

Hundred-dollar notes were folded neatly inside one of them; on the outside was written *one thousand dollars*.

'This your writing?' he asked Amelia. She nodded and he put the money bag into one of the evidence bags, then asked, 'Do you recognise these money bags?'

'Yeah. That was how I was certain it was from the rodeo. It's exactly how I packed it for the bank, except the plastic bags were held in big calico sacks.'

Dave was silent as he added up the amounts. 'There's a hundred k here,' he called across to Andy and Jack. 'Can you write it down?'

'What? Where's the rest of it?' Amelia asked.

Dave squatted down and stared at the placid spring. 'Could be lots of reasons it's not here,' he answered. 'How deep is it?'

Amelia shrugged. 'Never seen the bottom.'

'Can you take this?' He handed her everything he'd bagged up and then started to scramble up himself.

There was fear and confusion in Amelia's face. 'It had to be Graham, didn't it?'

'Let's get all the information first,' Dave said kindly.

'How could he do that, though?' she burst out. 'Did he hurt me? I'm his sister. How *could* he?'

'Tell me a bit more about Graham,' Dave said. 'Did he go out much, who are his friends, that sort of thing.'

Amelia grabbed hold of a bottlebrush branch and pushed it out of the way so she could get down towards the little beach. 'Yeah, he went out a bit. To the pub, mostly. Played footy during the season, mucked around with his sheep, that sort of thing. Loved living the high life with Dani recently.'

'What do you mean "high life"?'

'Just that Dani expected a higher standard than just the pub—oh, she'd go there, but only for a drink. I think it was a little beneath her. She preferred to go over to Barker where there was more variety, some restaurants and bars. That sort of thing. And Graham liked that side of life too.'

'And friends?'

'Well, he had some good friends from high school, but a lot of them moved on from town. He's . . . he *was* mates with the Andrews boys and the blokes from his footy team.' She stopped and thought about it. 'But you know, they weren't that close—he'd just have a beer or two with them at the pub.'

Dave nodded, his mind beginning to work overtime.

Chapter 34

Dave sat hidden in the depths of the bushes, his night-vision goggles on. He picked up every movement: the gentle rustle of a tree branch and the rabbit that hopped out to get a drink at the pool.

Tomorrow he was due to get a call from Coops about the truck and the taser cartridge, so he hoped that might lead somewhere. And after a hurried conversation with Steve, he'd managed to get all the more recent fingerprint and forensic work fast-tracked. He'd also requested Graham's full phone and internet records. Hopefully he'd have that information some-time in the next week. It frustrated him that fast-tracking still meant up to a week's worth of waiting, but there was no choice. At least the police divers would be up from Adelaide tomorrow to see if anything had sunk to the bottom of the springs.

For now, Dave watched and waited. Earlier in the day, he'd set up some static alarms along the track, just in case someone else knew the money had been hidden at the springs. If it was linked to Graham's death, they might be stupid enough to come sniffing around for it—and the best way to nab them would be red-handed. Yes, it was a long shot, but the only thing Dave could do for the moment.

He found himself thinking about a case he'd worked a while ago. Gemma Sinclair, from Billbinya Station, had had stolen stock planted on her land. Dave and Craig, the officer he'd been working with, had spent a fair bit of time examining the land and stock, thinking Gemma was the culprit. The investigation had included a stakeout: it was the way they'd caught one of the offenders. If only it would turn out to be that easy here.

Dave unscrewed his thermos and took a sip of coffee. Kim had packed him enough food to last weeks, and he was grateful; food would help keep him awake. It was easier doing a job like this with two people, he reflected. One slept while the other kept watch, or at least they could keep each other alert.

Dave looked around again, but there was nothing. Stretching out, he lay back and looked at the stars. Out here, away from the city lights, they looked like diamonds encased in black velvet. He watched a satellite scurry across the sky, all the while listening intently. A gentle breeze made the leaves rustle together.

And then he heard something.

Quietly, Dave rolled over onto his stomach and cased the area. It all looked the same. He listened so hard, he began to wonder if he was imagining something. Then a vibration started in his pocket. It was the static alarm going off! His hand flew down to switch it off, then reached slowly for his video camera. He pushed himself upright, trying not to make any noise.

A *thump, thump* like heavy footfalls sounded.

Dave readjusted his night-vision goggles and stared at the path, expecting the intruder to appear. There was movement at the path's entrance, but Dave couldn't see who it was. He didn't move his eyes from the spot and he held his breath as the shrubs shifted again. It was like someone was hiding behind them and moving the branches out of the way to check what was on the other side. Who was it?

Come on, come on, he thought.

As Dave leaned forward in anticipation, all was revealed.

A young kangaroo hopped cautiously into view, its nose twitching as it looked around.

☙

Amelia drifted in and out of sleep all night. Past dawn she was still lying on her bed with her arms around herself, trying to fight off her disbelief and horror. Her brother might have been involved in her attack. Had his been the familiar voice? She couldn't comprehend that. Oh, she could see the reasoning behind it. Graham had needed money; he always overspent and didn't know how to plan ahead.

A thought hit her. Who was the woman her attackers had mentioned? Could she be Dani? Amelia remembered the young woman's anger towards her on the night of the brawl: *You're the reason this has happened.* And then there was all that time Graham had been on the phone outside his engagement party. She'd known something was off with that. Dani and Graham had argued that night, too.

Another thought struck her. Where was his phone now? Had it ever been found after the party? It hadn't been mentioned at all, not since she'd talked to Graham for the last time. Maybe it had turned up. There could be something on the phone that would help her work out what the hell was going on.

Getting up, she walked quietly to her mother's bedroom. She was careful to press open the door without making it creak. The curtains were drawn, and the room was dark and smelt stale. 'Mum?' Amelia asked gently, going in and sitting on the bed. 'Mum, are you awake?'

Natalie mumbled something that Amelia didn't catch, so she leaned forward, only to be struck by the odour of an unwashed body. *Oh, Mum*, Amelia thought sadly. Out loud, she said, 'Mum, how about I bring you a cup of tea and you get up and have a shower? Let me strip the sheets and put clean ones on the bed.'

Her mother rolled over and looked up at her, the dark circles under her eyes obvious even in the murky light. 'Why?' she asked in a dead voice. 'What's the point? There isn't a point to anything now.' She rolled away. 'We can't even organise a funeral yet. Dave said that it might take ten days. Ten days!'

Amelia stroked her shoulder and wondered what to say. She wanted to take offense. Wanted to cry out: *What about me?* Aunty Kim had told her to expect something like this and not to take it personally. It was all part of the grieving process. Of course, things were more complicated now. The selfish voice inside Amelia also wanted to yell: *Hey, I miss him too, but I'm angry as hell with him and wish he was here so I could ask him a whole lot of questions.* But someone needed to be the strong one, and at this point it had to be Amelia.

She struggled to find something positive and wise to say. In the end she settled for: 'There's a point, Mum. Dad is still here, I'm still here and I'm really sure that Graham wouldn't want you to be like this.' It sounded lame, even to her ears. She stood up. 'I'll bring you that tea.'

In the kitchen Amelia went through the motions of making the tea, while her mind was full of her mother and Graham's mobile phone. Her thoughts flicked back and forth between the two. She needed to ask Natalie if the phone had been found and handed back by someone, but why would she be asking about Graham's phone at a time like this? Maybe she should just ring Dave and ask him.

Putting the cup onto a tray, she went back down the passage to find her mother up and opening the curtains. But the effort tired her and she sank down onto the camphorwood chest, her hands trembling. Amelia put the tray next to Natalie and turned to start stripping the bed.

'Do you remember how he was always smiling, Milly?' Natalie asked, staring out of the window. 'Always such a happy child.'

Amelia didn't answer. Death turned everyone into a saint, and Graham certainly hadn't always been happy. He was moody and temperamental, sometimes downright irritable and arrogant. But he did have a charming side to him, which he could turn on whenever he wanted. And he'd been kind and thoughtful to Amelia after her bashing.

Although that hadn't really been kindness, had it? *Guilt*, Amelia thought, scowling. *That's what that was all about. Bloody guilt.*

She stood up and gathered the sheets and doona cover. 'I'll

just pop these in the washing machine, Mum, and be right back.'

When she returned with fresh sheets, Natalie hadn't shifted. Quickly, Amelia started to make the bed, still trying to work out what to say.

'Such a quiet boy, too,' Natalie muttered. 'And gentle. It was no wonder Dani fell in love with him.'

Amelia turned to her mother. 'Have you spoken to Dani, Mum?' she asked. 'I'm sure she's having a tough time too. Maybe you'd be good for each other. You know, be able to talk about the man you both loved.'

Natalie didn't seem to hear, so Amelia went back to the bed-making.

'Maybe you're right.'

'Sorry?' Amelia asked as she tucked in the sheet.

'I should go and talk to Dani.' Natalie stood up. 'I must have a shower.'

'I'll take you over there if you like,' Amelia said, pleased that she'd suggested something worthwhile.

'Thanks, Milly, I'd like that.'

'Mum, I've got something to ask you,' Amelia said tentatively. 'When the hospital . . . when you were given . . .' She stopped and looked over at Natalie, who was staring at her. 'Have you and Dad put all of Graham's things in his room?'

'Yes. But don't touch them.' Although Natalie's voice was quiet, it had a steely quality to it. 'Don't even go in there, Amelia. That is *not* your space. I want it left exactly as it is.'

Amelia was silent for a moment. She knew the room wouldn't be staying as it was for long. Dave and the cops would be in there sooner or later, picking through Graham's things. She was surprised they hadn't come already. The day before, at Emerald Springs, Dave hadn't given much away. He'd asked her some standard questions, then told her to head back to the house and not return to the springs until he gave permission. 'Might be a few days,' he'd said regretfully.

Amelia had shrugged. 'If you get to the bottom of everything, it's worth it.'

Now she wanted—no, *needed* to get into Graham's room and look for the phone before Dave did. It wasn't that she didn't trust that he'd do a good job, but she wanted to know who Graham had been talking to, and Dave might still be looking at her as a suspect. For all she knew, he could even suspect Natalie.

Bloody hell, Amelia thought, *that's the most ridiculous thing you've come up with yet. You're paranoid.*

Struggling to clear her head, she turned to her mum. 'Go and have a shower, Mum. I'll ring Dani and see if she's home.'

If there was any chance that Dani was involved with all of this, then Amelia would just have to trust that Dani would never hurt Natalie, especially while her own parents were in the house. Good thing she still lived at home.

Then a comforting thought occurred to Amelia. There was an opportunity here for her to take her mind off things by losing herself in numbers and calculations as she'd always been able to. 'While I'm out that way,' she said, 'I might ring Anne and see if I can go check over her accounts. Make use of the time while you're with Dani, since their places are so close together.'

Natalie shook her head sadly. 'I don't know how you can continue on as if nothing has happened.'

Opening her arms, Amelia hugged her mum. 'I don't know either. All I know is if I don't keep going, if I stop, I'll be in trouble.' She let go and picked up the tray before walking out to the kitchen. Then she went into her room and waited; within minutes, she heard the shower running. *Ten minutes from now*, she thought, glancing at her phone clock.

She ran to Graham's room. Pushing open the door, she stopped dead in her tracks. The smell of his aftershave hit her and she had to gulp down tears. Then she reminded herself of what he'd done, and anger coursed through her.

On the bed was a box holding his car keys, his wallet, a handkerchief, and some other odds and ends—no phone.

Amelia was about to leave when she had an idea. Could Graham have hidden the phone in his room and pretended to lose it for some reason? To conceal evidence, or use it against someone?

She threw open the wardrobe door and felt in the pockets of his clothes. His desk! She pulled open the drawers and sifted through papers, but it netted her nothing. Then she peered under the bed and felt around beneath the mattress.

The shower stopped. Amelia shut the drawers, tried to make the room look like she hadn't been there and slowly backed out, closing the door tightly behind her.

So where was the phone? Had it really been stolen?

⁂

Sitting at his motel room table, Dave had just taken his first bite of Weet-Bix when his phone rang. He snatched it up when he saw the forensics number.

'What did you get, Coops?' he asked by way of a greeting.

'The cartridge is as clean as that paper was. Sorry, Dave. And since you didn't find any of the pellets, that's a bit of a dead-end too, because they have the serial number on them.'

'Bugger.' Dave thought quickly. 'So, going back to the cartridge, how does someone get hold of a taser gun?'

He could hear Coops scratching his scruffy chin, a habit he had when he was thinking. 'I guess,' he said slowly, drawing the words out, 'you can buy them online. Black market-type jobs.'

'So a civilian can access one easily enough?'

'Sure can.'

Dave frowned. 'What about the oil?'

'We can certainly match that if you ever find the truck. Now, speaking of the truck, it has a rigid body. I've run a check on the regos out there and emailed it to you.' Coops paused for a second. 'You do know how to get emails, don't you?'

'Smart arse,' Dave muttered under his breath. 'Many hits on the regos?'

'Surprisingly, yes. Farmers usually prefer tippers, but there are quite a few rigid trucks up that way.'

Dave groaned. 'Great. Cheers, Coops. At least I can check the oil. And I reckon the tyres are missing a chip of rubber.'

'But who's to say it's even registered?' Coops asked.

'Geez, who made you the detective? Any other info?'

'Not from me.'

'Thanks for rushing this through. Buy you a beer when I get back?'

'Up for it anytime. Hey, and Dave, before you go? Don't stay too long up there in the sticks, will you? We're beginning to think you like it.' Coops gave a short bark of laughter and hung up.

'So what if I do?' Dave muttered to dead air.

He scoffed the rest of his Weet-Bix and pulled on his jacket. The first thing to tackle this morning was the unpleasant task of disturbing the Bennetts and going through Graham's room. Then the divers would be arriving.

Chapter 35

Amelia knocked on the front door of Anne's house. Reaching down, she patted the cat who was winding himself around her ankles. A few moments passed. She didn't hear footsteps approaching the door, so she knocked again and was greeted with silence. She walked around to the side of the house, calling out, 'Hello! Anne?'

There was no answer. That was strange—she'd called ahead and Anne had told her to just knock at the front. Was the older woman all right?

Hearing the sound of barking dogs, Amelia walked towards them. Maybe the Andrews had all been caught up doing sheep work over in the yards. But no, there was still no one to be seen. Two dogs were tied up near the shearing shed, straining at the end of their chains. When they saw her, they let out another great round of barking.

'Sorry boys, can't let you off,' she told them, 'but I'd be real appreciative if you could tell me where Anne is.'

A noise came from inside the shearing shed. Was it just a chain banging against tin? *Maybe Anne's had an accident and needs help.* Amelia eyed the shadows inside the shed warily. Anyone could be in there. A shiver went up her spine. *No,* she told herself, *you have to get over this!*

Her footsteps echoed around the shed and it quickly became apparent that there was no one inside. Instead of leaving, Amelia walked towards a shaft of sunlight that streamed through a dirty window. Shimmering dust particles seemed to dance in the golden light, and she swished her hand through them, making them twirl in agitation.

She felt a little bit like they did. One minute floating peacefully through life, with everything going according to plan—and the next, with the slash of a hand, everything in chaos.

Breaking away from her dark thoughts, Amelia glanced around, hoping to see some fleeces. She loved the smell and feel. Stepping around the wool table and running her hands along the work-worn bench against the wall, she made her way towards the back of the shed where the wool bins were, but they were empty.

A gleam caught her eye. Near the grinder sat a pile of steel ear tags.

Amelia froze. Steel ear tags were really unusual. Only sheep owners who couldn't afford to lose their record number used them. That meant stud sheep.

She walked over to them, tucking her hand behind her back, and looked them over. The name of the stud and the identification number were clearly engraved into the long side of the tag.

'Oh my . . . Bloody hell!' she whispered, as everything began to make sense.

These were the tags from the ewes that had been stolen from Paul.

Images flashed through her mind. Graham hanging out with the Andrews boys over the past year, when they'd never been friends at school. Will befriending Chrissie, then dumping her just before the robbery. And Mike and Tony, security guards on the first shift. They would have known or at least heard what was happening during the night of the rodeo.

So, now it seemed there was Graham, Mike, Tony, Will and Dani involved. What a clever little crew.

Amelia's mind raced ahead as she tried to connect the dots. Dani's words on the night of the brawl might make sense if Graham had got cross with the other men for hurting his sister. The Andrews boys had been in the scrum, seemingly trying to calm things down. But of course, Jim Green had been at the centre of it.

Maybe he was involved too. Jim had a truck. Jim had money problems.

'Bloody hell, bloody hell, bloody hell.' Her whole body was trembling, and she could hear the fear in her own voice. She had to get out of here.

Amelia pulled out her phone to ring Dave, but there was no signal. Shit, she'd forgotten this farm was in a dead spot. Thinking quickly, she opened the camera app and started snapping pictures of the tags.

Hearing a noise behind her, she spun around fearfully. Just the cat, rubbing himself against the doorway. She stuffed her phone back into her pocket and, after one last glance at the ear tags, almost ran down the stairs, out of the shed and back towards the house, keeping her eyes open for the boys.

She needed to find Anne. But how could she tell her friend that she thought her sons were involved in the robbery? How would Anne react? She'd be furious! And devastated. She was so honourable and upright. Didn't tolerate lies of any size.

'I can't believe it,' Amelia muttered, as she stalked across the yard. *Maybe Dave would be the better option*, she thought. She pulled her phone back out and looked at it once again. Yep, that was what she'd do. She'd get in her car and drive away right now. Let the police deal with it. As much as she wanted to clear her name and confront these bastards, she didn't need to get hurt or die being a hero.

A little voice niggled in the back of her mind. *You don't know that they've done the other crimes*, it said. *Maybe they just stole Paul's sheep. Maybe it was opportunistic.* That could be what Dave would say. Or he could accuse her of planting the ear tags in the shed . . .

'Milly! Hey, Milly!'

With her heart thundering, Amelia turned around and saw Anne heading towards her, holding a bucket. She took a deep breath, her mind racing, trying to work out what to do. What if Anne didn't believe her, or got angry? No, Amelia was still sure that Dave was her best bet. Maybe the old Amelia would have told Anne: the one who did things without thinking them through. The ditzy one.

Summoning up her best smile, Amelia called out to Anne: 'Hello! I've been looking for you. I couldn't get anyone to hear at the house, so I went for a bit of a stroll trying to find you.'

'Sorry about that,' Anne said. 'I thought I'd have time to feed the chooks before you got here, then I found the trough was overflowing so I had to fix it.' Anne swung an arm over Amelia's shoulders and gave her a gentle look. 'How are you, love? You're looking like you're having a hard time of it.'

What? How could Anne know? Then Amelia remembered. Graham's death. She swallowed hard. 'Fine,' she answered, hoping her voice didn't shake. 'I'm fine. I've taken Mum over to Dani's. I thought it might help with the grieving process. It's horrible seeing her like this, Anne. Not getting out of bed.'

As Amelia said Dani's name, she wondered again if her mother was safe there, then dismissed the idea. Of course she was. Wasn't she? Why would Dani hurt Natalie?

Anne patted Amelia's arm. 'It's hard when you can't organise the funeral straight away,' she said with feeling. 'It gives you something to do, something to focus on. I know. And look, I'll be coming down to help this week, however I can.'

Against her feelings, Amelia smiled and squeezed the older woman's arm. 'Thanks, Anne. You would have to be the most perfect person to offer. After all, you know what it's like to lose someone you love.'

Anne's expression changed to deep sadness. 'Yeah, I do,' she answered softly. 'When Greg was killed, I didn't think I could ever get over it, but time moves on and lessens the pain.' She shook her head and Amelia knew talking about her dead husband was hard—in fact, Anne almost never did. 'But once the funeral is over, you don't have any option but to start moving forward. Speaking of, I think it's a great idea that you came out here to do some office work. Keeping busy is a big help.'

'Yep, that's what I'm hoping.' Amelia looked around as they walked towards the house. 'That rain has been great, hasn't it?' What had started as a green tinge was now a thick carpet of feed. The sheep in the paddock next to the shearing shed were out grazing contentedly in the sun, while the milking cow sat in the shade of a large gumtree, chewing her cud. 'Makes such a difference.'

'That it does,' Anne answered, smiling cheerfully. 'I love it when the land comes to life.' They walked up the steps and she held the door open, motioned Amelia inside. 'Have you had breakfast?' she asked.

'Yeah, I'm fine, thank you.' Amelia realised she was still holding her phone in her sweaty hand. She slipped it into her back pocket and looked around the sunlit house. 'Where are the boys?'

'Mike and Tony are out in the boundary paddock, fixing up a fence. Had some cattle trample it when that brief storm came through on Sunday night. And Will said he had to go to the doctor, though goodness knows what for! He's a fit young lad. But I don't suppose his mother needs to know everything about what he's up to, do I?' Anne grinned and shook her head fondly.

Amelia tried to smile, then turned the conversation back to the weather. Another half-inch of moisture had been much appreciated and the thunder had been so loud, the glasses in the cabinet at Granite Ridge had rattled together, and the light had flicked on and off as the power surged.

'Right, well,' Amelia said, 'I'll get on with reconciling the bank account, if you like.' She was keen to get finished and leave before any of the brothers came home.

Turning on the kettle and getting a cold roast lamb out of the fridge, Anne said, 'I've left the statement and the few invoices that came in the last mail on top of the computer keyboard. Should all be fairly self-explanatory.'

'No worries.' Amelia headed towards the office and let out a breath as she sat down. Working quickly, she opened the mail and ran her eyes over the statement before opening the accounting program on the computer and entering some details. As she worked, she realised the bank statement hadn't been imported from the bank's website. She shifted a few papers, looking for the security token that would allow her access, before pulling open the top drawer where it was usually kept if it wasn't on the desk.

Amelia rummaged about, then stopped. She stared into the drawer and then started to breathe very fast.

After glancing over her shoulder, she grabbed the familiar phone from the drawer and pressed a button. There was a photo of Graham and Dani taken at a footy club wind-up. It *was* Graham's phone.

Staring in confusion, Amelia wondered how on earth it could have got there, then realised Will must have stolen it on the night of the engagement party.

She heard Anne open and shut the fridge again, and quickly shoved the phone in her front pocket with shaking hands.

Surveying the office with new interest, she wondered if there was any other evidence hidden there. Nothing looked different to how it usually did and Amelia knew she couldn't go through filing cabinets without Anne wondering what she was doing. But she *could* open the cupboard door . . .

Kicking back the chair, Amelia leapt up and opened the tall timber cabinet in the corner, where Anne kept her stationery supplies.

'What do you need, Milly?' Anne asked from the doorway.

Amelia jumped at the sound of her voice. 'Just looking for some printer cartridges and more paper,' she stammered, as her eyes fell on a John Deere GPS guidance system. The small screen and cords were tucked away under a pile of papers, but Amelia was certain about what it was.

She also knew one had been stolen in the robberies. Was this it? Normally a GPS guidance system wouldn't be hidden away in a cupboard—it would be in the tractor being used for spraying and then seeding. Bending over to get a better view, she pretended to fumble with some paper, while her eyes made certain of what she was seeing. When she couldn't pretend anymore, she shut the door with a sheaf of paper in her hand and held it up for Anne to see.

'I only filled that printer up a couple of days ago,' Anne said. 'Those boys! I never know what they get up to in here.'

Obviously, Amelia thought. She smiled and said, 'It's a bit like the fridge. It seems to get emptied as soon as it's full. I'll get on.'

Anne looked at her strangely. 'Are you sure you're okay, Milly? You seem a little tense, love.'

'I'm fine. I think it's just all the . . .' A lump in her throat appeared from nowhere and genuine tears formed in her eyes.

'Oh, Milly. It's all a bit overwhelming, isn't it?' Anne gave her a hug. 'Don't worry, it gets better. Look, how about we give this a miss now and you go and pick up your mum and head home to your dad? You need to be with family at a time like this.'

Amelia nodded, allowing a tear to slip down her cheek, then let herself be led out of the office. As she walked she could feel Graham's phone digging into her thigh. She had everything she needed. She'd go straight to Dave and he'd piece it all together. The nightmare would finally be over and done with.

'Now look, before you go, do you want some pork chops?' Anne asked. 'The boys killed a couple of pigs and they're all cut up in the coolroom. I just haven't had time to bag and freeze them yet. Come and take them home to your folks.'

'That would be lovely,' Amelia said in a low voice.

'Follow me.' Anne led the way out past the laundry and into the garage next to the shearing shed, where a mobile coolroom was stored. The motor clicked on just as Anne opened the door.

Amelia could see at least four carcasses hanging there. 'Done a big kill, Anne?' she asked as the older woman grabbed some plastic bags from inside the door.

'Yeah, we did pigs first, then started on some lamb. That's the lamb you can see hanging there. Can you just hop up in there and hold back that carcass? I won't be able to get to the back otherwise.'

Amelia stepped into the coolroom and did as she was asked. Then, sensing movement and hearing a strange *click*, she turned her head.

Anne was holding a gun, pointed at Amelia's head. 'Give me your phone,' she growled, her eyes narrowed.

Amelia, wide-eyed, stared at the woman she called a friend. 'Wh—what?'

'Your phone. Now.' Anne held out her hand.

Amelia tried to put her foot forward and get out of the cool-room with force, but Anne waved the gun at her. 'It's loaded,' she said calmly. 'And I will use it. Give me your phone.'

With trembling hands, Amelia reached into her pocket and handed Anne her phone. 'It doesn't work here anyway,' she said, with a bravado she certainly didn't feel. 'There's no signal.'

'Well then, you won't mind not having it.'

Anne slammed the door and bolted it from the outside. In the frozen darkness, surrounded by dead animals, Amelia began to scream.

Chapter 36

Will Andrews parked his ute in the main street of Torrica and blew out a breath. He'd told his family he was going to the doctor. Acting quickly, so he didn't have time to back out, he jumped from the ute, walked across the road to Torrica Farm and General, and yanked open the door.

Inside he looked for Chrissie's curly red hair. There she was, in the back office. Swallowing hard, he strode over, walked in and shut the door behind him. Chrissie looked up, her mouth opening into an O before Will started to talk.

'Sorry I haven't been in contact. I wanted to call you. But I couldn't.' His words came out in short, sharp bursts. 'I'm really sorry. I like you a lot.'

Chrissie half-rose from her chair and then sat down again. 'Okay . . . ?'

'I've got to go and fix something. And when I've done that, you're not going to want to see me again.'

Chrissie tilted her head and looked at him. 'What are you talking about?'

'Look, I've got to go now. Go and fix it. I just want you to know that I'm sorry and I'm trying to make it right.' His heart was pounding. He left the room, rushed out of the store and strode back across the street, where he got into his ute and turned towards Barker. He had a date with the police station.

છ

'I'm really sorry, John, but this is something we have to do.' Dave's voice filled with sympathy as the man in front of him seemed to crumble.

'But I don't understand why you need to look at Graham.'

'We've found some evidence to suggest he may have known who was behind the rodeo robbery. I have a warrant to search his bedroom.'

John just stood there as Dave, Jack and Andy walked past him, down the passageway and into Graham's room. Quickly and quietly they searched under the mattress and bed, then through the drawers and cupboards.

'Upend the drawers and see if there's anything taped to the bottom of them,' Dave instructed after rifling through Graham's desk. 'I'll be back in a minute.'

He went in search of John, who was now sitting at the kitchen table, staring into space. Dave cursed himself for not bringing Kim with him. He hadn't considered that Natalie and Amelia wouldn't be home. It was clear John needed someone with him.

'Can I call anyone for you?' Dave asked as he sat opposite the man.

John shook his head.

'John, do you know if Graham had any financial problems?'

The ticking of the clock above the stove seemed loud in the silence. Finally John shifted his gaze and looked straight at Dave. 'Yeah, he did. About six months ago he asked me to go guarantor for a loan. It was twenty thousand dollars. Because he didn't have any assets of his own, and the fact that the wage he gets from us is quite small, the bank weren't prepared to take him on without a backer. So he asked me.

'I wasn't comfortable with it. I couldn't see how he could make the payments with the little cash he had, but he was convinced that he could. He said his wool sales would be enough and that he wanted to expand his business. I asked him to get Milly to help him draw up a budget, but he wouldn't hear of it.' John's eyes filled with tears. 'I wish I could have made it rain. Given him a bigger share of the profits, but it just didn't. And I couldn't.' His voice broke and he put his hands over his eyes.

Dave waited him out.

'He came to me . . . only a few days ago.' John took a tremulous breath. 'He said he was having trouble with the payments. I could have almost promised you that would happen, and part of the reason behind me agreeing to back him was wanting him to take responsibility for his own actions. He was a great one for going into a store, grabbing what he wanted and booking it up on our account without any thought of the cash flow or budget. Made it very difficult for us, some years.

'So I said to him I wouldn't make the interest payment. He had to go to the bank and try making other arrangements with them. Oh yeah, the bank would have come to me in the end. After all, I was the one who signed on the dotted line. I'm responsible for that. But I wanted Graham to take responsibility for his own money. So I said no and hoped he'd come through.' John looked down at his worn hands.

'Dave?'

Dave turned and saw Andy standing in the hallway. He motioned for Dave to follow him. Back in Graham's room, Dave gloved up and looked at the map that was spread out on the bed. Routes were marked in black texta and the farms that had already been robbed were ringed.

Dave sighed unhappily. 'Bag it up for evidence. Anything else?'

'There's this.' Jack handed over a phone bill. 'See these four numbers? They're the ones that are rung most.'

'Know whose they are?'

Both men shook their heads.

Dave copied the numbers down and felt a glimmer of excitement in his chest. 'I want to get traces run on these numbers.' Alone, they wouldn't be enough to convict anyone—but surely they'd lead in the right direction, and then the other evidence would come into play.

„”

Joan was sitting in her usual spot at the front of the police station when Dave walked through the door. He rushed past her, throwing a quick 'Hi!' over his shoulder.

'I'm pleased you're back,' Joan said. 'I had young Will Andrews in here a while ago—'

'I'm a bit busy at the moment, Joan. Can I catch up with you about this in a while?'

'Well, you can, but I sort of had a feeling it was important.' She held out a piece of paper to him.

Dave backpedalled, holding out his hand. 'Did he say what he wanted?'

'Only that he wanted to talk to the bloke who was the detective. He had some information he wanted to pass on.'

Dave stopped. 'Anything else?'

'I wrote his number down there,' Joan said. 'He wasn't really keen on you ringing back. Said he'd rather get in contact with you, but I insisted he give it to me. Knew you'd want it.'

'Great job! Thanks, Joan.' Dave began to walk off again. 'Don't suppose he said when he'd try to get in contact?'

'He'll be back tomorrow if he can, was all he said.'

Dave sat down at the desk and, using his two-finger typing method, wrote Steve an email, asking him to run checks on the numbers that had been found on Graham's phone bill. Then Dave turned his attention to Will's phone number. As he stared at it, excitement buzzed through his chest again. He quickly compared the number to the ones he'd just emailed through to Steve. One of them matched.

Dave's eye caught on the email from Coops about the regos and he clicked on it. There, right at the top of the alphabetical list of names, was *Mike Andrews*.

Leaning back in his chair, Dave let his mind race as it all fell into place.

The Andrews boys and Graham were friends. Graham had money troubles. Mike and Tony were security guards—they'd had access to the rodeo, to the money, to Amelia. They would have had the means to find a taser gun.

336

Dave shot off his chair and ran out of the office, telling Joan to call Andy and Jack and ask them to get back as quickly as they could.

❧

Amelia was shaking from head to toe and had tears running down her cheeks. She was cold and terrified. After Anne had left, she'd thrown herself against the door and shaken the whole coolroom. There was no way out.

'Oh no! No! *No!*' she screamed again, but knew there was little chance of anyone hearing. Even if someone was outside, the thick metal walls of these things were stuffed tight with insulation. Not soundproof, but close enough.

As Amelia banged her fists against the door, the carcasses rocked back and forth. One hit her on the head. She gave another little cry, then slid down the door and curled up in a ball. She was in shock, and couldn't understand what was happening. She couldn't make sense of what she'd just learned.

Unable to sit still, she stood up, once again knocking into the lamb carcass, and paced to the end. The cold air blew through her hair and sent shivers across her body. The hairs on her arms were standing up and she was covered in goosebumps.

Was Anne coming back to kill her, or would everything just slow down for her and she'd die slowly from hypothermia? How would they get away with it? They'd have to hide her body. Maybe they'd cut it into pieces, bag it up and store it in here.

She shuddered, pushed the sickening thought out of her head and decided to concentrate on staying alive. Images of everything she loved flooded into her mind: her parents' grief-stricken faces, Kim's smile, her precious Paul, the beauty of Emerald Springs, her three best friends. The quote they'd helped Chrissie put up on her wall, two weeks and another lifetime ago, came into Amelia's head: *At any given moment, you have the power to say: this is not how the story is going to end.* She was determined to do everything she bloody well could to survive.

Amelia rubbed her arms up and down and wrapped them around herself. She jumped on the spot to keep the blood flowing. Then she tried star jumps. Finally, she sank to the floor and wrapped her arms around her knees, conserving body heat.

Then she felt it. The hard lump against her thigh. Graham's phone! She leapt up and pulled it from her pocket, knowing there wouldn't be any signal, but it would give her light for a little while. The screen lit up as she pushed a button, and for a long moment she stared at the picture of Graham and Dani. Amelia traced the outline of her brother's face before noticing the words in the bottom corner.

Emergency Call Only.

Amelia held her breath as she pressed the button. Then she cried out when she heard the words: 'Police, Fire or Ambulance?'

༒

Dave pressed the phone closer to his ear and listened intently as his boss, Steve, explained the situation. He pushed his foot down on the accelerator and the car sped up. Steve paused for a second and Dave barked, 'When did the call come in?'

338

'About half an hour ago. It took the bloody call centre that long to work out where to direct it.'

'I'm on it,' Dave said. He was about to hang up but Steve kept talking.

'I'm going to send up the STAR Group.' The Special Tactics and Response Group. 'I know they'll take a while to get to you, but you *must* wait for them, Burrows. You have no choice. That criminal gang is unravelling. You won't stand a chance against them with just you and the locals.' Steve rushed on. 'There's four of them against three of you and I'm pretty sure they won't go down without a fight.'

'I hear you. But there's no way I'm going to leave Amelia where she is.'

'Don't get involved, Burrows,' Steve commanded again. 'Where's your sense of professionalism?'

Dave hung up on his boss. *That went out the window when I started loving Kim*, he thought. He dialled Andy's number and drummed his fingers on the steering wheel while he waited for him to pick up. 'You following me?'

'Can't keep up with you.'

'Got a kidnapping situation.'

Andy was silent.

'Amelia has been locked in a coolroom at the Andrews place. Now, do you or Jack know anything about that farm?'

'Nothing. Haven't ever been on it.'

'Damn it, we know absolutely nothing about what's going on out there, the layout—anything! We're going to have to assess when we get there. You've brought your bulletproof vests with you?'

'Yes, sir.'

Dave swore. He knew he was going in without enough information. Going in too soon. But he had to get to Amelia.

Steve had said she'd spoken with the operator for about five minutes. In that time she'd told them where she was, who'd locked her in and why they were responsible for the robberies throughout the district. Then the phone had cut off. Dave hoped it was from a dead battery and nothing else.

☙

Anne drove the battered old ute out to where her boys were fencing. It had taken her several minutes of pacing around the house—and a nip or two of gin—to pull herself together. Now she knew exactly what she had to do.

She was cursing herself for not being at the house when Amelia arrived. She'd only realised when the dogs started to bark that the stupid girl must be around. Then she'd hurried back from the chooks, but it was too late: Amelia had gone up into the shearing shed. Anne had followed her and seen her taking photos of the ear tags. Good thing they didn't get mobile phone reception out here, or that bloody detective would be on his way.

Anne let out a roar of frustration. Why hadn't Will got rid of the tags like she'd ordered? And why hadn't she checked on him? 'Stupid bloody woman,' she muttered to herself. 'You should have known. That lazy mongrel kid.'

Immediately Anne had known that she'd have to get her hands on that phone, but she still hadn't been sure what to do with the girl. Leaving Amelia in the office, she'd had the opportunity to take the gun out of its secure cupboard. The way she stored the gun was perfectly legal, everything above board. That was how Anne liked to keep her whole house. She'd always seemed to be following the rules. Of course, Amelia had gone and seen the GPS guidance system hidden in the cupboard. Badly hidden—by the boys, of course. Now they were in big bloody trouble. Especially since the interfering little bitch would soon be missed. Her mum was with Dani and her family, not so far away.

In a sliding stop, Anne jumped out of the ute and stood in front of her sons. Will had turned up at some point and was looking even more sullen than usual. They'd all looked around at the noise of the ute, and Mike threw down the pliers he was holding.

'We've been caught,' Anne said. 'We need to shift the truck to its hiding spot and put everything we've still got in it.'

'How—?' Mike started to ask.

'Don't interrupt me,' she spat. She watched as all three boys recoiled into themselves. *Good.* 'It's Amelia. She saw too much. I had to lock her in the coolroom.' She pointed at Will. 'Back from ninnying around at the doctor? You are a princess. Why didn't you get rid of the sheep tags? You're as useless as your father was.' She pointed at Mike, then Tony. 'And *you*—I can't even begin on the two of you.' After taking a couple of steadying breaths, she said, 'All right, you three know what you've got to do. Get on with it. Oh and Will, when you're done helping here, come straight to the shearing sheds to deal with those bloody ear tags.'

Anne climbed back in her ute and drove towards the house, her chest heaving. She had to be tough with them sometimes, she reasoned. Put her foot down. Her boys needed her to control them. How would they cope in the real world without her? She'd done everything for them. Always told them what to do and when to do it. No, she needed to keep them with her so she could help them through life. And by doing what she had done, she'd made sure that they would never leave her side, or make the same mistakes she had.

It chased her around, her past. No matter how hard she'd tried to put it behind her, she couldn't. Her affair with Brian Barnes was the reason she'd become who she was today. She still sometimes dreamed of him rising above her, moving into her, sweat on his brow and love in his eyes. He'd liked to watch her while they made love and she'd liked to be watched. She'd lived for those stolen moments with him, and now she was trapped, consumed by thoughts of him for the rest of her life.

He'd made promises and Anne had believed every one of them. She'd believed he loved her, deeply. Until she'd realised that she was just a cliché: the younger woman with an unsympathetic husband, looking for attention, for love, for affection.

She'd been flattered by Brian's advances. They'd been offered unexpectedly one evening when he'd come across to give Greg a hand in pulling a calf. Greg left to take care of the new mum and baby, telling Brian to call in at the house and have a wash and a drink. He'd be there soon.

But Greg was gone too long, because by the time he arrived back, Brian had run his fingers down Anne's face, told her she was beautiful and said he'd been admiring her from afar for many months. Tired from running after a small child—a thankless task—and receiving no attention from Greg, Anne had fallen into Brian's arms.

When they met again in secret, Brian promised to leave his wife and Anne promised to leave her husband. He promised to look after her, to sleep separately from his wife, and leave as soon as he could to be with Anne—and she promised him the same. Soon they would be together forever.

Then Anne fell pregnant.

Telling Brian was the easy part. They were sitting in the dappled sun, under a tree in an isolated parking bay where they often met. Brian was looking after his son Paul, who was not quite one.

'We're going to have a baby,' Anne said without preamble. She watched as a mixture of excitement, joy and fear spread across Brian's face. His dark blue eyes flicked from hers, to her stomach and then over to Paul, who was lying on his tummy on a rug.

'Are we?' Brian said softly.

Nodding, Anne reached for his hand.

Brian drew away. 'That's a piece of news,' he said, frowning. 'Unexpected.'

Right from that moment, Anne knew there was something wrong. But she didn't yet understand that every promise he'd ever made was never going to come true.

'Are you sure it's mine?' he asked.

Anne's mouth dropped open. '*What?*' she hissed. 'You know Greg and I are sleeping in separate bedrooms. How can you ask that?' Angry and bewildered, she stood up and walked away from him.

Brian shrugged. 'Well, I said that too, but look . . . it wasn't entirely true.'

Her eyes filled with tears. 'So what, Brian? What about all the times you've told me you love me, that you want to be with me?' Her throat closed over and she wasn't able to speak for a moment. 'You can't be serious. Please tell me you're not.'

'No!' Brian stood up and walked towards her.

'Don't touch me unless you're going to stay and acknowledge our child.' She held up her hands to ward him off, then tucked them around her stomach as if to protect the life growing within her. 'Tell me you will,' she pleaded.

'I do enjoy your company, but I can't give up everything I've got here. I'd lose the farm. My kids. Jan and I have a . . .' he paused, searching for the right words, 'comfortable relationship. An understanding. It suits me.' He sighed and ran his fingers through his thick dark hair. 'I'm not going to lose my farm and my family, Anne. I'm just not.' He paused before saying, 'Why weren't you more careful?'

'Me?' Anne yelped. 'Brian, you are half of this! You are half of this child.'

'Now don't be like that—' Brian said, trying to soothe her.

'Like what?' Anne asked angrily. 'Don't be hurt, don't be angry, confused? Just because you don't want me to be?'

'Anne, I do love you . . . but in a different way. And not enough to give everything up. I'm sorry, but that's just the way it is. I'll look after you, though. Get you money for the child.'

'Don't bother. I'll manage just fine. I don't need you.' She turned and walked away in the direction of her house.

That was their last meeting as lovers. Of course they ran into each other in public, where they acted polite and distant. Anne moved back into the marital bedroom and a bouncy, beautiful baby boy was born a little earlier than her dates suggested. There was one more son before Greg died in an accident, and Anne was left alone with three boys under the age of six.

Mike and Tony grew into the spitting image of their father. Big, strong bodies paired with weak, feeble and pathetic personalities. They were easy to control.

Will was different: kind and gentle, willing to love and wanting to be loved. Anne had tried to love him. After all, he'd been made in love, and just because that love had crumbled didn't mean she shouldn't still love what came from it. On her good days, that was exactly how she felt. On her bad days, she hated Will. He was the reason she couldn't be with Brian anymore. It was Will's fault.

Whenever she felt like that, she'd remind herself of that little brat, Paul—less than two years older than Will, and so similar to him. But Paul was the acknowledged son, the one Brian had chosen to raise. She couldn't stand the sight of him.

After Greg's death, Anne struggled financially. There had never been any money and it was hard, exhausting work to keep the farm afloat. Exhausting to pretend that they were doing well, that she was happy and managing. She wasn't. But she made it through and no one would ever take that away from her.

Five years after Greg's death, she opened the door to find Brian standing there. His eyes were red and bloodshot, his skin pasty. He was no longer the handsome man she'd loved.

'I'm sorry,' he said. 'More than you'll ever know. You put on a brave face, but I know you must be struggling. I wish I could have made it easier for you. For Will.' He held out his hand, which she ignored. Sighing, he dropped it down. 'I'll leave something in my will for you. I know it'll be too late to help you, but there it is.' He held her eyes for a moment longer, then backed away from the door and left.

After that, from a distance, she watched Brian drink himself into an early grave. He'd always been a big drinker, but she guessed that his addiction had worsened after their split. He became bitter and mean, isolating his family. And she was happy about it. She enjoyed watching him self-destruct, knowing it was because he was unhappy. She would have made him happy—they would have been happy together—if only he'd been strong enough to let himself love her.

As time went on, word came to Anne that Brian was sick and not expected to live. At his funeral she snuck in to sit at the back of the church, scornful of his children—especially of Paul. *If only they knew*, she thought. She left before the end of the service, realising there were too many 'if onlys' for her to stay.

After hearing of Brian's death she waited, but nothing came her way. Then she heard rumours that there'd been nothing left to give. He'd drunk it all away.

Well, she decided, she wasn't going to struggle anymore. She was strong and as wily as a fox. Resourceful. And so the idea for the robberies had been born. If not for Paul's meddling fiancée, everything would have gone smoothly.

Anne pulled up at the house, got out of her ute, ran into the office and started gathering up the evidence to hide or destroy. Soon Amelia would fall unconscious in the coolroom and it would be easy enough to put her back in her car without a struggle. The boys would send her off the road into a tree. Another tragic accident.

Anne froze as she heard the cocking of a gun.

'Stop! Police!' said a male voice. 'Put your hands where I can see them.'

She turned slowly, her heart pounding. There stood that blasted detective.

'Hands where I can see them, Anne,' Dave repeated. 'It's over.'

Chapter 37

As Will walked from his ute towards the shearing shed, he cast a nervous glance around. He was pretty sure his brothers were still off hiding the truck. And he could hear his mother in the house, muttering loudly to herself and crashing around in the office. It had been a long time since he'd seen her as unhinged as she was now. It happened occasionally—when she went off her medication or was completely stressed. Usually she managed to live a completely normal life, but during the times that depression and irrationality hit, she was nothing short of mean.

Rather than continuing to the shed, Will ducked into the garage. Cracking open the coolroom door, he whispered, 'Amelia?'

There was no answer.

'Amelia? It's me, Will. Come on, I'll help you get out of here.'

Still nothing. Then Will realised she was probably scared

of him. He stepped inside and held his hands palm-up. 'Listen, I know you think I'm one of the bad ones. I'm not. I've tried to stop them so many times. I tried to go and tell the police this morning, but there was no one at the station. Let me help you get out of here. But we've got to hurry. Before Mum and the others come back.' He jiggled on his feet, turning to cast a furtive glance out the door. *Come on, come on, come on.*

&

Driving back in the ute from where they'd hidden the truck, Mike and Tony had just rounded a bend and were passing through the shadows of a group of trees, when Mike slammed on the brake. 'Holy shit, Tony! Look, they've got Mum!' He stared in disbelief as Dave escorted Anne out of the house, her hands cuffed behind her back.

'No!' The word shot from Tony, and he moved to get out and run to her.

Mike grabbed his shoulder in a vice-like grip. 'Don't be so fucking stupid,' he said in a low voice. 'You want to end up like that?'

'What about Will?'

'He'll have to fend for himself.'

'Well, what the fuck are we supposed to do?'

'Get away from here.'

The two boys sat still, filled with horror. This was much worse than they could have ever imagined.

'C'mon,' said Mike, letting his brother go, 'we have to get back to the truck and get the fuck outta here.'

'Why don't we keep driving in this?' Tony asked.

'It's stolen—there's probably a notice out on it, you idiot. No one will know about the truck yet. We can probably get away in that.'

⁊

There was still no answer from Amelia. Fear welled up in Will as he realised she could have fallen unconscious. Or worse. Fumbling for his phone, he pressed a button and the screen lit up. He held it out like a torch and saw Amelia crouched in the far corner, her eyes wild and a bag of meat in her hands, held up like a weapon.

'Stay away from me,' she said.

Holding out his hand, he said, 'I know you don't want to trust me, but I'm about your only hope at the moment.'

Amelia looked at him with terror. 'It was *you* the night of the robbery. It's your voice I recognise. Not Graham's. Thank God.' Then she frowned. 'Why . . . why do you sound so much like Paul?'

Will was getting agitated. 'Come on, Milly, we've got to get out of here! Yeah, I was there, but it's not what you think. I was trying to stop them from hurting you.' He reached forward quickly, needing her to get up, needing her to move right away.

Finally Amelia dropped the meat, uncurled her body and tried to stand up, but stumbled and fell against a lamb carcass, then onto Will. She let out a little squeal and he clapped a hand over her mouth. 'Shh! It's okay, it's okay. Don't make any noise!'

Amelia's eyes widened in fear, but he couldn't stop. They just had to get out of there. Half-dragging, half-carrying her towards the door, he bumped into frozen carcasses and they tumbled into the garage. Then, peering out into the sunlight,

350

he let his eyes adjust to the brightness before working out there was no one around.

'This way,' he said in a quiet voice. He hurried Amelia as quickly as he could along the side of the house. When they rounded the corner, they both froze when they saw a car in the driveway.

'Dave,' Amelia gasped out, and started to cry.

☙

'If you're not going to talk, I'm not going to make you,' Dave said as he sat opposite Anne in the Barker station's one and only interview room.

The sour-faced woman crossed her arms and stared straight ahead.

'But you know the judge will make it a lot easier on you if you cooperate.'

She huffed at him. 'The judge won't listen,' she said. 'The judge won't care. No one has cared about me for *decades*. Nothing's gonna change now.'

Dave thought she sounded almost manic and wondered if they should get a doctor to her. 'So you're not going to tell me anything? Not where the sheep tags came from, not where the GPS system came from. Not why you locked Amelia Bennett in a coolroom and threatened her with a gun. Nothing?'

Anne sat still for a moment, then brought her head up and looked him in the eye. 'I'd tell you everything,' she said, 'but there's no point. You won't listen, you won't give a shit. You, my friend, can get fucked.'

☙

'We've taken two suspects into custody, Anne Andrews and her son Will,' Dave reported back to Steve.

'And the girl in the coolroom?'

'We've got her too. She's okay. Cold and frightened, but okay. She's at the hospital with her family now.'

'Good,' Steve answered curtly. Maybe he was still annoyed that Dave had disobeyed a direct order.

'I want a plane put up,' Dave said. 'To follow the Andrews brothers. I have the driveway being watched to see when they leave—I want them on the road. We won't try to stop them until the STAR Group gets here.'

'Expensive. Why not just give chase and set up some road blocks?'

'We're going to have to let them think they've got away,' Dave replied. 'One of them is violent, as you know, and they probably have access to firearms like most farmers. I'm not sure, but Anne won't talk, other than to spit obscenities at us. I'd rather just watch and wait. Take 'em down when it's safe.'

'Sure. I'll get a plane on standby from Port Augusta.'

Dave ended the call, picked up his cold coffee and drank the last mouthful. 'Joan, can you make sure Anne has something to eat and drink?' he asked.

She nodded, looking pale. 'I just can't believe . . .' She walked off in a daze.

Dave squared his shoulders and strode into the interview room, where Will was now sitting, looking down at his hands folded on the table in front of him.

'Got yourself in a bit of a fix, haven't you?' Dave asked as he sat down and crossed his legs. The boy seemed lost and found at the same time. His face held fear but also anticipation, his body language was open and it was clear to Dave that he was keen to talk. Unlike his mother.

'I tried to come and talk to you earlier,' Will said softly.

Dave nodded. 'I know.'

'I even left evidence around where you blokes would find it. But it seems that Amelia did, instead.' He put his face in his hands.

'So why don't you start at the beginning?' Dave asked.

Will looked up and met his eyes. 'There were two types of robberies. The ones where we stole things to put a crop in, and the one where we knew we could sell the goods with our produce. There were other reasons for that one, too.' He rubbed his eyes. 'Mum had her reasons.'

'Are you admitting you were involved? If you are, I need to caution you.'

Will nodded and then listened while Dave reeled off the caution. 'Do you want a lawyer?'

'No.'

'Okay. For the benefit of the tape, present are Detective Dave Burrows of the Adelaide Metro Police interviewing William Andrews and the time is 5.37 p.m. Right-o, tell me all about it.'

'The diesel, chemical, GPS system and rodeo money was so we could get a canola crop in. We wanted to because that's where the money is. But that crop's so bloody expensive to get in the ground, and the first few months you always need to be on the boomspray getting rid of insects and so on. Money was really tight.' He sighed. 'We needed a boost and Mum came up with this idea.'

'Okay, and the other robbery? The ewes?'

353

The door opened and Andy stuck his head in. 'Good to go, Dave,' he said.

Dave stood up and told Will he'd have to wait, then locked the door and turned to Jack, who'd been standing outside. 'You all right to sit in with the suspect?' The young cop nodded.

Hurrying into the main office, Dave asked Andy for the information. 'They started to move in a rigid truck about half an hour ago. They're taking the back tracks towards Port Augusta. The bird is up and watching them from a distance.'

'Any firearms?'

'Can't tell.'

'Show me on the map,' Dave instructed.

Andy pointed out the route the brothers were following, and Dave then indicated a couple of corners on the map. 'We need to put road spikes here and here. Can we get some there before the truck hits that part of the road?'

Shaking his head, Andy said, 'Can't get there in time.'

'Okay, tell me where you can get to.' Dave stared intently at the young man, willing him to have a go and give him a spot.

'There's a couple of patrol cars sitting about here,' Andy said, hesitantly, as he pointed to the place. 'They're about twenty k's from your preferred spot. The STAR Group aren't far away from there, either. We can get there too, if—'

'Right,' Dave said. He hurried out of the station with Andy close behind.

৩

Dave adjusted his headset and held his binoculars to his eyes.

'Suspect vehicle is approximately one kilometre from road spikes,' the voice said from the plane.

354

'Affirmative,' Dave said. 'Tell everyone to get ready,' he instructed Andy.

They both watched the corner where the truck was about to appear.

'On the countdown, boys and girls,' Dave said. 'And five, four, three, two . . . Suspect sighted! Wait for my call.' He watched as the front tyres burst and the driver struggled to control the truck, then brought it to a halt. 'Go, go, go!'

The STAR Group raced out of their bus, pulling open the doors of the truck before the two men inside had a chance to react. Within seconds each of the Andrews brothers was lying face-down on the ground with two officers on top of him. They were cuffed and hauled upright, and put into the back of the waiting patrol car.

'Good job, team,' Dave said as he gloved up and looked inside the truck. Lying in the centre console was a taser gun. He snapped a couple of pictures and then put it in an evidence bag. 'Circumstantial, but useful,' he muttered.

He then went to the back of the truck and examined the rear left tyre. There it was, the chunk of rubber that was clearly missing in all the tread photos he'd taken at the crime scene on Saturday. He'd been right when he'd told Anne it was over.

As soon as he'd made sure everyone was okay and the truck was secure for the trip to Adelaide, he took out his phone and dialled Kim. 'I'm on my way down to the city,' he told her. 'We've arrested the Andrews family and we're in the process of transporting them to the Adelaide holding cells.' He listened as Kim let out a breath. 'How's Milly?'

'That's the first time you've called her that, Dave,' Kim said, the pleasure in her voice clear. 'She's going well. We can take her home in a couple of hours.'

'Good.'

The silence stretched out between them like the distance between Torrica and Adelaide.

'So . . .' Dave started, as Kim said, 'What about us?'

Something tightened in Dave's chest. 'I don't know, Kimmy. I'm going to be pretty tied up for the next while with this case. I'll call you, okay?'

Epilogue

The picnic table had been jammed into the sand at Emerald Springs so it wouldn't wobble and spill anything. Amelia had wanted party music, but there wasn't a power source to run it from, so she'd opted to go with nature and hoped the birds would sing up a storm. The laughter and chatter was music enough anyway, she decided.

Her whole clan was there. Paul, of course. Her parents and Kim. Chelle and Chrissie. Sav, Dean and their kids. Pip, Gus, Cappa and other friendly committee members and their families. Even the two local policemen, who'd helped so much and been so supportive. Amelia had noticed with interest that Jack and Chelle were spending a lot of time talking, at very close proximity.

Of course, Graham was still missed constantly, but as Amelia looked around, she reflected that her family had made it through the past weeks of devastation with strength and grace. To have her loved ones hanging out at the springs, just as they'd once done, was a wonderful feeling. To have Paul with her and a sparkling engagement ring on her finger was even better.

Amelia still had many shaky days and the occasional nightmare, but she was doing okay. Her paranoia had stopped soon after the arrests and she felt safe in Torrica again. She'd been through a lot and come out the other side so much stronger. With that came a new sense of comfort in her own skin. She no longer cared what people thought of her and carried herself with more confidence.

Her parents had gone through an even more difficult time. John had made the hard choice of hiring a workman to take Graham's place, and was beginning to make other choices that were good for him and the farm. He'd decided to sell some shares that they had been saving for retirement: life seemed a lot shorter than it had before Graham had died. John and Natalie were going to take their first overseas holiday—there were brochures about Italy, Greece and Spain in the home office. Amelia wasn't sure when they were planning on going, but she'd make sure they wouldn't have to think about the farm while they were away.

Amelia's main concern at the moment was Aunty Kim. She'd been keeping herself busy, but her bright smile had dimmed. When Dave had called her and said he was on his way back to Adelaide, he'd made no mention of seeing Kim again. And there'd been no word from him since. That had been a month ago.

All their information about the progress of the case had come through Jack and Andy, and it hadn't been much. The judge wouldn't give Anne, Tony or Mike bail, while Will's bail was set quite high and there was no one to pay it. Paul had been thinking about going down to visit his half-brother and potentially pay the bail with some of the money recovered from insurance on the ewes, but of course he was wary. As for the investigation, the police would only say that it was ongoing, and that a court date hadn't been set yet.

'Milly!' Paul startled her out of her reverie. 'Hey, Milly.' He waved her over to the barbecue where he was cooking some lamb. 'Taste this.' He put a piece of lamb into her palm and watched her chew it.

'Ohhh,' Amelia moaned. 'That is so yummy.' She grinned at Paul, knowing it was his lamb from Eastern Edge.

'Paul love, did you want me to get the rest of the meat from the esky?' Natalie asked as she walked past with a smile. He nodded to her, smiling back.

Amelia slipped her arms around Paul's waist and gazed up at him. 'So, sexy, what else is for lunch?' she whispered.

'Dessert, you asked about?' he murmured in her ear. 'Well, I'll start here—' he put his hand on her bum '—and move to here, and here, and here.'

Amelia's stomach twirled in a very good way and she put her lips on his.

She was so glad that they'd been able to move on from her terrible misjudgement. It had certainly taken some talking, often into the small hours of the morning, exploring why it had happened and how it never would again. They both admitted they'd made mistakes and, at the end of it, they both knew they were so much closer than they had been before.

'Hang on, we can't start lunch yet!' Natalie called to everyone. 'Our guest visitor isn't here.'

They all stopped talking and looked at her.

'What do you mean?' Amelia asked, looking around. 'We're not missing anyone.'

'Well, actually, we are.' Natalie went to the pathway and said loudly, 'You can come out now!'

Everyone turned to watch as Dave entered Emerald Springs.

Amelia's grin widened, while Kim squealed and hurled herself towards him. He wrapped his arms around her and kissed her soundly, and there was applause and wolf-whistles. Then the rest of the gathering crowded around him with questions.

Kim and Dave disentangled themselves and he held up his hands, gesturing for silence. 'They're all still in custody. The evidence against them is overwhelming—the truck was full of it. The panels used to steal your ewes.' He looked over at Paul. 'Taser gun, ropes, everything they ever needed. And the best part is there were fingerprints on all of them.'

Paul looked over at Amelia and she knew at once what he was thinking. She nodded. 'What about Will?' he asked. 'Is he in as much trouble as the others?'

Dave shook his head. 'Certainly he's being charged as an accessory, but it's his evidence that's put the nail in the coffin for the others.'

Paul slipped his arm around Amelia's shoulders. 'How much is the bail? Maybe we could pay it.'

Dave regarded him before nodding. 'All right, we can talk about that later. The only other thing I have to tell you is that the Andrews were involved in quite a few other, smaller robberies in order to stay afloat—that's why they always seemed financially stable. They were very clever with the way they sold off the goods and made it all seem legit to you, Milly. Anne also had her boys steal your bank statement from your mailbox and try to frame you by anonymously slipping it to me.'

Amelia shook her head in bewilderment, still struggling to reconcile the kindly older woman, the one she'd considered a friend, with the truth.

'What about Graham?' Natalie asked in a trembling voice, her eyes filling with tears. John moved to stand beside her and take her hand.

Amelia gave her parents a sad look. 'Yes,' she said to Dave, 'have you found a way to link his death to the crimes? Surely it wasn't a coincidence.'

Dave sighed. 'That's one thing I can't talk about at present. I know you must be anxious for a conviction on that score, and believe me, we're working on it. I can confirm that Graham wasn't there for the rodeo robbery—he drew the line at that— and then he threatened to come forward when the brothers hurt you. That's when they tried to pay him off. Will has been very helpful.'

Amelia and her parents nodded. These were things they'd talked and speculated about many times since it had all happened.

'What was Jim's involvement in it all?' Amelia asked.

'Other than just being a nasty piece of work? Nothing,' Dave answered. 'He just always seemed to be in the mix, but there is nothing to suggest he had anything to do with it.'

Then Kim smiled at Dave, her hand firmly around his waist. 'So what's your plan now?' she asked.

Amelia watched as Dave looked into Kim's eyes. 'To stay here and love you forever.' He leant down and kissed her.

Paul pulled Amelia closer and as she looked over his shoulder, she saw Jack lay a kiss on Chelle. She turned to Paul and kissed him, which lasted all of about two seconds before the kids started making sucking noises and screwing up their noses.

Amelia broke away, laughing. 'Here's to us!' she cried, happiness flooding through her. 'To Granite Ridge and all who set foot on her, may you always be happy.'

'Cheers!' everyone said.

'And to Graham,' she added softly, looking up at the stunning, clear blue sky.

Acknowledgements

Mae Flynn, once again your help, friendship and advice has been paramount in helping me type 'The End'!

Kathy Mexted, for always being at the end of Facebook. Thanks for helping out when I was so seriously stuck!

The AMAZING Kate Goldsworthy. I am one hundred per cent sure *Emerald Springs* wouldn't have reached the finish line in this polished state if it hadn't been for your constant support, Skype calls and editorial skills (thanks, Louise, for letting me have Kate!). I'll forgive you for pushing me to write chapter summaries. I'm so sad I won't be working with you next time and I wish you the best plus every ounce of good luck for your next venture.

Thank you to all the crew at Allen & Unwin—especially Louise, Sarah and Amy—for your understanding and patience with me during trying times. Your support and belief in me is overwhelming. Siobhan Cantrill, even though I'm not working with you anymore, you're still there!

Gaby Naher, my incredible and supportive agent. From the bottom of my heart, thank you. Your generosity with your time and expertise is greatly appreciated.

Anthony, for making sure I had the time to finish this book.

Rochelle and Hayden, I am so proud of you both. Your maturity and sensitivity during the last year have been so impressive. You are both wonderful human beings and I am totally blessed you are in my life.

Cal, I love you. I love knowing you are happy and smiling so much more these days. And to Aaron, for making that happen for my darling friend.

My incredible friends (old and new) who have never let me fall. Special mentions to Carolyn and Aaron, Heather, Shelley, Tiffany, Amanda, Ann, Robyn, Chrissy, Jan and Pete (I couldn't have asked for more loving and beautiful neighbours), Jenny Mac and my other friends who have strong hands; you will always have my heart. Also, my sister, Susan.

The girls from Outback Paparazzi, Amanda and Ann. (Please check us out on Facebook at www.facebook.com/outbackpaparazzi.) When you started this group, Amanda, I could never have foreseen the bond and friendship we have all formed. I love you both more than you could ever realise. Even when you're both yelling at me in caps lock! ('Ann, don't yell, darling!') Can't wait to visit you both.

My writing friends who double as real ones! Fiona Palmer, Angela Slatter, Rachel Treasure, Nicole Alexander, Margareta Osborn and Tony Park.

To the 'real' Dave Burrows, Dave Byrne. Thanks for all your help, mate. Beer next time I'm in Perth.

Finally, but most importantly you, the reader, and my Facebook and Twitter friends. I can't express how grateful I am that you have supported me by reading my books. It's all because of you.

You can friend me on Facebook at www.facebook.com/FleurMcDonaldAuthor or follow me on Twitter: @fleurmcdonald.